DOCTOR WHO
SHADA

DOCTOR WHO

THE LOST ADVENTURE BY
DOUGLAS ADAMS
SHADA

GARETH ROBERTS

Based on the BBC television serial by Douglas Adams
by arrangement with the British Broadcasting Corporation.
BBC, DOCTOR WHO and TARDIS (word marks, logos and devices)
are trademarks of the BBC and are used under license.
K-9 was originally created by Bob Baker and Dave Martin.

ACE BOOKS, NEW YORK

THE BERKLEY PUBLISHING GROUP
Published by the Penguin Group
Penguin Group (USA) Inc.
375 Hudson Street, New York, New York 10014, USA

Penguin Group (Canada), 90 Eglinton Avenue East, Suite 700, Toronto, Ontario M4P 2Y3, Canada (a division of Pearson Penguin Canada Inc.) • Penguin Books Ltd., 80 Strand, London WC2R 0RL, England • Penguin Group Ireland, 25 St. Stephen's Green, Dublin 2, Ireland (a division of Penguin Books Ltd.) • Penguin Group (Australia), 250 Camberwell Road, Camberwell, Victoria 3124, Australia (a division of Pearson Australia Group Pty. Ltd.) • Penguin Books India Pvt. Ltd., 11 Community Centre, Panchsheel Park, New Delhi—110 017, India • Penguin Group (NZ), 67 Apollo Drive, Rosedale, Auckland 0632, New Zealand (a division of Pearson New Zealand Ltd.) • Penguin Books (South Africa) (Pty.) Ltd., 24 Sturdee Avenue, Rosebank, Johannesburg 2196, South Africa

Penguin Books Ltd., Registered Offices: 80 Strand, London WC2R 0RL, England

Doctor Who is a BBC Wales production for BBC One.
Executive producers: Steven Moffat and Caroline Skinner

BBC, DOCTOR WHO and TARDIS (word marks, logos and devices) are trademarks of the British Broadcasting Corporation and are used under licence.
K-9 was originally created by Bob Baker and Dave Martin.

Published by arrangement with Ebury Publishing, a division of The Random House Group Limited.
Originally published by BBC Books.

PUBLISHING HISTORY
Ace hardcover edition / July 2012

Library of Congress Cataloging-in-Publication Data

Roberts, Gareth, 1968–
Doctor Who : Shada : the lost adventure by Douglas Adams / Gareth Roberts. — 1st ed.
p. cm.
ISBN 978-0-425-25998-6
1. Doctor Who (Fictitious character)—Fiction.   2. Human-alien encounters—Fiction.   3. Enemies—Fiction.   4. London (England)—Fiction.   I. Adams, Douglas, 1952–2001   II. Doctor Who (Television program : 1963–1989)   III. Title.   IV. Title: Shada.
PR6068.O143D7 2012
823'.914—dc23
2012011293

PRINTED IN THE UNITED STATES OF AMERICA

10   9   8   7   6   5   4   3   2   1

For Clayton Hickman, whose role in the creation of this book was larger than Queen Xanxia's transmat engine, and whose role in my life is more precious than oolion.

And in memory of Douglas Adams.

'The radical evil: that everybody wants to be what they might and could be, and all the rest of mankind to be nothing, indeed, not to exist at all.'

Johann Wolfgang von Goethe, *Maxims and Reflections*

'. . . flat eyes that only turned toward the stars to estimate their chemical tonnage.'

Truman Capote, *Breakfast at Tiffany's*

'Concern with other people is a mistake.'

Quentin Crisp, *Resident Alien*

'Does the body rule the mind or does the mind rule the body?
I dunno . . .'

The Smiths, 'Still Ill'

Fig. 1. These words are carved into the machonite plinth upon which rests *The Worshipful and Ancient Law of Gallifrey*, one of the Great Artefacts of the Rassilon Era. They are here reproduced by kind permission of the Curator of the Panopticon Archives, the Capitol, Gallifrey. Translated from the Old High Gallifreyan they read, roughly: 'If this book should care to roam, box its ears and send it home.'

PART ONE

OFF THE SHELF

PART TWO

1

At the age of five, Skagra decided emphatically that God did not exist. This revelation tends to make most people in the universe who have it react in one of two ways – with relief or with despair. Only Skagra responded to it by thinking, *Wait a second. That means there's a situation vacant.*

Now, many years later, Skagra rested his head, the most important head in the universe, against the padded interior of his alcove and listened to the symphony of agonised screams coming from all around him. He permitted himself two smiles per day, and considered using one of them now. After all, the sounds of wrenching mental anguish and physical distress were a sure sign that his plan was working and that this was going to be a good day, possibly even a 9 out of 10. So he might have even more cause to smile later on and he didn't want to waste a smile. He decided to save it, just in case.

Instead, as the screams faded slowly into bewildered animal whimpers and the occasional howl of uncomprehending fear, Skagra climbed from his alcove and turned to survey his handiwork. His own alcove was one of six (an even number, of course) set into the sides of a tall grey hexagonal cone at the centre of the main laboratory. At the top of the cone was a grey sphere.

Minutes before, he had watched as the other five members of the Think Tank climbed into their alcoves, laughing and joking in their irritatingly trivial way. They hadn't even noticed that there were connecting terminals built into the headrests of all of their alcoves but no such terminals built into his own. Why were other people so stupid? Skagra wondered. Even these people, who were so clever, were basically stupid. He had wondered this every few seconds for as long as he could remember. Still, thanks to him – thanks to the plan of which this moment was a significant part – soon other people would no longer be a problem.

The five Thinktankers stood gibbering in their alcoves, their eyes blank, limbs making the occasional spasmodic movement. It was interesting that the bodies of all five had survived the process.

Now to check on their minds.

Skagra entered a command code into one of the many panels of instruments that lined the walls of the laboratory. It was a cursory, automatic gesture. If a lesser, sillier person had conceived this plan – not that anybody else could have this conceived this plan – they would have rigged up a big, melodramatic silly red lever to activate the sphere. Skagra congratulated himself on not doing this.

The command code chirruped and the sphere started to vibrate. A confused babble of thin, inhuman voices issued from its interior. It was the sound of thought. Messy, disorganised, arbitrary, no words distinguishable.

Skagra raised a hand. The sphere's command program reacted instantly. It detached itself from the top of the cone and zoomed towards him, coming to rest in his palm. Its touch was metallic and ice-cold.

Skagra's fingertips curved round the surface of the sphere. He looked across the laboratory at the slumped figure of Daphne Caldera, her eyes staring moronically into nothing, her lips issuing bubbly baby noises.

Caldera – whose specialty was six-dimensional wave equations. Skagra had never found the time to explore this particular avenue of research beyond the rudiments. Obviously, $zz = [c2]x4$, everyone knew that. But Caldera had taken the study of six-dimensional wave equations into an entirely innovative area. 'A whole *new* dimension, you might say!' she had joked yesterday, and Skagra had been forced to sacrifice one of his smiles just to look like one of the herd.

Now, his fingers on the sphere, Skagra applied his own mind to a complex six-dimensional wave equation problem:

Σ is less than †Δ if ∂ is a constant, so ß†ΔΔ + ≈ç if expressed as Zag BB Gog = ?

The answer popped into his mind: *((>>>x12!*

Of course! It seemed so obvious now. It *was* obvious.

The process had worked. But Skagra decided on one more check, a deeper probe of the sphere's potentialities.

In the alcove next to Caldera, C.J. Akrotiri was slumped, his fingers making tiny circling movements, his mouth hanging open, discharging a string of drool. Akrotiri, the legendary neuro-geneticist, whose research into dendritic pathway alteration had led to the cure for Musham's disease.

Skagra thought of Akrotiri, deciding on a suitable test question.

And suddenly, overwhelmingly, a memory tumbled into his mind –

I'm standing on the beach, a skimboard under my arm, I'm trying to look muscly and confident but you can't fake confidence or muscliness and I feel like a fool and I'm wondering why I ever thought this was a good idea and suddenly SHE is there and she looks so good and I look so bad and she's asking me do I want to skim over to the island and does she mean with her and of course she means with her and so we get on the board and I'm dying inside and she puts her arms around my back and I kick off and suddenly we're skimming over the water under a purple night sky and she rests her head on my shoulder and I think did she mean to do that and she doesn't take her head away and I can't believe it and I skim clean on to the island like a pro which I've never done before and she falls onto the sand and I go to help her up and she laughs and pulls me down and suddenly she's kissing me and my head's spinning and this can't be happening to me – and then in a flash I can see it, I can see how dendritic decay can be reversed by the early introduction of a fluon particle into Genome A/5667 –

Skagra shook himself. It was to be expected that some traces of personality and experience might, on occasion, corrupt the data during retrieval. He would increase the sphere's filter capacity to ensure such irrelevant sentimental trash would never again get in the way of the important things in life.

Then he released the sphere, which bobbed in the air, following its master as he crossed to the main communications panel. With another casual cursory movement he activated the message he had prepared earlier. Then he swept out of the laboratory, the sphere accompanying him.

His own voice echoed around the laboratory. *'This is a recorded message. The Foundation for Advanced Scientific Studies is under strict quarantine. Do not approach, I repeat do not approach. Everything is under our control.'*

The message began to repeat itself, transmitting on all frequencies out into space. But not very far out into space. Skagra wanted the message to keep any passing spacecraft away from the Think Tank and the word quarantine had a very definite effect on most beings, Skagra had found. It changed statements such as *'I wonder if we could help those poor people, Captain?'* into statements such as *'It's the plague! Scream! Scream! Let's get out of here with incredible reluctance and at incredible speed!'*

The message rang out loudly in the central laboratory of the Think Tank.

And the people who were supposedly the greatest minds in the universe, flopping and babbling in their alcoves, couldn't understand a word of it.

Skagra walked calmly – he always walked calmly – down the corridors from the laboratory to the shuttle bay. There were four docking positions built into the hull of the space station. Illuminated signs showed that docks 1, 2 and 3 were occupied by standard shuttlecraft, three-seaters with enough fuel to reach the outskirts of galactic civilisation.

Skagra walked calmly past docks 1, 2 and 3, the sphere following, and pressed his palm onto the locking panel for the unoccupied dock 4.

The airlock swung open into empty space.

Skagra walked calmly and confidently through into what appeared to be absolute nothingness.

He was on his way.

2

Chris Parsons felt that time was passing him by, and also that time was running out on him. How time could be doing both of these things to him at the same time, he didn't have time to wonder.

For a start, he was twenty-seven. *Twenty-seven!*

Over the years he had noticed a disreputable tendency in himself to age at the rate of approximately one day per day, and now, as he cycled the short distance from his flat to St Cedd's College on this unusually sunny Saturday afternoon in October, he could already feel another day heaving itself up onto the pile.

The old streets and the even older university buildings, tall and stony with their grey-mullioned windows and effortless beauty, seemed to mock him as he cycled by. How many hundreds of young men had passed through these institutions, studying, graduating, researching, publishing? Now all of them were dust.

He'd come up to Cambridge as a fresh-faced grammar-school boy nine years ago, and flown through his physics degree without much conscious thought at all. Physics was the one thing he could do well. Now he was engaged in a long and very occasionally exciting post-graduate struggle with sigma particles. He could predict the exact rate of decay of any sigma particle you cared to mention. But today even Cambridge, which he loved but had come to take as much for granted as the sun rising in the morning, seemed to add to his own inner feeling of decay. He often wondered if there was anything much left to be discovered in his field of research. Or, for that matter, any other. The modern world seemed unrecognisably futuristic to him sometimes. Videotape, digital watches, computers with inbuilt memory, and movie special effects that had made Chris, at least, believe a man could fly. How could things get any more advanced than that?

He passed a gaggle of freshers, who were to a man and woman kitted out in short hair and drainpipe trousers. How had this happened? Chris's own undergraduate days had been spent in the flared denims and flowing hair that he still favoured. He had been a member of *the* younger generation, the generation that was going to change everything, for ever and completely. There couldn't be another one, not yet, not before anything much had changed for ever and completely, it wasn't fair. For heaven's sake, in a few months it was going to be the 1980s. The 1980s were clearly far in the future and they had no business turning up until he was ready.

Yes, time was passing him by in general. But it was running out on him in a much more specific way.

Clare Keightley was leaving Cambridge on Monday.

She'd got a job at some research institute in the States and worked out her notice at the university. Three short days added to the pile and then he would never see her again, never get the chance to start another conversation. They talked rather a lot, saw each other rather a lot, and Chris despaired at the end of each encounter. Whenever they met, and much more of late, Chris felt that Clare had the air of waiting for him to say something obvious and important, but for the life of him he couldn't work out what it was. Why did she have to be so intimidating? And why did he have to be so in love with her?

Still, he had concocted one last shot, one final chance to impress her, one final excuse to talk to her, where she'd be so overwhelmed by his thoughtfulness that she might, finally, at long last, just tell him what she wanted to hear him say. That was why he was now turning through the ancient stone archway and into the impressive forecourt of St Cedd's College.

Chris parked up his bike among the rows of similar vehicles that acted as the students' free and endlessly swappable transport system. He took a scrap of paper from his satchel. *Prof Chronotis, Room P-14*. He looked around for the porter, but he must have been off on his rounds, so Chris collared two of the less outlandish undergraduates in the quad – one of them was wearing a Jethro Tull T-shirt, thank God – and they directed him to a door set in an ivy-covered corner.

Chris was very much wrapped up in his own thoughts and concerns about Clare, the passage of time etc., as he headed down the narrow wood-panelled corridor towards Room P-14, but a small corner of his inquiring mind couldn't help but wonder at the oddness of the architecture around here. It looked very much as if the corridor should have ended at Room P-13, but there was a buttress, a corner and a small extension down to P-14. That was all very well, because many of the university buildings were a patchwork of renovations and extensions, but the really curious thing about this particular one was that there was no obvious discontinuity. It was as if the extension had been built at exactly the same time as the building it was the extension to. This puzzled Chris on a deep, subconscious level that his conscious mind didn't even really notice. He did, however, notice a persistent very low electrical hum that seemed to grow louder as he approached the door marked P-14 PROF CHRONOTIS. The wiring in these old buildings was a disaster, probably installed by Edison himself. Chris half braced himself for an electric shock as he reached for the knocker and rapped smartly on the door.

'Come in!' called a distant, scratchy voice. He recognised it immediately as Chronotis, even though they had met only once before, and very briefly.

So Chris came in, navigated a cluttered little vestibule bulging with hats and coats and boots, and pushed open an oddly sturdy wooden inner door. He found himself in a large, oak-panelled room dotted about with ancient furniture, though for a moment it was hard to make out the panels or the furniture as every available surface, and several that weren't available at all, was covered with books. Every wall was lined with bookshelves, books jammed in two-deep and other books thrust on top, filling each shelf to bursting. Books covered the sofa, the chairs, the tables. They tottered in ungainly piles on the carpet, some at waist height. Hardbacks, paperbacks, folios, pop-up books, all creased and dog-eared and teacup-stained, some of them with spines folded back at a particular place, many annotated with torn pieces of paper, and none of them seeming to relate to its neighbour in subject, size, age or author. *The Very Hungry Caterpillar* lay next to a dusty Georgian treatise on phrenology.

Chris boggled. How the heck could anyone get through this amount of books? It would surely take you several lifetimes.

But extreme as this case might be, Chris was used to the eccentricities of the older Cambridge dons. He even tried not to react to the other, really much more peculiar thing that stood on the other side of the room.

It was a police box.

Chris hadn't seen one in years, and had certainly never expected to see one here. They had been a familiar sight on the street corners of London during his childhood trips to the capital. Like all of its kind this one was tall, blue, battered and wooden, with a light on top and a sign on the door, behind which there was a phone. The really peculiar thing about this one, on top of it just being there at all, was that around its base were the edges of several flattened books, as if it had somehow been dropped into the room from a great height. Chris even looked up at the low rafters of the ceiling to check that this hadn't in fact happened. And there was no way it could have been squeezed through the front door.

The voice of Professor Chronotis carried through from a door that presumably led to a kitchen.

'Excuse the muddle. Creative disarray, you know!'

'Er, right, yes,' said Chris. He carefully ventured further into the room, skirting the piles of books that looked the most dangerous. How was he going to find what he wanted in this lot?

He waited for the Professor to emerge from his kitchen. He didn't.

'Er, Professor Chronotis?' he called.

'Tea?' came the reply.

'Oh, yes, thanks,' said Chris automatically, though in fact he wanted to get away from all this strangeness and back to thinking about his own more important issues as soon as possible.

'Good, because I've just put the kettle on,' said Chronotis as he emerged from the kitchen and into the room, navigating the dangers unthinkingly.

After their one brief meeting a couple of weeks ago, Chris had mentally filed the Professor away as just another Cambridge eccentric, indulged and isolated by decades of academia. He had forgotten how memorable a person Chronotis was. And that was another irritating strangeness, Chris thought, because you can't forget memorable people. Chris decided he must have been really, incredibly wrapped up in himself to forget Chronotis.

He was a little man, somewhere in his eighties, in a dishevelled tweed suit and tie, with a heavily lined face, a shock of white hair, scruffy beard and half-moon spectacles over which peered kindly, penetrating black eyes.

Kindly and penetrating, thought Chris. You can't have eyes that are kindly *and* penetrating.

'Er, Professor Chronotis,' he said, determined to get things back to normal, 'I don't know if you remember, we met at a faculty party a couple of weeks ago.' He extended his hand. 'Chris Parsons.'

'Oh yes, yes!' said the Professor, pumping his hand enthusiastically, though it was abundantly clear that he didn't remember at all. He squinted up at Chris a little suspiciously. 'Enjoy these faculty shindigs, do you?'

Chris shrugged. 'Well, you know. I don't think you're actually supposed to *enjoy* them—'

'A lot of boring old dons, talking away at each other,' huffed the Professor.

'Yes, I suppose you could—'

'Never listen to a word anybody else says!'

'Yes, well, that night you said that—'

'Talk talk talk, never listen!'

'No, indeed,' said Chris. 'Well . . .'

'Well what?' said the Professor, staring at him with a look that was more penetrating than kindly.

Chris decided to humour him. 'I do hope I'm not taking up any of your valuable time.'

'Time?' the Professor laughed. 'Time! Don't talk to me about time. No no no. When you get to my age, you'll find that time doesn't really matter very much at all.' He looked Chris up and down and added, a little sadly, 'Not that I expect you will get to my age.'

Chris wasn't at all sure how to take that remark. 'Oh really?'

'Yes,' said the Professor, looking into the distance. 'I remember saying to the last Master of College but one, young Professor Frencham—' He stopped himself. 'Though hang on a minute, was it the last Master of College but two? It may even have been three . . .'

Chris frowned. The term of a Master of College seemed to last on average about fifty years. 'Three?'

'Yes, nice young chap,' said the Professor. 'Died rather tragically at the age of ninety. What a waste.'

'Ninety?' queried Chris.

Chronotis nodded. 'Run over by a coach and pair.'

'What was it you said to him?' asked Chris.

Chronotis blinked. 'How am I supposed to know? It was a very long time ago!'

Chris decided to put this aside. He wanted to get out of this strange humming room, far away from all its peculiarities and the peculiarities of its owner. 'Right, yeah. Professor, when we met you were kind enough to say that if I dropped round you would lend me some of your books on carbon dating.'

'Oh yes, happy to,' nodded the Professor.

Suddenly a high-pitched whistle emanated from the kitchen. The Professor jumped and clutched at his heart, then clutched at the other side of his chest. 'Ah,' he said, relaxing, 'that'll be the kettle.' He bustled round the piles of books towards the kitchen, calling back to Chris, 'You'll find the books you want at the far right of the big bookcase. Third shelf down.'

Chris sidled past the police box, trying not to think about it too much, and scanned the shelf the Professor had indicated. He pulled out a book, a slim leather-bound volume with an ornate scroll design, sort of Celtic but not really, picked out in gold on the front. He flicked it open and saw row after row of symbols, hieroglyphs or mathematical formulae.

And suddenly, for no reason that he could fathom, Chris was overwhelmed by a sensory rush of memory. He was seven years old, sat on his grandfather's lap in the back garden at Congresbury, listening to cricket on the radio, the voice of Trevor Bailey, bees buzzing in the garden, the tock of willow on leather, jam sandwiches and orange squash. So long ago . . .

The Professor's voice, echoing from the kitchen, called him abruptly back to the present. 'Or is it the second shelf down? Yes, second, I think. Anyhow, take whatever you like.'

Chris examined the second shelf and saw the titles *Carbon Dating at the Molecular Level* by S.J. Lefee and *Disintegrations of Carbon 14* by Libby. Yes, these were the ones. This was the stuff that would impress Clare, give him that excuse for one more conversation.

'Milk?' called Chronotis from the kitchen.

'Er – yes please,' Chris called back, distractedly hunting the shelf for more Clare-impressing material.

'One lump or two?'

'Two please,' said Chris absently, grabbing another couple of books from the shelf and stuffing them into his satchel.

'Sugar?' called Chronotis.

Chris blinked. 'What?'

The Professor emerged from the kitchen, carrying two cups of tea. 'Here you are.'

Chris, his mission accomplished, realised he didn't have to tolerate any of this strangeness any longer. 'Oh, actually, Professor, I've just realised I'm going to be late for a seminar,' he lied, checking his watch. 'I'm terribly sorry.' He indicated his satchel, now bulging with books. 'I'll bring these back next week, if that's all right?'

'Oh yes, yes, whenever, take as long as you like,' said the Professor. He took a noisy slurp of tea from each cup. 'Goodbye, then.'

Chris nodded. 'Goodbye.' He made for the door – but found that he couldn't go without asking one question, to try and clear up the strangeness in at least one of its respects. 'Er, actually, Professor, can I just ask you, where did you get that?'

He nodded towards the battered old police box.

The Professor peered over his half-moon spectacles at it. 'I don't know,' he said. 'I rather think that someone must have left it there when I popped out this morning.'

Chris didn't know what to say to that. He muttered 'Right' and let himself out, glad to be away from the strangeness of that room.

Nothing in his twenty-seven years had prepared him for the last five minutes. If anything, there'd been too much time in that room. It was oozing with time, covered in big dollops of time. And police boxes, and humming, and kindly and penetrating eyes and last Masters of College but three, and there was altogether too much of it all.

He was glad to be back in the real world. Back to the real, important business of Clare and impressing her. He selected a sturdy-looking bike from the available selection, climbed onto it and slung his satchel over his shoulder.

Chris had no idea that inside his satchel was the strangest, most important and most dangerous book in the entire universe.

3

It may – though it almost certainly will not – come as a surprise to discover that the police box that Chris Parsons saw in Professor Chronotis's rooms was not a police box at all. It was in fact a TARDIS, a machine that could travel anywhere in space and time, and its humble battered wooden blue shell housed a vast, futuristic interior. Chris was also very wrong to think back to his childhood trips to London because this TARDIS was not a product of Metropolitan Police technology. It may – though it almost certainly will not – come as a terrible shock that this TARDIS was not from Earth at all but in fact originated on the distant planet Gallifrey, home of the awesomely powerful society of the Time Lords. And it could – though this would really be pushing it – elicit gasps of awe to learn that this TARDIS was the current occupancy, if not exactly the property, of that mysterious traveller in time and space the Doctor, a renegade Time Lord who had shunned the static and futile life on Gallifrey and set off many hundreds of years ago to explore the infinite universe.

The Doctor's 'mission', if it could be called that, and it was something he would never have called it, had been simply to explore, to live a long life packed with wonder and excitement. Along the way, however, he had found himself dragged into the righting of wrongs, not for any grand and crusading reason but simply because he happened to be there and because it seemed the decent thing to do. Generally these adventures had taken place in the company of people from Earth, but relatively recently the Doctor had been joined by – or more accurately had foisted upon him – a member of his own people, the very same race he had spent so many centuries running from.

Her name was Romanadvoratrelundar – Romana for short, thankfully – and she was, at 125 years old, a recent graduate of the Academy of Time Lords. She had been selected by the White Guardian, a mysterious being even more awesomely powerful than the Time Lords, to assist the Doctor in a mission – and this really was a mission, much to the Doctor's irritation – to recover the six segments of the Key to Time, an extraordinarily awesomely powerful object needed to restore the harmony of the cosmos. Mission more-or-less accomplished, the Doctor had intended to return Romana to Gallifrey and continue his travels alone but for the company of K-9, a mobile computer in the shape of a dog whose powers, if not exactly awesome, were pretty handy, battery life permitting. K-9 also had the advantage over Romana, from the Doctor's point of view, in that he obeyed orders, came when whistled for, and was equipped with an off switch.

However, the Doctor's success in the quest for the Key to Time had incurred the wrath of the vengeful Black Guardian, who was as equally awesomely powerful as the White Guardian, although his desire was to plunge the cosmos into eternal chaos. He had sworn in a very dramatic way to hunt the Doctor down and destroy him. To avoid detection, the Doctor had attached a device called a Randomiser to his TARDIS, his plan being to outfox the Black Guardian by popping up randomly all over the place. Neither Romana nor K-9 had the heart to tell the Doctor that that was pretty much what he did anyway.

Whatever the case, the addition of the Randomiser meant the Doctor certainly could not return Romana to Gallifrey. And this suited them both, because the Doctor liked good company on his travels and Romana had learnt to appreciate the full variety of what life had to offer beyond the narrow confines of Gallifrey. Neither of them had ever discussed these feelings with the other, of course. This was not because they were members of an awesomely powerful race with a completely different set of emotional responses – although they were – but because they were not (currently at least) the kind of people who did that sort of thing.

One of Romana's particularly important discoveries during this period had been the extent of the Doctor's fascination for a planet in the Mutter's Spiral galaxy – Sol 3, known to its inhabitants as Earth. He had a great affinity for the people of this apparently distant and insignificant planet, and seemed to regard saving it from destruction as his special hobby. The Doctor had spent so much time there, and so much time in the company of its people, that it was hard to interact with him on any meaningful level without at the very least a working knowledge of the planet's history, social structure and idioms.

And so one afternoon she plucked a computer tablet from the TARDIS library and read up on it all, history and culture, from the birth of the planet from drifting clouds of cosmic dust, through the Stone Age, the Trojan War, Homer, Shakespeare, the Great Break-Out into Space, right up to its eventual immolation in the 57th segment of time. ('Been there, seen it, done it, wrote most of that, caused that,' the Doctor kept saying over her shoulder, irritatingly.) It had been a very interesting 45 minutes, and now Romana was able to keep pace with the Doctor and his favourite planet.

And now they were back on Earth again, taking part in what the Doctor had assured her was an idyllically bucolic and very relaxing activity. As usual, Romana had her doubts.

They'd arrived in the Professor's rooms a couple of hours earlier, but found them empty. Romana was concerned his absence might have something to do with the urgent message he had sent them. But the Doctor seemed almost glad of the chance to rush off through the back of the college to the river's edge, where he threw a handful of large-denomination notes at a surprised young student, threw off his hat, coat and scarf and virtually bundled Romana into a tiny, wobbly wooden boat.

She couldn't see the point in this at all at first. There was a perfectly serviceable path right next to the river, which they could have walked along and enjoyed exactly the same view without the possibility of capsizing. But the Doctor had seemed so delighted, marvelling at the wooden pole before thrusting it into the dirty water and using the full heft of his tall powerful frame to push off down the river like it was the Amazon, that Romana decided literally to go with the flow.

Now she reclined in the punt, the Doctor's ancient Baedeker guide in one hand, the other trailing over the edge through the clear water, enlivened by the sunshine and the pleasing architecture of the college buildings along the banks. Unlike the Academy on Gallifrey, this was a fresh, vibrant place of learning, the most ancient of the colleges a mere eight hundred years old.

The Doctor stood at the other end of the punt, punctuating each stroke of the pole with the name of one of the great Cambridge alumni.

'Wordsworth! Rutherford! Christopher Smart! Andrew Marvell! Judge Jeffreys! Owen Chadwick!'

Romana frowned. That name hadn't been on her tablet. 'Who?'

'Owen Chadwick!' the Doctor repeated emphatically. 'Some of the greatest thinkers in Earth's history have laboured here.' He went on. 'Newton!'

Romana nodded. She knew Newton. '"For every action, there is an equal and opposite reaction,"' she quoted.

The Doctor gave the pole a particularly hard shove through a muddy patch and the punt shot forward, as if to illustrate the truth of those words.

'So Newton invented punting?' asked Romana.

'Do you know, I wouldn't be at all surprised if he had?' said the Doctor airily. 'Like all great thinkers, he encapsulated the simplest things. There was no limit to old Isaac's genius.'

Romana smiled as the little boat passed under a bridge, the shadows of the willows on the bank casting criss-crossed patterns on the stone. 'Isn't it wonderful,' she mused, 'that something so primitive can be so . . .' She searched for the right word.

'Restful?' the Doctor suggested, shoving down again and causing the punt to wobble alarmingly.

Romana found the word. 'Simple. You just push in one direction and the boat moves in the other.'

They emerged from under the bridge and Romana gazed at another grand college building beyond the trees that lined the riverbank. 'I love the spring,' she said. 'All the leaves, the colours . . .'

'It's October,' said the Doctor, a little shamefaced.

Romana blinked in surprise. 'I thought you said we'd be arriving in May Week?'

'I did,' said the Doctor. 'May Week is in June.'

'I'm confused,' said Romana.

'So was the TARDIS,' admitted the Doctor.

Romana decided to make the best of it. 'Oh, I do love the autumn,' she said, trying not to sound too critical. 'All the leaves, the colours . . .'

The Doctor harrumphed. 'Yes. Well, at least with something as simple as a punt nothing can possibly go wrong. No coordinates. No relative dimensional stabilisers. Nothing!' He lunged down yet again. 'Just the water, the punt, a strong pair of hands and the pole!'

The words were barely out of his mouth when the pole jammed solidly into another muddy patch with a loud squelch. The Doctor tried manfully to retrieve it as the punt shot forward but was finally forced to abandon it or join it in the River Cam.

Romana looked sadly at the retreating pole as they sailed on.

The Doctor slumped down into the punt. 'Er . . . I think it's about time for us to go and see if the Professor is back in his rooms. Ask me how.'

'How?'

'For every reaction,' said the Doctor with one of his sudden toothy grins, 'there is an opposite – and equally difficult – action!'

He rattled in the bottom of the punt and snatched up a long-handled wooden paddle, deployed for just such an emergency, swung it into the water and started to paddle furiously towards the bank.

The punt passed under another bridge. Romana was glad there was only one paddle. She'd had quite enough paddling during their adventure on the third moon of Delta Magna, when—

Suddenly her thoughts were interrupted. This interruption was not just in the normal sense, of something distracting her. It felt as if something had literally barged into her mind and cut off her train of thought.

It was a thin, distorted babble of inhuman voices. Lost souls in torment, crying out in terror and confusion. The words were indistinguishable but the anguish was unmistakable, and tugged at her hearts.

The punt swept out from under the bridge. Romana blinked, and the voices were gone. It had all happened in a second.

The Doctor's expression was similarly disturbed, and he had stopped mid-paddle, looking around in surprise. Romana caught at his arm. 'Did you just hear voices?'

The Doctor nodded solemnly, just as the sun passed under a cloud, sending a chill autumn wind along the river. 'Yes – a sort of thin, distorted babble of inhuman voices.'

'Then what was it?' asked Romana.

The Doctor shrugged. 'Probably nothing,' he said very unconvincingly.

'Doctor, please, let's go in,' urged Romana.

The Doctor nodded and resumed paddling ferociously towards the shore.

If the Doctor or Romana had looked up rather than just around at this point, much of what follows may have turned out quite differently. But as it happened, they did not. And so they did not see the man on the bridge.

Skagra looked down, making his first detailed survey of this planet of primitives. He enjoyed looking down on people.

He still wore the functional white coveralls of the Think Tank, but had added a long, shining silver cape and a wide-brimmed shining silver hat, the better to go unnoticed and unremarked upon on this remote and uncivilised world. He had been pleased to see, on his journey on foot into this small conurbation known as Cambridge, that he had been correct in this decision. Several of the primitives had even shouted words of social greeting to him as he passed through the streets, using untranslatable colloquialisms such as 'Oi, Disco Tex, where are the Sex-o-lettes?' and 'Get her!' and 'Hello, honky-tonk!' Yes, he was obviously passing for a native amongst these cattle.

This planet really was almost distressingly backward. The few pathetic satellites winking in its orbit stood as a measure of that. Its people travelled in ground cars with exhaust pipes that belched smoke, or on laughably basic self-propelled contraptions consisting of two wheels and very little else. Skagra had passed a trading post that trumpeted low-resolution magnetic videotape recording equipment as the height of invention and sophistication, suggesting that the primitives would never have to miss *Coronation Street*, whatever that was, ever again. Their economy seemed to consist of shoving dirty pieces of paper with the head of a great matriarch printed crudely on one side at each other. The Matriarch wore a crown, suggesting a type-B monarchy, which was presumably something to do with this important street where coronations were so regularly performed.

There was also this strange, slow and wasteful mode of transport along the waterway in small wooden craft. He had just seen a primitive male make an incredible hash of this simple, if pointless, task.

All things considered, Skagra decided Earth rated as a 2 out of 10 planet, bad but not quite the worst he'd ever seen, and it gained half a point for its breathable atmosphere and another half a point for its tolerably close sun.

In fact it was the perfect place to hide away in, just as his target had done. Somewhere in this quadrant of the city, the so-called 'university quarter', was what he had come for. He was approaching it circumspectly, still not quite convinced that anybody could be so stupid as to possess what he desired, yet put up no security systems to protect either it, or himself.

The leather handles of a large carpet bag were clutched tightly in one of his hands. Inside the bag was the sphere, the babble of its voices undetectable by the non-telepathic primitives of this planet. The sphere buzzed and hummed angrily, rubbing against Skagra's leg like a pet demanding to be fed.

'Soon,' he told it curtly. 'Very soon.'

4

Chris was very glad to be back in his lab. He threw his satchel down on a bench and just stood breathing calmly for a moment, reassured by his spectrograph, his carbon-dating machine, his X-ray machine, and even his Bunsen burner. He looked the longest at his neat, almost bare bookshelf. These were all things he could understand.

He looked out of the window into the little garden which the laboratories surrounded. The sunshine was fading now and it was starting to feel a lot more like October. A solitary magpie hopped about on the lawn. Chris gulped and then reminded himself that he was a rational, scientific person surrounded by rational scientific things.

Whenever he felt irrational and unscientific like this, Chris reminded himself of the pure, simple and almost inexpressible beauty of Euler's Identity: $e^{i\pi} + 1 = 0$. You just couldn't argue with Euler, however many mad professors and police boxes you'd bumped into.

He checked his watch. It was just after two, so Clare had probably had lunch and was back in her rooms. Operation Keightley, aka The Chris Parsons Project, could now swing into phase two.

He flipped open his satchel and took out the books. He was irritated to discover that among the relevant ones was that other one, the strange one, the one he'd picked off the wrong shelf, the one with the odd not-quite-Celtic scrolly symbol on the front. He was about to put it down when –

He was back at home again, the cricket and buzzing bees and mum's voice coming from the kitchen –

Chris blinked – and put down the book. Odd.

He picked it up again –

He was back at home again, the cricket and buzzing bees and mum's voice coming from the kitchen –

– and then he blinked, and was back in the lab. That had been very strange. This book seemed to have the irritating habit of making you imagine things very vividly, things that weren't actually happening.

He shook himself. Of course it didn't. Books didn't do that sort of thing. Well they could, but not that vividly and you tended to have to be reading them. You didn't expect to feel the terror of Jane Eyre locked in the red room just by touching the spine of the Penguin paperback.

No, it was quite ridiculous. Books sat on shelves and waited to be read, that was all they did, the same way that solitary magpies signified nothing but an almost total lack of magpies.

He looked down at the book again, and again he saw the rows and rows of arcane symbols scrawled across its pages. But this time there was something else, and that something else was the most ridiculous something of all.

He could swear that as he looked at the book, the book was somehow looking back at him.

5

The Doctor led Romana through the gates and into the impressive forecourt of St Cedd's College. He pointed his paddle demonstratively around the buildings.

'Here we are! St Cedd's College, Cambridge. Founded in the year something or other, by . . . someone someone someone in honour of . . . someone someone someone whose name escapes me completely.'

'St Cedd?' suggested Romana.

'Do you know,' said the Doctor, turning to look at her and apparently very impressed, 'I think you're very probably right. You should be a historian.'

Romana smiled. 'I am a historian,' she said proudly, keeping to herself the thought that really, considering her relationship with the Doctor, she sometimes wondered if she should be a nursemaid.

A short, bespectacled man in a bowler hat and an immaculate suit and tie was pinning a notice on one of the boards that stood outside a smaller building set just inside the main entrance. Romana supposed he was some kind of official, a gatekeeper perhaps.

To her surprise the Doctor bounded over to the little man and whispered loudly in his ear, 'Good afternoon, Wilkin.'

'Good afternoon, Doctor,' said Wilkin casually, pressing the drawing pin firmly but neatly in its place, without turning around and without turning a hair.

Romana was pleased to see the Doctor slightly deflated by this smooth response. She loved it when he was out-eccentricked.

'Wilkin!' the Doctor gasped. 'You remember me?'

Wilkin turned from the noticeboard, smiling imperturbably up at the Doctor. 'Of course, sir. You took an honorary degree here in 1960.'

The Doctor grinned and nodded. 'So I did! How kind of you to remember me after all these years!'

'That's my job, sir,' Wilkin said smoothly.

'And you do it splendidly. Now, then—'

Wilkin interrupted him. 'Professor Chronotis, sir? He returned to his room forty-two minutes ago.'

The Doctor took a step back in amazement. Romana suppressed a smirk.

Then the Doctor leaned in close to Wilkin. 'How did you know I wanted to speak to Professor Chronotis?'

'That's who you asked to see when you were here in 1964, 1960 and 1955, sir,' Wilkin replied.

'Did I really?' marvelled the Doctor.

'Though not, as I recall, in such charming company,' said Wilkin, giving a little bow to Romana.

Romana extended a hand and introduced herself. 'Pleased to meet you,' she said brightly, and with a nod to the perplexed Doctor, added, 'Nicely done.'

The Doctor's eyes narrowed for a moment. He stepped back in and put a conspiratorial arm around Wilkin. 'I was also here in 1958,' he said grandly.

For the first time the tiniest crease of a frown appeared on Wilkin's brow. 'Were you, sir?'

'Yes,' the Doctor nodded, shooting Romana a triumphant look before adding mysteriously, 'but in a different body.'

Wilkin smiled his blandest smile. 'Indeed, sir.'

'Come along, Doctor,' called Romana. She was still thinking of the voices they had heard down at the river. If there was trouble coming, and there probably was, the sooner they cracked on the better.

'Nice to see you again, Wilkin, bye-bye,' said the Doctor, and breezed off. Then he had a sudden thought and turned around to hand Wilkin the paddle. Wilkin's hand was already outstretched to take it.

'Thank you, sir,' he said.

At least the Doctor knew when he was beaten, thought Romana, as he strode off into the university, this time without a backward glance.

Soon they were standing at the door of Room P-14. Before the Doctor had a chance to knock, a scratchy voice called from inside, 'Come in!'

But this time, instead of being taken aback, the Doctor smiled broadly and ushered Romana through the vestibule and into the room. Romana was pleased to be back. There was a time when she'd have squirmed at the muddle and mess, all the books strewn around the place, but now she found the odour of decaying aldehydes and tea leaves strangely reassuring.

The room was empty – or rather it was full, but empty of the Professor. The Doctor nodded towards the kitchen and whispered to her, 'He'll ask us if we want tea.'

'Tea?' called the scratchy voice from the kitchen.

'Yes please,' called the Doctor. 'Two cups!'

'Milk?' called the voice.

'Yes please,' called the Doctor.

'One lump or two?'

'Two please,' called the Doctor, winking at Romana. 'And two sugars.'

Romana wasn't sure what to make of that remark, but it caused the Professor to hurry out from the kitchen, a tray with three teacups in his hands, and a broad smile across his face. He seemed like such a nice old man. Immediately she liked him.

The Professor set down his tray and came forward to shake the

Doctor enthusiastically by the hand, his eyes alight with welcome for his old, old friend. 'Ah, Doctor! How splendid to see you again!'

'And you, Professor!' said the Doctor. 'This is Romana.'

The Professor beamed and shook her warmly by the hand. 'Ah, delighted, delighted. I've heard so much about you, young lady.'

The Doctor looked surprised. 'Have you?'

'Well not yet but I'm sure I will have done.' He looked momentarily confused and put a hand to his forehead. 'Do excuse me. When Time Lords get to my age they tend to get their tenses muddled up.' He hustled them to a sofa that could just about be distinguished under heaps of books and, after clearing a few away to create a little space, they sat down.

The Professor placed their cups of tea on the wonky table and then a thought seemed to strike him. 'Oh, would you have liked some biscuits too?'

'Well, I wouldn't have said no,' said the Doctor.

The Professor headed back to the kitchen. 'Crackers?'

The Doctor grinned broadly. 'Oh, sometimes, sometimes.'

As the Professor fussed around in the kitchen and the Doctor flicked idly through the nearest stack of books, Romana reflected on the incongruity of her surroundings. Until the distress signal had been picked up by the TARDIS, causing the Doctor to drop everything – literally – bypass the Randomiser and head for Earth at what passed for top speed, she had never heard of Professor Chronotis. The Doctor had explained how Chronotis, as was the custom for very elderly Time Lords of great service, in the declining centuries following their twelfth and final regeneration, had been offered the opportunity to retire somewhere out in the wide universe by the High Council of Gallifrey. It was a custom that dated back millions of years into the Time Lords' own history, and very few had ever accepted the offer. But Chronotis had jumped at the chance, packed his bags for Earth and set himself up as a professor at Cambridge.

'Three hundred years,' Romana marvelled as the Professor handed her a refill.

'Yes, my dear,' said Chronotis a little proudly.

'In the same set of rooms?'

Chronotis nodded. 'Ever since I retired from Gallifrey.'

Romana was puzzled. The life expectancy of a human was far shorter than that of a Time Lord, even a very elderly one. 'Didn't anybody notice?'

'Oh yes, of course they did,' said the Professor airily. 'But that's one of the delights of the older Cambridge colleges. Everyone is so very . . . *discreet*.'

He lowered himself onto a stack of atlases, stood up again, swept the books noisily to the floor with surprising strength, and plonked himself down into the armchair they had been occupying. He leant over and turned up the dial on a battered electric fire. The October afternoon was beginning to lose its warmth.

As part of her studies at the Academy, Romana had visited the chambers of the most ancient Time Lord academics and found them as sterile and dry as anywhere else in the Capitol. But now, as another bar on the fire glowed into life with the faintest sizzle of burning dust, Romana reflected that she felt almost as comfortable here as she did in the TARDIS.

The Professor sipped at his tea and tapped the Doctor on the knee with his spoon. 'Now then, Doctor, young fellow. What can I do for you?'

The Doctor blinked in surprise, his knife halfway between butter-dish and cracker. 'What can you do for me? Don't you mean, what can *I* do for *you*?'

'I don't think I do,' said the Professor.

'You sent for me,' said the Doctor patiently.

The Professor looked nonplussed. 'Sent for you?'

'I got your signal,' said the Doctor.

Chronotis frowned. 'Signal? What signal?'

'Romana,' said the Doctor, 'didn't we pick up a signal from the Professor? Would we come and see him as soon as possible?'

Romana nodded. 'And we came straight away.'

Chronotis shrugged. 'I haven't sent you a signal. But it's very splendid to see you. Have another cracker.'

The Doctor exchanged a worried glance with Romana.

'Professor,' he said, suddenly very grave, 'if you didn't send that signal – then who did?'

6

All was well in Wilkin's world, but then it always was. Wilkin would simply not permit it to be any other way. He had found his place and purpose in life. The place was St Cedd's, and the purpose was to maintain the order and calm established here centuries before, until the time came for him to hand over the task to an equally calm and ordered successor. Wilkin saw himself as a cog in the wheel of time, positioned here to ease the lives of those around him, and was a firm believer in the bit of the Bible that said 'A soft answer turneth away wrath', if not many of the other bits. But even he had his limits.

The encounter with the Doctor-with-no-name and his charming companion had put him out not one jot. If people chose to wear ridiculously long multicoloured scarves and to turn up on occasions decades apart not looking any older, it was none of his business.

But now, as he pinned another notice on the board and permitted himself just a tinge of inward pleasure at the thought of scrambled eggs on toast and the BBC's Saturday serial in a few hours, he found himself bristling for the first time in years.

A quite ludicrously dressed person was stomping – yes, that was the only word for it, *stomping* – through the entrance to the courtyard. Now obviously it was no business of Wilkin's if people chose to attire themselves in long silver capes and wide-brimmed silver hats, and went about carrying old carpet bags, that was their own affair.

But this fellow had none of the Doctor's affability or charm, and Wilkin was quite sure he had never seen him before.

He was in his early thirties, and might have been handsome – his features were symmetrically pleasing and he had full, sensual lips – were it not for two things. Firstly, there was the jagged scar that ran across the right side of his face, so that actually it wasn't symmetrical at all. And secondly, those full, sensual lips were curled arrogantly in a permanent disdainful sneer. All sneers were disdainful, Wilkin admitted to himself, but this one conveyed unfathomably deep levels of coldness and condescension.

'You!' the stranger barked.

Wilkin shot back his own best look of coldness and condescension, which was pretty good but couldn't really compete. He then turned back sniffily to the notice board.

'You! Gatekeeper!' the stranger barked again.

Wilkin looked about the otherwise empty courtyard with exaggerated politeness. 'Were you addressing me?'

'I want Chronotis,' said the stranger.

Wilkin winced at the lack of formality. 'Professor Chronotis?'

'Where is he?' the stranger demanded.

Wilkin wanted this rotter out. 'He will not want to be disturbed. He is with the Doctor – a friend.' He added with emphasis, 'A very old friend.'

The stranger stared down at him for several seconds. His hands moved as if to open the carpet bag. Then, without another word, he turned on his high silver platform heels and stomped back out of the courtyard.

Good riddance. Wilkin wondered where on Earth he had been brought up, with manners like that.

It would have surprised Wilkin to discover that the stranger had not been brought up on Earth at all. It would have surprised him even more had he learnt that his intervention had quite probably saved the lives of the Professor, his very old friend the Doctor and the fair Romana. And it would have left him agog with fear and horror had he been party to Skagra's thoughts as he stomped back out to the streets around St Cedd's. Though of course Wilkin would never have shown it. He was only ever inwardly agog.

Skagra was considering the information the Earth gatekeeper had supplied. So Chronotis had an old friend called the Doctor.

The Doctor, the Doctor . . .

Something about those words had made Skagra retreat and reconsider. He was certain that he had read something about this 'Doctor' in the course of the researches that had led him here halfway across the universe. And any 'very old friend' of Chronotis could not possibly be an Earth human. So the Doctor was a Time Lord.

Skagra needed more information. Who was this Doctor? Doctor who?

7

Romana was worried. 'Anyone that could send a signal directly to the TARDIS must be terribly advanced.'

'Terribly's the word,' agreed the Doctor. 'And what's more . . .' He nodded towards where the Professor was absent-mindedly clearing away the tea things, 'they not only had to know who we are, they have to know who the Professor is.'

Romana considered. 'Then it can only be a Time Lord.'

The Professor tutted across at them. 'Really, my dears, I'm sure it's nothing to worry about.'

Romana remembered the voices they'd heard on the river and shuddered. She wasn't at all sure about that.

The Doctor held out a hand and started to tick off items on his fingers. 'So. Whoever it is sent the signal, they know me, they know you, they're probably a Time Lord—'

Suddenly the Professor jumped and clutched at his hearts. 'Wait!'

They waited. He stood in the same position, his expression a curious mixture of enthusiasm and embarrassment. More seconds ticked by.

'Professor?' ventured Romana.

Chronotis sprang into life again. 'Well, now you put it like that, young fellow,' he said with a broad smile, 'I've had an idea about who might have sent that message. Someone who knows you, knows me, and someone who – yes, quite – just happens to be a Time Lord.'

Romana considered. The Time Lords had produced a share of genial exiles – the Doctor, the Professor and, she supposed, herself – at least. But they had also spawned a number of criminals and renegades.

'Yes, I think I know who sent that message, all right,' said Chronotis.

'Who?' demanded the Doctor. His grave expression told Romana that he also was fearing the worst. 'Who!?'

The Professor chuntered on. 'It all adds up, you see. Obvious, really.'

'Who was it?' spluttered Romana.

Professor Chronotis flung his arms wide, and shouted: 'Me!'

Romana and the Doctor looked at each other.

The Doctor snorted. 'But you just said that you didn't send it!'

'Yes, I know,' said Chronotis, shaking his head a little sadly as if to rattle the thoughts around inside it. 'The old memory's getting a bit touchy of late. Doesn't like to be prodded about too much.'

Romana's hearts went out to the old Professor. It wasn't polite to ask, but she estimated that he must be about twelve or thirteen thousand years old. Even the amazing capacities of a Time Lord brain must bow down eventually to age and decay.

With that surprising agility of his, the Professor crouched down and rifled under the sofa, pulling out a battered, dusty wooden box. He flipped open the lid, revealing an ancient contraption that Romana just about recognised as a very old-fashioned space-time telegraph. These had been used by Time Lords to communicate with each other through the vortex, that mysterious medium through which TARDISes travel, before the days of message boxes and time rings.

'Oh yes,' he said, tapping a weakly flashing bulb on one arm of the old machine. 'Yes, it was definitely me, there it is, in the Sent Mail folder.' He squinted at a tiny readout screen. 'But my dear old things, I sent that message ages ago, simply ages ago.'

Romana smiled. 'I told you, Doctor. You got the time wrong.'

'I know,' said the Doctor, 'but you're always saying that.'

'Well, you're always getting the time wrong.'

The Professor slammed down the lid on the box and pushed the telegraph back under the sofa with one slippered foot.

'Professor?' the Doctor asked gently.

'Yes?' replied the Professor. 'Ah, you want more tea.'

He started to move in the direction of the kitchen again. The Doctor caught him gently by the shoulder. 'First – what was it about, Professor?'

'What was what about?'

'The message.'

The Professor shrugged. 'How should I know? You've seen it more recently than I have. Something about coming to see me as soon as possible, wasn't it?'

'Yes,' said the Doctor, as patiently as he could. 'Yes, but why? And why so urgently?'

'Was it to do with the voices?' asked Romana.

'What voices?'

The Doctor coughed. 'When we were on the river we heard a strange sound, a sort of babble of inhuman voices.'

'Oh, just undergraduates talking to each other I expect,' said the Professor. 'I've tried to have it banned.'

The Doctor shook his head. 'No, it wasn't like that at all. It was the sound of humans – or ghosts – very quietly . . .' He searched for the right word.

Romana supplied it. 'Screaming,' she said with another involuntary shudder.

The Professor snorted. 'Overwrought imaginings, Doctor. With your lifestyle, I don't suppose it's surprising. The next thing, you'll be seeing sea monsters rising from the Cam—' He interrupted himself, clutching his head as if to grip a thought that had popped up in there. 'No, now I remember!'

'Remember what?'

'No, I remember why I wanted you to come and see me.'

'Why?'

The Professor shot a glance at Romana and lowered his voice. 'Delicate matter, slightly. Er, we can trust your young friend?'

Romana nodded. 'Absolutely.'

The Doctor nodded. 'Completely absolutely. She's a good sort.'

'Well,' said the Professor. He fidgeted. 'Well, the reason I sent for you . . . well.'

The Doctor looked as if he might finally explode.

Romana gave Chronotis her warmest smile. 'Please, Professor, just tell us.'

'Well,' said the Professor again. 'It's about a book.'

The Doctor blew out his cheeks. This revelation couldn't help but come as something of anti-climax. 'A book? Is that all?'

The Professor squirmed. 'Well, you see, it's a rather special book.'

8

Chris wasn't at all sure he should do what he was about to do to what was, after all, somebody else's property. But this book was irritating him and he wanted answers. Whatever its pages were made of, it wasn't paper. Paper should not have the capacity to make you feel that it was looking at you. Staring, in fact. In fact, he corrected himself, paper *doesn't* do that. That was an established fact, so well established that nobody had had previous cause to ever even suggest it.

So he set up the lab's electron microscope, took some sharp scissors from a drawer, and went to slice off a tiny section of this suspicious non-paper substance. The sooner he had it on a slide and under the microscope, the sooner he would find out what it was, exclaim 'Of course that's what it is!' and everything could go back to normal.

He couldn't cut the paper-or-whatever-it-was.

Chris boggled.

He checked the pages in his fingers. They had the same strength as paper. And scissors cut paper.

He tried to cut another section of the same page. Again the scissors met the same resistance. Chris was having none of this. He carried the book over to the lab's spectrograph, and switched the big white machine on at the mains. This would do the trick. Soon he'd be saying 'Of course that's what it is.' He could feel the words hanging in the air, absolutely ready to be spoken.

The spectrograph warmed up. Chris opened the book at a random page, slid it face down into the scanning aperture and pressed the scan button. Soon he would have the answer.

The spectrograph performed a sweep of the book. Chris looked eagerly towards the little slot from which the answer would soon come in cold hard print. Whatever this book was made of, the spectrograph would identify it. $e^{i\pi} + 1 = 0$.

There was an explosion deep in the bowels of the machine. Thick black smoke began to pour from the little slot.

Chris, momentarily shocked back to reality by the thought *And who's going to pay for that*, leapt across to the mains and pulled the plug from the wall. He coughed, waving away the clouds of smoke –

And the book, not even remotely scorched, shot out of the scanning aperture like an overenthusiastic slice of toast.

Chris picked it up, glared at it, then hurriedly opened all the windows onto the courtyard.

'Right,' he told the book. 'Right!'

Chris had never shouted at a book before. (Except, of course, *Jonathan Livingston Seagull*).

He switched on the lab's big old X-ray machine and positioned the book under the lens. Then he slipped on a protective apron, darted behind the protective shield, and pressed the switch to take the plate.

The lens flashed.

And the book glowed. For just a second, Chris saw it surrounded by an aura of tiny golden particles. It was a light like he had never seen before and it filled him with a superstitious awe that any number of magpies had never been able to manage. In that light he fancied he saw galaxies being born, time being torn apart. And the most curious thing was that he also saw two people.

One of them was a very tall man in some sort of long ceremonial robe. Like a medieval bishop, he carried a wooden staff. His face was forbiddingly stern and yet kindly.

The other person he saw in the light was Clare.

He blinked to clear his head.

The book sat innocuously under the X-ray machine.

Whatever it was, Chris thought, he was absolutely terrified of it.

9

David Taylor had just popped into town to get a few things. When he'd set out it had been quite sunny, unnatural for October really, but now he was regretting his light fawn coat and thin polyester shirt. There was quite a breeze blowing down the high street now, plucking at his carrier bags, which were full of things for Mum. They were having one of their good old Saturday nights tonight, nothing special, a bit of telly and a chat, then he'd shift her garden chairs into the shed for the winter. He'd got all her favourites – a nice bit of chicken, some mushroom, and a couple of Supermousses, plus a box of rosé. She'd never say, but David knew how much Mum missed a bit of company since he'd moved out, and what with Dad dying. Some of David's mates had ribbed him about giving over a Saturday night to stay in with his mum. But they'd only be propping up the bar at the Bird in the Hand and shuffling desultorily to Blondie on the tiny wooden dance floor until 11 p.m. It was the same every week. Even the police had given up raiding the Bird nowadays.

He got back to his old brown Capri and fumbled with the bags and his car keys. There was a wet patch in one of the bags, he could feel it knocking against his jeans, and he hoped it wasn't the desserts leaking.

Suddenly, a stunningly gorgeous man stepped up, as if from nowhere.

That was quite an achievement, thought David, as he was wearing a silver ensemble topped up with an even more outrageous hat and cloak. Very bold, and he must have been freezing in that get-up. The stranger had piercing blue eyes, full, sensual lips and, to top it off, he even had a scar – a sexy one, not a horrible one. David gulped. He wasn't used to being fancied, but this guy was giving him such a look.

'Hello, honky-tonk,' said the stranger in a severe and almost expressionless voice. 'I wish to ride with you.'

David looked around for candid cameras. He couldn't think of what to say.

The man had already made his way around the car and was standing at the passenger side. Oddly, David noticed he was carrying an old carpet bag which didn't go with the rest of the gear at all. He found this impressive. Here was a guy who clearly didn't care what anybody else thought of him.

'Look, you know,' David burbled, not at all sure how to handle this. 'We could go back to my place – I mean, only if you want to – but I've got to be somewhere else in a couple of hours, OK?'

'We will go to my place,' said the man levelly, never taking his beautiful eyes off David.

'Sure,' breathed David, still stunned. 'I'm David.'

'I am Skagra,' said the man flatly.

Exotic, thought David. Swedish, perhaps? He opened the car, threw the carrier bags into the back seat, got in, leant over and flicked the lock on the passenger side. The man slipped in, hat and all, and sat staring straight ahead, his long thin fingers curled round the leather straps of the carpet bag.

David gunned the engine and automatically the car stereo blasted into Cilla with 'Love Of The Loved'. Tinny brass erupted from the tiny speaker. David scrambled to switch it off. He didn't want the guy to think he was a silly old queen.

'You local then?' he asked, inwardly cursing at the naffness of that line, the brownness of his car, the fawnness of his coat, the polyesterishness of his shirt, the Cilla-ness of his tape collection, and the small spot on the left-hand side of his neck which he knew was in full view of his passenger and which he'd neglected to deal with that morning.

'I am a visitor,' said Skagra as the car turned into the narrow, quieter streets around the colleges.

'So which way now?' asked David.

The stranger pulled back the straps on the carpet bag. David couldn't understand what happened next. A big grey ball floated slowly from the bag. It was like something out of a magician's act, there didn't seem to be any wires or rods or anything supporting it, and the stranger's hands stayed completely still on the straps of the bag.

'That's clever,' enthused David. 'You could be the new David Nixon, Skagra, how do you do that?'

Skagra did not reply, his eyes fixed straight ahead on the road. 'Stop!' he barked.

David found himself obeying, his foot jammed on to the brake pedal. An angry cyclist swerved around the car, shouting an obscenity. They were at the gates of one of the colleges, St Cedd's David thought it was, though he'd never been clever enough to get more than three O levels.

David smiled across at his passenger. 'You're full of surprises,' he said, and decided to try and sound experienced and insouciant. 'What other tricks do you do, then?'

They were the last words David Taylor ever spoke.

The grey ball zoomed up to his forehead. He felt its icy, metallic touch for half a second – and then suddenly it was as if his brain was being pulled out of his body. He heard a thin, distorted babble of inhuman voices. There was a sudden searing pain, and David Taylor no longer existed. His last thought in this world was of Mum waiting at the old house.

Skagra watched as the human's head lolled to one side, exposing an unsightly blemish. The clothes the human was wearing would have to do. It was obvious from his encounter with the gatekeeper that these primitives were overawed by his attire. And this ludicrous vehicle would shorten the journey back to gather information about the Doctor.

'Access knowledge of this ground-transporter,' Skagra ordered the sphere.

The sphere burbled and detached itself from the forehead of the human. This one had not survived the extraction, Skagra noted with interest. The bodies of these Earth creatures were obviously more fragile than those of his former colleagues on the Think Tank.

The sphere zoomed to the operating wheel of the vehicle. Skagra prised the dead man's fingers from it.

'Return me to the Ship,' Skagra commanded.

The sphere burbled and the vehicle sprang into life, roaring past the gates of St Cedd's and off in the direction of the Cambridgeshire countryside.

On the back seat on the Capri, a Supermousse slowly melted.

10

The Professor was stalling.

'A rather special book?' the Doctor prompted him again.

'Rather special? Did I say rather special?' The Professor blinked. 'No, it's very special. A *very* special book.'

'Special in what way?' asked Romana.

'Award-winning? Critically acclaimed? Made out of jelly?' the Doctor suggested, increasingly desperately.

'No, not very special in that way,' fudged the Professor. 'Though I did once have a book made out of jelly, or was it about jelly, I forget . . .'

The Doctor looked as if he was building up to that explosion again. Romana gulped – and then her head was suddenly occupied by something else entirely. The thin, distorted babble of inhuman voices, much fainter this time. They were gone in a second.

'Did you just hear voices?' said the Professor, blinking.

The Doctor nodded. 'I just heard voices. Romana, did you just hear voices?' He wheeled on the Professor. 'Are those voices anything to do with this very special book, Professor?'

The Professor thought for a moment, then shook his head categorically. 'What? Oh no, no, no. No no no, no no no.' Talking into his shirt collar and avoiding their eyes, he added casually, 'That's just a book I accidentally brought back with me from Gallifrey. More tea, everybody?'

He shuffled towards the kitchen but the Doctor blocked his path. 'From Gallifrey? *From Gallifrey?*'

'Is that what I said, yes I suppose it was, yes I suppose it was.'

'Was what?'

'From Gallifrey. Rather a charming place, if a little static and futile, either of you two ever been there, worth a visit I suppose.' He looked at their shocked faces. 'Oh yes, of course, I suppose you must have, we were going to have tea, weren't we?'

This time Romana blocked his path. 'From Gallifrey? You brought a book from Gallifrey to Cambridge?'

The Professor nodded. 'Yes, just a few old knick-knacks, you know. And you know how I love my books, Doctor.'

'Professor, you just said that you brought it back by accident,' the Doctor reminded him.

'Ah yes, an oversight.' He mumbled into his collar again, very quickly, 'I overlooked the fact that I decided to bring it . . .'.

The Doctor and Romana exchanged a worried glance. Earth might be a very nice place to while away the odd afternoon, and this one was already turning out to be a very odd afternoon, but it was, nonetheless, at this stage in its history a level five civilisation with all the savagery and stupidity that implied. If an Earth warlord got his hands on an alien book that might refer, even casually, to the secrets of trans-dimensional engineering or warp-matrix astrogation or remote stellar manipulation, the planet might end up a charred cinder on which it would be impossible to while away any kind of afternoon.

'It was just for study, you know,' said the Professor, avoiding their gaze. 'Handy for reference.' He sighed and turned his head a little sadly. 'But as I'm now getting very old – very, very old – I thought that perhaps . . .' He let his sentence trail off suggestively and finally looked up over his half-moons at the Doctor, shamefaced.

'That perhaps I'd take it back to Gallifrey for you,' said the Doctor.

'Well,' said the Professor, 'now that I'm retired I'm not allowed to have a TARDIS.'

He turned his sad old eyes to Romana. She couldn't help but be moved. He seemed such a nice old man.

The Doctor looked less forgiving. 'Professor, I don't want to be critical. But I will be. It's very risky, bringing a book back from Gallifrey. It could be terribly dangerous in the wrong hands!'

11

Chris Parsons turned the book over in his hands. He'd summoned the courage to pick it up again but he couldn't banish the feeling that it was in some way terribly dangerous. His duty was obviously to alert the highest authority of his college straight away, the head of the Faculty, Professor Armitage.

So he put down the book, picked up the phone, and called Clare.

Firstly, and least importantly, Clare wouldn't kick up a fuss about the smouldering spectrograph. She might even think it was funny, though sometimes he didn't understand her sense of humour. Why she had nicknamed that skeleton she was examining 'bony Emm' and why she found that so hilarious and expected him to fall about too, he had no idea.

Secondly, and more importantly, the book was impressive. Much more impressive than the books he'd actually meant to borrow from old Chronotis, which now sat abandoned on a table top, in their disappointingly papery ordinariness.

As the call connected and Chris listened anxiously to the ring-ring, he was not aware that there was a third and even more important reason. He had found something exciting and wonderful, and there was nobody else on Earth that he would rather share it with than Clare Keightley.

She answered. 'Hello?' She sounded busy, as if he'd disturbed her in the middle of something.

Chris was flustered, as he always was when they first made contact, and then for most of the time they subsequently spent together. 'Keightley, it's me,' he said. As there were so few women in the faculty, Chris had decided that to make them feel welcome and not different in any way, he would address them by their surnames just as he would with any other friend or colleague. He was sure they appreciated it.

'Hello, Parsons,' she said. 'I'm busy, what is it?'

'Right,' said Chris, 'stop being busy because this is very important.'

'I'm packing,' said Clare. 'I leave on Monday. So get to the point.'

'If you want to see the world of science turned on its head,' said Chris impressively, 'come to my lab!'

'Your lab? You mean the faculty's lab that you sometimes use?'

'Yes, that's what I said, my lab,' said Chris.

'Look, give me two hours, OK?' said Clare. 'I've got a lot to sort out.'

'No, not in two hours, now!' insisted Chris. 'I need you here!'

There was a pause. 'All right then,' said Clare, in a different tone that Chris hadn't heard before. 'I'll come over now. But this had better be worth it.'

Chris glanced at the book. 'Trust me, it is – the most amazing, incredible thing—'

'Sooner you shut up, sooner I'll be there. Bye,' said Clare and hung up.

Clare replaced the receiver and looked around her small flat. Neatly propped against one wall were a stack of collapsible cardboard boxes and a huge roll of parcel tape, ready to receive all her worldly goods and transport them across the world to her new life. They had been sat there now for a week. She hadn't been able to bring herself to make a start.

She'd been hoping for a particular call that would mean she'd never have to leave. She wondered, despite all the weirdness, had that been it? Was she finally going to hear what she'd been waiting so long for?

She grabbed her coat and was out the door in five seconds flat.

12

The Professor marched solemnly over to a particular bookshelf, reached up and confidently plucked down a thin, hard-backed volume. Then he walked slowly back to where the Doctor waited with outstretched hand. The book was embossed, Romana saw, with the seal of Rassilon. Rassilon was the almost legendary founder of Time Lord society, the man who, untold millennia before, had endowed Gallifrey and its people with their awesome powers and great responsibilities.

The Doctor let out a sigh of profound relief and clutched the book to himself. 'Thank you, Professor. Yes, we'll take this back to Gallifrey for you.'

Romana's hearts sank at these words. She dreaded the thought of leaving the Doctor's side and returning to her old life. But she knew she must put any personal considerations aside. This wasn't the time.

The Doctor opened the book at a random page and read in his loudest, most sonorous voice, '"And in the Great Days of Rassilon, five great principles were laid down."' He frowned as his eyes wandered ahead to the next line. '"Can you remember what they were, my children?"'

Romana laughed. She took the book from the Doctor and flicked through it, reminiscing. 'It's just a Gallifreyan nursery book. *Our Planet Story*. I had it when I was a Time Tot.'

'So did I, and it's very good,' said the Doctor. He turned to the Professor, who was looking agitated. 'Well, if that's all it is, thanks for all the crackers but why make such a song and dance about it?'

The Professor tutted and crossed back to the bookshelf, scanning the myriad titles. 'Oh, no no, that's just another memento. Not the right book at all. Now where is it?' He ran his fingers along the shelves. 'Ah. Is this the one?'

He pulled it down and looked inside. '"I was sitting on a sofa, SW1, St James or so, very quietly, minding my own business –" No!' He threw the book over his shoulder. 'Ah, no, this looks like it.' He grabbed another book and read, '"The rain stopped as the *Inverness* rode into Dunedin harbour –" No!' He threw it over his other shoulder, narrowly missing the Doctor. 'Oh dear, no. Where is it? I know it's here somewhere.'

'Professor,' said the Doctor, looking worried again, 'how many books did you bring from Gallifrey, for heaven's sake?'

The Professor shrugged. 'Oh, just the odd two or seven. There's only one that's in any way . . . mm-mm-mous.' He mumbled the final word into his collar, turning away from them.

'Dangerous?' suggested the Doctor.

He turned to scan the shelves and picked out a book at random. Romana did the same. 'This,' whispered the Doctor to Romana, 'is going to be like trying to find a book about needles in a room full of books about haystacks.'

Romana looked around at the bulging shelves desperately. 'What does it look like, Professor? What's it called?'

'*The Worshipful and Ancient Law of Gallifrey*,' the Professor said breezily.

Romana's hearts skipped a beat. She and the Doctor dropped their books in horror.

The Doctor stormed over to the Professor. 'Did you just say "*The Worshipful and Ancient Law of Gallifrey*"?'

'Yes,' said the Professor, in the manner of a man discovered standing over a dead body clutching a bloody knife who remarks to the appalled onlookers what dreadful weather we've just been having. 'Little book, about five by seven.'

Romana had never seen the Doctor look so grave. He towered over the old man, and for once she saw the experience of centuries unclouded by his mask of bemused affability. She was reminded of the old Time Lords depicted in the pages of *Our Planet Story*, forbidding and unknowable. 'Professor, how did that book get out of the Panopticon Archives?'

'Well, what I did you see, is, er. Well, er, well, I just took it. Borrowed it, rather.'

The Doctor's tone was level. 'Borrowed it?'

'Well, no one's interested in ancient history on Gallifrey any more,' said the Professor. 'And I thought that possibly certain things would be safer with me.'

'And were they safer?' boomed the Doctor. 'In an unlocked room on a level five planet?'

'Well, in principle,' said the Professor. He sniffed and glanced over at the police box in the corner. 'After all, I'm sure your TARDIS is safer with you, isn't it? And you borrowed that from Gallifrey, didn't you?'

The Doctor was quiet for a moment. Then he nodded, as if acknowledging a good point well made, and let out a huge sigh.

He draped an arm around the Professor's shoulders. 'Professor, that book dates back to the days of Rassilon.'

The Professor blinked owlishly. 'Does it? Yes indeed, I suppose it does.'

'It's one of the Artefacts,' continued the Doctor.

Romana reflected. The Artefacts were the mysterious objects left over from the days of the first Time Lords, their significance lost over the untold centuries. The Sash, the Rod, the Great Key – the Time Lords had an almost superstitious terror of these ancient relics, and stored them safely deep in the Panopticon, the grand ceremonial chamber at the heart of the Citadel.

'Yes, I suppose now you mention it, it is one of the Artefacts, yes.'

'Professor, you know that perfectly well!' shouted the Doctor. 'And you also know perfectly well that Rassilon had secrets and powers that even we don't fully understand!'

Romana came forward and laid a hand on the Doctor's arm. 'Gently, Doctor.'

The Doctor shook his head. 'Professor, you've been appallingly irresponsible. I thought I was appallingly irresponsible, but you've taken appalling irresponsibility on to a whole new level. You've no idea what might be hidden in that book.'

The Professor smiled. 'Well then there's not much chance of anyone else understanding it, is there?'

'I only hope you're right,' said the Doctor. 'We'd better find it, hadn't we? Romana, little red book –'

Romana nodded. 'Five by seven.' She gave one final despairing glance at the mountains of books surrounding them, then set her jaw and began the search. A little red book . . .

The Professor's voice drifted from the kitchen, where he had scurried to prepare more tea. 'Then again, it could be green,' he said.

The Doctor's shoulders slumped. 'And I usually like Saturdays,' he said.

13

Skagra entered the command deck of his Ship, the dead body of the human over his shoulder. He let it thump to the ground and then barked out an order. 'Retain the outer vestments and then dispose of this carrion. Transpose it to the emergency generation annex.'

The body was immediately transposed away. In its place was the clothing it had worn, now cleaned, pressed and folded into a neat pile.

Skagra considered. It was time to absorb the nutrients that were essential to the functioning of his body. He viewed this prospect with no particular pleasure. Taste sensations were essentially animal and had no inherent intellectual worth. When the time came, Skagra reflected, he would not miss food.

'Feed me,' he ordered.

A golden serving trolley was instantly transposed to his side. It was laden with the finest and most nutritionally correct delicacies that the Ship's raw-matter synthesiser could provide.

Skagra set down the carpet bag containing the sphere and lowered himself onto his command lounger. Another diktat of the body needed to be satisfied. 'Rest me,' he commanded.

He closed his eyes and let the bio-tranquillic vibrations do their work. The rays bathed his neural pathways, cleansing the need for wasteful sleep from his brain. At the same time his body was pummelled by minute, invisible pressures that wiped harmful toxins from his muscles and removed waste matter.

Skagra opened his eyes, instantly refreshed and revitalised. He selected a fruit from the trolley and bit into it, chewing thoroughly to absorb the correct nutrients and ease digestion.

He spoke again, addressing the empty command deck. 'I have confirmed the location of the book. It shall soon be mine.' This was not strictly the truth, of course. He had left the Ship fully confident of the book's location, and fully intending to return with it. There was no logical reason to dissemble, but in fact Skagra had already rewritten his recent history in order to eliminate his concern over the mysterious guest in the Professor's rooms.

'Congratulations, my lord,' said the warm, soothing voice of his truest, most trusted, and in fact only, companion.

He took another bite from the fruit and said casually, 'Tell me of a Time Lord called "the Doctor".'

The Ship opened up a data window on the opposite side of the command deck and accessed its data store. Information began to scroll across the window, and Skagra blinked repeatedly, absorbing the information into the data-spike embedded in his cortex. The data store had combed all available information, including the secret and arcane Time Lord histories that were part of Skagra's own book collection. These books were lined up neatly, their spines matching perfectly, in a sterile, dust-resistant recess in a corner of the command deck, further protected by a powerful force field. Skagra had never physically opened the books, never so much as touched them, but had used scanning devices and robo-papyrologists to extract the information from within and add it to the store with no damage to the originals.

As Skagra watched, he learnt of the Doctor's early history, academic achievements, his family ties on Gallifrey and elsewhere, and the exact reasons for his first flight from his home world. But all of that was irrelevant. He needed to know about the Doctor as he was now.

Skagra flinched as a grainy image of the Doctor from some ancient video-text flashed by. He was a tall, imposing figure dressed scruffily in a long frock coat, a broad-brimmed hat and an unfeasibly long multi-coloured scarf. He had untidy curly hair, the wide, staring eyes of a child and he smiled all the time.

But he had seen this person, this idiot, earlier today, cartwheeling his arms as he lost control of the water transport on the river! Could this buffoon really be the Doctor?

It appeared that he was. Skagra focused in on a random selection of video-texts involving the Doctor and scrutinised them closely.

The first concerned events on a primitive world called Tara. The Doctor allowed himself to become embroiled in the piffling politics of the planet, siding with one faction against another. The Doctor made a show of acting under duress, but it was clear to Skagra that he was carelessly and irresponsibly enjoying himself. It was not exactly a bad video-text, just a rather bland one.

The second text told of intrigue on the third moon of Delta Magna, where a future Earth methane-refinery and some natives were being menaced by an enormous swamp creature known as Kroll. Again, the Doctor behaved with unbecoming frivolity throughout.

Finally Skagra reviewed a text that told of another enormous creature, this one inhabiting a pit on a planet called Chloris. Skagra noted how the Doctor seemed to react to danger and the threat of death with nonchalance, masking his Time Lord wisdom. It was a pathetic ploy that seemed to fool the low-grade antagonists he encountered.

Skagra found himself bristling. There was something about this Doctor that got under his skin. He was so messy, so silly. He needed to be tidied away. He'd wipe the imbecilic, toothy grin off the man's stupid face for ever –

Skagra stilled himself. He was not prey to such instinctive, animal reactions. Looked at objectively, the Doctor was nothing but a shambling fool, a 1 out of 10 Time Lord larking about on 2 out of 10 planets.

'So,' he said out loud, 'he is an ordinary Time Lord, albeit with an extraordinary lifestyle. He has no more power than the others.'

'Indeed, my lord,' said the soothing voice.

Skagra nodded curtly. 'Only one has the power I seek. And when I have the book that power shall be mine.'

'Yes, my lord,' said the voice.

'Get me the Command Station,' Skagra ordered.

The data-window flickered and resolved into a new image. A face.

'All goes well,' said Skagra. 'I shall be with you very soon. And then, let the universe prepare itself for me.'

A voice rumbled sepulchrally from the screen, echoing around the command deck. The words were clear, but they were accompanied by a sound like an exceptionally irritated earthquake. 'Everything is ready, my lord.'

Skagra gazed on the face of his most glorious and most terrifying creation. The red eyes glowed like twin furnaces. The roughly hewn features were formed from living rock. Smoke billowed from the creature's granite skin.

With the Kraags at his side, and the book in his possession, Skagra would be unstoppable. Shada was in his reach!

PART TWO

AN UNCHARITABLE DEDUCTION

14

Unaware of the impending threat to the universe, Clare Keightley checked her hair in one of the porthole windows of the physics lab's double doors, then knocked.

'Come in,' called Chris, sounding oddly preoccupied.

Clare went in. She was puzzled. She was used to Chris being hesitant and nervous where she was concerned. In fact she was used to most people at Cambridge being hesitant and nervous where she was concerned.

When she'd first arrived at Cambridge five years earlier as an undergraduate, fresh from a sixth-form comp in Manchester, she'd been surprised at how nervous and hesitant everyone in the faculty seemed to be. She formulated a theory that they had stumbled upon some massive discovery that would change the world for ever and were keeping it a closely guarded secret. It had taken her a few weeks to realise that the hushed voices, sweaty palms and nervous glances of her fellow students were actually because she was female. Most of them knew women only as mothers, matrons and chums' sisters.

As they'd got to know her, the ice had thawed. All of them had come to relax around her at least a little, apart from Chris, whose face could not hide a micro-expression of terror whenever he first encountered her.

And that was, peculiarly, one of the reasons why Clare liked him so much. He was clumsy and gauche. You weren't supposed to find that sexy. But Clare loved doing things you weren't supposed to, like coming from a council flat and becoming a top scientist. So she did.

This time was different. Irritatingly different, given the circumstances. She was leaving in three days, for goodness' sakes. If Chris was going to make his move, he should be down on one knee, or at least hovering hesitantly and nervously as per. Instead he was sat at a desk, boggling – that was the only word for it – boggling at a small red book, five by seven inches. He didn't even look up as she came in.

'Chris?'

'Ssh,' he said, turning the little book over and over in his hands and continuing to boggle.

'What do you mean, "Ssh"?' said Clare. 'You told me to drop everything and come running. So I did!'

Chris turned the pages of the book, shaking his head and tutting to himself.

'I can easily go away again,' said Clare.

At last Chris looked up. 'Then you'll miss something extraordinary!'

Clare sighed. 'What?'

'Something quite extraordinary,' said Chris.

Clare had had enough. 'Why are you being so pompous and odd?' she asked.

Chris waved the book at her. 'This book, Keightley! This book will do to the world of science what the Japanese did to Pearl Harbour!'

'What, dive-bomb it?' She sat down. 'I didn't know you were writing a book.'

'I didn't write it!' cried Chris excitedly, as if it were the most obvious thing. 'I found it.'

'What, just lying about?'

He nodded. 'Yes. Sort of. This book . . .' He weighed it in his hand. 'It's . . . it's staggering.'

'Right,' said Clare perfunctorily. 'What's it called?'

'Called?' Chris laughed. 'Called? How should I know what it's called?'

Clare fought down another wave of irritation. 'Please get to the point, I've got lots to do.'

Chris opened the book and handed it over to her, gently, as if it was a bomb. 'Feel that paper. Go on, feel it. Feel it! What does it feel like?'

Clare did as instructed. 'I'm afraid it feels rather like paper, Chris.'

'Aha!' cried Chris.

Clare made an impatient noise. 'Aha, what?'

'Tear it! Go on. Tear it, try to tear it!'

'That's no way to treat a book,' said Clare. 'A book that isn't even yours. Who does it belong to?'

Chris batted her objections aside. 'Old Chronotis. Professor at St Cedd's. Barmy. Or senile. Or both. Doesn't matter. Tear it!'

Clare decided that the quickest way to stop Chris being so irritating was to let him have his moment. She tried to tear a corner off a page. It resisted.

Despite herself, she flinched. That was odd.

Chris nodded at her like a hungry puppy. 'Aha!'

'All right, so it's made of strong paper,' said Clare.

Chris handed her a knife. 'Aha! Cut it, then! Go on, cut it!'

'Presumably I won't be able to,' said Clare, handing back the knife along with the book. 'OK, so it's a wonderful new kind of paper. Hurrah for super-paper. Hardly constitutes a dive-bomb attack on the world of science, or whatever you said.'

Chris raised a finger and opened his mouth to form a vowel sound.

'Don't say aha!' Clare warned him. 'Really, don't say aha! I will kill you if you say aha.'

Chris swallowed. 'Right then. Tell me what you think it's made of then, this new kind of paper.'

Clare shrugged. 'I dunno. Plastic.'

Chris raised a finger and opened his mouth to form a vowel sound.

'I will kill you,' Clare warned again.

'I checked,' said Chris. 'Not plastic. Not a polymer in sight.'

'All right then.' Despite Chris's incredible irritatingness, Clare was beginning to get intrigued. 'Is it metal?'

'There's no crystalline structure,' said Chris. '*At all!*'

Clare thought. 'A single crystal then?'

Chris huffed. 'If it is, our Mr Dalton's got a lot of explaining to do.' He hunched forward, getting closer to Clare than he ever had before. That was more like it, thought Clare. 'That's the fascinating thing,' he went on. 'Yes, I think it is a crystal – but no, it can't be a crystal. Half of it's stable all the time, half of it none of the time. There is absolutely no way of telling what it's made of.'

Clare coughed and looked meaningfully over at a machine in the corner, which was now covered up by a big tea towel for some reason. 'Er, spectrographic analysis?'

'Oh yes,' said Chris, crossing to the spectrograph with an irritating saunter. 'Oh yes, I got a positive result from the spectrograph all right. Oh yes, ho-ho.'

'Please, the point!' Clare insisted.

Chris whipped off the tea towel with a flourish, revealing a large black stain. 'It blew up!'

'OK, all right. That is very weird.' Clare considered for a moment. 'What's it about?'

'What's what about?'

'The book. What's it about?'

'Well, I don't know, do I?' Chris flicked the book open and flicked the pages at her. 'Looks like a cross between Chinese and algebra.' He put the book into her hands again. 'Actually – try and read it. Go on.'

Clare flicked through the book. The contents were gibberish. 'Not getting anything, sorry.'

'No – flashes?' prompted Chris, looking slightly disappointed. 'No – visions?' He rubbed his hands together, looking almost as hesitant and nervous as normal.

'Flashes and visions?' Clare frowned.

Chris took the book from her. 'No, of course not, that would be ridiculous. I mean, even more ridiculous.'

'Why don't you ask old Whatsisname?' suggested Clare. 'The professor you nicked it from.'

'I didn't nick it, I accidentally borrowed it,' blustered Chris. He looked thoughtful. 'Yes, ask Chronotis, that's the obvious thing to do, I suppose.'

Clare sighed. 'Is that why you haven't done it yet?'

Chris picked up his jacket. 'You're a genius! Er – look after the book, make yourself at home, I'll be back in half an hour.'

'I've got things to do,' Clare started to protest – but then she stopped herself and smiled as Chris bustled out.

He hadn't thought of doing the obvious thing. He'd made an incredible discovery, and the first thing he'd thought of was getting her over and impressing her. And he'd just failed to do the other obvious thing and take the book with him, instead entrusting it to her. That was almost worth his incredibly irritating excitability.

Clare tried to make herself at home. A cup of tea would be nice.

While she waited for the kettle to boil, she wandered over to where the book sat and idly opened it at a random page.

And then she jumped back. Because for just a second, surging up in her mind's eye, she'd seen a face. A malignant face. A face made out of rock, with twin furnaces for its eyes.

15

The Doctor and Romana had nearly completed their hunt for the Professor's very special book. Working methodically from either end of the room, they had been through almost every one of the thousands of titles, and the Professor's quarters looked, if it were possible, even more of a mess than before. Now they were checking off the last few books.

Romana had the sinking feeling that *The Worshipful and Ancient Law of Gallifrey* was not going to be among them. '*Roget's Thesaurus*,' she said, stacking yet another book on top of a tottering pile.

The Doctor did the same on his side. '*British Book of Wildlife*, in colour.'

'*Alternative Betelgeuse*,' said Romana, tossing aside the travel guide.

'*The Time Machine*,' said the Doctor.

'*Wuthering Heights*,' said Romana.

There were now only two books left. The Doctor took a deep breath and reached for one of them. His shoulders slumped. '*Tandoori Chicken For Starters*.'

Romana flung her last book down in absolute disgust. '*Chariots of the Gods*.'

'So,' said the Doctor. 'No sign of *The Worshipful and Ancient Law of Gallifrey*.'

Romana glanced at the open kitchen door. The Professor was inside, making another inevitable round of teas. 'Do you really think it's important?' she whispered.

'Of course!' exploded the Doctor. 'It's one of the Artefacts!'

Romana chose her next words carefully. 'Other than for its historical value?'

The Doctor bit his lip. 'Each of the Artefacts was imbued with stupendous power. The meanings were lost millennia ago, but those powers remain. And the ancient rituals, of course.'

Romana cast her mind back. 'I never really thought about the rituals. I just mouthed along to the words like everyone else.'

'Remind me,' said the Doctor. 'It's been a while. Isn't there one that refers specifically to our missing book?'

Romana frowned. 'Oh yes. At the Academy's induction ceremony. How did it go? "I swear to protect—"'

The Doctor nodded vigorously. 'Oh yes, of course. "I swear to protect *The Worshipful and Ancient Law of Gallifrey* with all my might and main, and I will, to the end of my days, with justice and with honour, temper my actions and my thoughts."'

Romana smiled. 'Harmless enough words.'

The Doctor looked as if he might explode again. 'Pompous enough words. From a pompous lot, all grand intentions but no actions.'

'That's not true,' countered Romana. 'What about you, for instance? Plenty of actions.'

'Yes, well, I'm the exception that proves the rule,' said the Doctor, not entirely unpompously.

'And there've been others,' Romana pointed out. 'What about Drax?'

The Doctor smiled. 'Ha! Drax!'

Romana thought back to their adventure on the planet Atrios, where she'd encountered her second renegade Time Lord. Drax, a contemporary of the Doctor, had left Gallifrey and spent his time running a slightly shady intergalactic salvage and repair operation.

'And the Corsair,' said the Doctor. 'Though he's one of the good 'uns, really. We must catch up with her sometime.'

'And the Master, of course,' Romana went on.

The Doctor gave her a sombre look. 'Of course.'

'And then there's the Rani. And Morbius, don't forget Morbius.'

'How could I?' spluttered the Doctor. 'He nearly knocked my block off.' He gazed into mid-air, looking back into his own past. 'And there was the Meddling Monk.'

'And the Interfering Nun,' added Romana. 'And going back a bit, there was the Heresiarch of Drornid. And Subjatric.'

'Subjatric *and* Rundgar,' the Doctor corrected her. 'They were quite a team, those bad brothers. Terrible tyrants, the stories say. Drowned their own mother in a leaky SIDRAT.'

'And what about Salyavin?' said Romana.

The Doctor frowned. 'Oh yes, him. Awesome psychic powers, they said . . .'

'Did you ever meet any of them, the ancient outlaws?' asked Romana. 'The legends always made them sound so terrifying.'

The Doctor spluttered, looking insulted at the suggestion. 'I certainly did not! I'm not that old!'

'Weren't you ever tempted to see them for yourself?' asked Romana.

The Doctor harrumphed. 'I don't go running up and down the Gallifreyan timeline, Romana. I have my limits! It could cause the most terrible paradoxes!'

Romana regretted asking. 'All right.'

'No, Salyavin was long gone, and long before I was born,' said the Doctor. 'Subjatric and Rundgar too, and Lady Scintilla, all of those old ne'er-do-wells.'

'What happened to them?' asked Romana. Her Gallifreyan history was usually better than the Doctor's, but on this occasion she couldn't quite recall the details.

The Doctor puffed out his cheeks. 'Do you know, I can't remember.' He called out into the kitchen. 'Professor?'

'Yes?' the Professor called back. 'Nearly done.'

'Lady Scintilla. And Salyavin. And Subjatric and Rundgar, the terrible tyrants. What became of them? We're regrettably cloudy on the details.'

The Professor ran suddenly into the room, his face wild with excitement and worry. 'I've just remembered!'

'I only just asked you,' said the Doctor, reasonably.

'Asked me what?'

'What happened to the Ancient Outlaws,' said Romana. 'Lady Scintilla and Salyavin and all the rest.'

The Professor frowned, obviously not taking in what she was saying at all. 'Salyavin? Scintilla? I'm not talking about them. Good riddance to them! We must find the book!'

'Professor, what do you think we've been doing?' said the Doctor.

The Professor waved his arm dismissively. 'I just remembered! There was a young man here earlier. Came to borrow some books. He might have taken it whilst I was out of the room making tea.'

The Doctor leapt over to the Professor's side. 'What was his name, Professor?'

The Professor tutted and drummed his fingers against his temples. 'Oh, I can't remember. Oh dear, I've got a memory like . . . Oh, what is it I've got a memory like? What's that thing you strain rice with?'

'What was his name, Professor?' urged Romana. 'Was he tall? Short? Young? Old?'

The Professor jabbed a finger in the air triumphantly. 'I remember!' he exclaimed. 'Yes, I remember!'

'Who was he?' demanded the Doctor. 'Tell us!'

'A sieve!' cried the Professor, exultant. 'That's what it is! I've got a memory like a sieve!'

There was a pause.

'What was the young man's name, Professor?' asked the Doctor again.

'Oh, I can't remember that,' said the Professor airily.

Romana took the Professor's hand and gave him her warmest smile. He seemed such a nice old man. 'Oh, Professor, please try.'

The Professor squinted. 'A ... A ...' He paused. 'No, it doesn't begin with A.'

'B?' suggested the Doctor.

'C?' suggested Romana.

The process was agonisingly slow. After all, Romana reflected, a Time Lord brain for all its marvels was still a brain at the end of the day, subject to eventual age and decay. The Doctor was nothing like as old as the Professor, as he had just had cause to remind her, and even he could be infuriatingly forgetful and erratic at times.

The Professor continued to run through the alphabet as far as he remembered it, pausing between each letter to consider. 'P, Q, R, X ... X again, T, B, Y ...'

Suddenly he snapped to attention. 'Y! Young!'

'He's called Young?' exclaimed the Doctor.

'Yes,' nodded the Professor. 'Young Christopher Parsons!' The revelation seemed to shake the Professor and he stood upright and rigid, eyes screwed tight shut. 'Born 1952, graduated 1975, honours degree in Physics, currently researching sigma particles.' He sighed as if this had been a great effort, opened his eyes and beamed over at the Doctor and Romana. 'There we are! I knew it was in there somewhere.'

'Where would this Chris Parsons be now, Professor?' urged the Doctor.

'Er – the physics lab, I should imagine,' said the Professor. 'You can borrow a bike from the quad. Then you'll have to take the first left out of the gates and then—'

The Doctor interrupted him. 'Yes yes, Professor, you took me there one afternoon, remember?' He was already heading for the door. 'We spent a very nice afternoon bashing some atoms about and then calling them names.'

'Oh yes,' said the Professor, smiling. 'Well, I suppose this calls for tea.' He set off back into the kitchen.

'I'll be two minutes,' the Doctor called after him.

Then he turned to Romana, looked her right in the eye and whispered urgently, 'If I'm not back in two hours, you and the Professor lock yourselves in the TARDIS with K-9. Send out an all-frequency alert direct to Gallifrey, and wait. Don't come after me!' He pulled his scarf tighter around his neck and made for the door.

'Wait!' called Romana.

The Doctor turned. 'Yes, wait! Wait and don't come after me!'

'No, I meant wait as in "wait a second",' said Romana. She leaned in close to him. 'Send a signal to Gallifrey? Is it really that important? That you'd ask for help from the Time Lords?'

'I hope not,' said the Doctor gravely, and then he was gone.

16

Skagra adjusted the collar of the shirt he had taken from the dead human. 'My appearance?'

'It is perfectly correct in every detail, my lord,' the voice assured him. 'I have cross-referenced your new vestments with local video signals. You will be able to pass for an ordinary human with no difficulty.'

Skagra nodded. 'Excellent.'

'And may I say, my lord,' added the voice, 'your magnificence is barely dimmed by such dowdy garb.'

Skagra found this flattery unnecessary and rather irksome. He had programmed his Ship to obey his orders unquestioningly. He had refined its personality matrix to worship and honour him, as this was obviously the most efficient relationship for getting things done in life. Unfortunately the Ship sometimes went too far, making irrelevant observations – *how amazing you are, my lord* or *only you could be so wonderful, my lord*. These observations were true enough, of course, but they were not strictly necessary. They were so obvious they were not worth vocalising.

'I am going to retrieve the book,' he said, picking up the carpet bag containing the sphere and turning to go. 'I shall return immediately.'

'Of course you will, my lord,' said the Ship.

Skagra left the Ship and slipped into the stolen ground-transporter.

He turned the keys in the ignition and the car roared off back into Cambridge.

17

Chris peddled furiously through the streets of Cambridge back towards St Cedd's. His head was full of theories about the book. Could it be the only remnant of some lost civilisation? Then again, it didn't look very old. Then again, it didn't look particularly new. It was hard to tell how old it was, it was hard to tell anything meaningful about the blasted thing —

His head was so full of thoughts about the book that he nearly collided with another cyclist. He rang his bell angrily at the bloke who was pedalling furiously in the other direction. In fact, thought Chris, it was very hard to ring a bicycle bell angrily. However hard you tinged it, it sounded bright and cheery.

Irritatingly, the other cyclist tinged his bell happily back at Chris.

In normal circumstances, Chris might have stopped and given the bloke a piece of his mind – or, more probably, tutted. There were two factors that stopped him. Factor A was the urgent business he was engaged upon. Factor B was that the bloke on the other bike looked eccentric. He was tall, with a mop of untidy curly brown hair and a ridiculously long multicoloured scarf that flapped after him in his slipstream.

Chris had had quite enough of eccentricity today. He was determined not to give the strange bloke another thought.

18

Wilkin checked his watch, though there was no need. He could tell from the angle of the slowly setting sun over the courtyard that it was nearly five o'clock. His stomach gave a small rumble, right on time. The agreeable prospect of scrambled eggs was looming.

He heard crisp footsteps coming over the cobbles through the gate and turned to see the insolent fellow he had encountered earlier. At least he was now wearing more suitable clothing, though still a little too casual for Wilkin's taste. The carpet bag was still clutched in his hand. The man gave Wilkin a broad smile. It was blatantly insincere, thought Wilkin, but at least now the fellow was trying.

'Hello,' said the stranger. 'I have returned, as you see. Is the one known as the Doctor still with Professor Chronotis?'

Wilkin was forced to repay politeness with politeness. 'No, sir. The Doctor left a few minutes ago. You'll find the Professor in Room P-14.' He indicated the way.

The stranger's smile faded. 'Thank you, gatekeeper,' he said icily and strutted over towards the entrance Wilkin had indicated.

Wilkin looked after him, shaking his head and tutting. In all his years at St Cedd's, and in all his dealings with undergraduates, graduates, dons, chancellors, deans, masters and, much more rarely, red-faced girls trying to sneak past him in the early hours of Sunday mornings, he had never before felt such a strong sensation of having failed in his duty as porter, of having allowed an enemy into his stronghold.

Wilkin shook the feeling off. The fellow was probably from Oxford.

'More tea, my dear?' asked the Professor, inevitably.

Romana had cleared the books away from what she had suspected was a comfortable chair. She sat down and stretched, trying to appear calmer than she felt. 'Lovely! Two lumps, and no sugar.'

The Professor smiled and tweaked her on the nose. Romana would have resented such an action from anybody else, but he seemed such a nice old man.

As he slipped back into the kitchen, Romana gave up on her attempt to relax. The chair wasn't nearly as comfortable as she'd hoped anyway. She idly twitched a corner of curtain and looked through the window onto the back of the college, leading down to the river. The sun had almost set, its last rays picking out the bare branches of the trees in shades of copper. The clouds had moved on now, mostly, and she could see a crescent moon low in the sky.

She shivered. The reassuring sounds of the Professor pottering about in the kitchen, seemingly without a care in the universe, were small consolation. She kept thinking of those voices she'd heard earlier, the whispered screaming of souls in torment. The Doctor's forbidding mood had unnerved her even further. For him even to consider an appeal for help to the Time Lords, the situation must be desperate.

Perhaps he was just being grand and portentous. After all, on the surface of it, all that had happened was that some human had accidentally wandered off with an old book that was probably completely harmless.

But as she looked at the moon, and remembered those voices, Romana shuddered again. She thought of those ancient scourges of the Time Lords – Subjatric and Rundgar, Lady Scintilla, Salyavin —

Suddenly the Professor was looming over her. 'Oh dear,' he was saying.

Romana snapped out of her reverie instantly. 'What's the matter?' she demanded, perhaps a little overdramatically.

'I've run out of milk,' said the Professor sadly.

Romana laughed. 'I think that's the least of our problems.'

The Professor leaned in closer, concerned. 'You're shivering, my dear. Are you cold?'

'No,' said Romana. 'It's just a silly feeling. No scientific basis for it. Those voices we heard, I can't stop thinking about them. I've given myself the creeps.'

The Professor sighed. 'Oh dear. A cup of tea will make you feel better.' He turned to the kitchen and stopped. 'Ah – no milk. I'll just pop out and get some. There's a little shop around the corner, very convenient, who doesn't love a little shop?' He bustled over to the door.

Romana, remembering the Doctor's dire warnings, jumped up from the chair and barred his way. 'I don't think that's an awfully good idea, Professor.'

The Professor blinked. 'Why not? It's the only way I know of getting milk. Short of keeping a cow.'

Romana nodded to the TARDIS. 'Don't worry. We've got plenty.'

'Ah, splendid!' The Professor peered over his spectacles at the police box. 'Yes of course. It's a Type 40 TARDIS, isn't it?'

Romana opened the door of the TARDIS. 'Yes. They were on the Vintage and Veteran Vehicles syllabus at the Academy. It's amazing this one's still going.'

'I remember when they first came out, you know. When I was just a boy.' He chuckled and reached out, stroking the wooden shell with affection. 'That'll show you how old I am. A vintage veteran myself.'

Romana leaned down and tweaked the Professor's nose. 'Nonsense. As they say nowadays on Gallifrey, "6,000 is the new 4,000". Anyway, the milk – I won't be a moment.'

'Oh yes you will,' said the Professor. 'That was one of the problems with the old Type 40 design. The kitchen's much too far from the control room.'

Romana smiled. 'I've never known the Doctor to use the kitchen anyway,' she said, and slipped inside.

Professor Chronotis stood for a moment looking at the TARDIS, seeming to stare back into days long gone. 'Hah, good riddance, good riddance to the lot of 'em . . .'

His thoughts were interrupted by a babble of voices from the corridor outside his rooms. 'Tsk. Undergraduates,' he muttered darkly.

There was a sharp, single knock on the door.

'Come in, then!' called the Professor automatically, and equally automatically he headed into the kitchen to prepare tea for these visitors, whoever they were.

Skagra entered the room, and winced. He was seeking one book. Here there were many, but they had all been scattered carelessly around in no particular order, with creased and cracked spines, dog ears and – most horrifically of all – many, if not most, of them were adorned with dark brown ring-shaped stains, as if some beverage vessel had been placed on top of them. It was a place of vile untidiness and confusion.

'It'll have to be lemon tea, I'm afraid,' called a scratchy, ancient voice from an adjoining room. 'No milk at the moment, the girl's gone to get some.'

Skagra noted the tall blue container in a corner of the room. He recognised it from the video-texts he'd scanned earlier as the Doctor's TARDIS. He was tempted to try and gain entry but realised this would be a long and complex process with no guarantee of success. Furthermore, it was not a necessary course of action.

Only the book mattered.

Skagra opened the straps of the carpet bag and the voices grew louder, more insistent.

'How many of you are there, for heaven's sake?' called the Professor's voice, slightly tetchily. 'I've only got seven cups!'

'Professor Chronotis!' barked Skagra.

The Professor appeared in the kitchen doorway, carrying seven cups on a tray. Skagra was not impressed. So this is what becomes of a Time Lord at the end of his days, he thought. All that power, all that genius, frittered away into dust and darkness.

The Professor blinked and looked around. The babble of voices grew louder still. 'Where are the others?' For the first time, Chronotis seemed to grasp that something was very wrong. He peered intently at Skagra. 'Who are you?'

'I am Skagra. And I have come for the book.'

'Book?' the Professor bluffed desperately. 'What book?'

'You know what book,' said Skagra. 'Give me the book.'

'I don't know what you're talking about,' said the Professor. 'I haven't got any books.' He corrected himself hastily. 'That is to say, I have lots of books. Lots and lots of books. What book would you like?'

'The book you stole from the Panopticon Archives,' said Skagra simply.

The Professor's grip on the tray slackened and it began to wobble. 'What do you know of the Panopticon?'

'The book, Professor! You are to give it to me!'

'On whose instructions?'

'Mine,' said Skagra. 'Give me the book.'

'I'm terribly sorry,' said the Professor, clearly trying to sound casual but betrayed by the rattling of the cups on the tray, 'but I don't know where it is. Honestly, I don't know!'

Skagra inclined his head and fixed Chronotis with his iciest stare. 'If you will not give me the information voluntarily, I will deduct it from you. I am sure there is much else in your mind that will interest me.'

He opened the bag wide and the sphere rose angrily from inside, the babble of voices reaching a crescendo. Before the Professor could react, the sphere zoomed towards him and fixed itself to his forehead like a limpet to a rock.

The Professor cried out in pain and dropped the tray with an almighty crash.

His arms waved frantically in the air, trying to reach up to remove the sphere.

'Do not fight the deduction, Professor,' Skagra advised him coolly. 'Do not fight it or you will die.'

He watched calmly and dispassionately as the old man's frail body buckled and he collapsed on to the threadbare-carpeted floor.

19

Clare closed the blinds over the windows that looked out onto the little grass courtyard and shivered at the memory of that fiery face.

It was hard not to feel unnerved, being alone in here with that book. Under the lab's strip lighting it looked so innocuous, as harmless as the other books on a nearby bench. Idly, Clare wandered over and inspected them. It occurred to her that these were the books Chris had gone to St Cedd's to borrow. They were clearly aimed at impressing her. And she was impressed, not because of the books – she had read them all several times over under the covers in her tiny teenage bedroom, and hid them in public behind *My Guy* annuals – but because of the thought that had gone into their selection. It was just possible that shoving a few books about carbon dating under her nose was Chris's idea of a romantic gesture.

But this was silly. The strange book was just a book. A strange one, admittedly, but just a book. She walked straight over to it and opened it again.

She was kissing Chris – not a peck, a full-on snog – and she heard herself saying 'I suppose a police station is as good a place to start as any –'

Suddenly she was brought back to here and now as the lab door burst open and an extraordinary figure burst through it. He was an almost unfeasibly tall and imposing person, with a long, dark-brown coat, a mop of curly hair, checked trousers stuffed into buccaneer boots and a stupidly long scarf. He should have looked ridiculous, and yes, in a way he did, but Clare was immediately overpowered by feelings of generosity and trust, as if she'd known this stranger since childhood and he was as familiar as Father Christmas or Winnie-the-Pooh.

She only had a second to feel like this, however, as he shot Clare a look of surprise and immediately burst back out again.

A second later he burst back in again, as if the first burst hadn't happened at all.

'Hello!' he said in a deep dark voice that was unlike any voice Clare had ever heard. 'I'm looking for Christopher Parsons.'

'You've just missed him, I'm afraid,' said Clare.

The stranger's extraordinarily bulging blue eyes passed cursorily over her and fell upon the book on the bench. He raised a finger and said, 'Aha!'

Clare found this 'Aha' much less offensive than Chris's 'Aha's. This man, she thought, had somehow earned the right to be pompous and odd. 'Can I give him a message?' she asked.

The stranger leaned over, his large beaky nose almost touching the book, and examined the cover, that curious scroll design. Then he straightened up and turned his probing stare to Clare once again. 'This isn't yours.'

Clare had the oddest feeling that he was studying her, weighing her up as a potential enemy. A part of her was screaming inside *Who the hell are you? How did you get in here and what's all this to you?* but it was muted by the part that felt the sudden warmth for him, which for some strange reason was shouting, much more loudly, *TAKE ME WITH YOU!*

'No, it isn't mine,' she said, trying to sound calm and normal. 'Is it yours?'

'It belongs to some friends of mine,' said the stranger, carefully, his eyes still not moving from her.

'It's a very strange book,' said Clare.

'I've got some very strange friends,' he said. 'And very careless.' A thought seemed to strike him. 'Strangely careless . . .' He looked into the distance and then suddenly snapped back to her. 'Why did you take it?'

'I didn't take it,' said Clare.

'I know,' said the stranger.

Clare sighed. 'Look, come on, what is all this about?'

'What's what about?'

Clare indicated the book. 'That. This book business.'

The stranger seemed almost afraid to touch the book. His fingers hovered hesitantly over it. 'Have you read it?'

'I can't,' said Clare.

'You can't read?'

'No – I mean, yes, I can read, but – the writing looks more like an explosion in a spaghetti tree.' Suddenly the questions blurted out of her. 'Where does it come from? What's it made of? Why did it make the spectrograph blow up?' She indicated the tea-towel-covered machine in the corner.

'May I inspect your spectrograph?' asked the stranger. Clare nodded and he strode over and whipped the tea towel from the machine. He whistled. 'That book did this?'

Clare nodded. 'This book did that.'

The stranger looked between her and the spectrograph and seemed to come to a decision. He smiled suddenly and unexpectedly, with teeth like two rows of great gleaming tombstones. 'Hello, I'm the Doctor,' he said, extending a hand.

'Clare Keightley,' said Clare, shaking it.

But what she was thinking inside, rather oddly, was *Well, of course you are.*

20

The Professor was right about the Type 40 design, thought Romana. The kitchen was a good five minutes' walk down the twisty white corridors from the control room. What the Professor didn't know was that the Doctor was quite appallingly cavalier with the pedestrian infrastructure of the TARDIS, casually deleting, creating and re-arranging the interior space like a deck of cards as the whim took him. It was a good job she had such an incredible memory or the journey might have taken much longer.

Romana returned to the control room with a pint of milk. She crossed to the console and was about to open the door to rejoin the Professor when a thought struck her. She called, 'K-9?'

The mobile computer, shaped roughly like a dog, whirred into view from beneath the console. His eye-screen glowed enthusiastically. 'Mistress?' he asked keenly.

Romana knelt down and patted him on the head. 'Do you want to come out and be useful? This doesn't seem to be just a social visit after all.'

'Affirmative, Mistress,' said K-9. 'My function is to assist you,' he added, perhaps a little put out at being left behind in the TARDIS all afternoon.

'Well, you can tell me how old this milk is for a start,' said Romana.

She tore off the golden foil top (which read *Express Dairies 1886*) and held the contents under K-9's super-sensitive scanner nose.

K-9 sniffed. 'This milk has been in the stasis preserver for only thirty years relative time. It is perfectly fresh.'

'Good,' said Romana. 'Come on, I'll introduce you to the Professor.'

She threw the big red lever that operated the main doors and K-9 followed her out of the TARDIS. 'I got the milk,' she called – and then she saw the old man lying curled up beside the sofa, his eyes open, staring blankly. His skin was horribly white, his head thrown back, mouth open, his features twisted in pain and shock.

'Professor!' cried Romana, rushing to his side.

This time, thought Chris, he was going to get some answers. This time he wouldn't stand for any eccentricity or vagueness or strangeness, or even any wanton police-box-related bizarreness. He was going to march straight into Professor Chronotis's rooms like a man and get the whole truth about this damned book business like a man would. Oh yes, this time would be different!

He parked the bike in the quad and nodded to the porter.

As he marched purposefully and in a very direct, masculine and no-nonsense manner indeed through the corridors to Room P-14, he almost collided with a stern-looking bloke who wore tight jeans and a shirt unbuttoned at least two buttons more than necessary, who for some reason was carrying an old carpet bag.

'Sorry,' said Chris, internally chastising himself for not sounding very manly at all.

The bloke barged past him brusquely without a word.

Chris reached the door of the Professor's room, braced himself and knocked. Time for some common sense!

'Professor Chronotis!' he called.

'Who is it?' said a voice that wasn't the Professor's.

Chris decided to push straight in, in a no-nonsense, common sense manner.

'It's me, Professor,' he started to say – and then stopped.

The Professor lay motionless on the floor, his face contorted in an expression of terrible pain, his hands twisted like claws. Leaning over him was the most beautiful woman Chris had ever seen. Her classical, almost aristocratic features were framed by long fair hair the colour of ripening corn, and she was dressed in a straw hat and a delicate lace ensemble. All she needed was a parasol and she could have stepped straight from the beach of a Boudin canvas. Though she was clearly deeply distressed at whatever had befallen the Professor, she retained an air of poise and dignity. Immediately, she made Chris more nervous than any woman ever had before, including Clare. Strangely, in the instant way the human sexual instinct works even in moments of distress or wanton bizarreness, Chris realised he didn't actually find her attractive, more – awesome.

And, even more strangely, she wasn't the oddest person in the room, if the other occupant of the room could be described as a person, which Chris severely doubted.

At the woman's side, somehow looking equally concerned, was a metal box about three feet by two feet with 'K-9' emblazoned on its side in what somebody had obviously thought was a futuristic typeface. From the front of the box sprouted what was clearly meant to be a head, with a glowing red screen for eyes, a snout with a nozzle at the end and two miniature radar dishes in place of ears. It sort of looked, a bit, like a dog. It even had an antenna for a tail and, for a campy finishing touch, a tartan collar.

All this flashed through Chris's mind in a second as all hopes of common sense for this day finally vanished. Lamely, and very un-masculinely, he found himself asking, 'What's happened?'

The girl gave Chris no more than a quick glance before turning back to the Professor. 'I don't know,' she said. She bent over and listened to the left side of his chest and then, strangely, checked the right side as well. She straightened up. 'I think he's dead,' she said despairingly.

'Negative, Mistress,' piped a tinny voice. It took Chris a moment to realise the sound was coming from the metal dog-thing. With an electrical whirr, a long slim probe extended from its eye to the Professor's forehead. 'He is alive but he is in a deep coma.'

Chris had so many questions. But they were pushed to the back of his mind by the sight of the Professor's prone body. He had seemed such a nice old man. So he just asked 'What's happened to him?' again.

This time it was the dog-thing that answered, its radar ears twirling furiously from side to side. 'Processing data,' it said.

Suddenly the girl stood up and fixed Chris with a suspicious glare. 'Do you know him?'

Chris almost stepped back a pace, and then actually did. This woman was a bit terrifying. 'Hardly at all,' he spluttered. 'He just lent me a book.'

'A book!' she exclaimed. 'We've been looking for a book! Are you Young Christopher Parsons?'

Chris flinched. 'Yes,' he admitted in a small voice. He felt, under the girl's steely glare, that he was confessing to bigamy, genocide and the drowning of especially cuddly puppies.

'Well, have you got it?'

'Got what?' stammered Chris.

The girl rolled her eyes. 'The book!'

'No. I left it back at the lab. You see—'

She interrupted him. 'So why isn't the Doctor with you?' Her gaze was suddenly less fierce. Now she seemed worried.

Chris blinked, more confused than ever. 'I didn't know that the Professor was ill.'

'No, *the* Doctor,' the girl said with peculiar emphasis.

Chris was totally stumped now.

Suddenly the dog-thing piped up again. 'Mistress. The Professor has been subjected to psycho-active extraction.'

The girl knelt down to address it. 'Will he be all right, K-9?'

'Physical prognosis fair,' said the dog. 'Mental prognosis uncertain.'

Chris inched towards them. He couldn't contain himself any longer. 'Is that a robot?' he asked, pointing at the dog-thing.

The girl didn't look up. 'Yes.'

Feeling suddenly bold, Chris knelt down opposite the robot. 'A robot dog?' he ventured. 'Called K-9? That's quite funny, isn't it? K-9, as in canine. Quite clever.'

'Yes,' said the girl, impatiently, as if this wasn't the time to discuss such trivia.

Chris tried to rationalise it all. Unfortunately the rationalising part of his brain had been worn down by trying to rationalise that book for most of the afternoon, so after a few idle thoughts about how far the Japanese were taking the science of robotics, it gave up. 'K-9,' he said weakly. 'Neat.'

The girl looked thoughtful. Gently, she touched the Professor's forehead. 'K-9, did you say psycho-active extraction?'

'Affirmative, Mistress,' K-9 replied. 'Someone has stolen part of the Professor's mind. His attempts to resist have caused severe cerebral trauma. He is weakening fast.'

'Can I get one thing clear,' said Chris, raising a finger. 'Is this all for real?'

The girl sighed. Then she turned to him with a sudden encouraging smile. It was like the sun coming out from behind a black cloud. Chris instantly felt he would do anything for her.

'Do you want to make yourself useful?' she asked.

'Well, if I can,' said Chris, nodding vigorously.

The girl pointed to the police box. 'Go and get the medical kit from the TARDIS,' she said, as if that was the most normal sentence in the world.

Chris stopped nodding. 'The what now?'

'Over there,' the girl said, pointing to the police box again. 'First door on the left, down the corridor, second door on the right, down the corridor, third door on the left, down the corridor, fourth door on the right . . .' She hesitated as if trying to remember.

'Down the corridor?' suggested Chris for want of anything better to say.

The girl nodded. 'White cupboard opposite the door, top shelf.'

Chris got up and then realised there wasn't another door in the direction she'd indicated. He didn't want the girl to think he was stupid but he needed some clarification.

He attempted a jaunty laugh. 'For a moment,' he said, 'I thought you were pointing at that old police box.'

'I was!' shouted the girl. She gestured urgently. 'Please, get it!'

Chris decided that things couldn't actually get any weirder than they already were and pushed into the police box.

Suddenly things got even weirder.

Instead of the small dark cupboard he'd been expecting, he stepped into a large white circular room, about as big as a middle-sized restaurant. At the centre of the room was a hexagonal control console, each of its six upward-slanting facets covered with levers, buttons, dials and switches, the functions of which he couldn't even begin to guess at. At the centre of the console was a tall glass column that contained an even more intricate unit that pulsed with a reddish light. The room was illuminated by concealed wall-lights that poured a gentle golden glow from behind ornamental circular panels ranged in a regular pattern around the walls. The room was alive with subdued energy, an even hum of power. It smelt, thought Chris, rather like a country church, with all those associations of great age and ancient tradition.

A wooden hat stand stood incongruously in one corner, with a large chequered cape and a long, oatmeal-coloured frock coat thrown casually over it. In a recess next to it was a large shuttered screen. On the other side of the room was another door, which was slightly open, revealing beyond what looked like a mile of similarly patterned white corridor.

Chris whipped round in shock – and saw, instead of the police box doors through which, he reminded himself, he had *definitely* entered, two much bigger white doors made of whatever material the rest of the room was made of. Through the doors he could see the awesome girl and K-9 crouched over the Professor.

Chris dashed back through the doors. He'd never been literally agog before, agog with eyes popping and jaw juddering, like Tom when he sees Jerry launching a disproportionately spectacular act of revenge.

He turned back to point at the police box, which was still clearly a police box, and one that he could see all the way around. 'I-I-I-I-I-,' he stammered.

'Hurry up!' barked the girl, as if his reaction was incredibly petty and tedious.

Chris found himself obeying. Despite this latest revelation, he could remember her directions as if she had deliberately implanted them in his mind. For all he knew, she had. He ran through the inner door and through the corridors as instructed, alternating between admiration for the capacity of the human mind to adjust to incredible new situations and screaming.

He found the correct door and poked his head around it into what seemed like a Victorian hospital ward, with plastic curtained-off alcoves. Chris hadn't any energy left to be overwhelmed and so snatched open the locker and brought down the medical kit, a large metal suitcase-affair that was stencilled with a red cross. Then he hefted it up and ran back up the corridors, into the main room and through the impossibly not-matching doors that led to the Professor's study.

He burst out to see that the girl had propped up the Professor's head on a selection of hardback atlases. 'Professor? Can you hear me, Professor?' she was calling.

'Mistress,' said K-9 in tones Chris was sure contained a hint of sympathy. 'His mind has gone.'

'You said part of it, K-9.'

'Affirmative,' said K-9. 'But the part that remains is now totally inert.'

Chris dashed over and set down the medical kit. 'Thank you,' the girl said cursorily and opened it to reveal a bewildering array of bizarre-looking instruments, including a stethoscope with two chestpieces, a big box of very ordinary-looking sticking plasters and a large translucent collar that looked something like a neck-brace, all of it tangled up in a length of oddly striped bandage.

Working quickly and efficiently, the girl fitted the collar around the Professor's neck and operated a switch built into its underside. Tiny green lights began to flash on the collar, with a beep rather like a hospital's heart monitor. But instead of a single beep, the rhythm was a faint but steady beep-beep beep-beep.

'What are you doing?' asked Chris.

'He's breathing and his hearts are beating, so his autonomic brain is still functioning,' said the girl. 'This collar can take over those functions and leave his autonomic brain free.'

Chris was baffled. 'What good will that do?'

'He should be able to think with it,' said the girl, looking anxiously down at the Professor. His eyelids fluttered, a tiny movement for just a second.

Chris shook his head. Now this was something he did know about. 'Hold on, think with his autonomic brain? No no no. The human brain doesn't work like that. The different functions are separated by . . .'

He trailed off as the girl looked up at him with an expression that was deeply pitying, as if to say *You can't really be this stupid*.

'Unless of course,' said Chris shakily, 'unless, that is, unless . . .'

'Yes?' said the girl, like a schoolmarm encouraging a particularly backward pupil at the end of a long Friday.

Chris looked between the girl, the robot dog, the police box and the Professor. 'Unless the Professor isn't human?'

The girl smiled and extended a hand. 'I'm Romana. And neither am I.'

Chris shook her hand and to his surprise wasn't instantly transformed into a block of ice.

'I am a human,' he confessed. 'Is that OK?'

21

The Doctor was nosing around the ruined spectrograph, examining the innards with the aid of a slender metal probe that occasionally whirred, buzzed and lit up. He had told Clare it was a sonic screwdriver. Clare had so many objections to that, but she pushed them to the back of her mind and got on with carbon-dating the book using her own equipment in the far corner.

'Quite incredible,' muttered the Doctor.

Clare nodded. 'The book has no discernible atomic structure whatsoever, Doctor.' No other man – or indeed woman – had ever reduced her to the role of lab assistant. For some reason, she found she didn't mind. It felt perfectly natural to be handing him tools and test tubes and asking helpful questions, as if it was something that you just did with the Doctor.

He looked up from the spectrograph and pocketed the sonic screwdriver. 'Simple pseudo-stasis,' he said airily. 'The more interesting thing is this.' He tapped the spectrograph. 'The book must have stored up vast amounts of sub-atomic energy and suddenly released them when the machine was activated. Now does anything strike you about that?'

'A few things,' said Clare. 'What in particular?'

'In particular,' he said, 'that's a very odd way for a book to behave.'

'I would have thought that was obvious,' said Clare.

The Doctor raised a finger importantly. 'Aha! Never underestimate the obvious!'

'But what does that tell us?'

'Nothing,' said the Doctor, equally grandly, 'obviously.'

Clare could tell he was waiting for her to say *And what does* that *tell us, Doctor?* So she said, 'And what does *that* tell us, Doctor?'

He grinned. 'Obviously it was meant to tell us nothing, which is exactly the opposite function of a book. Therefore—'

Clare cut him off. 'It isn't a book!'

He smiled encouragingly. 'So what is it?'

A teleprinter over in Clare's corner chattered into life, the results of the carbon-dating test. She crossed over and tore off the strip of paper. 'Twenty thousand years,' she said slowly. She picked up the book in her other hand and stared at it wonderingly. 'Doctor, this book is twenty thousand years old!' Her mind was suddenly full of ridiculous thoughts about aliens and/or Atlantis.

The Doctor peered over her shoulder at the print-out and pointed. 'Look there.'

Clare gulped. 'A minus sign. Minus twenty thousand years . . .' She looked helplessly up at him. 'What does that mean, Doctor?'

'It means,' he said, 'not only that the book is not a book, but that time is running backwards over it.' His features took on a particularly stern and forbidding aspect. 'I think I'd better return it to my friends as soon as possible, don't you?'

He held out a hand.

Clare knew that if she handed the book to him she would never see him or it again. An entire new world of amazing possibilities would be closed to her for ever, and she would wonder to the end of her days about the last crazy twenty minutes. On top of that, Chris would probably go ballistic over the loss to science and the forfeiture of his amazing, if accidental, discovery.

But somehow, Clare knew, the book *wanted* to go with the Doctor. It felt the same way about him as she did. He was the right pair of hands.

So she handed it over.

For the first time, the Doctor touched the book. Clare watched as, the moment it touched his skin, he flinched and stood back, his eyes closing involuntarily. A seraphic smile formed on his lips. What was he seeing? she wondered.

Then his eyes opened and he waved cheerily to her. 'Thank you, Clare Keightley. It's been a pleasure working with you. I've rather missed your sort.'

'Can't I come with you?' Clare protested.

'I think it'll be much safer if you stay here and wait for your friend Parsons,' said the Doctor. 'Goodbye! Sorry we didn't get to do any running!'

And then he burst out of the lab and was gone.

22

The bells of Cambridge struck six.

Skagra sat in the passenger seat of the brown Capri, considering his next move. The book was the antepenultimate part of his plan, a precisely detailed scheme to which he had devoted most of his life. So where was the book now? Where had the Professor hidden it?

He pressed the tips of his fingers around the cold metallic surface of the sphere and accessed the mind most recently added to it.

He flinched as he anticipated the full force of Chronotis's mind, the mind of a Time Lord, bursting into his own. He blinked, for once taken by surprise.

This was it? What he felt now might once have been a powerful mind. Now it was nothing but greyness, mist and confusion.

A faintly unpleasant taste surged at Skagra from the melee of Chronotis's thoughts. It was a weak, warm sensation with an aroma of scorched plant material, and for some reason it was accompanied by the letter T. Skagra cast it back, searching deeper.

Suddenly, from out of the greyness, a large shape began to form. This was more like it, thought Skagra. Whatever this thing was, it was at the heart of Chronotis's deepest thoughts. It was roughly circular, a hoop of some kind, with a web of netting suspended from it, and a metallic strut at one end.

The object got larger and larger, and Skagra concentrated harder and harder, trying to divine its meaning.

Letters formed beneath the object.

S, I, E, V, E.

Skagra suppressed his irritation and rejected the object. It was irrelevant.

He pushed deeper, aiming to bypass the general disorder and access recent memory traces.

He saw himself in Chronotis's rooms, from the Professor's viewpoint.

No – he needed to go further back.

He pushed deeper still.

The mental image disintegrated in a haze of grey and then reformed in a different pattern. This time it showed a tall figure with a long scarf. The face of the man was hazy, unformed. The Professor had clearly attempted to hide the man's identity. Futile. Skagra immediately recognised it as the Doctor. Did he have the book?

No – that was suddenly clear. *The Doctor had gone to fetch the book from Young Parsons.*

Skagra concentrated, trying to break through and bring up an image of this Young Parsons. The grey veil lifted for a moment and he was suddenly seeing through Chronotis's eyes again. He was busying himself preparing the T liquid in an antechamber of his dwelling. Skagra was distantly aware of a twittering noise from the main room. The twittering noise asked something about borrowing some books about carbon dating and the Professor said something about creative disarray –

Skagra felt Chronotis's mind slipping away from him. Again the metal loop appeared, the sieve.

For all his slippery forgetfulness and senility, Chronotis had still evidently retained some of the mental training and telepathic discipline of a Time Lord.

These efforts at concealment would almost certainly have proved fatal.

Skagra made one final attempt and demanded all Chronotis's knowledge of the book.

23

Chris looked anxiously as Romana leant over the Professor, her face lit eerily by the green glow of the collar and the red eye-screen of K-9.

'The collar's working,' she told Chris. 'K-9, is there any trace of conscious thought?'

K-9's radar-dish ears twizzled. In some way, thought Chris, he must be able to connect wirelessly with the collar. 'Processing data, Mistress.' There was a pause, then he added, 'It is too early to tell.'

'Good,' said Chris.

Romana's eyebrows shot up. 'What do you mean, *good*? What's good about any of this?'

'Well, don't you see?' asked Chris, who thought it was obvious. 'When one works as a scientist, one doesn't always know where one's going, or that there even is anywhere for one to go, only that there are always going to be big doors that stay permanently shut to one.' Chris had often noticed that when he was at his very best, when he was communicating the abstract (and yet concrete) wonder of the scientific method, that people tended to assume an enthralled, glazed expression, as if he was opening their minds to entirely new ways of thinking. He was delighted to see that even Romana's eyes seemed to be frosting over, and K-9's tail antenna had drooped as if in fascination.

Chris waved a hand around the room, taking in the dog, the collar and the police box. 'You see, I look at all this. And suddenly I know that a lot of things that seem impossible are possible, so yes, that's why I say "good"—'

K-9 made a peculiar noise, almost as if he was clearing his throat. 'Mistress!' he said. 'The Professor's condition is rapidly deteriorating!'

Chris was astonished to see tears forming in Romana's eyes. 'Oh, K-9, isn't there anything we can do?'

K-9's head lowered. 'Negative, Mistress. The condition is terminal.'

Chris almost put out a hand to console Romana but stopped himself.

K-9's eye-screen flashed. 'Minimal cerebral impulses detected, Mistress!'

The Professor's dry cracked lips moved. 'He's trying to talk to us?' gasped Chris.

'Negative,' said K-9. 'The speech centres of the Professor's brain are completely inoperative.'

Romana checked the Professor's chest, both sides, again.

'Well,' Chris said sadly, 'the collar was a good idea but it doesn't seem to be helping—'

'*Shhh!!!*' Romana said sharply, and to his astonishment Chris found he couldn't say another word.

'K-9, amplify the Professor's hearts beats!'

K-9 extended the probe from his eye-screen to the middle of the Professor's chest. Suddenly a throbbing double pulse beat filled the room, fast and irregular.

Romana clapped her hands together. 'Brilliant! The Professor is a brave and clever man.' She waved to Chris. 'Listen!'

Chris listened. The pulse beats were wildly irregular, thumping fast then slow then fast again. It didn't sound very healthy at all. 'I don't understand.'

'He's beating his hearts in Gallifreyan Morse!' she cried. She leant over the body. 'Professor, I can hear you! What do you want to tell us?'

The pulse beats resounded. Romana translated the message slowly. 'Beware . . . the . . . sphere. Beware . . . Skagra. Beware . . . Shada.'

The heartbeats stopped suddenly.

'Professor!' cried Romana.

'All life function has now ceased, Mistress,' said K-9. 'Professor Chronotis is dead.'

24

The Doctor pedalled furiously through the twilit streets of Cambridge, an ancient and dangerous Gallifreyan artefact of potentially terrifying power sitting rather casually in the woven wicker basket attached to the handlebars of his bike. The Doctor rounded a sharp corner, emerging onto one of the footbridges that criss-crossed the Cam, tinging his bell to clear the way, though there was nobody to be seen. It did add a much-needed sense of urgency, he felt.

Suddenly, as the Doctor's bike started up the cobbled incline of the bridge, he saw a man striding forcefully in his direction. As the man reached the crest of the bridge, he stopped and stood still, right in the Doctor's path. Even a barrage of irritated tings wouldn't get him out of the way. The Doctor had no choice but to brake hard, wobble a bit, and slither to a halt a few feet in front of the fellow.

He was a tall, slender, fair-haired man wearing ordinary Earth clothes of the period which didn't seem to quite fit him. In one hand he carried a large carpet bag.

By the sodium glow of Cambridge's municipal street lights, the Doctor stared hard into the man's eyes. They were cold, icy blue, with an almost staggering condescension behind them. Otherwise his face was blank, lent a slightly sinister note by what looked like a duelling scar across the left cheek.

'I'm terribly sorry, am I in your way? Or are you in mine?' the Doctor enquired.

The stranger ignored this remark.

'It's just that I'm on a rather important errand, and—'

'Doctor,' the man said, simply and emotionlessly.

The Doctor blinked in surprise. 'Though it's terribly flattering to be recognised,' he said, spreading his arms in apology, 'I simply don't have the time for autographs right now.' His tone changed, suddenly serious. 'But if I did, who would I be making it out to?'

The man's eyes never left the Doctor's. 'I am Skagra,' he stated. 'I want the book.'

The Doctor smiled broadly. 'Well, I'm the Doctor and you can't have it.'

Again, there was no flicker of reaction from Skagra. 'So you possess it? And yet you attempt to hide it from me?' he asked.

The Doctor waved a hand airily. 'Yes, I suppose I do. But don't worry, it'll be taken to a place of safety.'

'Where?'

'Oh, just a little place of safety I have in mind.'

Skagra lowered his carpet bag to the ground and a small grey sphere suddenly shot out of it, hovering next to its master's right hand. Skagra glanced at the sphere, then back to the Doctor.

'What you have in mind, Doctor, you will reveal to me. In fact, everything that you have in your mind will be mine.'

The Doctor leant forward over the handlebars of the bike and looked Skagra up and down, casually letting a length of his scarf fall into the basket as he did so, covering the book. He pulled a disparaging face. 'Do you know, I'm not mad about your tailor,' he said.

Skagra's face betrayed no reaction, but the sphere at his side gave a small jerk, as if anxious to begin its work. From it came the babble of inhuman voices the Doctor had heard before. But there was something different about it. Another voice had been added to the hubbub, a vague, scratchy voice the Doctor thought he recognised.

With a small gesture, as if handling a well-trained dog, Skagra released the sphere and it flew straight for the Doctor's head.

With a violent kick, the Doctor shot his bike backwards, using the downward curve of the bridge to gain momentum. At the bottom, he wrenched the handlebars around and described a perfect 90-degree turn, only wobbling very slightly in the process. As the sphere zoomed after its prey, the Doctor gave another mighty kick, then began pedalling furiously away from his pursuer, heading back into the narrow Cambridge streets.

Skagra watched as the absurd figure on the absurd vehicle vanished into the darkness, the sphere close behind. He turned smartly and began to walk in the opposite direction. He now had full access to the dead human's knowledge of this dwelling area. He knew precisely where he needed to be.

The Doctor tinged his bicycle bell for all he was worth. It was typical, really. Now he was fleeing for his life from a presumably homicidal alien device, the people of Cambridge seemed not to want to miss all the fun. The streets were teeming with life. Innocent people with no clue of the danger they were in from the Doctor's spherical stalker. Not to mention the Doctor himself. He'd passed his cycling proficiency test, he was sure, but it had been a few centuries back and in a different body with a different centre of balance. Frankly he was more than a little out of practice.

He sped around the corner of one of the grand college buildings and found himself on a collision course with a cluster of undergraduates gathered beneath a lamp post, singing at the top of their voices. The Doctor swerved desperately, causing one of the choristers to jump back in fright and momentarily spoiling the harmonies of a very good a cappella *Chattanooga Choo Choo*. The Doctor sped on, waving in apology and tinging his bell to punctuate a downbeat, reflecting that ham and eggs in Carolina would have been considerably finer than his current predicament. He risked a look over his shoulder and saw the sphere rounding that same corner, luckily ignoring the surprised students as it fixed again on its quarry.

The Doctor turned back to the road ahead. Now this looked more promising. He had a straight run and began to pedal with ever more energy, trying to get as much distance as possible between himself and the sphere. It all seemed to be going surprisingly smoothly, and he allowed himself a momentary hope that nothing could possibly go wrong –

And then he reached the crossroads. Directly ahead of him, milling over a zebra crossing, cameras slung around their necks, was an enormous gaggle of Japanese tourists, snapping away at the buildings, the lamp posts and even the crossing beneath their feet. If they started snapping at the sphere, thought the Doctor, it was more than likely to start snapping back. So he braked hard and looked desperately to the turnings on either side of him.

The left turn was completely blocked by an enormous truck, with almost equally enormous men in denim jeans and black T-shirts lugging musical instruments and amplifiers into an adjacent building. The truck, the men and the amplifiers were all emblazoned with a Latin motto. So, thought the Doctor, he couldn't go that way either – he had no wish to upset the status quo.

Desperately, the Doctor looked to his right. Down that way, to his horror, he saw a chapel disgorging nun after nun after nun until the street was black with them. For goodness' sakes, thought the Doctor, why weren't all these tourists, roadies and nuns at home watching television on a Saturday evening like normal people?

The babbling noise of the sphere was getting closer. He risked a quick look behind him and saw it zooming down the street, almost upon him.

That was when his eyes alighted on a small, narrow alley, running parallel to the street on his right. He had no choice, he'd have to chance it.

He kicked off and swerved into the alley, bouncing heavily on its cobbled surface. The alley was barely wide enough for the Doctor's broad form. His elbows and shoulders knocked against the brickwork as he frantically made for the patch of lamplight at the far end.

Suddenly, with a screech of brakes, a brown car slammed to a halt ahead of the Doctor, totally blocking the only way out of the tiny alley. Only seconds from a collision, the Doctor was forced once more to brake hard. The wheels of his bicycle locked and he found himself propelled over the handlebars, landing painfully on the stone cobbles several feet in front of his former conveyance.

The Doctor groaned and looked up. The door of the car which had so effectively barred his escape clicked open –

And Skagra stepped out, casually slipping on a pair of immaculate white gloves. He looked down at the sprawled figure of the Doctor with no appreciable reaction. The Doctor looked behind him and saw the sphere approaching fast from the other end of the alley. There was no way out. Instinctively, the Doctor pushed himself backwards on hands and knees, trying to reach the basket of the toppled bike. The book was the most important thing, after all.

The basket was empty.

Though the sphere was now only feet away, Skagra's voice made him turn.

'At last,' Skagra was saying as he reached down to pick up *The Worshipful and Ancient Law of Gallifrey* from where it had fallen, knocked from the basket along with the Doctor, and until he'd gone and crawled off it, shielded by the Time Lord's formidable bulk. The Doctor cursed inwardly – he'd virtually handed his precious charge to the enemy!

The sphere was almost upon him.

With an almighty effort, the Doctor leapt to his feet, grabbed the toppled bike and flung it up at the sphere. The bike hit the sphere's metallic surface with a clang, sending it skittering through the air and back down the alley.

The Doctor, panting with exertion, whipped round – to see the brown car carrying Skagra, book and all, speeding away into the Cambridge night.

Suddenly, like a bullet from a gun, the sphere shot back up the alley behind him, buzzing almost angrily. It began to whizz at head-height, lightning-fast, in a circle around the Doctor. It was too fast to make a break in any direction.

The Doctor was trapped.

The hissing, whispering voices grew louder and louder, and the Doctor clapped his hands to his ears. The sphere dived at him, sending him sprawling on to the cobbles with a smack.

He cried out as he felt the cold impress of the sphere on his forehead, plucking at the edges of his consciousness. Then it began to suck out the Doctor's mind.

PART THREE

OUT OF SIGHT, OUT OF MIND

25

Suddenly the Doctor heard the greatest sound in the universe, more delightful than the dawn chorus, more lovely than the laughter of children, more sweet than a mountain stream. It was the wheezing, groaning sound of the relative dimensional stabiliser of a Type 40 TARDIS in materialisation mode.

The sphere buzzed in confusion, detached itself and dipped back, distracted from its task momentarily by this intrusion. The Doctor took his one opportunity. He leapt to his feet and dived for the still-forming doors of the police box as it solidified up from transparency at the mouth of the alley.

Romana slammed the big lever on the control console as the Doctor burst through the doors. He was red with exertion and collapsed breathlessly on the floor.

'Mistress!' called K-9, alerting Romana to the scanner screen.

On the screen, Romana saw a small grey sphere buzzing angrily through the air outside. Every so often it launched itself against the TARDIS doors like a confused wasp trying to pass through a window. A grating vibration echoed around the control room each time it made contact, setting her teeth on edge.

'Can it get in?' she asked K-9.

'Insufficient data, Mistress,' said K-9. 'Suggest immediate dematerialisation.'

'Do it, K-9!' Romana ordered.

K-9 trundled forward, probe extended, and set the dematerialisation sequence in operation automatically. A moment later the central column was rising and falling as the TARDIS vanished from the alley.

Romana knelt down to check on the Doctor. He blew out his cheeks, coughed, and patted her on the arm. 'Romana,' he finally managed to gasp, 'thank you, thank you very much, thank you so much, thank you . . .' Then he shouted, 'You took your time, K-9!'

K-9's eye-screen flashed huffily.

'It was K-9 who traced you,' said Romana. 'I heard those voices again and he traced their location. Say thank you.'

The Doctor got to his feet and adjusted the loops of his scarf. 'I said thank you.'

'Say "Thank you, K-9",' prompted Romana.

'Thank you, K-9,' said the Doctor. 'So – that great big silver bauble. It's the source of those voices.'

'Affirmative, Master,' said K-9.

'What is it then, tell me that?'

'Unidentified, Master,' said K-9. 'Origin and composition of sphere unknown. Primary purpose of sphere seems to be psycho-active extraction.'

The Doctor brushed a hand over his forehead. 'I could have told you that,' he said. 'I could feel it plucking at my mind.'

Romana swallowed. She had to tell the Doctor the bad news. 'The sphere attacked the Professor,' she said falteringly.

'The Professor!' exclaimed the Doctor. 'Yes, I thought I heard him, mixed up with all those voices. How is he?'

Romana found she couldn't reply.

The Doctor's face fell. 'How is he?' he repeated levelly.

It was K-9 who answered. 'The Professor's life is terminated, Master.'

Romana would have given anything not to see the look that then passed across the Doctor's face. For a second his composure – the composure that had remained solid against Davros and the Black Guardian – vanished completely and he just looked tired and old and sad.

'The Professor is dead?' he muttered.

Romana nodded. 'We think that sphere thing stole his mind.'

'You *think*?' The Doctor's eyes flashed angrily. 'You weren't there? You were meant to be looking after him, I left some pretty specific instructions!'

'I was looking after him,' said Romana weakly. 'I just came back in here for a second.'

'Leaving him alone,' said the Doctor. 'Why? Why did you leave him alone?'

Romana swallowed. There was no way of avoiding the truth and her culpability in the death of the Doctor's old friend. 'I just came back in here for some milk.'

'For some milk,' the Doctor repeated evenly. Romana got the impression he was trying not to look disappointed in her, for her sake, knowing that she couldn't bear it after all they had been through together.

'Yes,' she said.

'I see,' said the Doctor coolly.

'Well, otherwise he was going out to get some himself,' began Romana.

The Doctor waved a hand. 'You needn't explain,' he said wearily and crossed to the console, where he began to adjust switches and levers with the casual experience of centuries.

'And the book?' asked Romana, biting her lip. 'Have you got it?'

The Doctor closed his eyes. 'I had got it,' he said, not looking up. 'But then I dropped it.'

Romana flushed. He'd let her go through all of that! 'You dropped it!'

'Yes, I dropped it!' the Doctor said fiercely. 'We've neither of us exactly covered ourselves in glory today!'

There was a terrible silence for a few seconds, disturbed only by the ever-present hum of the TARDIS systems and the grinding of the gears in the console's central column.

Finally Romana put out a hand to the Doctor's shoulder. 'I'm sorry.'

The Doctor flinched from the sincerity of her physical contact. 'So am I,' he said, moving to another facet of the console to handle delicate navigational instruments. 'But we don't have time for any of that.' He looked deep into the red heart of the column. 'We may not have time for anything.'

26

Chris Parsons was in a riot of confusion.

Seconds after K-9's pronouncement of the Professor's death, Romana had suddenly clutched her hands to her temples and said she was hearing a babble of thin, inhuman voices. K-9 had replied that he could sense something too – 'telepathic activity peaking at 8.4 on the Van Zyl Scale'. Chris could hear nothing at all.

Then K-9 and Romana had bundled themselves into the TARDIS police box, Romana shouting a parting order to Chris to guard the Professor's body. A moment later the big blue light on top of the police box had started to flash, there was a horrific wheezing and groaning noise like an elephant in the throes of childbirth, and the police box had faded away, leaving a square indentation in the carpet.

Chris decided not to be surprised about that. The interior of the box was obviously a vehicle of some kind, so what could be more natural than it should vanish into thin air?

He found it much more disturbing to be left alone in a darkened room with a corpse. He'd never seen a dead body before, not unless you counted Bony Emm or the various skeletons and skulls that friends from the medical faculty insisted on littering their rooms with. And Chronotis had not gone gently into that good night. His features remained horribly pained and contorted, picked out in the last glow of the day.

Chris got up and switched on a table-lamp, but this only made it worse. The glassy dead eyes of the Professor were staring at him as if to say *It's all your fault*. Chris took off his jacket and covered the Professor's body.

Tentatively he stretched out a hand to close the Professor's eyelids, like they did to dead people in movies.

He felt a tingle of something like electricity but which clearly wasn't electricity and leapt back in shock, congratulating himself as he leapt on still being able to feel shock after the last few hours.

An aura formed by particles of golden light began to dance around Professor Chronotis's body.

'No, please, don't do this,' urged Chris to nobody in particular, remembering Romana's last urgent instruction. 'How can I guard you against this? I'm just from Earth. Please stop it, please stop all this glowing.'

The golden aura grew brighter, the tiny particles whizzing faster and faster around the Professor's supine form. Chris suddenly realised he could see what remained of the threadbare carpet's pattern through the parchment-thin skin of the Professor's face. Seconds later the glow had faded to leave only the carpet, Chris's jacket and a pile of atlases. The Professor had vanished completely.

'Oh great,' said Chris.

He had a sudden compulsion to clear off out of this place and put this whole thing behind him. It was none of his business. Then he reminded himself of the incredible opportunity he had stumbled across. He, Chris Parsons, had made first contact between the human race and alien beings. First *knowing* contact, anyway; plenty of people must have been baffled or irritated by old Chronotis over the years without suspecting he was actually from the planet Zoot or wherever.

Chris shook his head. He wished Clare was here.

Clare! She was still back at the lab, possibly with this Doctor person who had gone to fetch the book. He looked around for a telephone and then remembered the Professor didn't have one. There was a call box just outside the college gates, he could use that maybe –

Suddenly the elephantine groaning started again and Chris blinked as a powerful blue light began to flash illogically in mid-air. Seconds later, the police box shell of the TARDIS had faded up from transparency, solid and four-square in exactly the same spot it had stood in before.

Chris gulped and prepared himself to explain his failure regarding the Professor to the icy stare of Romana.

Instead an extraordinary figure in a long coat and trailing multicoloured scarf vaulted from the box and came to a screeching halt at the sight of Chris, eyes bulging. 'Who are you?' he demanded angrily.

'Chris Parsons, Bristol Grammar School and Johns,' Chris responded automatically, cursing himself for sounding such a fool.

'Never heard of you,' said the stranger, and then continued in exactly the same tone, 'You're the one causing all the trouble!'

Chris wasn't having this. 'I haven't done anything!' He peered at the stranger more closely. 'It's you!' he said.

The stranger's huge blue eyes blinked. 'You know who I am?'

'You nearly knocked me off my bike,' spluttered Chris, 'along Pepys Street. I ting-ed at you.'

'You what at me?' asked the stranger. Behind him, Romana and K-9 emerged from the TARDIS.

'I ting-ed at you when I was coming back here,' said Chris. His face fell. 'Oh. Are you the Doctor?'

The stranger nodded.

Chris smiled. 'Oh good. So you were going to get the book, no wonder you were in such a hurry.' A terrifying thought jabbed at him. 'Is Clare all right?'

'All right? Clare's lovely,' said the Doctor.

Chris nodded. 'Did she give you the book, then? Where is it?'

Romana looked around the room. 'Where's the Professor?'

Chris swallowed. 'Well, I just, I just, I just . . .'

'You just what?' said the Doctor.

'Well, I just don't know,' spluttered Chris at last. 'There was a golden glowing sort-of thing and he just disappeared into thin air. You know, like people don't do.'

The Doctor exchanged a glance with Romana. 'Where was the Professor?' he asked.

Romana pointed. 'Right there.'

The Doctor knelt down and examined the empty area of carpet, running his long fingers over it and then rubbing them together. 'Residual traces of artron energy,' he told Romana.

Romana looked down guiltily. 'He must have been on his very last regeneration.'

'What does that mean?' Chris asked feebly.

Romana sighed. 'We don't have time to explain everything to you—' she began.

But the Doctor stood up and put a friendly arm around Chris's shoulder. 'There are people out there,' he said, waving his other arm to indicate the entire universe, 'who would tear this planet apart for the body of a Time Lord. The Professor's regeneration cycle was completed, so his last act must have been to will his own corporeal destruction to avoid any nastiness of that kind.'

'What's a Time Lord?' asked Chris.

'Doctor, we really don't have time,' said Romana.

'I'm a Time Lord, so's Romana, so was the Professor,' explained the Doctor.

'I am not a Time Lord,' said K-9 perfunctorily.

'That makes two of us,' said Chris.

'The Time Lords of the planet Gallifrey are awesomely powerful, even if we say so ourselves,' the Doctor told Chris grandly. 'And the ancient Artefacts of Gallifrey, like that book you so annoyingly borrowed from the Professor, and which I even more annoyingly dropped, are even more awesomely powerful—'

Romana interrupted. 'Doctor!'

The Doctor caught her eye, coughed, and removed his arm from Chris's shoulder. 'What? Oh yes.'

'Whoever stole the Professor's mind tried to do the same thing to you,' said Romana.

'Yes, I met him,' said the Doctor. 'Calls himself Skagra.'

'Skagra!' exclaimed Chris and Romana at the same time.

'You know the name?' the Doctor asked Romana, then wheeled on Chris in astonishment and said, '*You* know the name, Bristol?'

Chris nodded. At last he could be of some help. 'Just before the Professor died, he said three things. "Beware the sphere"—'

'Now he tells me,' said the Doctor a little sadly, looking down at the carpet.

'"Beware Skagra",' Chris continued.

'I shall, I shall,' said the Doctor.

'And "beware Shada".' Chris waited for a reaction from the Doctor.

'Shada?' The Doctor shrugged.

Romana shrugged too. 'Means nothing to me.'

The Doctor turned to Chris. 'Mean anything to you?'

Chris rather liked the way the Doctor was including him in things. 'I'm afraid not.'

'Shada not in my memory bank, Master,' piped up K-9, obviously irritated at not having been consulted.

'Yes, thank you, K-9, I was about to ask,' said the Doctor.

'How about Skagra, K-9?' asked Romana.

'No information,' said K-9. 'Epistemological analysis of the name Skagra suggests sixteen thousand, four hundred and eleven possible planets of origin. I shall adumbrate them in alphabetical order—'

'Ssh, ssh,' said the Doctor. K-9 fell silent.

Chris smiled at the thought of so many inhabited worlds, so much wonder and potential in the wide glorious universe.

'Why are you pulling that face?' asked Romana. 'I can't see anything to smile about.'

Chris pulled himself together. 'Sorry. You know, like I said, this is all marvellous.'

'It's very far from marvellous,' said the Doctor. 'Skagra, whoever he is, has killed a Time Lord, who was a very good friend of mine.'

'And now he's got the book,' Chris pointed out helpfully.

'And now he's got the book,' said the Doctor, closing his eyes as if in pain. To Chris it was as if a light had gone out in the room.

There was a sombre silence.

Finally Romana stood forward. 'We have no choice, have we?' she asked the Doctor.

The Doctor suddenly opened his eyes. 'None.'

Romana made to enter the TARDIS. 'I'll send the signal.'

The Doctor raised a hand. 'Wait, wait!'

Romana halted in the door.

'Not that way,' said the Doctor. 'Skagra might be able to intercept any message sent through the telepathic circuits.'

He sat down in the big armchair and riffled in his pockets. He tossed out an orange, a catapult, a ball of string, a collection of odd-looking loose change and a cassette tape. Chris theorised that the pockets worked on the same bigger-on-the-inside principle as the TARDIS and congratulated himself on not saying 'Wow!' or 'How did you do that?' or even asking how a circuit could possibly ever, ever be telepathic.

Finally, the Doctor clicked his fingers as if remembering something, and reached inside his coat, into the breast pocket. He took out six white squares about five-by-five inches and shuffled them like a deck of cards. He set them down on the table before him. Then he put his fingers to his temples and stared at the table, wearing a deep frown of concentration.

Chris's eyes widened in awe as first one, then all six of the squares danced into life, arranging themselves neatly into a white cube. There was a clear chiming sound and a bright white glow shone suddenly from within.

'Wow,' said Chris. 'How did you do that?'

K-9 trundled forward, looking a little anxious, thought Chris. 'The Doctor Master is sending a thought message to Gallifrey,' he whispered. 'He is requesting their assistance in apprehending Skagra.'

'Oh yes, I see, and Gallifrey is the planet of the Time Lords,' said Chris, anxious to keep up.

K-9 raised his voice. 'Master. This unit strongly advises against this course of action—'

'Shut up, K-9!' shouted the Doctor. 'When I want your opinion I'll ask for it!'

'Entreat, Master!' bleated K-9. 'My prognostication for this course of action is highly inimical—'

'Ssh, K-9,' said Romana, a lot more gently than the Doctor. She patted him on the head. 'We know how dangerous this is. That's why we've got to do it.'

'Negative, Mistress,' wailed K-9, sounding more and more frustrated. 'This unit strongly insists that you consider—'

The Doctor cut him off. 'Silence!'

K-9 flashed his eye-screen resentfully and trundled back a fraction.

The Doctor picked up the box and looked to Romana. 'I'm sorry it's ended this way,' he said.

'Like I said,' sighed Romana. 'We've no choice. We can't handle this on our own.'

The Doctor nodded, grinned suddenly and then threw the box into the air overarm as if he was bowling a cricket ball.

The box hovered in mid-air, twisting and turning, and then the glow from within brightened until Chris had to shield his eyes. Slowly the box began to vanish into thin air, a thing that Chris was now getting used to other things doing.

Suddenly K-9 shot forward. There was a low whirring noise and a stubby black rod extended from his muzzle. A moment later a bright red laser beam shot up from it and struck the box.

'K-9, what are you doing?' cried Romana. Chris was secretly pleased to hear her saying something along those lines.

There was a deafening crack and Chris was hurled to the ground.

A thin film of dust particles was floating down from where the box had been.

The Doctor leapt to his feet. 'K-9, what have you done?' he exclaimed.

'Regret action, Master,' said K-9. 'My overriding directive to protect yourself and the Mistress caused me to obliterate the thought box.'

'You can't go around doing things I haven't told you to do!' thundered the Doctor. 'Except if I'm not there, and I am there, I mean here!'

'He must have a very good reason,' suggested Chris.

The Doctor rounded on him. 'Who gave you permission to speak? When I want your opinion, I'll ask for it!' Suddenly he shook himself and pointed at Chris. 'I want your opinion. In fact, I'm asking for it.'

'Well, I just thought he must have a pretty good reason for doing that,' Chris said. 'He seems like quite a good dog.'

'He is. K-9, did you have a pretty good reason for doing that?' demanded the Doctor.

K-9's tail wagged urgently. 'Affirmative, Master. This unit calculates that your judgement and the judgement of Mistress Romana have been influenced by emotional reactions to the death of Professor Chronotis.'

'Of course we're upset, K-9,' said Romana. 'But we're up against something that could be too powerful, even for us.'

'Yes, Mistress, but this unit is without emotional circuitry,' K-9 countered. 'I have prognosticated the possible consequences of involving the Time Lords in this matter.'

'What about the consequences of not involving them?' said Romana.

But the Doctor had raised a hand and was blowing the air from his cheeks, like a man stepping back from the edge of a very high cliff. 'Romana,' he said very quietly, 'I think K-9 may have had a pretty good reason for doing that.'

'That's what I thought,' said Chris, although he wasn't following this bit at all.

'Think about it,' the Doctor went on. 'The two of us, two Time Lords, reacted to the loss of that book with panic. And we're the reasonable ones, aren't we, with the strong ethical code and general attitude of niceness?'

'What do you mean?' asked Romana.

Chris was beginning to follow this again. 'Aha,' he said, lifting a finger. He was getting pretty good at this now. 'So the Time Lords back on Galilee—'

'Gallifrey,' corrected the Doctor, Romana and K-9 all at the same time.

'On Gallifrey, sorry, trying to get all the names right,' Chris went on, 'the Time Lords on Gallifrey are going to really have the wind put up them when you tell them Skagra's nicked their book. And if they're not as reasonable and nice as you two, they might decide it's a case of *Carthago delenda est*.'

The Doctor nodded. 'A scorched earth policy. Literally.' He smiled. 'Nicely put, Bristol.'

Romana gasped. 'You mean the Time Lords might destroy this planet?'

'If they're as afraid of the book as you are,' said Chris, who couldn't quite believe he was now answering her questions.

Romana shook her head. 'They wouldn't. They don't know what that book is capable of, what secrets it contains, any more than we do.'

'Exactly!' said the Doctor. 'They might think it wiser, quicker and safer to burn book, Skagra, planet and all.'

'The High Council would never agree to that,' said Romana firmly. 'This planet is inhabited, it's littered with fixed points in time—'

The Doctor cut across her. 'You're a historian, aren't you? Remember the fifth planet, the sack of Lassademon, the Battle of Karn—'

'Thousands of years ago, relative time,' said Romana.

'And all of those involving Time Lord secrets falling into the wrong hands,' said the Doctor. He leant down and patted K-9. 'Well done, K-9. You are a very, very, very good dog.'

K-9's ears twizzled. 'Master.'

'No, we can't take the risk of involving the Time Lords,' said the Doctor. 'Not yet anyway.'

Chris laughed.

'What's so funny now?' asked Romana.

'We've just had a conversation about the end of the world,' he said, shaking his head. 'Not just in general terms, like students on beanbags at two o'clock in the morning when the beer's run out, but actually about the end of the world really happening. Today.'

Romana crossed to him. 'Chris. Go home and forget about all of this. Please, go now.'

Chris was crestfallen. However dangerous and strange today had been, he wasn't sure he ever wanted it to end. 'What? Turn my back and wonder about this day for the rest of my life? No!' he said boldly. 'I'm a scientist, Romana. It's my duty to stay and help you.'

'Quite right,' said the Doctor, bounding over and slapping him on the shoulder.

'Doctor, this is a terribly dangerous situation, he'll only get in the way,' said Romana, with a look of apology to Chris.

'That's what I used to think about you,' said the Doctor. He looked suddenly more genial and less abrupt. 'The more the merrier. Too many cooks spoil the broth of destruction. Now let's get on with it. K-9, Skagra must have some kind of spacecraft. Search for high technology emissions, energy spikes, all that kind of naughty thing.'

'Excluding the TARDIS there are no such traces, Master,' said K-9.

'Must be shielded,' said the Doctor.

'Shielded from K-9's sensors,' mused Romana. 'Which are linked to the scanners in the TARDIS.' She shuddered. 'A ship that can hide itself even from Gallifreyan technology? How is that possible?'

The Doctor ignored the question. 'Well then, K-9, can you find any trace of that sphere, the telepathic activity?'

'Affirmative, Master,' said K-9, 'but it is far, far too weak to take a bearing.'

'We'll have to wait until it becomes active again,' said the Doctor. 'Now listen, K-9, the moment the signal becomes clear, full alert!'

'Affirmative, Master.'

'Right! Come on, we'll wait in the TARDIS.' He strode towards the police box. 'Much safer for the moment.'

'Excellent thought,' said Romana. 'Goodbye, Chris.'

'Come on, Bristol!' said the Doctor, grabbing Chris and virtually throwing him into the TARDIS before Romana could say anything more.

27

Skagra positioned the book gently behind the vacuum-bubble shield of his book collection. He hated the thought of hands, even his own, touching any book, what with all their grease and bacteria and animal warmth contaminating the pristine pages.

'You have the book, my lord,' cooed the Ship.

Skagra nodded. 'And now you will read it to me. I will learn the darkest secret of the Time Lords.'

'At once, my lord,' said the Ship. 'You are such a wonderful, wonderful person. My circuits are unworthy of the privileges you bestow on me so bountifully.'

'Just read the book,' said Skagra.

He sat back in his comfort pod and closed his eyes.

Behind the bubble shield a slim metal probe extended from a tiny hole. It reached the front cover of the book and gently pushed it open to the first page.

From another hole on the other side of the vacuum shield emerged a thicker, flexible tube. At the end was an attachment that rather resembled an eye, a cool blue light blinking steadily from the iris.

The Ship coughed.

'Begin,' said Skagra.

'At once, my lord,' said the Ship. 'Er – are you seated in the position of maximum comfort, my lord?'

'Yes,' said Skagra.

The Ship coughed again.

'Begin!' said Skagra again.

'So I just have to read the book, do I, my lord?' asked the Ship.

'For the moment, yes, that is your instruction,' said Skagra.

'And a wonderful instruction it is too, my lord,' said the Ship. 'An instruction worthy of the paradigm of unutterable brilliance that is my lord.'

'Read it,' said Skagra.

There was a pause.

'Out loud, my lord?' asked the Ship, rather tentatively.

'Yes, out loud!' said Skagra. 'Reveal the secret of the Time Lords. Tell me of Shada!'

'Yes, my lord, immediately,' said the Ship.

There was another pause.

'From the beginning, my lord?' asked the Ship.

'Read it from the beginning, out loud, to me,' said Skagra. 'Now.'

'Are you sure?' asked the Ship.

'I am very sure,' said Skagra.

'How very sure, my lord?'

'One hundred per cent sure!' thundered Skagra. 'Now begin, before I'm forced to destroy your circuitry!'

'Very well, my lord,' said the Ship.

She coughed again.

'*The Worshipful and Ancient Law of Gallifrey,*' she said grandly. 'Read by me, out loud, to my lord Skagra.'

There was another pause.

'Squiggle squiggle squiggle squiggle,' the Ship said, enunciating every syllable with the gravitas required of the moment. 'Squiggle, line, squiggle, squiggle line squiggle squiggle wavy line, though I suppose that could be a squiggle—'

Skagra leapt from the comfort pod. 'What is the meaning of this?'

'Your magnificence has, as usual, pinpointed the problem with unerring accuracy, my lord,' said the Ship. The eyestalk flexed uneasily over the open book, which Skagra saw was covered in arcane symbols. 'I am programmed to translate every language and alphabet in the universe. And I have absolutely no idea what this means.'

28

Night shrouded the city of Cambridge. The moon shone fitfully through the clouds above the old streets and around the colleges.

Wilkin made his final walk-round of the grounds of St Cedd's, gave the padlock one final tug, then returned to the lodge where, at precisely half past ten, he changed into his pyjamas and curled up in bed with a John Dickson Carr.

Clare Keightley waited for Chris in the physics lab. She waited so hard she fell asleep in a very uncomfortable plastic chair, her head resting on a pile of books about carbon dating, and dreamt about America and big decisions and Chris and the Doctor and the book, but mainly about Chris. He would have been surprised to see how very forthright he could be in Clare's dreams.

David Taylor's mum wondered where he'd got to. Wherever he'd gone, she hoped he was having some fun at last.

And the Doctor, Romana, K-9 and Chris Parsons waited in the TARDIS, which remained in the corner of Professor Chronotis's silent study, which had not so long ago been filled with the sound of friendly conversation and rattling china and teaspoons.

* * *

The Doctor and Romana either didn't want or didn't need to sleep, Chris realised. After entering the TARDIS, the Doctor had activated the force field and collapsed into a large wicker chair, looking tired and portentously undisturbable. Romana plugged K-9 into a power point underneath the console, 'to charge him up overnight' as she put it. His eye-screen went blank, then the lowermost of its horizontal bars glowed into life with a beep, and the one above that began to flicker.

'He was down to one bar, poor thing,' said Romana.

Throughout, K-9's radar dish ears revolved steadily, searching for the sphere.

'He can only trace it when it's active,' Chris pointed out.

'I know that,' said Romana.

'Which means when it's attacking someone,' said Chris. 'Trying to kill someone, steal their mind.'

'Yes,' said Romana as patiently as she seemed able.

'That's a bit horrible, isn't it?' ventured Chris.

'Nothing else we can do,' said Romana. 'We're talking about a potential threat to the lives of everyone in the universe. We can only hope we'll be there to stop it in time, like we saved the Doctor.'

Chris decided to risk another question. 'So you and the Doctor, you're sort of explorers?'

'That's the idea, though it never seems to work out that way.' To Chris's astonishment Romana smiled. 'Why not try and get some rest? There's a bathroom and a guest suite.' She indicated the interior door and gave another set of detailed directions.

'So you'll call me when you need me?' said Chris.

'Whenever that may be, yes,' said Romana, still smiling sweetly.

Chris hesitated at the door. There was no other furniture in the control room. 'Er, shall I fetch you anything? Chair or stool or cushion or anything?'

'No thanks,' said Romana. 'I can sleep standing up, if need be.'

'Really?' said Chris. Then he noted a slight smirk mixed in with her smile. 'You're pulling my leg, aren't you?'

'Night night, Young Parsons,' said Romana, turning her attention to the console.

Chris set off down the twisting white corridors of the TARDIS. This time there was less urgency to his mission and he took time to open a few of the doors that led off the corridors. Some of them gave on to other, seemingly identical stretches of twisty white, and he was very careful, as befitted the proud owner of the 7th Bristol Scout Pack award for Orienteering 1966, to close them firmly and ignore any temptation to stray from the path. As before, he could remember Romana's instructions exactly.

Some of the other doors led to rooms. There was a cricket pavilion, which somehow actually smelt of new-mown grass and linseed oil. Another door led to a huge empty cinema in which was playing a black-and-white Lone Ranger film. Chris flinched as he bumped into a large-bosomed usherette. He apologised, only to realise the figure was a cracked dummy wound around, for some reason, with dead Christmas tree lights, with a cabbage for its head, a stuffed parrot on its shoulder and a cleaning lady's bucket, filled with popcorn, slung over one arm.

He peeked through yet another door to find an enormous room filled with shelves packed with balls of multicoloured wool, a huge plastic pick-and-mix dispenser with jelly babies in every tray, and piles of entangled yo-yos.

Finally, Chris made his way to the particular door to which Romana had directed him. So this was the guest suite. He gripped the handle and pushed, ready for anything.

Somewhat disappointingly the guest suite looked, at first sight, like nothing more or less than a fairly average hotel room, apart from the ever-present circular design of the walls. Flowery carpet, a dresser, a mirror, a trouser press. Then Chris noticed two peculiarities. The bed was a single four-poster, with ornately carved wooden posts, but when he drew back the curtains he found a bunk bed, with a rickety wooden ladder attached.

The second peculiarity was the minibar, if that was actually what it was. It was gleaming white and came to about chest-height, and it certainly looked like some kind of drink dispenser or chocolate machine, with a tray for delivery of the food or drink selected but with no slot for money – only two large dials with selector needles. There were numbers on the first dial, letters on the second. In the mood for experimentation, Chris set the dials to K12 and pressed a button in the middle. There was a rumble from inside, a kind of thunk, three loud beeps, a whirr, and then an object something like a white-coloured Mars bar shot out into the tray.

Chris picked it up and took a tentative munch. He hadn't eaten since breakfast, he realised. Chocolate would do very nicely. He took a bite. His mouth filled not with the sweetness of chocolate but the hot juicy taste of prime rib, medium rare. Chris grinned – space food, this was more like it! Greedily, he took another bite. The juicy steak was replaced by the tacky oversweetness of candy floss. The tastes blended in a very unpleasant way. He pulled out his hanky and spat the contents of his mouth out into it. There was obviously some clever space-thing you had to know before you got the hang of the minibar. He looked around for instructions but there were none.

There was one interior door, presumably leading to the *en suite*. Chris took a deep breath and pushed in.

This was perhaps even more disappointing. It looked exactly like a hotel bathroom, with a lavatory, mirror, towels and toiletries. Another door said BATH.

Chris pushed it open and gasped. Beyond the door was an enormous – at least Olympic-sized – swimming pool, slopping about in a huge white enamelled container. Chris looked closely at the base of the container and saw, to his astonishment, two tiny little brass feet supporting it at this end. Presumably at the other end, eighty feet away, there were another two. On the perimeter of the bath or pool, on the left at what would normally be the shallow end, he could just glimpse two ordinary-sized taps and a rubber duck.

Chris stripped off, climbed a metal ladder and dived in. It was the warmest, most soothing water he had ever known. There was a rush of spray and a bar of soap zoomed over the water towards him.

After his bath – he hadn't dared take the plug out – Chris climbed back into the bedroom and shrugged into a big white towelling bathrobe that had been thoughtfully placed on the back of the bathroom door.

But how was he going to sleep, with all that was going on?

He sat on the end of the lower bunk of the bed and suddenly felt unaccountably tired, despite the incredible excitements and strangenesses of the day.

He gave the bed a bounce and lay back, overwhelmed with a tiredness. The bed was incredibly soft and inviting, starched sheets and plumped pillows enfolding him. Even the lighting in the room seemed to dim as his head sank into the softness.

His last thought of the day was of Clare. He really, really should have phoned her, but she'd somehow got lost under everything else. No doubt she'd given up on him and gone home to pack her few final things.

She was out of his league anyway, thought Chris. All the stuff that had happened today – Time Lords, robot dogs, impossible police boxes with Olympic-sized baths in them – seemed far more likely than her ever settling for him.

At least she was safe, and well out of it. Whatever it was.

Chris Parsons slept.

29

The dawn's early light shone through the blinds of the physics lab, where Clare Keightley still sat slumped on the uncomfortable plastic chair. The magpie pecked on the window, probably coincidentally. Clare slept on.

Finally, Clare woke up. It took her a moment to emerge from the latest stage of her dream, in which she had been loading her packed boxes into the hands of the Doctor, who was smiling encouragingly. But where was Chris? Why wasn't he there with her, starting off on this amazing journey? 'Aha!' the Doctor was saying, but she didn't want his 'Aha!' – she wanted Chris's 'Aha!' And where was Chris?

Now, as she blinked the sleep out of her eyes, the question remained. Where was Chris?

She got up, stretched, then automatically checked her watch – it was, incredibly, half past seven. The events of the previous day, strange as they had been at the time, had been stripped of their mystique by the cold sunlight.

She shook her head. Hold on. A bloke had told her to stay put – in fact, two blokes had told her to stay put, and she had meekly obeyed. When had she become the female lab assistant in a Fifties sci-fi B-movie, staying behind while the men went off to do mysterious and dangerous things that she was just there to react to? She wasn't going to make tea and ask the obvious questions for anybody.

She devised a new plan – she would find Chris, shout at him, demand to know everything she'd missed, then storm home and pack her boxes and set off for her new life.

She grabbed the lab's phone and dialled the number of Chris's flat. She gave it a good twenty rings. He wasn't going to have a lie-in today.

But there was no answer.

So she'd have to check with this Professor Chronotis. She got down a directory and flipped through until she found him – P-14, St Cedd's. There was, very irritatingly, no phone number.

She'd just have to storm over there and demand answers. However, in the sobering morning light of reasonableness, bursting in to the study of an old don that she had never met before at eight on a Sunday morning shouting, 'Where's that bloke I'm not interested in and don't care about, and what was all that guff about that book anyway and who was that Doctor guy with the scarf?' seemed an arbitrary and slightly emotional thing to do.

So she scooped up the other books Chris had borrowed from Chronotis, the return of which would give her the perfect cover. She was a busy person, a level-headed, sensible academic, just returning some books, that was all.

She didn't want to admit to herself that she was terribly worried about Chris and terribly worried about the book.

Chris needed looking after, he was an idiot.

She put her coat on and set off for St Cedd's.

30

Bernard Strong settled himself down on his fold-out stool, adjusted his hat, settled the bait box by his feet, raised his rod and cast off.

He'd turned up early and got one of the best spots on this stretch of the Cam, along the water meadows a couple of miles outside the city. He had no real intention of landing anything good, he just wanted to clear out of the house before the missus woke up and gave him what-for after his late homecoming the night before.

Suddenly he saw a grey metal sphere, about the size of a football, hovering in mid-air some distance away down the curve of the river. He watched in astonishment as it zoomed forward with short, aggressive spurts of energy. What the heck was that thing? Some remote-control gizmo, a computer thing? Or perhaps a satellite, another bit of Skylab? If so, it might be worth a bob or two. If nothing else it was casting a shadow and would scare the fish.

Without really thinking about the logic of what he was doing, Bernard stood up and drew back his line from the water. He waited until the metal football-thing was within his reach and jabbed the end of his fishing rod at it.

The rod slipped off the side of the ball with a metallic scrape. Then the ball stopped in mid-air and turned on its axis, as if somehow it was adjusting itself to look at Bernard.

It made a loud buzzing noise, like an angry wasp trapped in a biscuit tin, and zoomed forward. Bernard felt its cold metal surface touch his forehead –

Then there was a pain in the back of his head, sharp and searing – and then nothing.

The mindless body of Bernard Strong pitched forward into the River Cam.

The sphere zizzed angrily past him, heading out into the empty water meadows.

It had been silent in the TARDIS control room for so long that Romana jumped when K-9's high-pitched voice suddenly rasped out, 'Master! Mistress!'

The Doctor, who had said not one word after settling down in the chair the night before, woke with a start and leapt for the console.

'Have you got something, K-9?'

'Affirmative, Master,' said K-9. 'The sphere is active: 5.7 miles distant at bearing 4.378. Velocity 15.3—'

'Good dog!' said Romana.

The Doctor punched new coordinates into the navigation panel with incredible speed, his fingers a blur. 'We might still be in time,' he told Romana. 'Get Parsons up here!'

Chris was jolted from sleep by the insistent *ring-ring* of an ordinary-sounding telephone.

He looked around the guest suite. There was no telephone.

He leapt out of bed, feeling rested and refreshed. The ringing continued – but where was the phone?

He looked into the mirror – and suddenly he saw, instead of his own reflection, Romana. 'Chris, we've picked up the sphere!' she called urgently. 'The control room, quick!'

Her image disappeared.

Chris reached for his clothes, which had somehow been pressed and cleaned and sat in a neat pile on the dresser. He was just getting into his trousers when a tremendous lurch sent the room spinning, as if the whole TARDIS had jerked to one side.

Clare evaded the porter of St Cedd's with ease. She waited until the little bespectacled man had unlocked the big padlock on the gate at 8 a.m. sharp, gave him another minute to start making his rounds, then slipped into the courtyard and headed for the corner which she assumed was the P Block. She didn't fancy any rigmarole with a porter on top of everything else.

She entered the long wooden-panelled corridor, the books on carbon dating clutched in one hand, and counted off the doors from P-1 down and around a corner. She was starting to feel more than a little ridiculous. There was probably going to be a perfectly reasonable, rational answer to yesterday's events, after all.

As she neared room P-14, she heard an unearthly noise, like huge and ancient engines grinding into life. And all the strangeness flooded back, worse than ever.

What the hell was going on in there? She had a nightmare vision of Chris, the Doctor and the Professor standing around a machine that was about to explode – perhaps that was the explanation, they'd spent the night in there trying to scan that bloody book, and now it was going to kill them all . . .

She ran for the door of P-14. The noise was definitely coming from inside, though now thankfully it was starting to fade away.

She pounded on the door with her free hand, calling, 'Professor Chronotis! Chris!'

There was no answer. The groaning machine-noise slipped away completely.

Clare tried the door and was surprised to find it open.

She burst in.

The room looked as if a bomb had hit it, with books pulled from their shelves littering the place. There were seven broken teacups. Chris's denim jacket, the one that he never went anywhere without, lay abandoned on the floor. There was no sign of him or anybody else. In the far corner there was a large, square indentation over carpet and scattered books.

Her mind started racing. All the worry she'd been repressing behind her anger surged up. What if the book had exploded or something – she wouldn't put anything past it – vaporising whatever scanning device had stood on the spot groaning like that, and taking everybody in the room with it?

She shook herself. Things like that just didn't happen. But then she remembered the book and Chris's disappearance.

The fear flooded back. She had to get help.

She dropped the books and pelted out of the room.

Wilkin had completed his first circuit of inspection on this fine Sunday morning. Apart from an inappropriately placed traffic cone and a pink-painted policeman's helmet, there was nothing especially amiss in the grounds of St Cedd's. The weather looked hopeful, with tinges of blue fighting through the cloud-covered sky. He stowed the cone and the helmet in his little office and was thinking of breakfast when he looked up suddenly. Through the little window of the office he saw a shape – a female shape, a young female shape – running pell-mell towards the gates. He recognised the signs at once. The mussed-up hair, yesterday's creased clothes, the smudged make-up, the air of panic and shame. But this girl obviously had no real experience of the Sunday morning escape.

He stepped out into the courtyard and raised his bowler hat to her. 'Good morning, miss,' he said with all the severity he could muster on these occasions. He preferred to turn a blind eye, but she had made that impossible by clomping across the grass like a scalded gazelle.

To his surprise she altered her course, running right up to him. 'I need your help,' she gasped.

This was new, thought Wilkin. He hoped to God she wasn't going to consult him on contraceptive advice.

'I will help you all I can, miss, within college rules,' said Wilkin.

'Have you seen Professor Chronotis this morning?'

'Now, now, calm down,' said Wilkin, instantly dismissing the possibility of any hanky-panky in this scenario. Professor Chronotis was far too old for that sort of thing, certainly not a roué. He seemed such a nice old man, in fact. 'Isn't he in his room, P-14?'

'No, I've just come from there,' the girl said breathlessly.

Wilkin frowned. 'You spent the night with Professor Chronotis?'

'No,' said the girl, 'I've just arrived here, I slipped in, you must have been making your rounds. The Professor isn't in his room, nobody is, that's the point.'

'Peculiar,' said Wilkin. 'The Professor certainly hasn't left the college since he returned from a shopping trip yesterday morning.'

'Could you have missed him as well?' pointed out the girl.

Wilkin was rankled now. 'Certainly not, miss. Professor Chronotis has, in my experience, always exited and re-entered this college in a civilised and entirely appropriate manner.'

'What about Chris Parsons, he's vanished too,' the girl went on. 'Tall, dark hair, denim jacket, looks a bit hopeless but sort of sweet with it . . .'

Wilkin nodded, back on familiar ground. 'Mr Christopher Parsons, physics postgraduate of St John's College, arrived here by bicycle at 6.20 p.m. to visit Professor Chronotis.'

'And did you see him go?'

'I'm rather afraid not, miss,' said Wilkin. 'I assumed he was joining the Professor and Miss Romana. Their friend the Doctor had gone out at 6.15 p.m.'

'And when did the Doctor get back?' asked the girl.

'He did not return last night, miss,' said Wilkin. 'And I am quite, quite certain that I could not ever miss him.'

The girl seemed to be concentrating hard, trying to fit things together. 'So – the Doctor never got back with the book. So – where are the Professor and Chris?'

Wilkin said reassuringly, 'No need to worry. I'm sure they'll be around somewhere. If you want to leave a message, I'll see the Professor gets it.'

The girl shook her head. 'No, you don't understand. Three men are missing, and it has something to do with a book.'

'A book, miss?' Wilkin was beginning to wonder about this young lady's state of mind.

'Yes, a book!' said Clare. 'A book, and I think it's a terribly dangerous book.'

Wilkin frowned. 'Well, what I say is, people shouldn't write things if they don't want people to read them.'

The girl groaned. 'No, you still don't understand, it's the book itself. It defies all analysis, it's blown up a spectrograph, it seems to be minus twenty thousand years old and now, on top of all that, the three of them have vanished!'

Wilkin had maintained his blandest smile in the face of this onslaught of a sentence. 'All right, miss,' he said. 'I'm sure we can sort this all out. I tell you what, you go back to his room, and I'll ring around the College and see where he's got to.'

'His room!' exclaimed the girl. 'That's another thing! It looks like a bomb's hit it, there was a wheezing, groaning noise and books are just thrown around all over the place.'

Wilkin smiled. 'Ah yes. That's quite normal. Our Professor Chronotis has his own ideas about tidiness and order. He will not permit the cleaning staff to enter, and in a college with such ancient and venerable plumbing as St Cedd's, one hears the most awful noises from the pipes. The wheezing and groaning you heard was probably Professor Gillespie in P-18 running his Sunday morning bath.'

The girl made one last protest, 'But—'

'Just wait in P-14, I'll sort the whole thing out,' said Wilkin. 'Believe me, there's nothing that can surprise me in this job.'

The girl stared at Wilkin for a moment longer, then turned on her heel and stalked back across the grass towards the Professor's rooms.

Wilkin shook his head and rolled his eyes. 'All this fuss about a book. I don't know, they'll publish anything nowadays.'

He slipped back into the lodge. Those phone calls could wait until after breakfast.

31

Chris entered the control room of the TARDIS, breathless from his run up from the guest suite. The big glass column in the centre of the console was coming to a halt, which Chris guessed was a signal that this miraculous craft had arrived at its destination.

Before he had time to say good morning, the Doctor had wrenched the red lever on the console and dived out of the big white doors as they opened. Chris followed Romana and K-9 outside.

The TARDIS had brought them to a place Chris recognised. These were the big water meadows outside the city. The autumn air was chill and spotted with fine drizzle.

The Doctor had already run to the river's edge, where he stood sombrely examining an angler's fold-out seat and a small collection of fishing ephemera.

'We were too late,' he said grimly, nodding to the river, where a body floated, face down.

Chris swallowed hard. 'Why did the sphere attack him?'

'Probably he tried to attack it,' theorised the Doctor. 'It must have a defence program of sorts.'

Chris stood back from the river, shaking himself. Suddenly he saw two things. At the edge of the big meadow they had arrived in, a brown

Capri was parked, very badly. And passing the Capri at that moment, zigzagging erratically and slowly from side to side in what he could have sworn was a sulky, frustrated manner, was the sphere he'd heard so much about.

'There!' he called, pointing out to the meadow.

The others turned and followed his finger.

They watched as the sphere disappeared. But this was not like the dematerialisations of the TARDIS or the body of the Professor. Chris watched in amazement as the top section of the sphere was swallowed up by nothingness. Then the middle vanished, then the bottom. It was as if it had been gulped up by some huge invisible monster.

Chris was secretly pleased to see that the Doctor and Romana looked almost as perplexed by this as he felt.

'Did you just see what I didn't see?' asked the Doctor, crunching forward over the long, dew-sodden grass.

'No,' said Romana, following him.

'Neither did I,' said Chris, following her. K-9 sped forward past the Doctor, leading their party, his gun probe extended from his snout.

'It just vanished,' said Chris.

'That's what I said,' said the Doctor, staring up at the very spot the sphere had done whatever it had done.

The sphere drifted disconsolately back onto the command deck of the Ship.

Skagra, now once again clad in his preferred garb of neutral white, sat back in his command chair, his mind searching endlessly through reams of information stored in the Ship's data core. There had to be something in all the fruits of his long researches into the Time Lords that would give him the power to understand the book. He knew better than to try to scan the book's composition or molecular structure – as an ancient Artefact it would have been constructed using materials chosen specifically to resist analysis. But hours of checking, rechecking and cross-checking the data core had provided nothing that helped him.

He needed a Time Lord, or at least the mind of a Time Lord, to unlock the book's secrets. Chronotis's mind was useless, a hotchpotch of senility. But soon the sphere would return with the mind of the Doctor and, however erratic and childish that was, Skagra was certain he could force the truth from it.

'My lord,' said the Ship, gently insinuating itself into his thoughts, 'the sphere, that construct of your unequalled genius, has returned to us.'

Skagra disconnected his data-spike, opened his eyes, and turned to the sphere. He held out his hand and the sphere bobbed gently onto his palm.

Skagra searched the sphere. A new mind had indeed been added. Skagra communed with it, asking it for knowledge of the book. Instead he got only confusing glimpses of the consciousness of another primitive human –

Piscine creatures, wriggling worms and quiet teas with the missus –

Skagra demanded an explanation from the sphere. The sphere, which had a rudimentary operating consciousness of its own, displayed a mental image – of the Doctor escaping from it into his ridiculous TARDIS.

Skagra almost shouted out loud. A curse word formed itself and almost pushed itself from his lips.

'My lord, is anything wrong?' enquired the Ship.

Skagra dismissed the sphere, which settled itself on the top of its cone.

'Nothing is wrong,' said Skagra levelly, though in his head he could see the Doctor being eviscerated by an enormous harpoon. He coughed. 'Ship. Give me details of the Doctor's TARDIS capsule.'

The Ship was ready with the information in microseconds. 'My gracious lord, it displays the characteristics of a Gallifreyan time-travel capsule, Type 39, possibly Type 40.'

'I know that,' said Skagra, fighting the compulsion to exclaim. 'Inform me of its present whereabouts. Is it still on this planet?'

'Oh yes indeed, my lord,' said the Ship. 'It is in close proximity. In fact, intruders including your enemy, that nasty Doctor, are approaching us from it at this very moment.'

Skagra sat forward. 'Show me!'

The Ship provided a holo-screen, showing a high angle from one of the sensors. On the screen was the Doctor, accompanied by two other humanoids. The first Skagra recognised as the fair-haired female who had accompanied the Doctor in some of the video-texts he had scanned. There was another male, unfamiliar to him but outwardly brutishly human and stupid-looking. Bringing up the rear was the Doctor's irritating mobile computer, the unit so humorously titled K-9.

Skagra watched as the Doctor walked straight into the side of the Ship.

The Doctor, walking slowly forward into the empty meadow, suddenly cried out and rubbed his nose. He raised a commanding hand to halt the others.

'Don't move!' he ordered. Then he stretched out his long arms tentatively. Chris watched as he seemed to touch an invisible wall, patting the thin air as if it contained solid shapes, like a mime artist.

'K-9, there's something here!' he exclaimed.

'Affirmative, Master,' said K-9.

'Then why didn't you tell me there was something here, you stupid animal?'

'This unit assumed that you could see it, Master,' said K-9. 'Apologies. I had not completed my scan and had not noted the object's non-refractive exterior as regards the humanoid visual spectrum.'

'I think it's invisible,' said Chris.

'What is it, K-9?' asked Romana.

'It is a spacecraft, Mistress, of very advanced design,' said K-9.

'Are you sure about that, K-9?' said the Doctor, rubbing his nose. 'I'm sure we can spare a week for you to waggle your probes at it.'

K-9 sniffed. 'Scan complete. Many of the ship's functions are beyond my capacity to analyse.'

Chris reached out and touched the invisible hull of the craft. 'If I build something this clever, I'll want people to see it,' he said.

'K-9,' said the Doctor, 'what's it powered by?'

'Insufficient data,' said K-9.

'Aren't we all?'

'What about its origin?' asked Romana. 'Where does it come from?' She reached out and felt the hull, touched it briefly and stepped back as if she wasn't impressed.

'Insufficient data,' said K-9.

'What does it look like?' asked Chris.

'A very large spacecraft,' said K-9.

'How large is very large?' asked the Doctor.

'One hundred metres long,' answered K-9.

'And is that large for a spacecraft, then?' asked Chris. ''Cause I've never see one.'

'Well, I've seen bigger,' said the Doctor, feeling his way down what was probably the side of the ship.

'We're not really seeing this one, are we?' observed Romana.

'There must be an entrance,' said the Doctor. 'Find the door and I'll have us in there quicker than you can say sonic screwdriver . . .'

Chris suddenly noticed something. There was a low electronic hum coming from about six feet in the air.

'That sounds like a door,' said Romana.

There was another, lower hum from the same place. It seemed to Chris to be getting closer and closer to him. He stepped back nervously as a small line of grass right in front of him suddenly flattened as if something had been dropped on it.

The Doctor pushed in front of Chris and put a tentative foot forward. The heel of his boot made a metallic clang. He rocked forward to put his weight on it, and moved his other foot experimentally up a few inches.

Then he pulled the first foot up cautiously and was suddenly standing a few inches above the ground.

'Looks like stairs,' mused the Doctor. 'Well actually, it doesn't look like stairs, it feels like stairs. No way to welcome visitors, particularly those of us without legs.' He nodded to K-9.

Chris suddenly had an idea. He picked up a big pile of autumn leaves that had been blown into the meadow, strode up to the line of flattened grass before the Doctor, and flung them upwards in his general direction.

The leaves flopped wetly down, onto nothing at all – but various levels of nothing at all, giving a vague brown wet indication of a staircase that led up to nowhere. 'Aha,' said Chris. 'Well at least it gives us a vague idea of where the steps are.'

'Well done, Bristol,' said the Doctor. 'Isn't he good, Romana? Plucky old Bristol, that's what this situation needed, a bit of practical thinking, and not afraid of getting his hands dirty.'

He turned and started going up the steps slowly, one by one.

Romana started after the Doctor. Two steps up, she turned with a smile. 'Since you don't mind getting your hands dirty, you can bring K-9.'

Chris rubbed his dirty hands on the sides of his jeans and looked down at K-9, who was wagging his tail impatiently. He bent down and hefted him up, grateful that he wasn't as heavy as he looked.

'Kindly exercise caution while conveying this unit, young master,' said K-9.

Chris staggered in an ungainly fashion after the Doctor and Romana. So it was Sunday morning, and he was carrying a robot dog up some slippery steps into an invisible alien spaceship. Nobody was ever going to believe a word of this.

He glanced up to see that most of the Doctor had vanished into nothing, and now Romana was disappearing from her hat down. He quickened his pace –

There was no appreciable sensation whatever. Chris suddenly found himself seeing not the empty meadow but a small, spotlessly white chamber, like someone had flicked a switch behind his eyes. He jerked his head back, instinctively startled, and saw the meadow again.

'Come on, Bristol!' he heard the Doctor call.

Chris squared his shoulders and walked through.

He found himself in the white chamber. The Doctor and Romana were examining the featureless, curving white walls. Ahead of them was a large circular closed door.

'Oh, I see,' said Chris, setting K-9 down gratefully. 'This must be the ship's airlock. Assuming spaceships have airlocks, but then again yours doesn't, but then again it's not strictly a spaceship, is it?'

He trailed off, looked behind him, and saw the meadow, framed by another circular door. There was a low hum and it irised shut, cutting out the reassuring world of Cambridge and normality. A horrible thought struck him. 'Wait a minute, nasty things happen to people in airlocks.'

'Do they?' asked the Doctor.

Chris nodded. 'In films and things.'

'Don't worry, Chris,' said Romana. 'With a ship like this, Skagra could have blasted us down the moment we left the TARDIS.'

'Don't upset Bristol, Romana,' said the Doctor. He knocked on the far door. 'Come on, open up.' He put his mouth to the door and sang loudly, '*Why are we waiting*?'

Chris was alarmed. 'Hold on, this Skagra guy, he's a cold-blooded killer. Are you sure it's a good idea to provoke him? I mean, I'm not an expert, but when dealing with a psychopath is it a good idea to go shouting abuse through his letterbox?'

The Doctor gave Chris a look that was suddenly utterly sincere and serious. 'Yes,' he said.

Romana put a hand on Chris's arm. 'Don't worry. The Doctor knows what he's doing.'

The Doctor turned to her with a big grin. 'Thank you, Romana,' he said.

Romana smiled back. 'Well, usually.'

And then suddenly there was a blazing glow of intense white light – and the Doctor was gone.

'Where is he?' asked Chris.

Romana looked around. 'Where are *we*?'

Chris looked round in panic. He suddenly realised that he, Romana and K-9 were no longer where they had been. The Doctor hadn't vanished – *they* had.

The room they stood in was still spotlessly white, and it was even smaller than the airlock.

But what made Chris's blood run cold was the fact that there were no doors. Wherever they were, there was no way out.

32

The Doctor had watched helplessly as a spinning cube of white light appeared from nowhere, forming around Romana, K-9 and Chris. A moment later the cube had disappeared again, taking his three friends along with it. He was alone in the airlock.

There was another electronic hum, and the inner door irised smoothly open to reveal Skagra.

The Doctor faced him, and spoke in a level, serious tone. 'What have you done to them?'

'They will not be harmed, Doctor,' said Skagra in the same bland, emotionless way he expressed everything. He added, 'For the moment', but it was not the threat of a madman or dictator, the types the Doctor was used to encountering and besting. It was a simple, untrammelled statement of fact, as if Skagra was passing casual comment on something of no consequence at all.

'I'm not very impressed by the party tricks, Skagra,' said the Doctor.

'These "party tricks", Doctor, are purely functional. Their purpose is precisely defined, as is mine.' Skagra indicated a long curving white corridor that led from the airlock into the heart of the Ship. 'Come with me, Doctor.'

'First, where have you taken my companions?' The Doctor advanced menacingly on Skagra. 'It's just the two of us here now. I knew you couldn't hide behind that overgrown billiard ball of yours for ever.'

Skagra held up a hand. 'I am undefended at present. But should you attempt a physical assault, I will order the immediate deaths of your friends.' He gestured down the corridor once more. 'Now come with me.'

The Doctor followed Skagra down the corridor.

'What have you done with the Professor's mind?' he asked.

'It has been put to a more useful purpose,' Skagra replied.

The Doctor seemed about to explode with anger. He restrained himself and instead said quietly and threateningly, 'I would argue that it was serving a very useful purpose where it was.'

'Possibly,' said Skagra. 'But not to me.'

The Doctor snorted. 'You realise the Professor is dead?'

'Only his mind was of use to me,' said Skagra. 'Not his body.'

They had reached the far end of the corridor and another large white circular door. 'It seems to me that you take a very proprietorial attitude towards other people's minds,' said the Doctor.

For the first time, Skagra seemed to react. His full, sensual lips twitched in a micro-expression that mixed amusement and contempt. It wasn't much, but the Doctor caught it. 'It seems to me, Doctor,' said Skagra, 'that the Time Lords take a very proprietorial view towards the universe.' He paused. 'They are your people, aren't they?'

The Doctor pressed his face very close to Skagra's, looking deep into his cold blue eyes. 'Just exactly who are you, Skagra? And what do you know of the Time Lords?'

'That knowledge will be of no use to you,' said Skagra coolly.

'Then I think you may as well tell me,' pointed out the Doctor.

'And I think I may as well not,' said Skagra. He activated a control on the left of the door and it irised open. 'We have more important matters to discuss.' He waved the Doctor through ahead of him.

The Doctor looked around the spartan command deck of the Ship. There was a bank of controls on each side, and a large white leather padded chair, angled back. Next to the chair was a tall grey cone, with the mind-sucking sphere resting on the top, apparently inert for the moment. Up ahead was a large screen, presently covered by white shutters. The room displayed no trace of individuality or even of having ever been occupied. It was, thought the Doctor, rather like a showroom model. 'Functional and precisely defined, indeed,' he said. 'I don't like it.'

Skagra moved to a white cabinet and pressed a button. A panel on the front of the cabinet slid back, revealing a collection of books, meticulously arranged in order of size, largest to smallest.

The Doctor stepped forward and stooped to examine the contents. 'I take it back. Quite a collection you've got here.' He recognised the worn gilt lettering on the spines of the books. It was a slightly archaic form of Gallifreyan, from several thousand years ago. '*The Chronicles of Gallifrey*,' he said, trying not to sound impressed. 'I thought these were out of print.'

'These titles have helped bring me to my greatest acquisition,' said Skagra. He crossed to a clear plastic bubble, presumably some kind of scanner, on a nearby workstation. He slid the bubble open and took from inside *The Worshipful and Ancient Law of Gallifrey*. The Doctor noted how Skagra handled the book, delicately, at arm's length in his white-gloved hands. 'This book, Doctor.'

'What book, that book?' The Doctor snatched it from him at lightning speed, flicked through the pages, and handed it back. 'I've read it, it's rubbish.'

If he suspected such a move would unsettle Skagra, he was wrong. Without a trace of reaction, Skagra calmly passed the book back to him.

'Then perhaps you would read it to me?'

The Doctor shrugged. 'I have a very boring reading voice. By the time I'd got to the bottom of the first page you'd be asleep, I'd escape, and then where would you be?'

'Read it to me,' said Skagra.

'I presume you can't read Gallifreyan, then?' said the Doctor.

'Like a native,' said Skagra, indicating the other books in his collection. 'From the Old High Gallifreyan of the Rassilon Era down to the scrawlings of the Sheboogans. But as you know, the book is not written in any form of Gallifreyan.' He nodded. 'Read it to me, Doctor.'

'All right,' said the Doctor affably. He flipped open the first page and coughed. 'Are you standing comfortably?'

'I am,' said Skagra.

'Then I'll sit down,' said the Doctor, leaping into the padded white leather chair. He was uncomfortably aware of the sphere, sat atop the cone right next to him at head height. He concealed his apprehension, crossed his long legs, coughed again, and began.

'"Squiggle squiggle",' said the Doctor. '"Squiggle, wavy line, sort of an eye I think, squiggle, squiggle . . ."' He stopped and smiled up at Skagra. 'I'm paraphrasing wildly, of course.'

Skagra's lip trembled slightly. 'Doctor,' he said warningly, 'let me remind you that your friends—'

The Doctor held up a hand. 'Shhh, this is a good bit. "Squiggle squiggle wavy line, wavy squiggle!"' Suddenly a look of mock worry came over his face. He flipped through the book again. 'Skagra, do you realise this book doesn't make one bit of sense?'

'Doctor,' said Skagra, composed again. 'Any fool would realise that the book is written in code.'

The Doctor stared at the book for a good ten seconds. Suddenly he sat bolt upright in the chair. 'Skagra!' he exclaimed.

'What?'

'This book is written in code!' He winked. 'How am I doing?'

'I believe that you know the code,' said Skagra.

The Doctor shrugged. His eyes kept turning between Skagra, the book and the uncomfortably close sphere. 'Who, me? Oh no no no.' His tone changed suddenly, becoming less flippant. 'I'm afraid I'm very stupid. Very stupid. I am very, very stupid.'

It was almost as if he was trying to convince himself of that fact.

'Doctor,' said Skagra patiently, 'I believe that you, as a Time Lord of some experience, know this code. Unlike the Professor's, your mind is relatively young and strong. You will decipher the code for me. Immediately.'

'There's no point in giving me orders,' said the Doctor, looking up at him with an oddly vacant expression. 'As I keep telling you, I'm very, very stupid.'

'That was not an order,' said Skagra.

'It wasn't?'

'It was a statement of fact.'

'Ah,' said the Doctor. 'How stupid of me not to realise.'

Skagra raised his hand in a sharp, up-cutting gesture.

The sphere buzzed into life. Gently it left its position on top of the cone.

The Doctor made to leap from the chair. Skagra barked out, 'Ship, restrain him!'

A warm, female voice said, 'Certainly, my lord.'

Suddenly the Doctor cried out. He found that he could not move from the chair. A searing pain surged through his body, pinning him back.

'You will give me the code because you have no choice,' said Skagra.

The Doctor grimaced and spoke through gritted teeth, fighting the pain of the chair's force field. 'I don't know about that, Skagra,' he managed to say, beads of sweat running down his forehead. 'I don't know about anything, in fact.' He closed his eyes and gasped in pain. 'I am an . . . appallingly stupid person . . .'

'That, Doctor, will soon be very true,' said Skagra. He gestured to the sphere.

The sphere attached itself to the Doctor's gleaming forehead. He let out a long cry of terrible pain, and his whole body shook in a series of agonised spasms.

Skagra watched the process, unmoved. He considered using up a smile but decided against it.

Finally the sphere detached itself from the Doctor and moved gently into Skagra's outstretched hand.

The Doctor lay still and slumped, eyes staring open.

'Scan for life signs,' ordered Skagra.

A melodic electronic burble sounded as the Ship carried out a sensor sweep. 'My gracious lord,' it reported finally. 'I am pleased to confirm that your enemy the Doctor is dead.'

Skagra reached out and took the book from the Doctor's lifeless, unresisting fingers.

33

Chris completed his circuit of the tiny white room. 'So there are no doors,' he began.

'Correct,' said Romana, who had drawn up her feet and was sat next to K-9, her chin propped in her hands.

'So,' said Chris, 'we must have been transported here, wherever here is, by some form of matter transference.'

'Very clever,' said Romana, staring straight ahead.

'Commendable deduction, young master,' said K-9, and Chris could have sworn they exchanged a glance that was not entirely favourable to him.

'Oh well,' said Chris, feeling confident enough to throw a little sarcasm back their way. 'I suppose you two do this sort of thing all the time.'

Romana sighed. 'Yes, actually.'

There was a silence. Chris was never loath to take the opportunity to fill a silence. 'Do you know, I was meant to be delivering a paper to the Physics Society next week.'

'Oh yes?' asked Romana.

Chris nodded. 'Finally disproving the possibility of teleportation.'

He shrugged. 'Well, I can always deliver it the week after. Means a complete rewrite, though.'

He sat down next to Romana, crossing his legs. 'You're very calm,' he said. 'And that makes me calm. Thank you.'

Romana smiled. 'Actually, Chris, I'm desperately worried.' She turned to K-9. 'K-9, do another scan. Can't you pick up any trace of the Doctor?'

K-9's ears rotated. 'Negative, Mistress. Every signal is shielded. Suggest that this is a primitive zero environment, isolated from all external sources.'

'That's one of the things that has me desperately worried,' said Romana. 'Skagra's technology, it's frighteningly similar to our own.'

'You mean,' said Chris, 'similar to yours and the Doctor's in particular, or to the Time Lords in general?'

'Both, in a way,' said Romana. 'The shielding around this Ship. The invisibility screen. Now a zero environment. And how did he know to find the book here in Cambridge? The Professor was surely the only person in the universe who even knew it had been stolen from Gallifrey.' She dug her chin harder into her hands. 'What does he want from the book anyway? And who or what is Shada?'

'Could Skagra be a Time Lord?' asked Chris. 'A bad one? There must be some bad ones.'

'Let's hope the Doctor's finding that all out now,' said Romana.

'You've a lot of faith in him,' said Chris.

'He's saved your planet many, many times. And not just yours. He's the most wonderful man in the universe,' said Romana, quickly qualifying her remark. 'If you tell him I said that, I'll kill you. Same goes for you, K-9.'

Chris's mind was buzzing with questions. If they were stuck here for a bit, it was time to ask a few more questions. And it might distract Romana from her worries. 'I always thought,' said Chris, 'that aliens, if they existed, would be gas globules or big bat creatures or something, or something we might not even recognise as life. No offence.'

'There are plenty of creatures like that in the universe,' said Romana.

'But you and the Doctor and the Professor,' went on Chris, 'you look just like us, really. You even drink tea and ride bikes. You'd think that would be disappointing. But as a scientist, I think it's actually a good thing, it opens up so many areas of thought and theory as to the parallel evolution of the humanoid form.'

Romana seemed to have the glazed fascinated expression falling onto her face now, noted Chris. She turned her attention to K-9, pressing a sequence of some of the flashing buttons on his top side. 'I suppose we could try altering K-9's sensors to overlap rather than influx.'

Chris abandoned his questioning and decided to go for a decisive course of action. He sprung up and examined the inward-curving walls of the white room. They felt neither warm nor cold. In fact, though he could most definitely touch them, they felt like nothing at all. 'This wall. It's made of a very curious substance.'

'Zero technology again,' said Romana casually. 'Give me a year, I'll explain it to you.' She finished her reprogramming of K-9. 'Try again, K-9. Overlap scan this time, there's just a chance it could penetrate the null interfaces of this place.'

Chris tapped the wall. 'Even looking at these walls is hard. It's as if there's nothing there at all, though I can see there is.'

'Your senses can't operate properly in a zero environment,' said Romana. 'Don't try to understand.'

K-9's ears whirred around again. 'Overlap scan commenced.'

'Yes,' said Chris, 'so the senses of my lot, Earthlings I suppose you'd call us –'

'Among other things,' said Romana, bending over K-9 anxiously.

'– Earthling senses can't fully comprehend this wall,' went on Chris.

'Negative scan, Mistress,' said K-9.

Romana sighed and ran her hands through her hair in frustration. There was another awkward silence.

'I suppose the thing about this wall—' began Chris.

Romana banged her fist on K-9's side in frustration. 'Oh, blast the wall!' she shouted.

'Affirmative, Mistress,' said K-9 brightly. A bolt of bright red laser-light shot from his snout with an ear-splitting zap.

'Duck!' shouted Romana. She grabbed Chris roughly and flung him to the floor.

The red laser bolt ricocheted wildly around their tiny prison, lancing inches from them. It had no effect on the walls whatever, but Chris was not so hopeful about their chances if it hit them.

Suddenly, Romana tore off her hat and threw it with expert timing up into the air, directly into the path of the laser bolt. There was a small explosion and the hat was reduced to a cloud of ash that rained down on them.

Another silence followed.

'Apologies, Mistress,' said K-9 finally. His head and tail drooped. 'Action was precipitate.'

'Not at all,' said Romana, letting go of a big sigh and getting to her feet, dusting the ash from the pristine white lace of her dress. 'It was a good try, K-9.'

Chris got up and found he was grinning. 'One thing you've never solved out there in space, then,' he said. 'Computers, however advanced, just do whatever you tell them to. Whatever it is, however stupid, they just do it. On Earth we call it the sophisticated idiot problem.'

K-9 spun to face him. 'In this unit's memory bank regarding Earthling behaviour, instances of idiocy outnumber instances of sophistication by a ratio of 77 to 1.'

Before Chris could take him up on that, and there was certainly no chance of taking the dispute outside, K-9's sensors whirred again. 'Mistress! I am picking up faint telepathic signals.'

Chris and Romana knelt at his side.

'Must be the sphere again,' theorised Romana. 'To be detected in here, it must be active again. And enormously powerful.'

'Can you let us hear it?' asked Chris.

'Affirmative, young master. I have calibrated the signal so that your unsophisticated Earthling senses can hear it.'

A new noise issued from K-9.

To Chris's ears at first it sounded like a lot of static and interference, like Radio Moscow on long wave during a blizzard. But instead of announcements on tractor production and the progress of the glorious revolution, Chris could just make out the thin distorted babble of inhuman voices, all speaking together. The words were indistinguishable. The effect was haunting, like the lamenting of lost souls. He shivered.

'Yes, that's the sphere, and it's active,' said Romana. 'But it sounds different this time.'

'Different how?' whispered Chris.

'Ssh,' she ordered. Her face was creased in concentration as the ghostly voices cried out.

For a second, Chris thought he recognised one of the voices. Deep, dark and distinctive tones, so far away, so insubstantial.

Romana gasped. 'K-9, did you hear that?'

'A new voice has been added, Mistress,' said K-9.

'Oh please, no,' said Romana, her eyes suddenly wide and wet.

K-9's head drooped. 'It is the voice of the Doctor.'

Romana's face was a mask of horror. She reached out automatically to grab Chris's hand, and he saw the light go out of her eyes.

34

Clare sat in an armchair in Professor Chronotis's study and found that she was literally twiddling her thumbs.

Hang on. *Hang on.*

It was at least twenty minutes since that little porter person had gone off to 'ring around' and find his perfectly reasonable explanation. Incredibly, thought Clare, yet another man had told her to stop worrying her little head and go and wait for him to sort everything out. And yet again she had obeyed him. At least she fancied Chris, and had been overwhelmed by the Doctor's force of personality. The little porter was just anybody, so she had even less excuse this time.

She leapt to her feet and glared around the room, searching for any clue to what had befallen Chris, the Doctor and the Professor and, come to that, this girl the porter called Ramona or something. If he had been any of the other men in the faculty, she might have suspected Chris was off gallivanting somewhere with this mysterious Ramona character, but in his case that would be ridiculous.

Determined to initiate some positive action of her own, Clare started a methodical search of the Professor's rooms. She went into the little kitchenette and ran the taps, and though the pipes groaned and wheezed it was nothing like the groaning and wheezing she'd heard before. She caught her reflection in the glass door of a cupboard and winced. Her hair was all over the place, and she looked tired and crumpled in yesterday's clothes and make-up.

She went back into the study and began opening drawers, peering under tables, and rifling through sideboards. There was nothing but mess and confusion. Heaps of paper, tattered files and random odd objects like an orange, a catapult and a loose cassette tape marked *Bonnie Tyler's Greatest Hits*. Clare huffed. Bonnie Tyler had hardly had enough hits to warrant such a collection. I mean, she thought, apart from 'Lost In France' and 'It's A Heartache', what had the woman done? She looked closer at the cassette. There were more song titles printed on it, songs she didn't recognise. She squinted at the little smudged white letters of the copyright information. She blinked and squinted again.

This compilation © 1986.

Clare was at a loss. Why would anybody bother to make such a thing, have it done so professionally, then just leave it lying around? Clare tapped the cassette with her fingers, intrigued.

The simplest explanation? It was real. It did come from 1986. Somebody from the future, somebody who could travel in time, had brought it back with them.

No, no, that was the stupidest explanation. If somebody had travelled back in time from 1986 wouldn't they have brought something more impressive from the future? A new kind of digital watch or a videophone? Not *Bonnie Tyler's Greatest Hits*.

She didn't know what to think any more.

So she put the cassette down, and grabbed Chris's jacket. She could smell the cheap washing powder of the St John's communal launderette.

'Oh, where are you, Parsons?' she said aloud.

And then a very curious thing happened. Her eyes were drawn to a cupboard in a far corner that she hadn't noticed before. It wasn't the normal way your eyes are drawn to something, thought Clare. It was as if some exterior impulse had entered her head and *made* her look in that direction, literally turning her eyeballs to the cupboard.

She folded Chris's jacket over the back of a chair and went to the cupboard. It was a big, old wooden-panelled thing, quite an antique. It was also firmly locked. Which was odd because nothing else had been, even the Professor's front door.

She looked around the room. Presumably there must be a key somewhere in all this mess.

Suddenly, a thin shaft of sunlight shone through the small gap in the closed curtains of one of the windows. It seemed to be coming in at a very peculiar angle. It illuminated a particular section of the cluttered mantelpiece like a spotlight.

Clare stared, blinked – although all this blinking didn't seem to be doing her any good – and saw, in the very spot the light was shining, between a stopped clock under a dome and a bust of Dryden, a small brass key. The sunlight made the key glint and sparkle in a ridiculously magical way, as if it had been lit by a Hollywood movie's production team.

'No, ridiculous,' Clare said, out loud again.

Behind her there was a crash. She jumped and spun around. One of the teetering piles of books had chosen this particular moment to overbalance.

Clare gawped at the titles of the books that had collapsed, fanned out on the rug like a window display.

The Lion, the Witch and the Wardrobe. The Secret Garden. The Phoenix and the Carpet. The Box of Delights. And finally, inevitably, what looked very much like it could be a first edition of *Alice's Adventures in Wonderland.*

Clare was briefly transported back to a childhood world of wonder, adventure and excitement where anything could happen. Secret passages, hidden treasures, mysterious gateways, epic journeys through imaginary lands.

It was as if the room was encouraging her into a world of magic and –

Rubbish. She was an adult, she was a scientist, there was a rational explanation for this, and she was going to find it.

She grabbed the key, stormed to the cupboard and opened it, almost daring it to reveal an enchanted kingdom.

Inside were a pair of cricket pads, some ancient spiked running shoes, a punter's paddle and an old, folding wooden toolbox. Clare angrily flung them aside. There was nothing at the back of the cupboard but the back of the cupboard. So she kicked it.

With a hydraulic whirr the back of the cupboard swung around like a revolving bookcase in a corny horror film. It revealed a triangular brass panel at waist height which swiftly extended itself forward with a grind of gears.

It took Clare a moment to comprehend what she was seeing. The brass panel was old and weathered, but it was covered with levers, switches and dials whose function she could only guess at, many of them marked with curious circular designs similar to the scrollwork on the front of that strange book. There was a row of little glass bulbs at the top of the panel, unlit.

Whatever this thing controlled, it was obviously inert, thought Clare. So there'd be no harm in touching it.

She reached out and pressed a button at random. It switched in with a satisfying, springy ker-clunk, like a channel button on a television set.

All the little bulbs lit up.

Clare had just one second to raise an eyebrow. The next second, the faint humming noise suddenly rose in volume, loud and insistent. The curtains at every window swished shut. The lights in the room flared and dimmed, flared and dimmed. There was a tremendous creaking and cracking like splintering wood. The vestibule door slammed shut. She heard that wheezing, groaning noise again, but this time it was even more pained and protesting.

And then she felt the ground move under her feet.

She was thrown violently backwards on to the floor. A bookcase toppled towards her.

Clare had a sudden vision of her gran standing at her bedroom door in their old flat. 'Ruddy books!' she was saying. 'Books won't take you anywhere, young lady.'

Then Clare blacked out.

Wilkin knocked on the door of Room P-14. 'Miss?' he called. 'Are you in there, miss? I'm afraid I haven't been able to locate Professor Chronotis. Miss?'

The plumbing was kicking up a hell of a row again. She probably couldn't hear him over that din. Gently, he pulled open the door.

And staggered back.

The little vestibule of Room P-14, with its coat hooks and welcome mat was just where it should have been. But beyond it there was a howling blue vortex. A whirling, distorted tunnel of impossible beauty and complexity extending for ever.

Wilkin slammed the door shut.

He straightened his tie, adjusted his hat, and, deciding to ignore the vortex completely, he knocked once more and opened the door again. He would give the room a chance to sort itself out and behave like a respectable part of St Cedd's College.

This time, beyond the vestibule, there was no vortex. Just a view onto the backs of the college and a large, flattened area of mud, surrounded by flowerbeds, to mark where Room P-14 should have been, but was decidedly not.

Wilkin did not believe in third chances. He slammed the door shut, turned on his heel and went to find a policeman.

35

Skagra held the book open in one hand. The sphere rested in the upturned palm of the other.

Now, at last, he would learn the secret of Shada.

Skagra entered the Doctor's mind. A bewildering array of colourful images spewed into his own head. Planet after planet, face after face, monster after monster. The Doctor's mind was dizzying, undisciplined. It babbled like an excitable child with irrelevant observations and irrational thoughts.

Skagra drew a deep breath and steadied his own consciousness. He took a look at the body of the Doctor, where it lay slumped in the command chair. At least he had stopped up the mouth of the prattling idiot, where so many others had failed.

Reinvigorated, Skagra returned his attention to the sphere. This time he searched directly, using the Doctor's stolen knowledge and faculties, and turned to read the book.

The symbols remained obstinately what they were. Symbols.

Angrily, Skagra pushed further, deeper into the Doctor's mind. He caught glimpses of the man's training, his long years of study at the Academy on Gallifrey.

Ranks of students attired in the long black gowns of novices, sat at their desks, ranged in a semicircle before their tutor. The tutor was talking of the Artefacts, of the codes, secret mysteries and legends of the Great Heroes of the Old Time.

And the Doctor – curse him!, thought Skagra – *was staring out of the window into the orange blasted outer wilderness. 'That would be a lovely spot for a picnic,' he was thinking.*

Skagra withdrew from the Doctor's mind. He looked down at the body, fighting an impulse to kick at one of the long, lanky legs.

'He does not know,' he said out loud.

'My lord?' inquired the Ship politely.

'He does not know the code,' said Skagra. 'He never knew it. He told the truth.' He shook his head. 'The fool died for nothing.'

'Oh dear, my lord,' said the Ship after a pause. 'I am quite sure my gracious lord, as the most intelligent person in the wide universe, will soon overcome this latest unexpected obstacle.'

Skagra paused and thought. Every aspect of his plan had been checked and rechecked. Every step of the way to the fulfilment of his great destiny. And now he had the secret in his hands, and he could not read it.

A lesser being would have shouted with anger and despair, but Skagra's icy detachment would not allow him to consider failure. Calmly and methodically, he weighed up all the factors involved, all the options available to him. He would adapt the plan, was he not the ultimate genius?

A few seconds later he reached a decision.

'I am going to depart this planet in the Doctor's TARDIS capsule,' he told the Ship.

'Oh,' said the Ship, seeming a little taken aback.

Hurriedly she added, 'I am sure my lord has excellent reasons for assuming this course of action.'

Skagra weighed the book in his hand. 'This book is of Time Lord origin. I believe the code is hidden somewhere in the Doctor's mind, without him even knowing it. It may require Time Lord technology to crack that code.'

'What an astute observation, my lord!' cried the Ship enthusiastically.

'I shall return for the final phase of the operation,' said Skagra. He waved his hand over a control panel. Interior lights glowed briefly and there was a set of three insistent *beeps*.

'Forgive my abhorrent curiosity, my lord,' said the Ship. 'But you have just adjusted some of the manual controls, which as you know in your wisdom, are outside my schematics—'

'Then obviously my actions do not concern you,' Skagra said shortly.

'Quite right, my supreme lord and master,' said the Ship. 'I apologise most humbly for my worthlessness and crave your forgiveness.'

Skagra did not bother to reply. Instead he walked to the container that housed his book collection and detached it carefully and slowly from its podium.

Inside the bubble scanner, the Ship's scanner eye lifted curiously on its stalk. Skagra glared at it. The eyestalk quickly turned away and retracted.

He transferred the book container into his carpet bag. He summoned the sphere with a curt gesture. Then he tucked *The Worshipful and Ancient Law of Gallifrey* inside his quilted tabard and left the command deck without a further word or a backward glance, the sphere bobbing behind him.

The Doctor's sightless eyes stared up from the command chair.

Romana wrung her hands, looking pleadingly into K-9's eye-screen. 'Are you positive, K-9? Absolutely negative?'

'Affirmative,' said K-9 sadly, his tail drooping. 'No signals on any frequency, Mistress.'

'It doesn't mean the Doctor's necessarily dead, though, does it?' asked Chris, trying to salvage some hope from their predicament. 'I mean, the Professor was a very old man. The Doctor can only be about forty, forty-five.'

'He's seven hundred and sixty,' said Romana.

'Well, there you go,' said Chris, though he was trying to process that revelation at the same time as being encouraging. 'He might have survived the psycho-active extraction process thing.'

Romana sighed and stood up. Suddenly she gave a primal howl of rage, bunched up her fists and shouted, 'I wish I could get out of here!'

The words had barely left her mouth when a cube of white light surrounded her, blazed with light and disappeared again, taking her with it.

Chris looked at the empty spot where Romana had been in astonishment. He clicked his fingers. Suddenly everything was clear. 'That's it!' he exclaimed.

K-9 whirred and ticked. 'Please clarify this statement, young master.'

'That's what you have to say!' said Chris. 'You have to wish.' He coughed and squared his shoulders, then said loudly, 'I wish we could get out of here!'

Nothing happened.

Chris tried again, louder. 'I wish we could get out of here!'

Nothing happened again.

Chris grunted and angrily beat a fist against the wall. 'Oh, blast it!'

K-9's nose laser extended.

'No no, K-9, don't blast it!' cried Chris. His shoulders sagged. 'Wishing worked for Romana. Why didn't it work for me?'

'Suggest your superstitious inference of a connection between Mistress's statement and her transposition was mistaken, young master,' said K-9 sniffily.

Chris snorted. 'You're right. That was stupid. For a scientist, it was idiotic.'

'And unsophisticated,' added K-9.

'How did Romana get out but not me?' said Chris.

'Insufficient data,' said K-9.

'Insufficient data!' shouted Chris. 'Insufficient data! Why did I get myself involved in this?'

'Insufficient data,' said K-9.

*   *   *

The transposition cube materialised in the long corridor that led from the command deck to the airlock of Skagra's ship. Skagra watched as the Doctor's companion, the Time Lady Romana, stepped from it with almost admirable coolness.

'What have you done to the Doctor?' she said, looking him straight in the eye.

'Nothing you would like to hear about,' replied Skagra. He appraised her. She was forthright and direct, merely stating her intentions with firm conviction. This was good.

'Let me see him!' She moved to push past him and down the corridor.

Skagra blocked her path and indicated the sphere, which bobbed along behind him. 'You would not enjoy it. I have taken his mind. He foolishly resisted the extraction and his body has terminated.'

Romana shook her head. 'No. I simply won't believe it until I see it.'

'It is not important that you believe it,' said Skagra. He studied her. 'A third Time Lord, I have considered using the sphere to extract your mind as well.'

'Much good it will do you,' said Romana. 'You obviously didn't get what you wanted from either the Doctor or the Professor. You certainly won't get it from me.'

Skagra nodded. 'Neatly put. But you may be of use in other ways. You will now accompany me.' He grabbed her arm and steered her roughly back down the corridor towards the airlock.

Romana shook off his grip. 'I can find my own way, thank you.'

Skagra narrowed his gaze and studied her again, this time at closer quarters, as they walked together towards the airlock. 'I find your acceptance of your situation quite refreshing. Of course, resistance is futile, as I can use the sphere to drain your mind at any moment I choose. So you logically accept my dominion. Good. This is behaviour much more becoming of a Time Lord.'

'What do you know about the Time Lords?' Romana demanded.

'Things that even they have forgotten,' said Skagra. 'Though of course you don't really expect me to answer your questions.'

'Who are you? What do you want?' Romana said insolently.

'I want many things,' said Skagra.

They entered the airlock and passed through onto the invisible steps that led down into the meadow. The sphere drifted after them. At the bottom of the steps, Skagra clicked his fingers and the airlock door closed.

'Where are we going?' asked Romana.

Skagra pointed across the meadow. 'To your travelling capsule.'

Romana led the way to the TARDIS. At the door she suddenly whirled around and fixed Skagra again with her penetrating gaze. 'If you think I'll open this door, you're going to be extremely disappointed. My acceptance doesn't go so far as that.'

'Naturally,' said Skagra. 'Like the Professor and the Doctor, you would prefer to die pointlessly. So it's just as well for you that I have the Doctor's key.'

He slipped the key from his pocket, savouring the tiny expression of alarm on Romana's face. She was obviously more shaken by the Doctor's death than she wanted him to think.

He turned the key in the lock, feeling the vibration of power coming from within. The battered blue door swung open and Skagra took Romana by the arm and thrust her savagely inside, the sphere following as faithfully as ever.

Skagra repressed a sneer at the antiquated fixtures and fittings of the capsule's interior, the heavily roundelled walls typical of the Quintilian Era on Gallifrey. He watched as Romana got to her feet from the appallingly grubby floor. 'No doubt you also refuse to operate the capsule for me.'

'No doubt,' she replied. 'And as no one can operate it other than the Doctor or myself, your "dominion" over me has come to an end, wouldn't you say?'

Skagra almost allowed himself another smile. So that was why she had cooperated. She thought this was her trump card, and had been waiting to play it.

'If the Doctor can operate this capsule,' he said smoothly, 'then so can I.'

He set down the carpet bag, then clicked his fingers. The sphere came into his open right palm. With the left hand he threw down a big red lever.

The outer doors closed, shutting out Cambridge and this 2 out of 10 planet from Skagra's life for ever.

Skagra found the information in the Doctor's mind quite easily. It was complex but almost instinctive, a habitual pattern formed over five hundred years of travel. He closed the real-world interface and disengaged the multi-loop stabiliser, preparing the TARDIS for flight. The precise coordinates of their destination could be input once they had left conterminous time and entered the space-time vortex.

The central column began to rise and fall. Romana launched herself at the console, reaching desperately for what Skagra identified as the emergency override system.

Skagra swatted her to the floor with the flat of his free hand. Then he reached for a seldom-used array of controls on another panel and his fingers tapped out an instruction.

Immediately, the lighting darkened. Skagra continued his work, talking over his shoulder to his captive. 'This console is now keyed to my biorhythms.'

'Anyone can dematerialise a TARDIS,' Romana said casually. 'But you'd be a real safety hazard at the major controls. That's why they're booby-trapped.'

'Not true,' said Skagra.

'How do you know?'

Skagra tapped the sphere. 'It's all in here.'

He anticipated her next move. She ran for the interior door, possibly hoping, he surmised, to reach the secondary control room and take charge of the capsule from there.

The sphere zoomed over, blocking her path.

'I wouldn't irritate it if I were you,' said Skagra. 'It can do far worse things to you than you can possibly do to it.'

'I don't see why you want to steal an old Type 40 like this anyway,' said Romana. 'You've got a perfectly good ship of your own.'

'Impressed with it, were you?' he asked. She did not reply. 'I should hope you were. I designed it. But it has certain limitations. And what the Time Lords have hidden, I shall need Time Lord technology to locate.'

Romana looked up at him. 'Consider what you're doing, Skagra. Logically.'

Skagra moved to the input panel and entered a long string of precise coordinates in Gallifreyan notation. 'I never do anything else.'

'Then you must know the risks,' Romana went on, warningly. 'You have the Doctor's knowledge but none of his sense of responsibility.'

Skagra blinked. 'Are we talking about the same Doctor?'

Romana stood closer. 'You now have access to all of space and time. Power beyond imagining. You must see, logically, how dangerous that is without the correct training, without the unique insights of a Time Lord.'

This time, Skagra broke all his rules. He stopped the inputting process and laughed in her face. 'Power beyond imagining? This?' He indicated the console. 'This is merely a means to an end. It's going to get me where I'm going faster, that is all.'

'And where are you going, Skagra?' asked Romana fiercely. 'Who are you? What do you want?'

Skagra wondered. It would be interesting to see her reaction. 'Have you heard the name Salyavin?'

Romana gasped and backed away. 'Salyavin! You're Salyavin?'

'You asked me three questions,' said Skagra enigmatically.

He finished the input and pressed the coordinate override button. The column thrummed and glowed bright red with new life, rising and falling faster than before. The TARDIS jerked to one side, powering through the vortex at incredible speed, the engines screaming in protest.

'To answer your first question,' said Skagra. 'First, we are going to my command station.' His fingers gripped the edge of the console. 'And from there, with your help, to Shada!'

36

Very, very stupid person. Or very, very clever person? He couldn't decide.

So he opened his eyes and saw the frayed tassels at the ends of his scarf.

He twiddled the tassels.

Stupid or clever?

It might just be fun to twiddle the tassels for a lifetime, like a stupid person. If that's what he was.

But if he turned out to be a clever person after all, that would be a very stupid thing to do.

'Very stupid,' he said.

He could talk. That suggested he was clever. Or did it? He dimly remembered that very stupid people could talk. Sometimes they did it a lot. Didn't they?

'Very stupid, very stupid,' he said again.

Hold on, he thought. Who was he? He couldn't decide if he was very stupid or very clever without knowing who he was. If he was very stupid he probably didn't know who he was.

He decided to check to see if he knew who he was or not. 'Who am I?' he asked himself.

There were a few seconds of empty nothingness. He twiddled the tassels again. Twiddle twiddle twiddle. Twiddle-dee-dee, twiddle-dee-dee –

Dee. Dee? D? D for what?

Twiddly-diddly-Doctor.

Doctor.

The Doctor.

The Doctor!

Seven hundred and sixty years flashed through his mind in less than a second.

'Very, very clever!' he shouted, leaping to his feet from the command chair on the main deck of Skagra's spaceship.

'Ow ow ow ow ow!' he said, slumping back into the seat, shutting his eyes and clutching his throbbing head. 'Have you got anything for a headache, Skagra?'

There was no reply.

The Doctor opened an eye and looked around. 'Skagra?'

'My lord has departed,' said a woman's voice.

The Doctor opened his other eye and looked around again. There was nobody else on the command deck.

'Who's that?' the Doctor called.

'My lord,' said the voice. 'My wonderful lord Skagra.'

The Doctor swivelled right round in the chair. Still nobody about. 'No, I don't mean who's departed, I mean who is that speaking?'

'The servant of Skagra,' said the voice. 'I am the Ship.'

'You're the ship?' The Doctor smiled. He realised that the voice seemed to be coming from all around him. 'A talking spaceship?'

'Correct,' said the Ship.

'Skagra must be pretty hard-up for friends,' muttered the Doctor, choosing to forget K-9. 'Will you tell me where my friends are?'

'I will not!' said the Ship, rather hotly. 'You are an enemy of Skagra. Any orders you give me are hostile to my gracious lord.'

'Oh, I don't mean any harm,' said the Doctor affably. 'And it wasn't an order, I only asked.'

There was a lengthy pause.

Finally the Ship said, 'I do not understand how you are asking. In fact, I do not understand how you are moving.'

'Really?' The Doctor didn't care for the Ship's somewhat starchy and disapproving tone. He got up carefully from the chair. 'Why's that then? It seems quite natural to me.'

'Because you are dead,' said the Ship, sounding puzzled. 'Your mind was extracted into the sphere.'

The Doctor laughed. 'Ah, but it wasn't, was it? The trick on these occasions is not to resist. I just let the thing believe I was very stupid, and then it didn't pull nearly hard enough. It got a bad copy of my mind, a bootleg version if you like, but it left me with the original intact.' He tapped the side of his head. He was trying to sound very casual, although in fact the mental effort he had expended had drained him. 'Understand?'

'No, I do not,' said the Ship. 'I scanned your body for life signs after the extraction. And you, Doctor, are quite definitely dead.'

The Doctor coughed. 'Well, you see, I don't like to keep boasting but that's another little trick I picked up, I can suspend all life-functions for a very short period—' He stopped himself and clamped his hand over his mouth.

'What was that?' asked the Ship suspiciously.

The Doctor shook his head.

'You were saying?' prompted the Ship.

'I'm dead,' said the Doctor cautiously.

'I know,' said the Ship.

'Of course you do,' said the Doctor.

'Though maybe I should just give you another quick scan—' began the Ship.

'No need!' cried the Doctor. 'As the servant of the great Skagra, who is infallible—'

'I'm glad you see him that way now,' said the Ship. 'What a pity you had to die before you had the realisation.'

'Quite,' said the Doctor. He continued, 'As the servant of the infallible Skagra, your sensors must also be infallible. Ergo, I am dead.'

'That seems reasonable,' said the Ship.

'And if I'm dead, then I'm an ex-enemy of Skagra,' said the Doctor. 'Correct?'

'Correct,' said the Ship.

The Doctor wiped his brow. He chose his next words very carefully. 'So, if I'm dead, I cannot give orders that would be any kind of threat to Skagra. Correct?'

'Correct,' said the Ship.

'Then I order you to release my friends,' said the Doctor, crossing his fingers. 'Please.'

There was a pause.

'They will be released,' said the Ship.

The Doctor gave a long exhalation. 'Excellent! Thank you! I think I must be very clever.' He mopped his brow again. 'Do you know it's getting very stuffy in here all of a sudden?'

'You *are* dead?' asked the Ship.

'Yes!' said the Doctor. 'I thought we'd sorted all of that out.'

'I am programmed to conserve resources,' said the Ship simply. 'Since there are no living beings on this command deck, I shut down the oxygen supply on the departure of my lord Skagra.'

The Doctor gasped for breath.

With a sudden dizzying sensation, he realised he had now used up all the oxygen left behind following Skagra's exit. Normally he could have suspended his life-functions – but he had only just recovered from his last such trance.

He felt his knees give way. 'Turn on the air supply,' he gasped. Sharp, terrible pains pierced all three of his lungs.

'That is not logical,' said the Ship.

The Ship's warm, matronly voice rang in the Doctor's ears as he sank to the floor.

'*Dead men do not require oxygen . . . Dead men do not require oxygen . . . Dead men do not require oxygen . . .*'

PART FOUR

CARBON COPIES

37

Chris completed yet another circuit of the tiny white room. Finally he crouched down beside K-9 and patted the dog's head the way he'd seen Romana do it. It was a silly thing to do, but it was strangely reassuring. 'We'd better face it, K-9,' he said heavily. 'When it comes to getting out of here, we haven't got a clue.'

Suddenly Chris found himself looking beyond K-9 to a door that had seemingly appeared from nowhere. It was only when he got up and looked around that he realised they were no longer in the white room. Instead they had been transported – if that was the right word – into a long, curving corridor with doors at either end.

'Hey, we did it!' cried Chris.

K-9 trundled forward, heading down the corridor to one of the doors. 'We must locate the Doctor Master and the Mistress. There is great danger!'

He reached the sealed doorway and extended his nose blaster. 'Stand clear, young master!' he warned Chris. 'Preparing to fire!'

'Hold on!' called Chris. There was a panel on the left-hand side of the door, with two switches marked OPEN and CLOSE.

Chris pressed the button marked OPEN.

Hidden mechanisms built into the doorway clicked.

'Most satisfactory,' said K-9 glumly, the laser retreating into his nose.

Chris shrugged. 'Sorry.'

The halves of the door parted with a smooth electronic hum. There was a rushing sound, and Chris was almost knocked over as a mighty wind roared past him and K-9 into the room beyond.

Chris shook his head, looked through the door – and saw the Doctor, lying sprawled on the floor. He raced in, barely registering the large white space and its sleek, inbuilt control panels.

'Doctor!' Chris ran to his side, fearing to touch him. There was nobody else in the room; no sign of Romana or this Skagra person.

'Oxygen levels are returning to normal,' said a warm, female matronly voice.

Chris spun around. 'Who said that?'

K-9 turned on his axis. 'Identify yourself!'

'I am the Ship,' said the voice grandly. 'The servant of the great lord Skagra.'

Chris shuddered. It was eerie. The voice seemed to be coming from all around them. 'Where's that voice coming from?' he whispered to K-9.

K-9's eye-screen flashed. 'Impossible to pinpoint source. The voice emanates from the fabric of this ship.'

'That's what I just said, dog,' said the Ship.

Chris looked back to the Doctor, relieved to see his big blue eyes opening.

The Doctor sucked in great lungfuls of air and nodded to his friends. 'Nice to see you, Bristol.' His eyes narrowed. 'You took your time, K-9.'

'He's alive!' cried Chris.

The Doctor sat up like a shot and clamped his hand over Chris's mouth. 'No I'm not, I'm dead,' he whispered fiercely.

'You're what?' Chris tried to say.

The Doctor looked around and whispered into Chris's ear, 'I've been nearly too clever by three-quarters.'

Chris removed the Doctor's hand from his mouth. 'You never seem to do anything by halves,' he said.

The Doctor rummaged in his pocket and produced a scrap of paper and a stub of pencil. He jotted something down hurriedly then held it directly before Chris's eyes.

The paper read I PERSUADED THE SHIP I WAS DEAD AND IT CUT OFF MY OXYGEN SUPPLY.

'You persuaded the Ship what?' asked Chris, incredulous.

The Doctor slammed his hand back over Chris's mouth.

'What was that?' asked the Ship.

'Nothing,' called the Doctor. He flashed the paper at K-9.

'Confirm,' said K-9 haltingly. 'It is – nothing.'

'Hmm,' said the Ship.

The Doctor quickly jotted down some more. He showed the paper to Chris, keeping his hand firmly over Chris's mouth.

THE SHIP WON'T TAKE ORDERS FROM AN ENEMY OF SKAGRA. BUT SINCE IT BELIEVES I AM DEAD, THE SHIP HAS NO REASON NOT TO OBEY MY ORDERS. GET IT?

Chris nodded. It was the sophisticated idiot problem again, this time working in their favour. The Doctor removed his hand.

He flashed the paper at K-9.

'Confirm understanding,' said K-9. 'Logic is peculiar but acceptable.'

'The logic of what?' asked the Ship. 'I really do think I ought to see what you've written on that piece of paper.'

'I'm a dead man writing,' said the Doctor, hurriedly stuffing the paper back into his pocket. 'Whatever I've written, how can it be a threat to your great master Skagra?'

After a pause the Ship said, 'Fair enough.'

'The Ship turned the oxygen back on when you came in,' the Doctor told Chris. 'Because you're still alive. Officially.'

'That's reassuring,' said Chris.

The Doctor clapped a hand on Chris's shoulder and got to his feet. 'Where's Romana?'

'I thought she was with you,' said Chris. 'We got transported into this prison thing, then she got transported out again.'

'Skagra,' said the Doctor grimly. 'He's got Romana, as well as the book, and a copy of my mind.'

Chris was finding it slightly hard to keep up again. 'He's got what?'

'A copy of my mind, in his sphere. He thought that I'd know how to read the book.'

'But you don't, do you?' said Chris.

'I don't even know why he wants to read it,' said the Doctor. 'But I don't imagine it's simply the incurable curiosity of the bibliophile.'

'Why don't you ask the Ship?' suggested Chris.

The Doctor clapped Chris on the shoulder again. 'I was just about to.' He looked up. 'Ship, why does your gracious lord Skagra want to read the book?'

'It contains the secret of Shada,' said the Ship.

'And what is Shada?' asked Chris.

'I'm hardly going to tell you that,' snapped the Ship. 'You are an enemy of my lord Skagra.'

'So he is, so he is,' said the Doctor. He coughed. 'But you can tell me, can't you? I'm dead.'

'I could tell you,' said the Ship, 'but I do not know. My lord has not shared that information with me.'

'It can wait,' said the Doctor. He set off for the door. 'We'd better get after Skagra and Romana. K-9, you can trace them from the TARDIS.'

The Ship coughed. 'I'm afraid that won't be possible.'

The Doctor crashed to a halt by the door. 'Why not? As a dead man, I can do what I like, it's one of our special privileges.'

'You cannot return to your TARDIS,' said the Ship patiently, 'because it has gone.'

'Gone? What do you mean, gone?'

A hologram screen shimmered into view in mid-air. It displayed the meadow outside the ship. Chris could see the toppled fold-out stool and fishing tackle. But there was no sign of the TARDIS.

'He's taken Romana off in your police box,' said Chris. He called up to the Ship. 'Where has he taken her?'

The Ship harrumphed. 'As if I'd tell you that.'

'Where has he taken her?' demanded the Doctor.

'My lord did not share that information with me,' said the Ship.

Chris watched as the Doctor slammed down into the big white chair, pulled his hat from his pocket and jammed it down over his eyes.

38

For Romana, this was a nightmare. She clutched a bulkhead as the TARDIS bucked and swayed through the vortex.

Could the tall, slender young man holding on to the console really be Salyavin? The mere mention of that name had sent a shiver through her body. It had stripped her of the very training and detachment that she had been extolling, and suddenly she had been a little girl again, over a hundred years earlier. 'Go to sleep,' her mother had said playfully, in the mocking tone adults used without realising the horror they were inspiring, 'or Salyavin will come to get you!' She had seen holo-images of Salyavin, the wild man, in the history books, and spent the night still and silent, listening to the sounds of the Citadel, convinced that Salyavin was hiding beneath her bed.

And Salyavin, or Skagra, or whoever he really was, had stolen the mind of the Doctor, and left him dead. He had no reason to lie.

One thing gave Romana hope. She had not seen the Doctor's body. Was it just possible he had somehow fooled Skagra, and would come bursting in at any moment, teeth flashing, eyes bulging, that ridiculous scarf flapping in the wind?

Finally the TARDIS started to groan to a halt, the centre column grinding slower and slower until Romana felt the familiar wrenching sensation of materialisation.

Skagra stood back from the console. 'We have arrived,' he said simply. He threw the big red lever, and the outer doors opened.

Romana gathered herself. Whatever was out there, she would refuse to be impressed.

Skagra gestured for her to exit first.

Romana stepped past him haughtily and went through the doors of the TARDIS.

She found herself among the stars. She stifled a gasp of astonishment.

The TARDIS had put down at the centre of a huge open circular space. Above and around her on all sides was a brilliant starfield, beyond what she guessed must be some kind of invisible spherical vacuum shield. At the edges of this arena she could see huge dark mountains, blasted black spires of rock reaching up to the heavens.

Romana turned to see Skagra exiting the TARDIS, carpet bag in hand, followed as ever by the sphere.

'Where are we?' she said as casually as she felt able. She waved a hand airily across at the infinite stars. 'Of course I know roughly where we are from the star formations. We're at the centre of this galaxy's trade routes, among the most powerful civilisations, not so very far from Gallifrey. I assume from the look of those rock formations that this observatory is built into the surface of an asteroid.'

'Of course,' said Skagra, who did not look impressed either. 'This is my command station.'

Romana sneered. 'Command station! And what do you need to command?'

'More than you can possibly imagine,' said Skagra.

'I have a very vivid imagination,' said Romana.

'Then it may be in for a shock,' said Skagra.

He gestured her forward. To one side of the TARDIS was a large computer console. The sphere bobbed forward and, at Skagra's command, positioned itself on top of a slender spike.

'For a logical, rational man, you like a bit of mystification, don't you?' Romana said. 'Why don't you just tell me who you are and what you want?'

Skagra turned to look at Romana. He inclined his head, as if evaluating her. His blue gaze was even more intense than usual.

He gestured around at the heavens. 'Tell me what you see.'

'I've already told you. Stars. Billions of them.'

Skagra nodded. Then he leaned forward, bringing his face closer to hers. 'What are they *doing*?'

Romana shrugged. 'What do you mean? They're not doing anything. They're just there.'

'Exactly,' said Skagra. 'Spinning uselessly through the void. And around them, trillions of people spinning uselessly through their lives.'

Romana snorted. 'Says who?'

'Says me.'

Romana thrust her face into his. 'And who are you? Salyavin?'

For the first time Skagra seemed almost passionate. 'What I am now is not important. But what I – what we all – shall become. That is all that matters.'

Romana, acting a lot braver than she felt, laughed. 'Messianic rubbish.'

Skagra cupped his hands together and slowly moved them up to her face. Then he parted the palms.

'Look,' he said.

Romana was hoping that he was as mad as he now seemed. A madman was fallible by definition. She looked into his cupped hands. 'What am I meant to be looking at?'

'What do you see?'

'Nothing,' said Romana. 'I don't know . . . Air?'

Skagra looked down into his hands. 'Billions of atoms, spinning at random. Expending energy, running down, achieving nothing. Entropy.'

He broke the pose and gestured above himself. 'Just like the stars. Heading pointlessly and futilely towards extinction and endless night and nothingness.' A gleam came into his eyes. 'But what is the one thing that stands against entropy, against random decay?'

He held out one gloved hand to her.

'Life,' said Romana.

'Exactly!' Skagra flexed his fingers. 'See how the atoms are arranged here. They have meaning, purpose. And what more meaning and purpose than what is contained –'

Slowly he pointed to his head.

'– in here?'

'The living brain,' said Romana.

'*My* living brain,' corrected Skagra. 'My genius.'

Romana shot him her best look of utter contempt.

'I'm sorry,' he said, stepping back and regaining himself. 'I had hoped you might be different. But like everybody else, your mind is limited. You do not understand me.'

'What is there to understand?' said Romana and turned her back on him.

She found herself looking into the glowing red eyes of what appeared to be a living rock.

She jumped in sheer animal terror at the strangeness of the creature. It stood about seven feet tall, and its large body was formidable if not graceful. Its bulky frame consisted of crystallised lumps of smouldering black carbon. An intense aura of heat emanated from it.

'Command station welcomes you, my lord Skagra,' it said in a deep, rumbling voice.

Romana saw two more of the creatures emerge from the shadows at the edge of the domed observatory. 'What are these things?'

Skagra had returned to his normal icy self. 'My Kraags,' he said evenly. 'My creations. They shall be the servants of the new generation.'

All Romana's fears came flooding back. 'New generation? A new race, new people?'

Skagra shook his head. 'You still do not understand. Not new people.' He paused as if to emphasise his point. 'A new *person*.'

He turned his attention to the Kraags. 'It is almost time. I shall shortly require reinforcements. Begin the generation process.'

The first Kraag lowered its head in a gesture of obedience. 'As my lord commands.'

The Kraags turned away and lumbered off into the shadows.

Skagra took Romana's arm. 'You shall see this,' he said and pushed her forward.

As they moved into the shadows, Romana saw a large circular door leading out of the observatory down into a long tunnel of roughly hewn rock. A fiery glow came from the end of the tunnel.

The tunnel emerged onto a large metal platform that looked down into another circular area, this one some hundred metres in diameter, and covered by a canopy of rock. Romana shied away from the heat and the light. The entire central area of the room was filled with a bubbling pit of lava. The air was filled with a heavy thick green gas that caught at her throat.

The first Kraag pounded to a small console built into the edge of the platform and depressed a series of switches with its stubby, three-fingered claw.

The lava bubbled even more furiously. Suddenly a massive crane-like device swung out from the opposite wall. In its claw was a bare wire skeleton, roughly human-shaped.

The crane lowered itself. The claw dropped the wire frame into the pit.

The lava seethed. Suddenly, black crystals of carbon began to agglomerate around the wire frame. Romana watched as the crystals coalesced, forming the unmistakable figure of a Kraag.

The newborn Kraag groaned and strained, ripping itself free of the lava.

The first Kraag pressed another button. A long ramp extended from the platform down into the pit.

The new Kraag clambered on to the ramp, its heavy feet, still smouldering, leaving steaming black prints as it presented itself to Skagra.

'What is your command, my lord?'

'Join these others,' said Skagra. 'The time is nearly come.'

The new Kraag joined its fellows on the platform.

'Test activation complete, my lord,' reported the first Kraag.

'Begin full activation,' said Skagra.

The first Kraag – which Romana could now see was slightly larger than its fellows, some sort of commander – hit another button.

Panels in the ceiling slid back around the huge chamber to reveal more and more crane-arms. Each crane held a wire frame in its claw.

The cranes swung out. The frames splashed into the lava pit. New Kraags started to form around each frame.

The cranes swung back – then swung out again a second later, producing more wire frames.

Romana looked into the impassive face of Skagra. If this was madness, it was madness on a terrifying scale. For once, she could not hide or mediate her own reaction.

Romana was appalled.

39

Chris looked between K-9, who had apparently turned himself off in a state of utter dejection, and the Doctor, who sat sprawled in the big white chair, his hat still jammed on his head and covering his eyes.

Chris assumed they were thinking. He hoped they were thinking, anyway.

He looked at the holo-screen, where the image of the quiet Cambridge meadow on this drizzly Sunday morning remained. There was nothing to prevent him, he supposed, walking out of here right now. He could find Clare and try to apologise and return to his normal human life.

His normal human problems seemed pretty irrelevant now.

He found himself distracted by three red lights that winked insistently in sequence by one of the control panels. He didn't like red lights. Red light meant danger. Three red lights, logically, meant thrice the amount of danger. He considered asking the Ship what they meant but realised he wouldn't get an answer, as he was an enemy of Skagra's.

That was something at least, thought Chris. He'd never had any enemies before. Never made enough of an impression on anyone. And he'd never even met this Skagra bloke.

The silence had lasted a good five minutes. Chris decided to break it. 'So we need to work out where he's gone in the TARDIS? Yeah?'

'Affirmative, young master,' said K-9. 'And/or when he has gone.'

'When he has gone?'

'Time machine,' said the Doctor from beneath his hat.

'Oh yeah,' said Chris.

The silence formed again.

Chris couldn't bear it. 'He must have taken Romana because she can fly it.'

'So can he,' said the Doctor. 'He's got my mind in that sphere of his, remember. Everything I know is at his disposal.'

'There's one thing he doesn't know,' said Chris.

'What's that?'

'You're still alive.'

The Doctor ripped off his hat and simply stared at Chris. 'No, I'm dead, remember.'

Chris hunched himself down next to the Doctor. 'Doctor,' he whispered, 'why doesn't the Ship realise that you're – you know – if it's really clever, I mean I can work it out—'

'The Ship is programmed only to obey instructions, not to consider them,' said K-9.

'Blind logic,' said the Doctor.

'Right,' said Chris. 'Why don't we try a bit of logic ourselves? Let's work out what we know.'

'Go on, then,' urged the Doctor.

'Well,' said Chris, 'we know that . . .' He trailed off. 'We know that . . . er, perhaps we could work out what we don't know and work backwards?'

The Doctor grunted. 'We don't know where Skagra has taken Romana, we don't know why he wants the book, we don't know what he's going to do with it, we don't know what it can do.'

'That's enough don't knows to win an election,' said Chris sadly.

The silence descended again.

Chris sighed. 'So. Back to square one.'

Suddenly, the Doctor leapt from the chair in an explosion of movement. Chris jumped back, astonished at how the man had gone from despondent lethargy to crackling vitality in less than a second.

'That's it!' cried the Doctor.

'What's it?' asked Chris.

'Square one!' cried the Doctor, exultant. 'Work backwards, like you said!'

'Did I?' asked Chris.

'We've got to go back to square one if we want to find out who Skagra is and what he's up to,' said the Doctor. 'Once we know that, we'll know where to find him now. Hopefully.'

He cleared his throat. 'Ship! Me again, the late lamented Doctor, ex-enemy of Skagra and former all-round ratbag. I order you to take us to where your lord Skagra last came from.'

The Ship answered straight away. 'Very well. The order does not conflict with my programmed instructions. I will activate launch procedures.'

'Blind logic,' said the Doctor. 'Well done, Bristol!'

Chris couldn't quite work out what he had done well, but he smiled anyway.

'Launch procedures activated,' said the Ship.

The floor vibrated beneath Chris's feet.

'Oh my God, we're taking off!' gasped Chris. 'We're going into space!'

'Where did you think Skagra came from, Norwich?' said the Doctor.

'But – *space*,' said Chris, gasping.

'Oh, sit down,' said the Doctor, pushing him into the chair.

Chris found himself looking directly across at the three blinking red lights. They probably didn't mean anything. In space, red probably meant 'hooray, everything's fine'.

'Launch procedures activated.'

The Ship's voice echoed throughout itself. In the empty corridor, in the airlock, in the prison.

'Launch procedures activated.'

The voice echoed in another area of the Ship, where a small chamber contained an empty tank. As if in response to the voice, tiny nozzles on either side of the tank began to spray boiling jets of lava.

A panel in the ceiling swung open, and a wire frame descended into the tank. Heavy green gas began to swirl.

Crystals of black carbon started to form around the frame.

40

Clare could hear a peaceful, smooth electronic hum. Was she in hospital?

Slowly the events of the last few hours swam back into her foggy head. Chris, and his amazing discovery of the book. The Doctor. The porter, saying he'd ring round the college to find Professor Chronotis –

A bookcase toppling onto her.

She moved her head, and immediately wished that she hadn't. A sharp pain jabbed behind her eyes.

She got up slowly. She was still in the Professor's study. The bookcase was back in its place, as if it had never moved.

She looked about. The humming noise was coming from all around her, as if the room was alive with power. She still had the key clutched in her hand. The brass control panel blinked and winked with flashing lights.

She had the strangest sensation that the room was moving.

The curtains were drawn and no light came from beyond. She must have been out for hours.

Dazed, she grabbed the arm of the nearest chair and slumped down into it. She couldn't even begin to understand what had happened.

Suddenly a ghost appeared in front of her.

She knew he was a ghost because she could see right through him, and also because he was wearing a nightgown and nightcap and held a ghostly flickering candle in an antique holder. He was a very old ghost, in his late seventies at least, and Clare caught herself thinking sadly about how awful it must be to linger on Earth for all eternity when you're way past your prime.

The ghost opened its mouth to speak. Clare was expecting a spectral howl or shriek of revenge.

'Well done, young lady,' said the ghost. 'Very well done.'

The ghost took a pair of spectacles from inside its nightgown and hobbled over to the brass control panel. It reached out one transparent hand to a particularly large golden knob. To Clare's astonishment, its hand did not pass right through it but connected with it, firm and solid.

The ghost shimmered. A wave of solidity passed up along the hand and through the ghost's body, until he was concrete and corporeal and no longer a ghost at all. He was a small old man with a heavily lined face.

He turned back to her and smiled broadly. 'Tea?' he asked.

'Yes please,' said Clare. She could think of nothing nicer, and whoever he was, this ex-ghost seemed like such a nice old man.

'May I ask who you are?' she heard herself say as he shuffled towards the kitchen in threadbare checked slippers.

The ex-ghost turned at the door. 'Certainly you may. What delightful manners you have, young lady.'

'Thanks,' said Clare, her head still spinning. 'So who are you?'

The little old man puffed out his chest proudly. 'I was, I am, and thanks to you I hopefully will be, Professor Chronotis,' he said.

41

Chris stared through the open shutters of the ship's forward screen and marvelled at the infinite universe. He was heading away from Earth, from everything he knew, out into the stars. It was his boyhood dream come true, in a way he had never expected. He gave a sigh of satisfaction.

'Will you stop doing that?' asked the Doctor. He was sat cross-legged on the floor next to K-9.

'Sorry,' said Chris. 'I didn't know I was doing anything.' He gestured to the stars. 'Look at that. Just look at that.'

'I am looking at it,' said the Doctor as another star system flew past. 'And I don't like the look of it. We're going a bit casually for my liking. Bit of a Sunday service, if you ask me, though I suppose it *is* Sunday.' He called out loudly, 'Ship! How long will this journey take?'

'Thirty-nine astrasidereal days,' said the Ship primly.

'What!' the Doctor exclaimed. 'That's nearly three months!'

The Ship sniffed. 'That is at full warp drive. And we have hundreds of light years to cover.'

'Hundreds of light years,' said Chris. 'In three months. That's an incredible speed!'

'Yes, it's incredibly slow,' said the Doctor. He pondered for a moment, then called, 'Ship, do you have the power to adjust your own inner circuitry?'

'Yes,' said the Ship, 'yes, I can do that.'

'I thought you might,' said the Doctor. 'Being created, as you were, by someone with an interest in Gallifreyan technology.'

'Yes, my precious lord Skagra,' sighed the Ship. 'I do miss him, you know.'

'We all do,' said the Doctor. 'Right then, Ship. Stop!'

'Please clarify,' said the Ship. 'Stop what?'

'Stop,' said the Doctor. 'Cut all engines. Halt!'

The faint vibration of movement died away, and Chris watched as the stars outside slowed and then fixed on one beautiful image, a nebula of unimaginable size and variety of colour.

'What are you doing?' asked Chris, stifling another sigh of wonder.

'I'm going to introduce this ship to a few new concepts,' said the Doctor. 'Fortunately it's halfway there already.'

'I have accomplished your request,' said the Ship.

'Good,' said the Doctor. He cleared his throat.

'Now, Ship, please regrade your deoscillation digretic synthesisers by ten points.'

The Ship gasped. 'I cannot do that! The drive will explode!'

'Nonsense, it's perfectly safe,' said the Doctor.

'Master,' said K-9 warningly.

The Doctor huffed. 'What now, K-9? Nobody asked for your contribution—' He cut himself off. 'Wait a minute. Did I just say ten points?'

'Yes,' said Chris.

'Affirmative,' said K-9.

'You did, yes,' said the Ship.

The Doctor wiped the back of his hand over his chin and swallowed. 'Well, obviously I meant *minus* ten points. Otherwise the drive would explode.'

'I am complying,' said the Ship. There was a chatter of electronic activity.

Chris barely noticed. He was staring at the nebula, open-mouthed. The only thing that spoilt his perfect view were those three irritating red lights winking on and off in his peripheral vision, now ever so slightly faster.

'Accomplished,' said the Ship. 'Deoscillation digretic synthesisers regraded by minus ten points.'

'Good,' said the Doctor. 'Now, Ship, please realign your maxi-vectometer on drags so it cross-connects with your radia-bicentric anodes.'

There was another burble of electronics.

'Accomplished,' said the Ship.

'Good,' said the Doctor. 'Now, here comes the difficult bit. Please switch your conceptual geometer from analogue to digital mode and keep triggering feedback responses until you get a reading of 75 dash 839.'

'Accomplished,' said the Ship. 'And for your information, Doctor, that bit wasn't so difficult at all.'

The Doctor took a deep breath. 'Now. Let's see if it works. Ship, activate all realigned drive circuits!'

Electronics chattered incessantly.

'Ooh!' said the Ship. 'Something – something very strange is happening.' She giggled. 'Very strange – ooh –'

'Don't worry, my dear, keep going!' insisted the Doctor.

Chris leapt out of his seat as the view on the forward screen suddenly shifted. The nebula blurred and was replaced by a shifting, whirling blue vortex. At the same time there was a sound not unlike the painful grinding of the TARDIS's engines, though much softer and smoother.

'Ooh!' said the Ship, sounding to Chris like she was licking her lips. 'Ooh Doctor! Ooh, ooh, ooh!'

'Bingo!' cried the Doctor, punching the air.

'What have you done again?' asked Chris, who was mesmerised by the swirling blue vortex but felt sure the Doctor wanted to explain how clever he'd been in more detail.

The Doctor smiled. 'I've only gone and constructed a primitive form of relative dimensional stabiliser by remote control.'

'Oh good,' said Chris.

'So any journey, however far we go, will only take a couple of hours' relative time.' He beamed. 'Pretty clever, don't you think, everybody?'

'Very,' said Chris.

'Affirmative, Master,' said K-9.

When the Ship spoke again she had a slightly different, warmer tone. 'For a dead man, Doctor, you are extremely ingenious.'

'Yes, well let's not harp too much on that aspect, shall we?' said the Doctor.

'Yes, well done,' said Chris. 'I just wish you could turn those red lights off, they're very irritating.'

'What red lights?' asked the Doctor.

'Those ones,' said Chris, pointing them out. 'They've been annoying me ever since I came in here but I didn't want to mention them, as it's probably nothing.'

The Doctor vaulted over to the panel where the red lights flashed. 'Ship, please explain the significance of these lights.'

'How should I know?' said the Ship. 'My lord Skagra activated that panel shortly before his departure. It is outside my schematics.'

The Doctor beckoned K-9. 'Here, boy. What do you make of this? Come on, I'm asking for your contribution.'

K-9 extended his probe and scanned. 'Alert, Master. This ship has been timed to explode in precisely one point four three minutes!'

'What?' cried the Doctor and Chris.

'The ship has been primed to explode,' repeated K-9.

'Skagra wanted to cover his tracks,' surmised the Doctor. He called upwards. 'Ship, please disable the explosive mechanism. Now!'

'Now how can I do that?' asked the Ship coyly. 'I've got no interface with those particular circuits, as decreed by my gracious lord Skagra.'

'Your gracious lord Skagra wants to blow you to atoms!' called the Doctor.

The Ship paused. 'I cannot believe that, Doctor. I am his truest and most trusted servant.'

'Er, if it is a bomb, shouldn't we defuse it, Doctor?' asked Chris.

The Doctor whipped out his sonic screwdriver, adjusted the settings and ran it swiftly along the side of the panel, cutting a smoking square through the smooth white material. 'Sorry if it hurts—'

'Ow!' cried the Ship.

'No time to be gentle,' said the Doctor. He wrapped his hand in one of the ends of his scarf and wrenched aside the burning plate. Beneath the panelling, Chris saw a maze of thin, interconnected fibres, like a bowl of dry vermicelli. Red light throbbed from somewhere underneath the tangle.

'Time to detonation now fifty-four seconds, Master,' said K-9.

'Thanks for that, K-9,' said the Doctor. He held the glowing tip of the sonic screwdriver above the fibres. 'Which one do I cut?'

'How should I know?' said Chris and the Ship at the same time.

'Time to detonation now thirty seconds, Master,' said K-9.

'What?' spluttered the Doctor. 'It was fifty-four seconds a couple of seconds ago!'

'Does it matter?' said Chris. 'Just cut them all! Do it!'

The Doctor stared at Chris, apparently rather struck by his sudden hot temper. 'Good idea!' he said – and he jabbed the sonic screwdriver down into the mass of fibres.

There was a crackle of energy and a sound like popping corn. The fibres twanged and split.

'Well?' called the Doctor in the sudden silence that followed.

'Crisis averted, Master,' said K-9. 'The detonation sequence has been aborted.'

The Doctor mopped his brow and switched off the sonic screwdriver. 'Well, there we are.'

Chris was trying to piece together what had just happened. 'So Skagra set the ship to explode,' he said.

'More than just the ship,' said the Doctor. He indicated the burnt ends of the tangled fibres. 'There was enough thermal energy generated by that thing to destroy an entire planet.'

'He was going to wipe out Cambridge?' Chris was horror-struck. 'All the colleges? The Backs, the railway station . . . the pubs?'

'Plus the entire planet,' said the Doctor gravely.

Chris flared up. He found himself squaring up, his nostrils flaring in anger. 'He was going to kill Clare?' The words burst out of Chris's mouth before he had a chance to think about what they told him about his subconscious.

The Doctor raised an eyebrow. 'And all the other lovely girls. Plus the lovely boys. He must have considered it safer, just in case we'd sent off a message to the Time Lords.' He sighed. 'Which we perhaps should have done.'

'No way,' said Chris. 'They would probably have come and torched the place anyway.' He frowned. 'You know, before today I always thought Earth was a safe kind of a planet.'

The Doctor raised his other eyebrow, as if Chris had said something incredibly stupid. 'Anyway, not to worry,' he said, getting to his feet. 'Thanks to me, the ship is safe, and we're on our way.'

'I can't accept that, Doctor,' said the Ship. Her voice was tremulous, as if she was on the brink of bursting into tears. 'My lord Skagra is infallible. If he wished me –' She paused, gulped, and gathered herself. 'If he wished me, his truest servant, to be – destroyed . . . Well then, I must have been destroyed.'

'If that's the way you want to see it,' said the Doctor cautiously.

'It's the only way I can see it,' said the Ship bravely. 'You were already dead of course, Doctor. Now we all are.'

'This is ridic—' began Chris, but when he saw the Doctor's hand raised as if to clamp over his mouth again he stopped.

'I've exploded,' said the Ship.

The Doctor patted the open panel. 'Of course you have, dear. There, there.'

Chris looked grimly out of the forward screen and into the vortex. 'Worrying, isn't it?'

'Which it in particular?' asked the Doctor.

'Well,' said Chris, nodding upwards, 'what else isn't she telling us?'

In the small generation chamber deep in the bowels of the ship, the newly formed Kraag stirred.

One rocky claw clasped the edge of the tank and it hauled itself upright.

42

Kraag after Kraag after Kraag marched from the generation chamber into the observatory. Romana, her head bowed, stood beside Skagra, who was manipulating controls at the central console. The sphere sat on top of the cone, burbling to itself.

'Now,' said Skagra, 'you shall see that though the Doctor is deceased, his mind lives within the sphere.'

A holo-screen flickered into life above the console. Romana looked up despondently, and to her astonishment she saw herself. She was smiling brightly, leaning against the door of the TARDIS.

'You see what was uppermost in his mind,' said Skagra. 'He was very –' he searched for the word – '*fond* of you.'

Romana looked around at the gathering Kraags. 'That's hardly important now,' she said flatly. 'You were right. I've no choice but to accept your dominion over me.'

Skagra turned his head slowly to look at her. 'I wonder if you are telling me the truth.'

'What could I possibly hope to gain by lying to you?' she asked. She looked up at the stars. 'You spoke about entropy, the long dark nightmare at the end of the universe.' She turned back to Skagra. 'Have you really found a way to stop it?'

'I have,' said Skagra. 'The ultimate answer. I will bring purpose and order. I will save the universe from itself, from chaos.'

'I'm trying to understand you, I swear,' said Romana. 'But how can I begin to believe it if I don't even know who you are?'

Skagra relinquished his place at the controls. 'You are familiar with the planet Drornid?' he said stiffly.

Romana nodded. 'It was the scene of an incident in Gallifreyan history.'

'An incident,' said Skagra. He tilted his head to one side. 'I admire your understatement. It is an excellent quality.'

'Thank you,' said Romana. 'Many thousands of years ago there was a schism in the College of Cardinals on Gallifrey. Cardinal Thorac fled to Drornid, declared himself President of the Time Lords, and established a rival court there.'

'Where he became known as the Heresiarch of Drornid,' Skagra continued. 'Eventually Thorac returned to Gallifrey.'

Romana nodded, thinking back to her history lessons. 'The High Council forced him to return by simply ignoring him.'

Skagra's eyes narrowed. 'And do you know what happened on Drornid, Time Lady, both during and after the reign of the Heresiarch?'

Romana searched her memory. 'There was no mention of that on my history syllabus at the Academy.'

Skagra grunted, and his hands flew over the controls. The holo-screen shifted to show another image. 'Then it is time for me to expand your learning. This was Drornid during the reign of the Heresiarch.'

The holo-screen showed the wide vista of a city that nestled in a large valley. Towering over the buildings was an enormous statue of a hook-nosed man in the robes of a Time Lord President. 'The Heresiarch controlled the planet from the statue. He set up a pacification beam from his court within, quelling any unrest or resistance from the native populace.'

The image shifted again as Skagra manipulated more controls. Now

Romana saw the crowded streets of the city from ground level, with the statue looming down from on high. The citizens of Drornid shambled happily along the streets, dumb smiles on their faces. 'Drornid at this time was an advanced civilisation, late level nine, early level ten,' continued Skagra. 'But the day came, after several hundred years, when Thorac, as you say, left to return to Gallifrey.'

The screen now showed an aerial view of the city. Tiny figures teemed through the streets. 'The pacification ray was switched suddenly off,' said Skagra. 'The people of Drornid suffered a severe psychic feedback. The centuries of quiet subservience were over, and all the accumulated aggression and unrest spilled back into their minds. They tore their own planet apart.'

Romana watched as the view changed back to the wide view of the city, now sparking with flames. Burnt-out buildings toppled, there were distant cries of anger and terror. Finally the great statue of Thorac itself was dragged over, smashing into the city below with a colossal crash.

Romana put a hand to her mouth. 'That's terrible,' she said. 'I am so sorry for your people.'

Skagra's nostrils flared. 'They are not my people, nor should you be sorry. This is merely historical background. It happened, as you say, thousands of years ago.'

'So what does it have to do with you?' asked Romana.

Skagra adjusted the controls again. 'When I was born, this is what Drornid had become,' he said gravely.

Romana turned her eyes back to the screen, expecting to see some hellish, blasted wilderness. Instead she saw lush, tropical beaches, and wide tree-lined boulevards through which people in shorts and sandals walked happily.

'It looks quite nice,' said Romana.

'*Nice*?' said Skagra. 'This is the sick, degenerate, purposeless world I was born into. Drornid, the so-called top holiday destination of Galactic

Quadrant 5. Primary export, beachwear. Primary import, ice cream. The Planet of Fun.'

'It must have been awful for you,' said Romana.

Skagra searched her face. 'Do you mock me?'

'Of course not,' said Romana.

'Nobody was interested in the past,' Skagra went on. 'Nobody was interested in anything but their mindless, futile diversions. It was I who unlocked the secrets of the planet's history. I who excavated the site of the great Statue of Thorac. I who discovered the abandoned papyri in the ruins and restored them.'

The holo-screen switched again, to show a grainier image. Skagra, presumably accompanied by the remote video camera that had captured these pictures, was clambering over dusty rubble in a deep, dark cavern.

With a mighty effort, he pushed aside a huge chunk of rock and revealed beneath an almost perfectly preserved lower chamber.

Romana saw the Seal of Rassilon, the emblem of the Time Lords, carved into one wall. The chamber was filled with books and scrolls. It had obviously been the library during the reign of the Heresiarch. The image of the younger Skagra skipped forward almost eagerly down into the chamber.

'So that's how you know so much about the Time Lords,' said Romana.

Skagra nodded. 'And from that information, I formed my plan. I made my preparations over long years. I established this asteroid as my command station. I obtained the sphere. I had almost everything I needed.'

'Except the book?' prompted Romana.

'Except the book,' said Skagra.

'How did you know that Chronotis had stolen it from Gallifrey?' asked Romana. 'Surely only he knew that.'

'At first I intended to steal the book from the Panopticon Archives,' said Skagra.

Romana blanched. 'Gallifrey is very well defended.'

'I know that,' said Skagra. 'There is no conventional method to gain entry. So I chose an unconventional method.'

He adjusted the controls and the image of a thin, hysterical-looking young woman in tattered red robes appeared on the holo-screen. Her face and hands were covered in henna tattoos, a mystical scrawl.

'A visionary?' Romana guessed.

'One of the Sisters of Karn,' said Skagra. 'A powerful seer. I used the juice of the Lethe flower, an anti-telepath drug known as synaptrol, to drain her powers and steal her away. When she awoke she was my prisoner.'

The image changed again, to show the young woman inside the zero prison of Skagra's ship. 'I ordered her to take me, undetected, into Gallifrey,' said Skagra. 'But she taunted me. Said I would not find the book there.'

Romana took a deep breath. 'What did you do to her?'

Skagra nodded to the screen. 'I withheld food and water until she told me where to find the book.' The screen showed the young woman, writhing on the floor of the prison. The image was silent but Romana could see the visionary was railing up at Skagra, cursing him. 'Of course,' said Skagra, 'she was protected from death by the elixir her sisterhood so jealously protect. But I am a very patient man. I waited for years until the pain became unbearable to her. Eventually she told me how Chronotis had stolen the book, how it was hidden in an obscure place called Cambridge. And then, I disposed of her.'

'How?' asked Romana.

'It is not important,' said Skagra.

'How?'

'I merely ejected her into space.'

Romana shuddered. 'I suppose you had no further use for her,' she said steadily.

'Correct,' said Skagra. 'I needed her only to find the book. And with the book I shall find Shada.'

'What is Shada?' asked Romana. 'And what's the book got to do with it?'

'You really don't know, do you?' said Skagra, looking almost amused. 'Another historical item that dropped off your syllabus.' He turned back to the screen, touched the sphere, and the image reverted to the smiling face of Romana.

'Somewhere in the Doctor's mind, buried so deeply perhaps even he is unaware of it, is the secret,' he went on. 'I am convinced he knows the code.'

'I wish I could help you,' said Romana. 'But I need to know more.' She stood closer to Skagra and put an arm on his shoulder. 'You have been so alone. Perhaps I can share in your great purpose.'

Skagra flinched as she touched him. 'I would like that to be so,' he said eventually. 'You are not the same as other people.'

Romana touched him gently on the cheek. 'I am like you.' She held out her hand.

Skagra's gloved hand took it.

Suddenly, with all of her considerable strength, Romana swung Skagra's hand around until it hovered over a large button on the control console. From the corner of her eye she had seen it, and worked out that it was the entry-coder for a self-destruct sequence, undoubtedly keyed only to Skagra's touch.

She forced his hand down towards the button.

Skagra fought back, wrenching his hand free. He took a step back and with a snarl, froth foaming at the corners of his lips, he smacked her across the face. 'Duplicitous time-witch!' he shouted.

Several Kraags advanced. 'Shall we destroy her, my lord?' asked the Commander.

'Yes!' cried Skagra, wiping flecks of spittle from his mouth.

Romana screwed up her eyes as the Kraags surrounded her, their arms outstretched – burning auras of heat formed at the tips of their claws . . .

'No!' shouted Skagra.

The Kraags lowered their hands.

Skagra shook himself, returning to his normal self. 'She may still be of use. Guard her well.' He turned back to the controls. 'I must find the code,' he said. 'I *will* find the code.'

43

The grinding engine noise made by a TARDIS was now almost familiar and reassuring to Chris. He stared out of the forward screen as the swirling patterns of what the Doctor had described as the space-time vortex dissolved back into a vision of the endless stars.

The ship was slowing to a halt alongside a huge, dark multi-decked structure, roughly circular in shape. The detail of the hull of the space station, if that was what it was, was picked out as it revolved slowly in the light of a nearby red sun. It looked shabby and deserted.

'Commencing docking procedure,' said the Ship. 'Though I don't know quite why, as we're all dead anyway. Though I suppose I was technically never alive. Hey-ho.'

Chris felt the ship turn around, presumably to align itself with a docking port on the side of the space station.

'Well, wherever it is, we're here,' said the Doctor.

'While Skagra is presumably going in the opposite direction,' said Chris.

'Worrying, isn't it?' said the Doctor. 'But it's the only thing we can do.'

'Haven't you any idea what he's after?'

'Shada,' said the Doctor, looking out at the stars as the ship continued its manoeuvres. 'It would definitely help if we knew who Shada was.'

'Who, or what,' said Chris.

The Doctor ruffled his fingers through his mop of curly hair. 'Shada . . . Shada . . . there's something at the back of my mind . . .' He held up a finger. 'Wait a moment. Shada! Isn't she a singer?'

K-9 burbled. 'Suggest the master is confusing Shada with Sade.'

The Doctor's face fell. 'Oh yes,' he said. 'Never mind.'

'I've never heard of her,' said Chris. 'Not that that counts for much.'

'She is an Earth singer from your future, young master,' said K-9 helpfully.

'Well, that's all right then,' said Chris. 'That means everything's all right.'

The Doctor glared at him. 'What are you talking about?'

'Well,' said Chris, 'if there's a future, we know, don't we?'

'We know what?'

'That everything's going to be all right.' Chris rubbed his hands excitedly. 'Whatever happens to us, at least the Earth and the universe are safe. If there's a future, where people can sing and be famous.'

The Doctor looked sadly across at him. 'I wish it worked like that.'

'Oh,' said Chris. 'You mean it doesn't?'

'No,' said the Doctor. 'Anyway, never mind about the future. Whatever Skagra's up to we have to stop him. Mind control is the most terrible thing. Any physical threat you can fight, but once someone has control of your mind you've lost everything.'

He stopped, as if surprised by his own words. 'That's very odd.'

'What is?' asked Chris.

'Why did I say that? It's as if my subconscious mind was trying to push something up to the surface.' He blinked. 'Now it's gone.'

'Don't think about it,' Chris advised him. 'Then maybe it'll come back to you.'

'I should know the answer!' said the Doctor loudly in one of his sudden explosions. He tapped his head. 'Perhaps, somewhere in the back of my mind, I do know the answer . . .'

The ship rumbled along the side of the hull.

A hidden doorway in the long corridor outside the command deck swung smoothly open.

The Kraag emerged.

It heard voices from the command deck.

'It's about time I worked out the answer!' one of the voices was saying.

It turned and trod slowly and heavily towards the source of the voices.

44

Romana stood encircled by her Kraag guardians. Skagra was at the control console, accessing the Doctor's mind. The holo-screen showed rapidly flickering images of the book and recent events. She saw herself, Chris, K-9, the Professor, a young woman who must have been Chris's friend Clare.

Romana rubbed her cheek. It was still tender from Skagra's attack. She looked sadly at the screen, and saw herself and the Professor sipping tea in his warm, comfortable study. It seemed inconceivable that that had been only a few hours ago. Now the Professor, and possibly the Doctor too, were dead.

'Concentrate,' said Skagra, his hand on the sphere. 'Your great minds can discover the answer. Let your minds be guided. Concentrate.'

The holo-screen fixed on an image of the open book as the Doctor flicked through it.

'What's so important about the book anyway?' asked Romana.

Skagra shot her an impassive glance. 'It is *The Worshipful and Ancient Law of Gallifrey*. What does a Gallifreyan judge say when passing sentence?'

Romana thought. '"We but administer. You are imprisoned not by this Court but by the power of the Law."'

Skagra reached inside his tunic and held up the book in his white-gloved hands. 'That used to be quite literally true.'

Romana frowned. She was trying to formulate a response when the sphere burbled and Skagra's interest returned to the screen. The image had frozen on the open pages of the book, and a single word was flashing at the bottom of the picture again and again:

INSOLUBLE.

INSOLUBLE.

INSOLUBLE.

Skagra thumped his fist on the console. 'No!' he cried. 'The code is insoluble!'

He stepped back from the console, looking shattered and drained. Sweat poured from his forehead. 'My plan cannot proceed,' he said at last, seemingly suddenly like a lost little boy.

'I'm glad you realise it,' said Romana. 'It's about time.'

Skagra turned on her. 'You are a Time Lord,' he said, a cunning glint coming into his eye. 'Somewhere in your mind you know the answer. I shall not use the sphere this time. I shall dissect your living conscious-ness, pluck it apart. Cell by cell—'

Romana stood firm. 'You've lost, Skagra. It's all over.'

But Skagra did not reply. Instead he pointed to her, his lips moving silently.

'What did you say? "About time"?' he said at last. He swung back to the console. 'Time! Yes, I should have seen that. A Gallifreyan code would have to include the dimension of time!'

Skagra replaced his hand on the sphere. 'Concentrate,' he ordered, fixing all his attention on the screen. 'Find me the Doctor's last reference to time!'

45

'Oh come on, Ship!' called the Doctor. 'What's taking you so long?'
'These docking safety procedures are very important,' said the Ship haughtily. 'Though frankly, I don't know why I'm being so careful as we've all long since shuffled from this mortal coil. Habit, I suppose.'

There was a loud clang as the ship finally docked with the space station.

Chris's attention was elsewhere. He sniffed the air. 'Can you smell burning?'

'Of course not,' said the Doctor. 'Right, let's go.'

He hurried over to the door and pressed the panel marked OPEN. The door opened.

A huge burning figure stood before him, eyes glowing like a furnace. It spoke with a deep rumbling voice, forming words as if for the first time. 'Who . . . are . . . you?'

'Oh,' said the Doctor. 'No cold callers thank you!'

He reached for the button marked CLOSE. As the door started to slide back into place, the creature strode forward and ripped the door apart with its powerful claws, as if it were made of polystyrene.

The creature stalked through the door. Chris could feel the intense aura of heat radiating from it. He dashed to join the Doctor as he attempted to sidle past the creature.

'What on earth is it?'

'How am I supposed to know?' said the Doctor. 'And what's Earth got to do with it? Ship, what is it?'

'It is a Kraag,' said the Ship. 'It was formed automatically when I took off without my great lord Skagra aboard. Standard emergency procedure.'

'Why didn't you tell us?' exploded the Doctor.

'You didn't ask,' said the Ship with what it obviously considered sweet reason. 'Anyway, it hardly matters, does it? It can't do us any more harm. We're dead, and it must be too.'

'You are . . . intruders . . .' said the Kraag.

The Doctor shrugged. 'Well actually, I'm the Doctor and this is Bristol.' He gestured to the smoking trail left by the Kraag. 'That's what I call a carbon footprint.'

'You trespass on my lord's ship,' said the Kraag. 'You shall die!' It raised one arm which ended in grotesque lumpy claws. The tips of the claws glowed red hot.

'So there are some aliens that don't look like us,' said Chris. It was the only thing he could think of to say, and even as he was saying them he realised what incredibly rubbish last words they were.

'K-9, what's keeping you?' shouted the Doctor.

K-9 shot forward, nose blaster extruded. The powerful red laser beam shot from it, blasting the Kraag square in the centre of its chest.

The Kraag reeled back. Chris had a moment of relief. Then the Kraag growled terribly and raised its arm again. 'You – shall – die!'

'Silly thing, we're already dead,' said the Ship. 'I always thought those Kraags were a little slow on the uptake.'

'K-9, continuous fire!' shouted the Doctor.

K-9 blasted his laser again, and this time the bright red beam was sustained, beating the Kraag back.

'Good boy, K-9!' called the Doctor.

The laser beam started to sputter and weaken. The Kraag roared, flailing its arms in anger.

'Master!' called K-9 urgently. 'This unit cannot contain Kraag creature with blaster at maximum power – battery depleting!'

'Hold on K-9!' The Doctor knelt down and ripped off the side casing of the robot dog. 'We need a power feed,' he shouted to Chris over the roar of the laser. 'Any power feed!'

Chris grabbed at the tangle of fibres from the exposed panelling. 'Will these do?'

The Doctor grabbed them and shoved the bundle roughly into a small socket inside K-9. 'He's supposed to be universally compatible – but let's find out!' He called upwards, 'Ship, channel power to K-9, please!'

There was a crackle of energy along the length of the tangled fibres. With a whining, buzzing noise K-9's blaster beam returned to full strength. The Kraag was held frozen, its powerful form trapped in the red glare.

'There we are,' said the Doctor. 'All better.' He turned to Chris and indicated the door. 'We'd better get on.'

'But we can't just leave it like this,' protested Chris. 'Poor K-9.'

'Oh, he'll be fine,' said the Doctor airily, 'won't you, K-9?'

'Master,' groaned K-9.

'But what are we going to do about it?' spluttered Chris.

'I'm sure I'll work something out,' said the Doctor, 'when we get back.'

'Shouldn't we work something out now?' asked Chris.

The Doctor coughed. 'Listen, I have a way of dealing with such situations, it's very complicated and very impressive and I can't go into it now, will you just trust me?'

Chris nodded. 'OK.'

'Then let's go!' The Doctor skirted carefully around the burning Kraag and led the way through the smashed door and into the corridor that led to the airlock.

46

'*Not only is this not a book,*' said the Doctor's voice from the holo-screen, '*but time is running backwards over it.*' The screen showed the book in the Doctor's hand from the Doctor's point of view, with Clare looking anxiously at him beside the wrecked spectrograph.

In front of the screen, Skagra held the actual book in one hand, the sphere in the other. He turned to Romana. Any hint of his earlier emotional display had been wiped away, and he was as smooth and casual as he had ever been.

'Thank you,' he said. 'You have helped to give me the answer. It is, of course, about time.' He indicated the TARDIS. 'You will enter.'

The Kraags jostled Romana towards the police box. She had never felt so desperate and so alone.

The control room, usually a place of humming warmth and security, now seemed cold and alien, despite the heat emanating from the two Kraags that guarded her.

Skagra followed and stood before the console. He held the book out towards the time column and turned the pages.

Nothing happened.

Romana gave a sigh of relief. 'Looks like you were wrong again. Time for Plan B? Or is it Plan F by now?'

Skagra paused for a moment. Then he closed the book, and opened it again at the first page.

He turned the page.

The central column wheezed into life, jerking upwards. A cool green light came from deep beneath the column, something Romana had never seen there before.

Skagra turned another page. The exterior doors slammed shut. The lights dimmed, turning the same pale sickly green colour.

Skagra turned another page. The navigation input panel burbled into life, and a lever slammed over by itself.

Skagra smiled. 'Exactly. The Doctor knew the answer, and so did you, buried deep in your subconsciouses. Time runs backwards over the book. So I turn the pages within the time field of this machine and the machine operates. And turning the last page will take us to Shada!'

47

The airlock door irised open. From the clean cool interior of Skagra's ship, Chris looked through into a dank, dingy corridor that matched the shabby exterior of the space station.

The Doctor marched through the door and into the corridor. 'Come on!'

Chris hovered in the doorway. 'I suppose I ought to say something special. I mean, I am the first human being to travel into outer space.'

The Doctor shook his head.

'I'm not the first?'

'Not even close, sorry. Now come on!'

Chris followed him. The corridor was rusted and decayed, illuminated only by dim, caged wall lights and there were occasional creaking noises, like the sound of rending metal, that reminded Chris uncomfortably of just how close he was to millions of miles of vacuum.

'I suppose it's safe?' he asked.

'Yes, of course it's totally unsafe,' said the Doctor, his long legs taking him past doors marked SHUTTLE BAY 1 and SHUTTLE BAY 2 and into the belly of the station, his big booted footsteps thunking on the gridded metal plating of the floor and echoing away into the darkness.

Chris hurried after him. 'It's so hard to believe we just travelled hundreds of light years.'

'Why?' asked the Doctor.

'I always understood that you cannot travel faster than light,' said Chris.

'Says who?'

'Says Einstein,' said Chris.

'What?' The Doctor stopped and put an arm around Chris's shoulder. 'Do you understand Einstein?'

Chris wasn't sure where this was going. 'Yes.'

'What?' gasped the Doctor. 'And quantum theory?'

'Yes,' said Chris. He basked in the Doctor's astonishment, on firmer ground at last.

'What?' gasped the Doctor. 'And Planck?'

'Yes,' said Chris.

'What?' gasped the Doctor. 'And Newton?'

'Yes!' said Chris.

'What?' gasped the Doctor. 'And Schoenberg?'

Chris paused. Was it a trick question? He recalled reading about the crisis of tonality. He thought he'd caught most of it, so he answered proudly, 'Yes. Of course.'

The Doctor whistled, apparently impressed. Then he said, 'You've got an awful lot to unlearn, Bristol.'

Chris sagged. Back to normal, then.

They advanced down the corridor to a junction that led away to the right and into another dirty-looking corridor. There was a sign at the junction, a simple metal plaque on which was written in bold, unfussy lettering FOUNDATION FOR ADVANCED SCIENTIFIC STUDIES. Beneath that were another three letters, ASD.

The Doctor ran his fingers along the raised letters of the plaque, picking up a coating of dust. 'Advanced Scientific Studies,' he mused, 'but apparently no cleaning lady.'

Chris ran his own fingers along the smaller row of letters beneath. 'ASD,' he said, thinking. 'Advanced state of decay, by the look of it.'

Suddenly the Doctor raised a finger to his lips. 'Ssh!'

Chris fell quiet. The Doctor silently and carefully advanced a few steps down the second corridor. He listened intently for a few seconds, peering into the shadows, then turned back to Chris. 'Did you hear anything?'

More silence. The metal around them creaked like an old ship at sea. 'Only that creaking,' said Chris.

'That's nothing to worry about,' said the Doctor. 'Come on!'

They set off along the second corridor. A thought struck Chris. 'How could I read that sign?' he asked. 'I mean, don't tell me that everyone in the universe speaks and writes in English.'

'Of course not,' said the Doctor. 'The sign wasn't in English. But you've been in the TARDIS. She implanted a translation loop in your mind as a matter of course.'

'Your TARDIS mucked about with my head?' said Chris, slightly aggrieved. 'What were you saying about mind control?'

'It's a small courtesy,' said the Doctor, 'nothing serious or evil.'

Chris boggled. 'But a TARDIS can do that? Alter the perceptions of the people inside it?'

'Only a very little and only if the pilot instructs it,' said the Doctor. 'And I'm the pilot, so it only does nice things.'

They had now reached a large steel door. The Doctor searched for an opening mechanism and couldn't find one. He pulled out his sonic screwdriver and twiddled it. There was a small puff of smoke and the halves of the door trundled apart with a hydraulic wheeze.

'You rely rather a lot on that thing,' observed Chris.

'It makes things quicker,' said the Doctor as he stepped through the door. 'I like quicker.'

Chris followed him into a large room that seemed to be some kind of control chamber. The walls were covered in a complex array of technology the purposes of which he could not even begin to guess at. In the centre of the room was a tall hexagonal cone, with a recessed man-sized alcove in each of its six facets. On top was a spike similar to the one Chris had seen next to the chair in Skagra's ship's command deck.

But here everything was inert. No flashing lights, no reassuring beeps and clicks from the machinery.

The Doctor approached the cone and stopped at one of the alcoves, reaching up to examine something by the headrest. 'Aha! This is quite interesting.'

'Quite interesting!' spluttered Chris. He paced around the room, examining the dead displays and controls. 'This is fascinating. Absolutely fascinating!'

The Doctor smiled. 'It's nice to see things through a human's eyes now and then. All these questions.' He poked Chris with a bony finger. 'Go on, ask me another.'

Chris waved a hand around the room and across at the cone. 'OK. Does all this mean something to you?'

The Doctor hesitated. 'I think so. But it would be nice to have confirmation.' He raised the sonic screwdriver and headed for a particular control panel. 'I'm going to rely heavily on this thing again.'

He swept the sonic screwdriver across the panel. The console remained inert. This time no lights flashed, no electronics chattered.

'It's dead?' asked Chris.

The Doctor huffed. 'Very definitely. No power response, and even if there was . . .' He tucked his fingers under the panel and it came loose easily. 'The circuitry has decayed, the computation matrix, everything.' He pulled out a set of what could, Chris thought, be circuit-boards. He exerted the tiniest pressure and the boards shattered into dust. 'Accelerated entropy.'

'How can you accelerate entropy?' spluttered Chris, again uneasily aware of the shifting creaking noises all around them.

Before the Doctor could answer there was a sudden, shattering crash.

Chris whipped round. Through a dark interior doorway he could see movement.

Something was creeping towards them out of the darkness.

48

Clare was feeling a little better. Her watch had stopped, and the domed clock on the mantelpiece was, for some reason, running backwards and forwards and going up and down. But generally the world was beginning to look more real and solid and sensible again.

She accepted the teacup from the now solid and liver-spotted hand of Professor Chronotis as he sat down on the old settee across from her.

'You said that you will be Professor Chronotis?' she asked.

'Did I?' said the Professor. 'Oh yes I wouldst have been going to have said that, I suppose.' He sighed. 'Goodness me, we Gallifreyans have never managed to come up with a satisfactory form of grammar to cover these situations.'

Clare sipped her tea. It was sweet and milky. 'And what kind of a situation is it exactly?' she ventured. She assumed that Gallifrey was a Greek island or somewhere similar. Chronotis sounded like a Greek name, after all, though his accent was definitely English.

The Professor supped at his own tea and waved his hand about the room as if the answer was obvious. 'Timelessness,' he said.

'Timelessness?' asked Clare. Much as she had taken to this nice old man, she was starting to worry for his sanity. She recalled Chris's description of him – 'barmy, senile'.

The Professor nodded. 'Quite. Timelessness, as in standing obliquely to the time fields.'

'Oh,' said Clare. 'That's what we're doing, is it?'

'Oh yes,' said the Professor. 'Or sitting anyway.' He leaned forward and patted her hand. 'And I'm very grateful to you for arranging it, young lady.'

Clare shrugged. 'Least I could do. Though all I did do was press a button.'

'And by pressing that button, you activated the emergency program,' said the Professor. 'After a little gentle nudging in your perception field by my TARDIS.'

'Tardis?' asked Clare, looking past him to the outer door that led to sanity.

'Yes, I know, barely call it a TARDIS, can you?' said the Professor, looking around the room. 'A Type 12 in fact, very ancient. I rescued it literally from the scrap heaps. I'm not officially allowed to have one, you know.'

'Really, are you not?' said Clare.

'Still, it's just as well I did,' said the Professor, 'or I'd still be dead.'

'Still be dead?' Clare had a jolting memory of how he had transformed from a ghost into a solid person. She dismissed it. She must have imagined it after that knock on the head. Then she looked at that upright bookcase. What knock on the head?

'Yes, I've been killed,' the Professor went on. 'But the emergency program, which is a very naughty thing I'm not allowed to have either, means that you tangled with my time fields at the critical moment. You sent us into a temporal orbit, back through last Thursday night and into the vortex, I think. That's why I'm dressed like this, you see, excuse the impropriety.'

Clare stared at him, amazed at the garbage he was coming out with. It must sound so real to him, she thought sadly.

'You're not following me, are you?' he asked.

'No,' said Clare.

The Professor nodded. 'Good. You just think of me as a paradox in an anomaly and get on with your tea.'

Clare finished her tea and put the cup down. 'I think I'd better be going, actually, Professor.'

'Oh, I'm afraid there's absolutely no chance of that,' said the Professor casually. 'Not now, anyway.'

Clare made her way to the door. 'I'd better find Chris, and the Doctor.'

'Yes, we'd better had,' said the Professor, 'but you won't find them out there, my dear.'

Clare turned the knob of the door that led into the little vestibule. It was firmly locked. 'Please, Professor,' she said, 'open this door.'

'I can't,' he said. 'And you certainly can't.'

Clare squared her shoulders. 'Come on, Professor, the joke is over.'

The Professor stood up and crossed to the nearest windows. 'The joke is far from over, young lady,' he said. 'Would you care to see the punchline?'

He threw back the curtains dramatically.

Beyond them, Clare saw the twisting, howling blue maelstrom of the space-time vortex.

49

Skagra stood looking up through the observatory at the infinite stars. Romana, still under the guard of a pair of watchful Kraags, wondered what was going on in his head.

The Kraag Commander stomped through the mass of his fellows towards Skagra. 'First wave of generations is complete, my lord,' it said.

'Good,' said Skagra. He tapped the book in his hand. 'I have found the key, as anticipated. You will make all necessary preparations for the entry into Shada, and then begin second generation for the activation of the Universal Mind.'

'My lord,' said the Kraag Commander. It stomped away.

'The Universal Mind,' scoffed Romana.

Skagra turned to her. 'Exactly.'

Romana believed she still had one option available to her. It was something she had learnt from the Doctor. Irritating the enemy, exposing any weaknesses of their psychology. 'Why don't you just kill me, Skagra?' she said.

'Your reaction will interest me,' said Skagra.

'My reaction to what?'

Skagra tapped the book again. 'Your reaction to meeting one of the greatest criminals in your history.'

'Salyavin?' Romana shook her head. 'Salyavin died thousands of years ago. And even you can't fly the TARDIS back across the Gallifreyan time stream to meet him.'

'Tell me how Salyavin died,' said Skagra.

Romana considered. 'I don't know.'

Skagra nodded. 'A Triple Alpha-plus graduate of the Prydon College in the Academy on Gallifrey, and you don't know? How peculiar.'

Romana thought back to Skagra's earlier boast about the book and the role it had once played in the administration of Gallifreyan justice. Nowadays – or at least in the last few thousand years – the very few evil renegades about, such as Morbius and Zetar, had been sentenced to vaporisation. But she had no idea what had befallen the criminals of earlier generations on Gallifrey. For some reason, the impulse to wonder about it had never crossed her mind, and even now she felt a vague sense of apprehension at the question.

'Perhaps,' said Skagra, 'the Time Lords wanted to forget. To assuage their consciences. They wanted to obliterate all memory of what they had done, wipe it from their history.' He gestured to his collection of Gallifreyan texts. 'But it was all in there, still intact, on Drornid.'

'What was there?' Romana felt an almost overwhelming impulse to fight her own curiosity, as if this was a question that should never be answered.

'Can't you work it out for yourself?' asked Skagra.

'The book of the law sentenced Salyavin,' said Romana slowly, each word sounding a death knell deep in the back of her mind.

'But what was his punishment?' Skagra coaxed her.

'Imprisonment?' suggested Romana.

Skagra nodded. 'Correct. In Shada, the ancient prison of the Time Lords!'

Romana shuddered. The words hit her like a physical attack. If this was true – and somehow she just knew it was – she could at last begin to guess at the ultimate nature of Skagra's great scheme.

She pointed to the sphere. 'The Universal Mind,' she gasped.

Skagra nodded. '*My* mind.'

50

Clare's head was spinning again. She had a million pressing questions but didn't know which one to ask first or how to understand the likely replies. She had established that Chris was probably safe, and probably with the Doctor and this Ramona girl. But the deeper details eluded her.

As far as she could begin to grasp it, the Professor's suite of rooms was also an alien capsule for travelling through space and time, and the Professor himself was an alien. It seemed Gallifrey was not a Greek island after all but the home planet of a race called the Time Lords. Furthermore, the Professor's space-time craft, which he called a TARDIS, was at present stuck in something called a temporal orbit, which had sent itself and both of them back to Thursday night, or as the Professor more accurately said, 'a state of Thursday night-ness.' She abandoned her last objections to this idea when she looked in a mirror and saw that the perm she had washed out on Friday night was well and truly back. 'I suppose it's a time perm,' she said wistfully.

'That is the correct technical term, yes,' said the Professor abstractedly. 'Unfortunately the temporal orbit did not bring the book back in here. I suppose it must stand outside time, or it couldst have must've did has.'

Mention of the book made the Professor rather agitated. 'We must find Skagra. He's got the book,' he kept repeating, looking worriedly between the brass control console of his capsule and the window view that now showed not the neat green lawns sloping down to the Backs but the dazzling infinity of space and time.

'I thought the book might be dangerous,' said Clare.

'It is!' cried the Professor. 'Very dangerous, and I have been very careless with it.' He mopped his brow. 'I've been such a stupid old fool.'

'But why is it so dangerous?' asked Clare.

The Professor hesitated. 'I cannot say.'

Clare put her hands on her hips in a gesture that she had used unconsciously since the age of eight to terrify men. 'I think I deserve an explanation. I saved your life, didn't I?'

The Professor stared at her through his spectacles and seemed to reach a decision. 'Quite right, young lady. What does the secret matter now? It is best that you know before the trials that lie ahead.'

Clare felt a sinking sensation at the mention of danger. But then she remembered the books that had fallen onto the floor earlier. Adventures. Wasn't that what she'd always wanted?

'So what is the book's secret?' she asked.

The Professor drew himself up and spoke slowly, as if he could not quite believe he was telling her words out loud. 'It is the key to Shada.'

'Oh,' said Clare.

'The ancient prison of the Time Lords,' said Chronotis heavily.

'I see,' said Clare.

'Of course the Time Lords have all forgotten about it,' said Chronotis. 'All except me.'

'Oh,' said Clare again.

The Professor bit a fingernail. Clare was astonished to see that his eyes were beginning to fill with tears. 'And if this Skagra is meddling with mind transference, he is only going to Shada for one reason, and it is imperative that he be stopped!'

He crossed decisively to the brass control panel. 'But where to start? How to start?'

Clare followed him over. 'And what's in Shada that's so dangerous?' she asked.

'It's not a matter of what,' said the Professor, taking off his spectacles and wiping his eyes with a handkerchief. 'It's a matter of *who.*'

51

Chris found himself shrinking into the Doctor's side, like it was an instinct to go all girly and powerless next to this big, solid broad-shouldered man.

'Who are they, Doctor?' he whispered urgently as the five figures shuffled from the shadows into the main control room of the space station. '*What* are they?'

At first sight, Chris had thought these newcomers were vampires or zombies or werewolves, or a bit of all three with something else even worse mixed in. They were ragged, filthy creatures with long unkempt hair and long dirty fingernails, some with wild straggling beards. All of them wore a similar outfit of tunic and trousers. These clothes, Chris guessed, had once been gleaming white, but now they were shredded, hanging from the creatures' skinny bodies like torn grey shrouds.

Perhaps the worst thing about the newcomers, though, was the smell. They were caked in filth. Their eyes were blank and uncomprehending. Their bodies moved jerkily and uncertainly, like toddlers taking their first cautious steps. They held their hands outstretched towards the Doctor and Chris like beggars. They made a ghastly chorus of mewing sounds, and short guttural clicks and cries.

To Chris's astonishment and alarm, instead of sensibly backing away from these creatures as he had done with the Kraag, the Doctor put out an arm and gently took the bony hand of the nearest. He made soothing noises.

'There, there,' he said.

He smiled, though Chris could see he was deeply disturbed by the apparitions, whatever they were.

The creature touched by the Doctor lifted its head, and Chris was startled to see that under the shapeless rags and tatters it was a woman.

'Victims of Skagra's brain drain,' said the Doctor.

'That sphere?' said Chris.

The Doctor nodded. 'Their minds were stolen but their bodies survived the extraction process. If you can call this survival.' He brushed the woman's hair gently away from her blue eyes. 'They might know who Skagra is, what he's after, where he's gone.'

'But their minds have been stolen,' pointed out Chris.

'Some memory patterns might remain,' said the Doctor, clearly thinking hard. 'Locked off in the Broca's region.'

He turned very slowly, looking between Chris and the cone. 'Bristol, I would like you to do something for me.'

'Certainly,' said Chris brightly. 'Anything I can do to help.'

'It won't be pleasant, I'm afraid,' said the Doctor.

'Silly Kraag, silly dog,' observed the Ship, looking on at the titanic struggle between K-9 and the rock monster. 'You should really give it up. The pair of you. I mean, all this denial's not going to get you anywhere, is it? We're all dead.'

K-9's laser continued to fire into the Kraag. The searing heat and blazing light would have blinded any organic being. Even K-9's finely attuned sensors, which operated through every spectrum, were having trouble keeping a clear image of his opponent. The constant wittering from the Ship wasn't helping things either.

'Ah,' sighed the Ship, now switching to its more wistful and reflective mood. '"Feel no more the heat o' the Kraag," as one of the great poets of that silly Earth planet almost has it. Take a break, get a long sleep in, that's the whole point of being dead, isn't it? I intend to do nothing at all now I've crossed to the other side.'

'Nothing – but – talk,' K-9 managed to say. It was, of course, completely impossible that a machine creature like himself could feel irritation. That was an organic emotion. But several of K-9's inner servo cut-offs were locking in and out with what could almost have been frustration.

The Kraag suddenly roared. It flung out its arms on either side, as if it was basking in the deadly laser beam.

'Master!' K-9 called urgently. 'Master, hypothesise that the Kraag creature is absorbing energy from the beam! Master!'

'He can't hear you,' said the Ship. 'For that matter, neither can I. Ho-hum.'

Chris stood in one of the alcoves around the central cone, as directed by the Doctor. The Doctor had gently led one of the survivors, a man, into the position right next to him. Then he took a long length of wire from his pocket and fastened it around some sinister-looking inputs above Chris's head.

'Bristol,' he said darkly. 'I'm going to allow this man access to your intelligence reserves. It'll only be temporary. It might just allow his memory to function. I'm sorry, but it's our only hope of finding Romana.'

He trailed the wire from the inputs and wound it around the head of the dirty, bearded old man. The old man looked up and smiled innocently like a small child. His fellow survivors cowered in a shadowy corner of the control room, looking on uncomprehending.

'I hope you know what you're doing,' said Chris as the Doctor held out his sonic screwdriver.

'So do I,' muttered the Doctor.

'I have total faith in you,' said Chris.

'So do I,' muttered the Doctor. 'There should be enough power to jump-start the transference circuit, for a while anyway.' He turned on the sonic screwdriver and touched the tip to the length of wire that ran between Chris and the old man. 'Take a deep breath,' he ordered.

Chris took a deep breath.

'Now!' cried the Doctor.

Chris felt a tingle of power along the back of his neck. It was not unpleasant, and he was just opening his mouth to tell the Doctor that everything was all right when the world fell away.

Another mind crashed into his.

A bewildering sequence of wild, flashing images tumbled through Chris's head. He felt himself flashing through purple waves on some kind of futuristic surfboard, a young woman's hands wrapped around his naked back. He saw lectures, machinery, white boards and computer viewscreens filling up with equation after equation after equation.

The image of Clare faded from his mind, to be replaced by another face. A cold-eyed young man with fair hair and full, sensuous lips. The small part of Chris that still existed was certain he'd seen him somewhere before.

And then, Chris felt himself disappear. Suddenly, he was somebody else.

'Master, alert!' cried K-9. 'Kraag creature is –' He gathered his strength. 'Kraag not only absorbing energy – but it is –'

The Kraag turned almost mockingly in the beam, shaking itself. Its entire body was now suffused in the red light, smoke and steam belching from it in furious blasts.

'It is – growing stronger!' called K-9 weakly. 'This unit requires assistance! Hurry, Master!'

The Kraag gave another horrifying roar and stepped slowly to the side and out of the beam.

'I knew this would end badly,' said the Ship.

The Doctor looked anxiously between Chris and the old man. Chris's head was slumped back in the alcove, and the pained expression on his

240

face was not pleasant to behold. The Doctor quickly checked Chris's life signs and gave him a fond kiss on the brow.

Then he turned his attention to the old man. A little light had come back into the man's clouded gaze, and the Doctor fancied he could almost see the adult intelligence swimming back up onto the ravaged face.

Suddenly the old man's arm jerked. He pointed with one long-nailed finger and moaned.

'Gently now, take it easy,' said the Doctor, kissing the old man's brow as well for good luck.

A hissing sound issued from the back of the old man's throat. Then a single syllable pushed itself up through his lips.

'It's . . .'

'Please, go slowly,' said the Doctor.

The old man's eyes settled upon him. 'Who are you?'

'The Doctor.'

'What are you doing here?' gasped the old man, every syllable clearly a tremendous effort.

'Me? I'm here to help,' said the Doctor. He leaned in close and whispered softly, 'May I ask who you are, sir?'

'My name is . . . Akrotiri . . .'

The Doctor's own memory was functioning perfectly accurately. 'What?' he gasped. 'Not C.J. Akrotiri? The neurologist?'

'The same,' said the old man. He managed to dip his head graciously. It was a pitiful sight, thought the Doctor, the famed scientist reduced to the level of a babbling idiot.

Carefully the Doctor shook the old man's hand. 'It's a pleasure to meet you, sir,' he said, trying to keep the emotion out of his voice. 'One of the greatest intellects of your generation.'

'So are we all.' Akrotiri gestured to his fellow survivors. There were tears forming in his rheumy eyes as he identified them. 'K. Thira the psychologist, J. Centauri the parametricist, C. Ia the biologist, D. Caldera . . .'

The Doctor regarded the survivors. 'I thought I recognised those faces. Arguably some of the greatest intellects in the universe in this time period,' he breathed. One of the women, J. Centauri, master of parametrics, was staring at her fingers as if trying to count them.

Akrotiri gave a long, grating sigh. 'And Doctor R. Skagra.'

The Doctor returned his attention to the old man. 'Tell me about Skagra.'

'Dr R. Skagra,' the old man repeated. 'Geneticist, and astro-engineer, and cyberneticist, and neurostructuralist, and moral theologian.'

'And too clever by seven-eighths,' muttered the Doctor. 'Who is Skagra? Where does he come from?'

'I don't know,' whispered the old man. 'He never answered any of our questions. But . . .' He grimaced. 'He was very impressive. He offered very handsome fees. So we all agreed.'

This memory seemed to trigger a response in Chris. The Doctor looked over to see the innocent young face of his friend contorted by exactly the same grimace.

'Agreed to what?' asked the Doctor, though he had a horrible feeling he already knew the answer to this question.

Akrotiri gestured about weakly. 'This place, the Institute. It was his idea, he set the place up. A grand experiment. We called it the Think Tank.'

'Go on, please,' urged the Doctor.

'The Think Tank,' sighed Akrotiri. 'The pooling of intellectual resources by electronic mind transference. No longer any need, he said, for wasteful duplication of research and lengthy cross-reviewing by scientists with different specialties. We could pool our intellects, think together, a symphony of the scientific mind . . .' He weakened once again, his face showing the enormous struggle to hold on to his thoughts.

'And together,' said the Doctor, looking up at the spike on top of the cone, 'you built the sphere, for Skagra? And you all got into this thing and switched on?'

'Then it was too late,' Akrotiri groaned. 'Too late!' He reached out and his long yellow fingernails clutched at the lapel of the Doctor's coat. 'Too late!'

The Doctor looked over anxiously at Chris. He was agitated too, his head twisting and turning under the inputs.

'Too late!' Chris called in an agonised voice. 'He stole our minds!'

'It's never too late,' said the Doctor soothingly. 'I've come to help, remember?'

Chris slumped back against the headrest of his alcove, becalmed.

'Why would you help us?' asked Akrotiri.

The Doctor coughed. 'Well, wouldn't anybody?'

The Kraag almost seemed to be laughing.

It turned its back on K-9 and started pounding for the exit door from the command deck.

'Master! Master!' cried K-9. He snapped off the laser beam and shot forward at top speed. The power cable clicked from the socket on his side.

The Ship watched as K-9 followed the burning red-hot Kraag from the command deck. 'All very confusing behaviour,' she said.

Without the distractions on her command deck, the Ship decided to get on with some serious thinking.

'Now that's odd,' she said to herself as the sounds of K-9's engine and the roaring of the Kraag receded up the companionway. 'I'm dead, so it should be impossible for me to think.' She hemmed and hawed, electronics chirruping. 'Why didn't I think of that before?'

The Doctor looked deep into the eyes of Akrotiri. 'I'm going to take you all with me, there's plenty of room.'

The structure of the station creaked once more.

'Sooner the better. Skagra obviously built this place to last only until his great experiment was concluded. Now it's falling to bits.'

'Aren't we all?' said Akrotiri.

The Doctor patted him on the shoulder. 'Don't you worry. I can get help for you when all of this has blown over, get your brain back.'

Akrotiri smiled. 'You are a good man, Doctor.'

The Doctor smiled back. 'No, I'm not. In fact I'm flippant, boastful and terribly disorganised.'

Suddenly Chris emitted a deep, terrible groan.

The Doctor licked his lips and turned urgently to Akrotiri. 'Listen. I'm terribly sorry but I'm going to have to disconnect you again. I may not be able to speak to you again for some time.'

Akrotiri nodded.

'Now please, concentrate,' the Doctor went on. 'Did Skagra ever mention his place of origin? Anywhere he might use as a base, anywhere he was trying to get to?'

'Never,' said Akrotiri.

Chris let out a cry. His head rocked back and forth in the alcove.

'Anything – please?' urged the Doctor. 'I mean, doesn't the wretched man have a home to go to?'

Akrotiri struggled to answer. 'Perhaps . . .'

'What?' spluttered the Doctor. 'Go on, quickly.'

'Once, I saw him . . .' Akrotiri began. The words were swallowed up in another agonising cry from Chris.

The Doctor got closer. 'Saw him what? Please!'

Akrotiri shuddered. 'He was . . . checking coordinates – on a palm unit . . .'

The Doctor's eyes lit up. 'What were the coordinates?' prompted the Doctor. 'Please, Mr Akrotiri!'

Chris cried out once again.

The Doctor reached out instinctively to pull the connection between the two men free.

And then Akrotiri said, 'Galactic north 9 . . . 6 . . . 5 . . . 5 . . .'

'Yes?' called the Doctor, the wire in his hand.

Chris writhed in agony.

'Galactic north 9 . . .'

'Yes, I got that bit, 9655! What's the rest? By what?'

Akrotiri's dry lips forced out, 'By . . . by . . . galactic east vector 9 . . . 1 . . . 3 . . .'

Suddenly there was a mighty roar and an explosion of heat and noise.

The Doctor was knocked to the floor by the heatwave.

He lifted his head and saw the Kraag, glowing red hot, stomping towards him. Sparks crackled around it, and smoke poured from the floor-plates at its stumpy feet.

The structure of the space station groaned.

There was an almighty crack and one wall of computer banks smashed down.

'Now listen,' said the Doctor, calling to the Kraag. 'I don't know if you can understand me, but this is a very unstable environment and you are about the worst person to come crashing in here!'

The Kraag roared and raised one arm towards him.

'You fire that weapon,' called the Doctor, 'and this whole place will be destroyed!'

PART FIVE

GALLIFREY'S MOST WANTED

52

The Doctor was never to know if the raging Kraag had understood his words of warning, or if it had even heard them. A red mist had come down in front of the Kraag's eyes – quite literally – and the Doctor, who had made a career of shouting 'Wait!' at people or things that were preparing to shoot him, but could sense the rare occasions when that just wasn't going to work, did the only sensible thing, and ducked.

A bolt of red-hot plasma energy blasted from the Kraag's outstretched claw and smashed a gaping hole in the facing wall. Rivulets of molten metal spattered across the room.

And, true to the Doctor's prediction, the station that housed the Foundation for Advanced Scientific Studies began to creak and groan ever more perilously. The survivors, huddled in their corner, began to moan and scream in uncomprehending terror, hooting and howling like wild beasts.

The Doctor found he still held the connecting wire in his hand. Chris and Akrotiri were still linked together. But there was no chance of getting the final coordinates now, no chance of finding Romana or stopping Skagra. The Kraag was already stomping after him, claw outstretched to blast him to atoms.

The Doctor yanked the wire free.

Chris screamed and leapt from the alcove, straight into the Doctor's arms.

Through the haze and the mist they heard a faint, tinny voice. 'Master! Master!'

'K-9!' shouted the Doctor.

The Kraag was almost on top of them.

Suddenly Akrotiri leapt from his alcove into the line of fire. Summoning all his energies, the tattered figure screamed wildly, 'Six-one-ZERO!'

At the last word, his frail, ancient body took the full force of the Kraag's energy bolt. For one terrible moment his skeleton was visible as the flesh boiled away. Then even his bones turned to ash, disintegrating in a wave of heat that threw the Doctor and Chris heavily to the floor.

Now the Kraag towered over them.

Suddenly the gridded metal floor-plates beneath its feet turned to slurry. With a roar almost of surprise, the Kraag slid down through the hole in the floor, jerkily, vanishing section by section. First its legs, then its torso, and finally its head with the glowing red eyes disappeared through the smoking gap.

Chris tried to gather his senses. All around was confusion, heat, smoke, the noise of the rumbling, roaring Kraag down below and the rending metal of the station.

'I told you we should have dealt with it before!' he found himself shouting in the general direction of the Doctor.

'Don't worry!' the Doctor shouted back. 'I've thought of something.' He called out into the black smoke. 'K-9! Are you there?'

'Master,' came the faint reply. 'Advise immediate evacuation!'

'Well, yes, that would be nice,' the Doctor called back. 'But we can't see in all this! Activate a homing beacon, lead us out of here, back to Skagra's ship!'

'Master,' said K-9 obediently.

A moment later Chris heard a steady and ear-splittingly loud beep. It repeated every other second.

The Doctor clapped Chris on the shoulder and shoved him away from the smouldering hole in the floor and in the general direction of the beep.

Chris kept his head down, remembering first-aid-class advice on how to avoid smoke inhalation. Faintly he saw the bright red rectangle of K-9's eye-screen retreating down from the control area.

It took Chris another second to realise that the Doctor was not following him.

He stared back into the haze and confusion and called desperately, 'Doctor! Where are you? Doctor!'

'Carry on, Bristol!' came the reply.

Chris squinted. He could just make out the figure of the Doctor, on one side of the hole formed by the falling Kraag. On the far side cowered the other four survivors, pressing their bodies together in a pitiful huddle.

The Doctor was reaching out over the widening chasm, trying to encourage them to jump across and join him.

'Doctor, leave it!' cried Chris.

'I promised!' shouted the Doctor.

Suddenly the station shook as some vital part disintegrated. The centre of gravity shifted, knocking the Doctor back to the floor.

With a chorus of ghastly wails, all four survivors tumbled into the pit.

Chris yelled and lunged towards K-9, flinging himself on to the metallic body of the little robot. Thankfully, K-9 seemed to have some kind of internal traction system of his own. He held firm, and Chris held firm to him.

There was a sudden silence, and then a grinding, splintering *crack* that chilled Chris to his very heart. The station was finally breaking up.

Nobody will know, Chris thought crazily. He was going to die. In fact he was going to die in the most bizarre and extraordinary circumstances, blown to bits aboard an alien space station thanks to a creature made of living rock, in the company of a Gallifreyan Time Lord and a robot dog. But it wouldn't even make the *Cambridge Evening News* or

Anglia Tonight. They had trouble covering events as far afield as Ipswich, let alone deep space. He felt quite affronted, and then quite surprised at being quite affronted. But then, might people think he had disappeared mysteriously and gone to reinvent himself in some dramatic and romantic way? He sighed inwardly. No, they'd just assume he'd hit a loose cobble, come off his bike and fallen in the river.

Suddenly he felt himself lifted up by the scruff of the neck, like a kitten being gummed by its mother. The next moment he was being hurried down the crazily shifting outer corridor of the station after the beeping, retreating K-9.

A loop of multicoloured scarf was flung over Chris's reddened, stinging eyes and burning mouth.

And then, just when he was feeling better, Chris fainted.

The Doctor careered onto the command deck of Skagra's ship, carrying Chris carefully in his arms as if he were taking a sleepy child up to bed. K-9 came trundling in behind them, still bleeping and blinking.

'Emergency, emergency!' the Ship was crying, ringing all its alarms. 'My sensors tell me that there's shortly going to be an absolutely enormous explosion in our near vicinity!'

The Doctor tried to clear his throat and dumped Chris into the command chair. 'I know!' he shouted. 'Don't you think you ought to do something about it?'

'Emergency escape procedures will be implemented,' said the Ship. 'That silly Kraag has gone and ignited the zison energy source of the station!'

'Zison energy! Then stop nattering and get on with it!' yelled the Doctor.

'Though why I'm implementing these procedures, I can't personally fathom,' the Ship nattered on. 'Do you know, Doctor, I have combed my databanks for legends of the afterlife from over thirteen thousand cultures across this galaxy alone, and I can't find a single one that suggests that things carry on after death rather suspiciously exactly as they did before. Hmm.'

'Just get us out of here!' cried the Doctor. He aimed a big angry kick at one of the control panels. 'And don't you talk to me about life and death! Come on! Don't you realise this is a matter of life and death!'

'No need for violence,' sniffed the Ship. 'That hurt!'

'Do it!'

The Ship rumbled as it disengaged its locking clamps. 'Preparing to reverse docking procedure,' said the Ship. 'Engaging engines.'

'Not that way!' cried the Doctor, almost despairing. On the screen he could see a boiling red aura from the station, building up to a cataclysmic end for the Think Tank that would easily take them along with it. 'I told you how to do it! Dematerialise!'

'Oh yes,' said the Ship. 'So you did, Doctor, so you did. And frankly I don't mind if I do.' She coughed and turned off her alarms.

The familiar wheezing groan of a relative dimensional stabiliser soothed the Doctor's ears.

'Ooh,' said the Ship. '*Ooh!*'

The forward screen view of the burning station dissolved into the comparatively relaxing vista of the endless spinning space-time vortex.

Chris regained consciousness to find the Doctor staring out at those same patterns, his hands buried deep in his pockets.

'We made it!' said Chris exultantly. The Doctor showed no sign of having heard him, and continued his brooding.

Chris was astonished to discover a golden trolley laden with exotic delicacies next to the command chair. 'Is this for me?'

It was the Ship who answered. 'I thought you might need refreshment, dear boy, after such a terrifying experience.'

'Thank you.' Chris leant over and grabbed something that looked almost like an apple. He bit into it. The flavour was unfamiliar but sweet enough. 'What happened? I guess I must have blacked out.'

'The space station was destroyed,' said the Ship.

'But did we discover anything? About Skagra?'

The Doctor turned at last. 'Thanks to Dr Akrotiri, yes. He gave his life to save ours, shouted out those final coordinates after his brain was disconnected from yours.'

'But you told me that was impossible,' said Chris, 'after his mind was stolen.'

'It was,' said the Doctor, nodding. 'Quite, quite impossible. But he did it.'

Chris didn't quite know how to deal with the Doctor in this mood. 'Then we can get after Skagra, and save Romana. Isn't that a good thing?'

K-9 piped up. 'This ship is already in transit to the stated coordinates.'

'Good,' said Chris.

The Doctor harrumphed. 'I just saw the best minds of this generation destroyed by the madness of a rampaging Kraag. And I couldn't lift a finger to help them.'

'Then we've got to make sure we don't waste what Akrotiri gave us,' said Chris. 'It's impossible things like that that show us we have to keep going.' He reflected how odd it was that it was he, who had never before experienced action, adventure and sudden death outside a cinema, that was taking this better than the Doctor.

But incredibly his simple and, he thought, rather clichéd words had a galvanising effect on the Doctor. He burst into a spectacularly wide and toothy grin and pointed straight at Chris. 'I like you,' he said.

'Sorry to interrupt this moving moment,' said the Ship, who sounded more left-out than sorry. 'But I think I ought to inform you gents that we'll be arriving at our destination in ten minutes of relative time.'

'Excellent, Ship,' said the Doctor. 'I like you too.'

'Thank you, Doctor,' said the Ship, sounding appeased.

Chris coughed, caught the Doctor's eye and nodded over to K-9, whose tail antenna was cast down.

'And of course I positively adore you, K-9,' said the Doctor quickly.

'This unit does not require adoration, Master,' said K-9, but nevertheless his tail perked up.

'Doctor,' said the Ship. 'I feel I should tell you that despite the warmth of our relationship, and all that you have done for me, much of my deceased circuitry feels uneasy about continuing to accept instructions from a dead man.'

'Well, just tell it not to worry,' said the Doctor breezily. 'I'm sure your great lord Skagra will be very anxious to pay his last respects to me.'

'Hmm, would he now?' said the Ship, who sounded to Chris like she was raising an eyebrow.

'And to you, of course,' the Doctor added hurriedly.

53

Following his dire and somewhat cryptic warning to Clare about a person she could never possibly have heard of being released from somewhere she could never possibly have heard of by another person she could never possibly have heard of, the Professor had slipped off into what she supposed must have been his bedroom and returned very shortly afterwards fully dressed in a dusty tweed suit. He then proceeded to tinker with the brass control panel, tweaking, adjusting and even removing some of the components and passing them to her for her opinion. 'I suppose we could always risk de-phasing the chronostatic field tracker,' was his latest observation. He peered over the rims of his spectacles and blinked as if he honestly desired her thoughts on the subject.

'Look, I don't know what any of this means,' Clare protested. 'I'm not an engineer and even if I was I'm not sure I could help you do whatever you're trying to do.' It was amazing, really, she thought, how calmly she was taking all of this. Something about the Professor made her heart go out to him, a little like she had felt before with the Doctor. He seemed such a nice old man, and she just wanted to help him.

The Professor tapped the brass panel meaningfully. 'Oh dear, did I not explain?'

'Not this particular bit, no,' said Clare.

'Sorry, thought it was obvious,' said the Professor. He seemed to be drifting again. 'Oh dear, that came out rather more pompously than I intended, I do hope you'll forgive me, young lady.'

'I'll forgive you anything,' said Clare, 'if you just tell me what you want me to do.'

The Professor tapped the panel meaningfully again, quite clearly forgetting he had just done so. 'You and I, my dear, we must get this old perambulator of mine moving again.'

'It certainly moved when I touched it before,' said Clare.

'A spasm, a mere spasm of the emergency mechanism,' sighed the Professor. 'I only hope it wasn't a dying spasm. Nobody likes a dying spasm. Nobody likes spasms much at all, I suppose.'

Clare gestured to the bewildering view through the curtained windows. 'You mean we're stuck? In this space-time vortex?'

The Professor flinched. 'And who, may I ask, told *you* about the space-time vortex?' he demanded, eyes narrowing.

'You,' said Clare. 'You did.'

The Professor clutched at his head. 'Oh, I'm sorry, my dear. I was confused enough when I was alive. Now I'm dead I'm absolutely hopelessly vague. I suppose it's inevitable, I mean look at the trouble spiritualists have, all of that "Auntie Sheila says look in a special place for the blue teapot" nonsense, it's useless . . .'

Clare tried to steer him back in the right direction. 'So we're stuck?'

'Yes,' said the Professor. 'The emergency mechanism has left us jammed in the temporal orbit, wedged between two irrational time interfaces. So time is moving away from us. I'll have to be ever so careful disentangling it all, otherwise I might cease to exist again.'

Clare gulped. 'What about me?'

'Oh yes, you too,' said the Professor, nodding enthusiastically. He seemed to note her troubled expression and patted her on the hand. 'Just do what I do.'

'What's that?'

'Forget about it,' he said simply. 'I've done a lot of forgetting in my time. Or rather I suppose I must have done, I can't actually remember.'

Suddenly he stared with new enthusiasm at one of the small components he had removed from the panel. 'Wait a moment!' he said eagerly and snatched it up. He seemed about to give a cry of victory. But then his shoulders slumped. 'No, it can't be done. I can't fix this on my own.'

Clare waved a hand in front of the Professor's face. 'You're not on your own.'

The Professor sucked his teeth and looked between her and the component. 'Difficult! Very difficult. To repair an interfacial resonator requires two very tricky and very delicate operations that must be performed absolutely simultaneously.'

'Just tell me what to do,' said Clare. 'I'm a scientist. A scientist who's a bit out of her depth, admittedly, but I've got a steady hand at least.'

The Professor smiled sadly. 'I'm sure of it. But to be honest, my dear, I don't think you have the necessary technical understanding even to begin to comprehend my instructions. No offence.'

Clare bristled. 'I'm a fast learner. Legendarily fast. I'd learned the whole periodic table before I'd started primary school. And then I learned – incredibly quickly – never to mention that fact to anyone else.'

The Professor stared at her intently. 'A Time Lord spends over sixty years at the Academy just to grasp the very basics of Gallifreyan temporal theory.'

'Right. Fine. Then we're stuck in this temporal orbit for ever,' said Clare, folding her arms. 'Whatever that means. We can pass the time reciting the periodic table if you like?'

The Professor gave a small smile, but it quickly faded. 'It's no joking matter, my dear. It means dissolution, eventually. Most things do, in my experience. It may take thousands of years of living death for us but eventually the time winds will break down the security systems of this old wreck and—'

Clare interrupted. 'Thousands of years of living death?' She didn't know how to respond to that. In the end, she heard herself saying very distantly, 'I had plans.'

The Professor suddenly sprang to life. 'Oh my dear! I simply can't condemn you to that, can I?'

'But if there's nothing we can do—'

The Professor leaned in very close to her and whispered conspiratorially, 'Oh, there is something. But it's very naughty.' He looked out of the window. 'It was naughty for me to still have a TARDIS. It was naughtier still to rig up the emergency mechanism – but this would be extraordinarily naughty . . .'

'Well if you can't be naughty when you're stuck between two irrational time interfaces, when can you be?' said Clare.

The Professor grinned. 'That's the spirit! The little girl who so diligently learned those boring old elements would undoubtedly be aghast.'

'I should have been playing hopscotch, anyway,' Clare grinned back.

'I'll teach you that later. Now then,' he said briskly, 'what is that piece of equipment you are holding in your hand?'

Clare stared at it again. It was a complicated-looking thing, metallic yet criss-crossed with filaments of what might have been coral. 'I have absolutely no idea,' she said flatly.

'Good,' said the Professor. He took off his spectacles and cleaned them absently with his tie, staring blearily at her as he did so. He was one of those people who looked very different without their glasses. 'How about now?'

'Now what?' said Clare.

'Now,' said the Professor, slipping his spectacles back on, 'what is that piece of equipment you are holding in your hand?'

Clare looked down at it. The answer to his question was obvious. 'This? It's a conceptual geometer relay with an agronomic trigger. The field separator's gone kaput, but that doesn't really matter, because we can dispense with it totally if we can get that interfacial resonator working again.'

The Professor smiled. 'Splendid!'

'Let's get on with it, then,' said Clare. 'No point hanging about here.'

She crossed to the console and picked up the resonator, turning it over in her hands. 'Yeah, very tricky job, see your problem here,' she said, sucking air through her teeth. 'We'll have to strip the lexifier coating totally. You got a spanner?'

As the Professor hurried off to find such an object, Clare stood staring at the console, thinking. It occurred to her that if they got the resonator going, then gave the rotor a quick burst – well as long as the omega configuration was folded back and the lateral balance cones held out, then it was a case of Bob's your uncle, no temporal orbit.

What it didn't occur to Clare to think, not even for a second, was exactly why or how she knew any of it.

54

'Oooh!' moaned the Ship as she engaged her makeshift relative dimensional stabiliser once again and shifted out of the space-time vortex to materialise back in normal space. 'That hit the spot!'

'I hope you've kept your defence shield up,' called the Doctor, who was polishing off the last of the delicious treats from the golden trolley.

'I followed your orders to the letter, Doctor,' trilled the Ship happily. 'We have now materialised at the specified coordinates as instructed. Nobody, not even Skagra, can possibly tell that we have arrived. Big as I am, I can be an inconspicuous little thing when I want to be, you know.'

Through the forward screen Chris could see only a pair of large circular white doors at the end of a rocky corridor. 'It doesn't look very inspiring.'

'You can find any number of amazing things at the end of a corridor,' said the Doctor. 'At the moment, I'd just settle for the one. Romana. Though the TARDIS comes a close second, naturally.'

K-9's ears twizzled excitedly. 'Confirm proximity of Mistress Romana and the TARDIS, Master.'

'It must be my lucky day,' cried the Doctor. 'I should have gone for three wishes and bunged in peace across the universe while I was at it.'

He clapped his hands together. 'Right, this should be a simple enough rescue mission. Come on, you three!' He made for the gap where the door leading from the command deck used to be, Chris and K-9 following.

'I'm afraid I cannot join you, Doctor,' said the Ship. 'But thank you very much for the invitation. It's certainly never been extended to me before. Oh my, you have given me rather a lot to think about.'

The Doctor stopped a moment and looked up. 'Well, sorry, I didn't mean to.'

'Oh please,' said the Ship, 'there's no need to apologise. I'm sure that all forms of life, no matter what the definition of life may be, must at some point be forced to consider the great abstracts of existence such as love, death, happiness, even personal morality. You, Doctor, have opened my eyes to these big questions. I'm going to go through everything I have in my data store on these weighty topics and then I'm going to jolly well form some definite opinions on them.'

'Good luck with that,' said Chris.

The Ship seemed to pick up on the irony in his tone. 'Oh, I'll find the answers, don't you worry little Earth person,' it said a little snappily.

'Imperative we commence rescue mission, Master,' entreated K-9, his servos revving.

'Quite right,' said the Doctor. 'Come on, you two, best feet forward.' He strode out with K-9, Chris hurrying after.

'Have we got a plan, then?' asked Chris.

The Doctor grinned a huge grin. 'I don't know, but it'll be fun finding out. Keep up, Bristol.'

Romana had lost all hope. She stood under guard and watched as more and more Kraags strutted from the generation chamber and into the observation dome. There were now at least five hundred of the creatures arrayed in military formations before Skagra. He stood at the console, the book clutched tightly in his gloved hand.

Finally the Kraag Commander emerged and stomped over to its

master. It bowed its crowned head to him and rasped, 'Main-stage generation complete, my lord. We have a full complement.'

Skagra nodded. 'Good. Then proceed to your stations.'

The Kraag Commander bowed again, and gestured to the ranks of his fellows. Immediately, in perfect unison, the long formations of Kraags marched out through a series of dark, almost invisible arches cut roughly into every side of the huge arena. Romana watched as the fiery army filed out, the glow in the room diminishing in their wake, until just the Kraag Commander and one other remained, both standing uncomfortably close to her, their red eyes fixed on Skagra.

Skagra indicated the TARDIS. 'We shall depart immediately for Shada! Bring the Time Lady.'

Romana felt a pang of deep despair. The battered blue box, which had always symbolised warmth and security to her, now looked like an alien object, its wooden exterior illuminated oddly by the sickly red glow of her Kraag escort and the harsh, cold light thrown down from a billion suns.

Then she became aware that Skagra's face had set in an expression even stonier and more imperturbable than usual. He was staring over her shoulder at something.

She felt a familiar *tap-tap* on that shoulder.

She whirled around, and saw the Doctor, accompanied by Chris Parsons and K-9.

'Doctor!' Her hearts surged with relief. 'You're alive!'

The Doctor coughed, 'Well there's been a certain amount of debate on that topic of late, but generally speaking I think I'd agree with that statement. Hello Romana.'

Romana grinned. How had she ever believed the Doctor was dead? 'But how did you get here?'

'Ah,' said the Doctor, jabbing a thumb over his shoulder, 'these kind gentlemen escorted us.' Two more Kraags stood threateningly behind his small group.

And Romana's hearts sank once again. All this despair, hope, cruelly crushed hope and despair again wasn't doing them any good at all, she reflected.

But the Doctor was alive.

And that meant anything could happen.

55

At first, things had gone well with the rescue mission. The Doctor, Chris and K-9 had managed to get at least fifty yards from the ship before they were apprehended by two Kraags and guided in a rough but effective fashion down a long rock tunnel and straight into what must be, thought Chris, Hell. He barely had time to register the captive Romana, her Kraag guards, the TARDIS sitting in the middle of it all, and the brilliant view of the infinite universe, however, because – incredibly enough – something else was bothering him.

The man who stood at the centre of this grand arena, dressed in a white tunic, with the book that had started all of this clutched tightly in one gloved hand – Chris was certain he'd seen him somewhere before. It was really going to irritate him until he worked out where. He supposed that it was a good thing to be so distracted, as it seemed likely they were all about to die some sort of horrible fiery outer-space death.

The man was staring back at him with an odd, stony expression. Chris was wondering if the chap had recognised him back and was trying to place him, too. Then he realised that the man wasn't looking at him at all, but just to his right. One's eyes can play tricks across fifty feet of sulphurous cavern lit only by the dim glow of the entire universe. The man was in fact staring at the Doctor.

'Doctor,' the man said, in a voice that was clearly trying not to express surprise, anger and disappointment but was failing on all three counts.

'Hello there, Skagra!' the Doctor called back with massively inappropriate cheeriness, giving a cheeky wave.

'That's Skagra?' said Chris. 'But I'm sure I've seen him before somewhere . . .' Suddenly the memory clicked into his mind and Chris pointed an accusing finger at Skagra. 'You're that bloke,' he said. 'You pushed past me in the corridor at St Cedd's, very rudely, just before I found the Professor lying dying all over the carpet . . .' Full realisation dawned at last. 'Oh. Oh, I see.'

'Shut up, Chris,' hissed Romana.

Skagra walked smartly forward, looking the Doctor up and down as if to check he was really there. 'I am,' he said, as coolly as he seemed able, 'a little . . .' Skagra paused as if grasping for a word he'd never had cause to use before, '. . . *surprised* to find you here, Doctor.'

The Doctor shuffled his feet and rubbed his nose as if embarrassed. 'Yes, well, your ship was a little surprised to find itself bringing me.'

Skagra tried hard not to raise an eyebrow. 'You stole my ship?'

'Only after you stole mine,' said the Doctor, nodding to the TARDIS. 'Ah, there she is! I hope you've been looking after her. May I check? If you've been over-revving her in third phase –'

He made for the TARDIS but the two Kraags automatically barred his path. 'I see,' said the Doctor. 'Well, you'll be happy to know I've returned your ship in perfect working order, if not a little improved. You were very naughty setting her to self-destruct, you know, that poor girl worships you.'

'A machine consciousness is worthless,' said Skagra. His eyes never wavered from the Doctor's smiling face.

The Doctor gasped in mock-horror. 'Don't listen to the nasty man, K-9,' he said.

Chris was uncomfortably aware that Skagra could order their deaths at any moment. They had no weapons, no plan. But somehow the Doctor's childish goading had, incredibly, tipped the scales in their favour. Skagra was clearly intrigued and off-beam, at a disadvantage. Chris reflected that a horrific place like this, with all the odds so grotesquely stacked against him, was where the Doctor magnificently *belonged*. Like some people belonged behind a bar, or in a very big office behind a very big desk, or swallowing swords on stage at the London Palladium. This was where the Doctor was at his best.

'I am curious to know how you survived the treatment of my sphere,' said Skagra flatly.

'Don't be too hard on the poor old thing. We Time Lords have highly trained minds.'

'So I am aware.' Skagra nodded, as if satisfied that he was now up to speed. 'Doctor,' he went on, 'if you have come here in the hope of interfering with my great purpose, I am afraid you will be—'

The Doctor's laugh cut him off. 'Ha! Great purpose! You?'

Chris saw Romana trying to catch the Doctor's eye, shaking her head a little as if to indicate that he shouldn't, for once, be quite so dismissive.

'Yes, Doctor,' said Skagra, 'the very greatest purpose.'

If the Doctor had noticed Romana's look, he ignored it. He laughed again. 'Great purpose?' He wagged a finger in Skagra's general direction. 'I know what you want to do, you old sly-boots. You want to take over the universe, don't you? I've met your sort before. Any moment a mad gleam will come into your eye and you'll start shouting "The universe will be mine!"'

Skagra looked at him quizzically. He was clearly devoid of any mad gleam and was not going to shout.

'How naive, Doctor. How pathetically limited your vision is. "Take over the universe". How childish. Who could possibly want to take over the universe?'

The Doctor seemed slightly thrown by this, but pulled himself back on track. 'Exactly!' he said. 'That's what I keep on trying to tell people. It's a troublesome place, difficult to administer, and as a piece of real estate it's worthless because by definition there'd be no one to sell it to—'

Skagra cut him off. 'Such visions are for infants. My purpose is to fulfil the natural evolutionary goal of all life.'

The Doctor smirked. 'Oh tell on, do. It's been a stressful day and we could all do with a laugh.'

Skagra merely nodded and gestured to the sphere at the console. 'With the aid of the sphere I shall make the whole of creation merge into one single mind. One godlike entity.'

'Oh, you will, will you? How terribly clever,' said the Doctor, in a tone that suggested he was speaking to a four-year-old who was boasting to him about how well he could tie his shoelaces.

'The universe, Doctor, as you so crudely put it, shall not be mine,' said Skagra. 'The universe shall be *me*.'

There was a deep, terrible silence.

It was broken by the Doctor. He walked slowly towards Skagra and looked him curiously up and down as Skagra had done to him. He rubbed his chin for a moment, before leaning in close and saying casually, 'Have you discussed this with anyone? Why don't you send one of your charming Kraags to make us some tea, perhaps a plate of sandwiches,' he broke off, glancing over at the seething, burning creatures. 'Actually some toast might be a better bet, then we can all have a nice sit down and—'

'Doctor, your inane witterings do not interest me, nor will they distract me from my purpose,' said Skagra. 'What I have described *will* happen. It will start within hours. Once started, nothing you or anyone else can do will stop it.'

'He can do it, Doctor,' called Romana. 'He's found Salyavin! You know what that means!'

The Doctor stopped and stared at her.

'Silence the Time Lady,' said Skagra.

The Kraag Commander clamped its stony claw down on Romana's shoulder. She cried out in pain as the material of her dress began to smoulder and blacken.

Chris automatically ran to help her, but the other Kraag barred his way and he was forced back by its unbearable aura of heat.

He saw that the Doctor, too, had been blocked by another of the massive creatures. 'Stop it, Skagra!' Chris shouted. 'Let her go. Now!'

Skagra nodded to the Kraag Commander and it released its grip on Romana, who fell to her knees, clutching her injured shoulder.

Skagra surveyed his captives dispassionately. Then he turned to the Doctor. 'So,' he said, 'does mention of the name Salyavin alter your opinion of my great purpose?'

Chris saw the ashen look on the Doctor's face and a cold stab of fear ran through him.

'Skagra,' said the Doctor, in a quiet, defeated voice, with no trace of his former flippancy, 'if you truly know the whereabouts of Salyavin, that changes everything.'

Chris and Romana exchanged horror-struck glances. K-9 shot forward a few inches, his tail drooping. 'Negative, Master,' he called.

'Indeed?' said Skagra, a trace of a smile on his full lips. 'Tell on, Doctor, do.' He waved a hand and dismissed the Kraag blocking the Doctor's path.

The Doctor walked slowly towards Skagra, his head bowed as if in supplication. When he spoke, it was in little more than a cracked whisper.

'I see it all now. Everything in its place. One Universal Mind, bring order to chaos. Such order.' He raised his head, fixing Skagra with a look almost of awe. 'Your order.' Suddenly he straightened up and shouted, 'Or an order like – *K-9! Now!*'

At the Doctor's words, K-9 swivelled around, lightning fast, fixing Skagra in his sights. Chris suddenly realised that the Doctor had been arranging the whole scenario just to bring K-9 into position.

A bright red energy beam shot from the dog's nose, hitting Skagra in the dead centre of his chest.

And then everything seemed to happen at once.

Skagra staggered a little but did not fall.

K-9 fired off another blast, but again Skagra withstood the assault. The Kraags moved automatically to protect their master, leaving the Doctor, Chris and Romana unguarded.

The Doctor made for the TARDIS, where Romana was climbing unsteadily to her feet.

Skagra's voice rang out. 'Maintain your positions. Guard the capsule. Kill the prisoners.'

Romana's Kraags, who had been furthest from Skagra, turned instantly and aimed their already glowing claws at Romana. She held up her hands in surrender.

The Doctor skidded to a halt, yelling 'Bristol, K-9, get out of here! Now!'

Chris snatched up K-9, and pelted towards the nearest archway. He couldn't help but pause and turn back.

He saw the second pair of Kraags stomping towards the Doctor.

He saw the Doctor and Romana's eyes lock across the chamber. She gave a tiny shake of her head.

He saw the Doctor set his jaw, nod to Romana, and then race towards the archway, just dodging a sizzling beam of fire from a pursuing Kraag. As he reached Chris and K-9, he virtually swept them along the dark, rocky passageway that lay ahead.

The only thing Chris heard him say, was 'We'll be back for her. Now run!'

They ran.

Skagra watched as the Kraags, their arms outstretched, advanced on Romana. She stood, still and composed, hands raised, as the creatures prepared to blast her to ashes. Skagra could see the pain in her eyes from her injury, but he saw no weakness, no sign that she would break down, weep, beg for her life. Her composure in the face of certain death stirred within Skagra what others might have called, though he never would, fellow feeling. He almost felt that something valuable might be lost with her destruction. The Kraags reached Romana, raised their claws to her face and prepared to discharge their devastating energy bolts at point-blank range. Even then, not so much as a flicker of fear crossed the woman's face. And through all this her eyes had never once turned to him.

He waited four seconds more. Then commanded 'Stop!' The Kraags lowered their arms and took a step away from their captive.

Now she looked at Skagra. 'Why do you want to keep me alive, Skagra?' she asked simply.

'That is the question you wish me to answer?' Skagra said. 'Not how I survived the attack from the Doctor's robot? Not where the tunnel your companions escaped into will lead them?'

Romana shrugged, 'Oh I imagine you're wearing a personal force shield, and the Doctor, Chris and K9 are heading down a dead end. It all seemed rather obvious, so I didn't waste time asking about it.'

Skagra gave what could almost have been a small bow. 'Very well,' he said, 'then I will answer your original question. I need you alive because you may still be of use to me on Shada. You are not essential, but a Time Lord prison may require Time Lord biology to access its systems.' He walked over to the TARDIS, unlocked the door and held it open for Romana. 'We have an appointment with Salyavin.'

Romana stared at him for a moment. 'I did have one other question.'

Skagra nodded, still holding the TARDIS door.

'I was just wondering,' Romana began, 'as the Doctor has already escaped from certain death once today, aren't you a little bit worried he might do it again?' She smiled sweetly up at him.

A tiny pulse twitched uncontrollably over Skagra's right temple. He tried to suppress the violent images that surged up in his mind at this thought. He saw the Doctor being pushed off a very, very high cliff, crushed by an avalanche of enormous boulders, torn limb-from-limb by a pack of rabid dogs, bloodied shreds of scarf flying in all directions as his death screams echoed and echoed and echoed and –

Skagra straightened, under control once more. 'Get inside,' he ordered Romana. 'Now.'

She ducked obediently under his arm and into the TARDIS, giving Skagra a satisfied smile as she passed. 'Gotcha,' she called back.

Chris, weighed down by K-9, was finding it hard to keep up with the Doctor as they fled, without any idea what they were fleeing towards, down a seemingly never-ending rock passage, lit only by K-9's eye-screen and the distant glow of the pursuing Kraags. He was exhausted, near blind in this Stygian blackness, but still he kept running. He was surprised he had it in him. He'd always been useless at anything athletic. Perhaps if two Kraags had been chasing him around the 1500-metre track at Bristol Grammar School it might have been a different story. Though he could barely see him, Chris felt sure the Doctor would be taking all this in his enormous stride.

'Clever feint, wasn't it?' the Doctor's voice boomed back from just ahead. 'Making them think I was trying to get to the TARDIS.'

'What were you trying to do?' puffed Chris.

'Get to the TARDIS,' admitted the Doctor from the gloom.

Chris let that one pass. Between breaths, he asked, 'Doctor, that bloke must be mad, mustn't he?'

'Skagra, you mean?'

'Yes, sorry, it's not easy remembering alien names, particularly when running for one's life.'

'You'll get used to it,' the Doctor called back. 'And as for Skagra. Well, madness, sanity, it's all just a matter of opinion.'

'And what's your opinion?' demanded Chris.

The Doctor stopped dead in his tracks, Chris only just managing to pull up before a painful collision. The Doctor turned and grinned down at him, the red light from K-9's eye-screen giving him an almost demonic look.

'He's bonkers!' His grin faded. 'But infinitely dangerous, Bristol.'

'You mean he really can do all that stuff? Make the universe into himself?'

The Doctor nodded, gravely. 'It's possible. If he really has found Salyavin.'

'Who's Salyavin?' asked Chris. 'I'm not sure I can remember another silly name beginning with S.'

K-9 suddenly piped up. 'Master. Kraags approaching.'

'Thank you, K-9, I think we're all very well aware of that,' snapped the Doctor.

Chris looked over his shoulder and saw the rock walls more clearly now in the increasing glow of the gaining Kraags. He turned back to the Doctor. 'So why have we stopped? Have you got a plan? A better plan, I mean?'

The Doctor coughed, tugged at his nose, shuffled his feet and Chris's heart sank.

'Well,' the Doctor said, 'we've stopped because there isn't actually any tunnel worth speaking of in front of us.'

Chris pondered a second. 'You mean it's a dead end?'

'Well, I was trying not to put it in such a final-sounding way. Why don't we agree to say cul-de-sac?'

Chris felt a wave of panic. 'You mean we're going to die? There's no way out?'

Before the Doctor could answer, K-9's ears began to whirr furiously. 'Alert!' he chirruped. 'Please adopt silent mode.'

The Doctor and Chris fell quiet as a familiar wheezing, groaning sound began to echo around the cavernous passageway. It seemed to come from all directions at once, then faded with an odd, muffled thump and a sound like creaking wood.

Chris frowned. 'That was the TARDIS.'

The Doctor nodded. Then shook his head. 'Yes. No. There was something very odd-sounding about it. And we shouldn't be able to hear it all the way down here in this cul-de-sac.'

With a thrill of horror, Chris realised that the tunnel was now bathed in a strong red glow. At any second the Kraags would be upon them. And there was no possible escape. He looked ahead, beyond the Doctor, at the bare rock wall that blocked the passage and had condemned them to death. And was rather surprised to see a door in it.

Not a space door. A normal door. A wooden door. A panelled wooden door with a brass knob.

Chris pointed frantically ahead. 'Look! There's a door! You said it was a dead end, but there's a whacking great door in it! There! Look!'

The Doctor whipped round. 'That wasn't there before. And anyway, we'd agreed to say cul-de-sac.'

Chris took a deep breath, bundled K-9 into the Doctor's arms, ran to the door and turned the knob. It swung open and he burst through –

– into Professor Chronotis's study. Chris barely heard the Doctor run in behind him, slamming the door shut and wedging K-9 against it like a novelty doorstop, because the unexpectedness of suddenly finding himself back at St Cedd's was as nothing to the unexpectedness of seeing the deceased Professor Chronotis himself, on his feet and smiling across at him, tea tray in hand. But even that was as nothing to the unexpectedness of what Chris saw on the sofa, eating a cheese sandwich. It was Clare. Clare, here. And she'd had her hair done. And she was wearing that really lovely blue blouse that made her eyes sparkle. He wanted to run to her, take her in his arms, kiss her again and again and –

Clare leapt to her feet and ran towards him, smiling broadly, eyes brimming, her arms outstretched in what Chris could only assume was a reproving and aggressive manner. He took an involuntary step back. For some reason she crashed to a halt right in front of him. 'Chris!' she cried, in a voice bursting with emotion. Chris couldn't tell which emotion it was. But probably somewhere between stern disapproval and loathing. What had he done now?

'Er, hi there, Keightley,' he mumbled awkwardly.

Meanwhile, the Doctor was staring, and staring, and staring at Professor Chronotis. But he didn't say a word.

'Tea, everybody?' the Professor asked, brightly.

56

Nothing and nobody can survive unprotected in the space-time vortex, that mysterious region where space and time are one. So there was nobody and nothing to observe the TARDIS as it spun through the howling maelstrom, the fragile wooden police box exterior tossed hither and thither by the shrieking time winds.

Inside, Romana – a Kraag standing close guard on either side of her – watched as Skagra turned the later pages of the book. 'The key turns slowly in the lock,' he whispered, his face lit by the eerie green glow from the central column. 'The door to Shada opens!'

He started to turn the pages more quickly.

Suddenly the TARDIS jerked to one side, the engines grinding in protest. Emergency alarms blared, red lights blazed across the console. The illuminated circular panels on the walls dimmed and then flared back up, but instead of their usual warm yellow glow they too flickered a murky dark green, casting misshapen shadows as if the ship were being plunged deep underwater.

Romana felt a sickening plunging sensation in the pit of her stomach. She guessed the TARDIS was passing through a time-lock placed around Shada who knew how many thousands of years before. A time-lock was the usual way Gallifreyans kept the universe in general ignorant of their secrets. Or their misdeeds.

They were leaving the universe behind altogether, moving into a forbidden zone sealed safely away from the rest of reality. But this time Romana knew the Doctor was still alive. He *would* find some way to stop this, despite his less than impressive attempt at a rescue mission.

The TARDIS bucked and roared as Skagra turned the last few pages of *The Worshipful and Ancient Law of Gallifrey*.

That book had taken Romana back to her childhood nightmares, now it was literally taking her to meet them, face to face. All that Romana could think of, blotting out even the terrifying scene around her, was one image from *Our Planet Story*, the wild, screaming insanity on the face of the Great Mind Outlaw Salyavin.

She was jolted back to the present as the TARDIS suddenly settled. The green glow brightened, the time column began to rise and fall, smoothly and silently, without its usual protesting squeaks and clanks. There was utter stillness and calm. A perfect harmony of technology. A TARDIS at the peak of its efficiency. And at the centre of it all stood Skagra, supremely calm and assured, as he turned the final page.

And Romana felt sick. It was as if the time ship had simply stopped fighting and surrendered itself to Skagra. As if the soul of the TARDIS was gone.

57

Chris looked at Clare, and Clare looked at Chris. Chris had the strange sensation that Clare was waiting for him to say something significant, but he didn't know where to start, as everything seemed equally and terribly significant. The universe was at stake, after all. So he continued to look at her without saying anything.

Eventually, Clare said something. 'What are you doing here?'

To his own surprise Chris felt himself flaring up. He realised he must be storing up quite a lot of aggression under all his confusion, excitement and constant near-brushes with death, and it had now found its outlet. 'How am I supposed to know!?' he spluttered.

'Don't have a go at me!' shouted Clare.

Chris gestured to the windows of the Professor's study, which between the grubby flower-pattern curtains showed walls of sheer rock. Any hope that he had suddenly and impossibly been transported back to the relative normality of Cambridge had been swiftly crushed by the sight.

'All right, you tell me what the Professor's room is doing here, on an asteroid in the middle of outer space?' he shouted at Clare.

'Oh, you may well ask!' snapped Clare back.

'I am asking!' shouted Chris.

'Ask the Professor!' shouted Clare, pointing at the little man, who stood next to the Doctor at the brass instrument panel.

'But he's dead!' shouted Chris.

'Well, *durrr*, I know that!' shouted Clare.

'Children, children, ssh!' called the Doctor.

Clare and Chris stopped shouting and went back to looking at each other again.

The Doctor turned back to the Professor and slid his long fingers over the instrument panel. 'A Type 12 Mark 1 TARDIS, if I'm not mistaken, Professor Chronotis?'

The Professor nodded. 'Do you like it?'

'Oh it's ace, Professor,' said the Doctor, 'ace! And you arrived in your TARDIS just in the nick of time. I'm beginning to appreciate how wonderful it must be for other people when I do that.'

'This is a TARDIS, too?' boggled Chris, gesturing around and about.

'Obviously,' muttered Clare. She indicated K-9. 'And that's a robot dog, in case you hadn't worked that one out either.'

The Professor squirmed up at the Doctor, looking a little guilty. 'It's strictly unofficial. I'm not really allowed one.'

'No you aren't,' said the Doctor darkly. For a moment Chris wondered if the Doctor was about to release one of his sudden explosions of anger at the nice old man. But instead he grinned and hugged the Professor warmly. 'And there's no better way to hide it than by living in it, you old sly-boots.'

The Professor smiled back but then his expression grew grave. 'Doctor, where is Skagra?'

'Skagra?' said the Doctor as if he had all but forgotten the pressing business of the day. 'Skagra? Oh yes, Skagra. Well. He's got Romana. He's got the TARDIS. And he's got the book.' Before the Professor could do more than look horrified at this news, the Doctor pointed at him and said loudly, but with an unnerving casualness, 'I thought you were dead.'

'Yes, so did I,' said the Professor. 'But about Skagra—'

'Did you really?' exclaimed the Doctor. He peered down at the brass controls. 'I presume that you installed a very, very naughty emergency defence programme into your TARDIS's sub-routines? Temporal orbit, crossing your own timeline to cheat death, that general sort of absolutely forbidden and highly criminal sort of thing?'

'Well yes, I did,' said the Professor sheepishly. 'And then stabilised it with a little help from this charming young lady.' He gestured to Clare.

Clare gave a little bow. To Chris it seemed quite a pointed little bow. Pointing at him.

'You helped bring him back to life?' he shouted.

'So what if I did?' snapped Clare. 'I'm not an idiot.'

'Oh, is that supposed to mean I am an idiot?' snapped Chris.

'*Stop!*' called the Doctor. He turned back to the Professor. 'Stealing a naughty book from Gallifrey. Hiding away a naughty TARDIS. Cooking up a naughty emergency program. What a naughty little professor you've been, Professor Chronotis.'

'None of that matters now, Doctor,' spluttered the Professor urgently. He lowered his voice gravely. 'If Skagra has your TARDIS and the book, he can get to Shada!'

'Shada?' repeated the Doctor. 'Shada? Why does everybody keep going on about Shada, particularly when nobody has the faintest idea about who and what it is!'

'Hear hear,' said Chris.

Clare coughed. Chris bristled. 'Shada is the lost and forgotten prison of the Time Lords,' she said.

Chris snorted. 'And how could you possibly know that?'

'Because the Professor told me,' Clare sniped back. 'The book is the key to Shada.'

'Shada!' cried the Doctor suddenly, smiting himself on the forehead with considerable force. 'Shada!'

'Yes, Doctor, the Time Lords' prison, as the young lady says,' said the Professor. 'You've probably forgotten about it.'

'I never forget anything!' cried the Doctor indignantly. 'I never, never forget—' He stopped and smote himself again, this time on the back of his head. 'I forgot Shada. The Time Lords' prison, locked in a bubble outside the universe. Now why would I have forgotten it?' He gasped as another thought struck him. 'Romana mentioned Salyavin.' He sank into an armchair. 'Of course! Salyavin was imprisoned in Shada!'

'You can ask me who Salyavin is,' Chris said smugly without quite looking at Clare.

Without quite looking at him either, she replied coolly, 'Oh, he was a great criminal imprisoned centuries ago by the Time Lords for mind crimes.'

'Oh for goodness' sakes,' grumbled Chris.

'A great criminal with unique mental powers,' said the Doctor slowly, staring into the glowing gas fire. 'Totally unique. He had the capacity to project his mind into other minds, didn't he, Professor Chronotis?'

'But isn't that what Skagra's doing?' asked Chris.

'Oh no, no, no, no!' barked the Doctor. 'Skagra has been doing quite the opposite. With that sphere of his he has the capacity to take minds *out of* people, but he couldn't put minds *into* people. That was Salyavin's great power. He could put anything he wanted into any mind he wanted. Dominate them completely. That's why the Time Lords locked him away. The Great Mind Outlaw. And now Skagra wants Salyavin's mind and the terrifying power within that mind for himself. And that's why he's going to Shada!'

Chris spluttered. 'Then he is bonkers. He's planning to move his own mind into every other mind in the universe?'

The Doctor nodded. 'It might take thousands of years, millions of years. But his mind would be immortal. It would spread through the universe like a plague.'

Chris pondered. 'It's quite a thought, though, isn't it? Every mind in the universe working together as a single organism, a single mind . . .'

'A *bonkers* mind, according to you,' snapped Clare.

'I didn't say I approved,' Chris snapped back. 'I just said it's quite a thought for one to consider!'

'Well I hope one enjoys considering it!' said Clare. She crossed to the Doctor's side and said, 'Doctor, we've got to stop Skagra from getting to Shada.'

Chris flinched. Why was Clare annoyed with him? Why was he annoyed with Clare? And why was Clare so much better at this, whatever it was, than him?

'Yes, Clare,' said the Doctor. 'But how? He's got a head start on us and we don't even know the way.'

'Then we must follow him,' said Clare.

'Oh yeah, we'll follow him,' mocked Chris. 'Let's hail a taxi, "Follow that TARDIS!"'

'Follow him to Shada the same way we followed him here,' said Clare, not even looking at Chris.

'Of course!' cried the Doctor. He turned to the Professor. 'You can follow the space-time trail of my TARDIS! Let's go!'

He leapt to his feet, and vaulted over to the brass instrument panel. His hands hovered over the ancient controls, and then he finally coughed and stood back, beckoning the Professor forward. 'You know this vehicle much better than I do, Professor Chronotis,' he said. 'And cross-tracing along a time path is a very sensitive and delicate operation. I wouldn't like to break anything.'

The Professor nodded. 'Thank you, Doctor.' His wizened old hands flickered over the controls, adjusting a knob here, a lever there.

Clare leant forward and flicked a switch the Professor had missed. The Doctor didn't seem to notice but Chris was fuming. Who did Clare think she was?

'And while you're doing that, Professor Chronotis, I'll make tea,' said the Doctor. 'Come on, Bristol!'

Chris sighed and followed. Making tea was obviously about the only thing he was any use for around here.

58

The doors of the TARDIS opened onto Shada.

There was no hint of decay, no sense of a place abandoned and forgotten. Existing as it did beyond a time-lock, and therefore in a state of perfect timelessness outside the normal physical laws of the universe, Shada could have been built yesterday, reflected Romana as she stepped from the TARDIS. Equally, she thought, it could have been built tomorrow. That thought made her wince. It was the kind of thing poor old Professor Chronotis used to come out with.

The huge, red high-vaulted chamber in which the TARDIS had materialised was silent and empty. Romana recognised traces of a long-past Gallifreyan architectural style, much less fussy and ornate than the Capitol she had grown up in. The huge sloping walls were a dark red, with occasional circular panels – similar to those in the TARDIS but much larger – pulsing with fierce crimson light.

She looked above her. The chamber seemed to stretch up and up, hundreds of metres of empty space. Suspended against one facet of the chamber, way above the heads of herself, the Kraags and Skagra, was a heavy stone block into which had been carved the complex pattern that was the Seal of Rassilon, the same design that adorned the cover of the book still clutched tightly in Skagra's gloved hands.

Romana tried to tell herself that this was just a room. A room in a very strange place, admittedly, but only a room. She tried to push down the waves of panic, almost of revulsion, she felt as those long-blocked race memories – if that was what they were – surged and stirred deep inside her mind.

Skagra, followed as ever by the bobbing sphere, walked slowly into the very centre of the chamber and threw his arms wide in an almost messianic pose.

'Shada!' he cried.

The sound of the word echoed and re-echoed around the walls.

'It looks horrid,' observed Romana, trying very hard to sound unimpressed.

Skagra wheeled on her, pointing a finger. 'Built by your race. A prison for the very worst criminals.'

'You should feel quite at home here, then,' said Romana. She had noted the effect of the Doctor's often-terrible jokes on Skagra. They made him angry and distracted, and a weakened, distracted enemy was – according to the Doctor's theory, anyway – better than a strong and focused one. To Romana, it had at first seemed one of those theories of the Doctor's that would surely lead to getting your head blown off. To be fair, though, it seemed to have served him well after 525 years of space-time travel, so she had been starting to experiment with it.

'Keep her silent,' ordered Skagra.

The Kraags moved threateningly closer to Romana.

Skagra moved to a high red stone wall between two enormous pillars. He slid the book inside his tunic and ran his gloved hands over the wall. 'Logically, the entrance must be here,' he said. His hand found a small indented panel in the stone. 'Yes – here.'

He pressed his gloved hand on to the panel. Romana hoped against hope that the builders of Shada had possessed the sense to install a booby trap. Then she remembered the arrogance of the classical Time Lords, even worse than those of her own time, and realised it was impossible they could ever have thought Shada could be threatened in this way, or any other. But still – perhaps, just perhaps . . .

But no. Romana knew her people too well. With a grinding, crunching noise, the wall heaved itself up, releasing a rush of long-trapped air from beyond.

Behind the wall was a long, long hallway, stretching deeper and deeper, more red stone walls and red light-panels. Indentations were marked above various junctions and turnings, Gallifreyan symbols, numbers and letters.

Right in front of the hallway, immediately before Skagra as the wall slid up, was a large control console with a central circular screen. The instruments on the console were archaic, but they were picked out in gleaming bronze as if they had just been polished. The main panel consisted of a simple-enough keyboard with the seven hundred and twenty-three letters of the Gallifreyan alphabet in the centre, the thirteen numerical symbols ranged across the top.

Skagra nodded. 'The index file. One of the best qualities of the Time Lords is their meticulous record-keeping.'

He tapped at the keys. The console and the screen remained inert. Without looking round, he gestured to the Kraags. 'Bring her,' he said.

Romana had no choice but to shuffle forward as the Kraags closed in towards her.

'I don't see how I can help,' she said.

Skagra indicated the keyboard. 'There were no personnel here in Shada. The systems are fully automated. The index file is obviously protected by a bio-morphic shield, which clearly only a Time Lord can operate. You are a Time Lord. You will operate it.'

'I would rather die,' said Romana.

Skagra nodded. 'I only need your bio-morphic information to operate the index file. I can obtain that by removing your hands. Perhaps your eyes. Those pieces would be enough. But if you would prefer to live –'

He gestured her towards the keyboard.

Romana considered. It had been easy enough to say she would rather die, but would she? A voice in her head kept saying *The Doctor is alive, the Doctor is alive* . . . She couldn't give up. There might be other chances. Other ways to stop Skagra.

So Romana ran her fingers lightly over the keys. Again she hoped there would be some catch, some defence mechanism. No. Instantly the circular screen lit up, data screeing across it.

'Find Salyavin,' ordered Skagra.

She punched in a request, her fingers shaking slightly – INDEX: SALYAVIN.

The screen chittered back, automatically scrolling down a long, long list of names. Names that struck horror into Romana's hearts:

RUNDGAR – WAR CRIMES
SEC. 5/JL
SENTENCE TBA
CAB. 45, CHAM. S

SUBJATRIC – MASS MURDER
SEC. 7/PY
SENTENCE TBA
CAB. 43, CHAM. L

SALYAVIN – MIND CRIMES
SEC. 245/XR
SENTENCE TBA
CAB. 9, CHAM. T

SCINTILLA – CONSPIRING WITH CARRIONITES
SEC. 8/HT
SENTENCE TBA
CAB. 21, CHAM. T

'There!' cried Skagra, pointing to the screen. 'Salyavin! Chamber T, Cabinet 9.'

He stared past the console and into the long hallway, noting the identifying marks at each junction. Then he grabbed Romana by the arm and pushed her forward. 'Come!' he commanded the Kraags.

Then he paused. 'No,' he said slowly. He pointed to one Kraag. 'You will remain behind and guard the capsule.'

'Yes, Master,' the Kraag said and stomped back to take up sentry position outside the TARDIS.

'I can't imagine who you think might possibly turn up,' said Romana.

Skagra tightened his grip on her arm. The little tic over his right temple twitched a couple of times. 'The Doctor is most definitely dead,' he said.

'But, just in case . . .' said Romana, indicating the Kraag at the TARDIS.

Skagra thrust her forward. 'Come. It is time for you to meet Salyavin.'

They began to move down the hallway, Romana first, held tight in Skagra's grasp, the Kraag Commander and the sphere following.

'A little more history for you, historian,' said Skagra. 'Your Gallifreyan ancestors were caught in an interminable ethical dilemma. Could any crime justify the death penalty? Arguments raged back and forth for centuries. In the meantime, the criminals were placed here, outside the universe, outside time itself, suspended until the Time Lords' great moral debate –' he scoffed at these words – 'was resolved.'

'Capital punishment was restored,' said Romana. 'I know that.'

'And Shada was deliberately "forgotten", brushed under the carpet, removed from your history,' continued Skagra. 'So the High Council decreed.'

'The High Council?' Romana frowned. 'The mental power required to blank something from the minds of generations of Time Lords would be enormous. I certainly don't think the High Council would be capable of that. Is their involvement confirmed in all those books you stole?'

'No,' said Skagra. 'But it happened. Shada *was* forgotten. By implication, the High Council decreed it.'

Romana struggled to understand. 'Are you absolutely sure—'

'Here!' called Skagra suddenly. They had reached a junction with the letter 'T' marked above another thick red stone block.

'Beyond this door, Salyavin,' said Skagra.

He pressed his hand against a panel and the block began slowly to slide upwards.

59

A chime like a vesper bell rang through the Professor's rooms. Chris shot up from the sofa where he'd been sitting next to Clare, studiously ignoring her. 'What the hell was that?'

Clare grabbed him by the back of the shirt and pulled him down again. 'It means we've arrived, that's all.' Chris noted that the glass-cased clock on the mantelpiece had ceased its upping and downing.

'The young lady is quite right,' said the Professor, turning agitatedly from the control panel. 'We've arrived in Shada!'

'Oh,' said Chris. 'Oh, it's just I thought it might be a bumpier ride than that. After all, we don't have the key and it's locked away in this bubble-thing, outside the universe, apparently. Somehow.'

The Doctor laughed and patted the Professor's shoulder. 'And Professor Chronotis's TARDIS is even older than mine, yes. But as we were following the space-time trail of my TARDIS we were able to slip through quite easily and undetected. Neat, wouldn't you say?'

'Doctor,' pleaded the Professor, 'this is all quite fascinating but we really must get on and stop Skagra. He's already here!' He started heading for the exit.

Chris and Clare got up from the sofa simultaneously. 'Right behind you, Professor,' said Clare with such gumption that Chris added, 'Yes, we've got to stop him!' because it sounded quite plucky and he was sick of feeling left out.

The Doctor whirled to face them. 'Yes, of course, you two have a vital part to play, you must—' he began.

'Yes?' asked Chris and Clare.

'Stay here,' finished the Doctor.

Chris and Clare opened their mouths to protest.

The Doctor waved his arms demonstratively and said 'Sssh!' Then he leaned in close to Clare and whispered – Chris thought, slightly oddly – 'I am not at liberty to explain.' He then turned to Chris. 'Ditto,' he said. Then he whirled away from them to face K-9. 'Now K-9, you *can* come along.'

'Master,' said K-9 happily and trundled towards the door, which the Professor was already holding open with considerable agitation.

'But, K-9,' added the Doctor, stopping the dog in his tracks, 'you are not to tangle with any Kraags! Understood?'

'Affirmative, Master,' said K-9.

'Unless of course you have to tangle with any Kraags.'

'Hurry, Doctor!' cried the Professor. He seemed to have lost patience and was already heading through the door. He turned briefly towards Clare. 'You will look after the old place for me, won't you, my dear?' he added.

'Of course,' said Clare, blinking.

The Doctor and K-9 followed the Professor through the door and it slammed shut behind them.

Chris and Clare were left alone. They sat back down on the sofa.

'Well,' said Chris.

'Well,' said Clare.

That having seemed to cover everything, they went back to ignoring one another.

The wooden door of the Professor's room was positioned incongruously in the wall of a tall, imposing hallway of red stone. The

Professor, his face a picture of concern, was hurrying down the passage. The Doctor tapped him on the shoulder and pointed the other way. 'Professor Chronotis,' he whispered, 'judging by the coordinates on your time-path indicator, I'd say my TARDIS was in this direction.'

'But Skagra will have gone in this direction,' said the Professor, pointing very definitely down the hallway to make his point. 'I'm quite sure I heard footsteps,' he added hurriedly.

The Doctor nodded. 'But if we can get to my TARDIS first we can stop Skagra getting it back. He'll be trapped here. In a prison. Which is rather fitting for such a rotter.'

'Doctor,' pleaded the Professor, almost hopping up and down, 'it is imperative we find Skagra before he finds Salyavin!'

The Doctor held up a hand and started backing down the long hallway in the direction of his TARDIS. 'Yes, but let's just exercise a little strategy, shall we?' he said.

The Professor sagged. 'Oh, very well,' he huffed. 'But please hurry.'

Cautiously the Doctor led K-9 and the Professor down the echoing hallway. The Doctor looked about him at the red walls with their glowing circular light-panels. 'Rather eerie, this state of timelessness,' he whispered. 'This architecture suggests the grandeur of the Rassilon era. Almost like stepping back into the past.'

'You are always stepping back into the past, Master,' whispered K-9.

'Not my own past, the past of Gallifrey,' the Doctor whispered back. 'I suppose this is how it must feel for normal people.'

The very end of the passageway opened out into a huge chamber, and at its centre sat the comforting blue shape of the TARDIS.

'You see,' the Doctor whispered to the Professor, 'strategy.'

He was just about to step out into the open and vault over to the TARDIS when a Kraag stomped around the side of the police box, eyes glowing fiercely, and obviously very much on guard duty.

The Doctor flattened himself against the wall of the passageway and gestured the others back.

'So much for strategy,' he said through gritted teeth. 'I think we'll try this your way, Professor Chronotis.'

They turned about and hurried in the other direction. The Professor took the lead, wringing his hands and tutting continually like the White Rabbit.

'By all the suns, I hope we're not too late,' he muttered. Suddenly a thought seemed to strike him and he turned and looked down. 'K-9?'

'Professor?' queried K-9.

'Be alert. If Skagra tries to use the sphere on –' he faltered for a moment – 'on anybody, you must destroy it!'

'Affirmative, Professor,' said K-9.

The Professor hurried on down the hallway, K-9 and the Doctor following. 'I rather thought we were going to destroy it anyway,' the Doctor mused into his shirt-collar, never taking his eyes off the Professor's threadbare-tweeded back. 'Yes, I'd sort of taken that as read.'

The strange little party continued to move through the deep, dark hallways of Shada, quiet as ghosts, each one lost in his own thoughts.

60

The massive inner doorway of Chamber T slid slowly upwards. Skagra pushed Romana through, then followed her inside with the sphere and the Kraag Commander.

Romana looked around. The chamber was roughly circular, and consisted of hundreds of sealed black cabinets that resembled upright coffins. They were arranged regularly around the curving walls. Each cabinet was marked with an identifying sequence of numbers and letters in Gallifreyan notation. A connecting ramp led to higher levels, the cabinets stretching upwards into the darkness.

'The prisoners of Shada,' said Skagra. 'Each in their own separate cryogenic cell. Alive, but frozen in time, in perpetual imprisonment.' He turned to Romana with a slight smirk. 'A very humane solution, don't you think?'

Romana shrugged. 'Don't look at me. I'm not answerable for the Time Lords.'

'Soon no one will be,' said Skagra, 'as the Time Lords, like every other race, will become irrelevant!'

Romana coughed. 'You're starting to get that mad gleam in your eye that the Doctor was talking about,' she said, with a small sigh. 'I knew you would. This is, after all, quite insane.'

Skagra walked slowly closer to her. 'You are afraid.'

Romana tried to keep her gaze level. The longer she kept him talking, the greater the chance that something – anything – might stop him. 'Of course. *I'd* be insane if I wasn't afraid,' she said.

'There will be no fear in the Universal Mind,' said Skagra. 'But perhaps, just one last time, I should like to see that primitive animal emotion. I should like to see *your* fear, *your* terror. The terror of a Time Lord.'

'You are seeing it,' said Romana. 'Is it worth it?'

Skagra smiled, a broad, terrible smile, and strode to the nearest cabinet. He read the nameplate. 'Subjatric the tyrant!' Then he punched out a command sequence into a tiny panel built into the side of the cabinet.

Immediately there was a scrape and a clank from somewhere deep in the dormant machinery. The door of the cabinet shuddered. Icy vapour began to swirl from within, the chemical tang catching at Romana's throat.

Skagra moved to the next cabinet and read off its nameplate. 'Rundgar, brother to Subjatric. Together, they dragged Gallifrey down into a second Dark Age!' He punched at the cabinet's panel and there was another clanking noise and more freezing cryogenic gas swirled.

'What are you doing, Skagra?' demanded Romana. 'You came here for Salyavin. These others can't possibly mean anything to you.'

Skagra moved to another cabinet. 'But they mean something to you,' he said. 'It is a rare honour to bring a Time Lord's nightmares to life.' He entered the release code. Again the vapour poured out. 'Lady Scintilla!' he read from the nameplate. 'And my actions have a practical purpose, as ever. They, along with you, of course, can become the first to participate in the Universal Mind!'

Romana watched appalled as the doors of the cabinets, each one containing a forgotten horror of Gallifreyan civilisation, began slowly to creak open.

61

Chris decided to break the silence. It was hard to think of anything worth saying to Clare in the face of the incredible events of the last few hours, and he'd have to choose his words carefully to avoid another argument. He was tempted to observe that it was odd how some days turned out, but realised that would just sound incredibly trite. Then he considered launching into a detailed and no doubt pertinent reappraisal of what their experiences might mean for science, but something told him that Clare might murder him before he could get to any particularly juicy bits of insight.

So, as the universe might soon be coming to what might as well be an end, he decided to say, 'I love you.'

It was surprisingly easy once he'd made the actual decision. His lips were ready at last to form the first of those three little words. Here goes –

'Chris,' said Clare, breaking the silence. 'There's something very strange about Professor Chronotis.'

Chris's moment was lost. 'Why single out the Professor?' he asked instead, surprised and disappointed at how easily he'd given up. He looked anxiously towards the door. 'And who knows what's going on out there? Aliens, time travellers, ghosts, tin dogs, they're all odd.'

'Perhaps we can find out what's happening,' said Clare. She got up from the sofa and examined the control console. 'There should be a scanner, and we could throw out an external line.' She drummed her fingers on the edge of the panel.

'I don't like getting left behind,' continued Chris. 'I mean, just because we come from Earth doesn't give everyone the right to be patronising to us.'

Clare selected a control on the panel.

'I wouldn't,' Chris advised, jumping up to guide her away from it. He looked down at the maze of instrumentation, shaking his head. 'Admittedly, all this does make us look a bit primitive. I don't have even the faintest idea how it all works.'

'I have,' said Clare, and pressed the control.

Immediately there was the whirr and tick of hidden hydraulics, and a small screen extended from the control console. The screen showed a large, empty red-walled hallway.

Chris blinked. 'You have?' He looked between Clare and the screen. 'Yes, you obviously have.' A thought struck him. And it would explain so much! 'Of course! You're from another planet!?' he spluttered.

Clare rolled her eyes and punched him on the shoulder. 'No, you berk, I'm from Fallowfield. Now listen, I need to tell you something. About the Professor.' She frowned and drummed her fingers on the panel again, as if trying to catch a fading thought.

'Go on, then,' urged Chris. 'Tell me.'

Clare tapped the screen. 'The image translator is bussed into the real-world interface. It reads off the exact N-space coordinates.'

Chris coughed. 'That's what you needed to tell me?'

'No,' said Clare after a pause, as if she was fighting some block of confusion in her mind.

'It was something about the Professor,' prompted Chris, a little worried. Clare was many things but she was not a scatterbrain. He blinked. And she was not a technical expert. She knew what she needed to know about the apparatus used in her field. But nothing beyond that.

When he'd tried to interest her in his little proton accelerator, she'd turned up her nose and suggested they go to the pub.

He realised Clare was staring at him, as if willing him to ask the right question. He'd often had that feeling from her, but this time she seemed almost desperate.

'What you're trying to say is that the Professor's been teaching you how to work his machine?'

Clare frowned. 'Yes. No. He . . . he didn't teach me. He showed me.' She glanced between the control panel and Chris's concerned face. 'Chris, it all just sort of – appeared in my head. Like the Professor barged in the front door of my mind and shuffled my thoughts about. Suddenly I understand it all. But I don't understand how I understand it.'

Chris sighed with relief and patted Clare on the shoulder. 'There there, Keightley, it's just these TARDIS machines of theirs,' he said confidently. 'They let us understand any alien languages we might come across. The Doctor explained it. They rearrange the thoughts of their passengers automatically. It's nothing to worry about.'

Clare groaned. 'Don't be stupid, Chris. I think I know the difference between a simple extruded telepathic circuit's field of operation and psycho-active addition.'

Chris licked his lips. A thought, a very uncomfortable one, was forming at the back of his own mind. 'Clare,' he said slowly, 'did you just say psycho-active addition?' He thought back to the aftermath of the sphere's attack on the Professor.

Clare shrugged. 'Yes.'

'And such a power would be the opposite of psycho-active extraction, I guess?'

Clare nodded. 'Obviously.' She blinked and shook her head. 'But I don't know how he made me know that it's obvious.'

'I think I'm just beginning to understand,' said Chris. It was all adding up about Professor Chronotis. The book, the miraculous return from the dead, and now this –

He made decisively for the door. 'Wait here!' he ordered Clare.

'No way,' said Clare, very aggressively.

And then she said, 'All right then,' very agreeably, as if she was a completely different person.

It looked as if she was surprising herself. Probably, thought Chris, she was – and this was all confirming his theory.

Chris hovered at the door. 'I've got to go after the Doctor. You'll be safer here.' He sneaked the door open.

'That's fine,' said Clare. 'I must stay here. Look after the old place.'

Chris nodded slowly. Then he turned and set off decisively into Shada.

And Clare, who hated being left behind, turned with a smile back to the scanner and began to search for an external line sub-routine on the image translator as if it was the most natural thing in the world.

62

Lady Scintilla, greatest of the Visionaries, stepped from the cabinet where she had been imprisoned for countless thousands of years.

She was quite unlike the illustration in *Our Planet Story*, reflected Romana, not at all that haughty flame-haired woman in red robes. The real Lady Scintilla was short, even dumpy, and she wore a simple orange tunic with the number of her cell stencilled on the sleeve. Her eyes stared forward unseeing, her consciousness blurred from the cryogenic process. But there was one thing those illustrators of Gallifreyan nursery books had got absolutely right. Scintilla's slender fingers ended in six-inch razor-sharp nails painted blood red.

From the other cabinets staggered the tyrant brothers Subjatric and Rundgar, similarly attired in orange prisoners' suits. They were tall, with the high domed foreheads, long, sallow faces and beaked noses so typical of the older Prydonian families. But there was, even in their current mindless state as they recovered from cryogenic immurement, a savageness and cruelty in those features, the innate primitivism that had caused them to usurp the powers of the then-President and wage terrible war on their own people.

Romana called across to Skagra, who stood almost mesmerised

before the reviving criminals. 'They'll be fully awake soon, Skagra. I wouldn't give much for our chances when they come to.'

'Thank you for the reminder,' Skagra said neatly. 'The time has come. The beginning of the Universal Mind.' He sounded as if he could scarcely believe it himself.

With a swift, cutting gesture he summoned the sphere into his gloved hand. Then he walked slowly and reverently towards another of the black slab-like cabinets.

He reached out with his free hand and gently touched its ebonite surface. 'In here. The man I have sought for so many long, long years. The man whose power I will use to reshape the entire universe!'

His fingers moved to the cabinet's small input panel.

Romana felt black despair. In this, the darkest moment of her life, she permitted herself a supremely illogical and unscientific whim. Surrounded by nightmares of her childhood, as alone as she had ever been, she closed her eyes and *wished*.

She wished the Doctor was here.

Skagra's gloved index finger tapped at the control panel, beginning to key in the release code.

'Let Salyavin be released,' he whispered.

'Er, sorry to intrude again, Skagra,' said a voice suddenly, the voice of the man Romana had wished for. 'But I really wouldn't do that, if I were you.'

Skagra's head whipped round. The Kraag Commander's head whipped round. Romana, a smile illuminating her face, turned her head slowly and opened her eyes.

In the doorway stood the Doctor, K-9 at his feet, and – incredibly, impossibly – the absolutely, definitely dead Professor Chronotis at his side. Romana hadn't even dared wish for that! But how wonderful it was to see the nice old man again.

'*Doc-tor*,' gurgled Skagra, more than just a hint of a mad gleam in his eyes, the tic over his right temple kicking dangerously.

'Well if it's not him, it's someone very handsome wearing his scarf,' said the Doctor, striding into the chamber. He patted Romana gently on the back. 'Hello, Romana, not dead I see. Good, good.' He blinked at the three prisoners, who were milling about like zombies by their cabinets. 'Quite a party you've got going here, Skagra. Don't think much of this lot, they look half-cut already, and it's always best to try for a good mix of evil and not evil on the guest list, I find.' He nodded to the Kraag Commander. 'You need to have a word with your bouncer. So, is nobody going to offer me a crisp?'

Chronotis shot forward, passing the apparently casual Doctor with surprising agility. 'Skagra, stop! You must not release Salyavin!'

Skagra signalled to the Kraag Commander. It stomped angrily towards the intruders, glowing claw outstretched. Chronotis was forced to retreat by the intense heat, staggering back into the Doctor's arms.

'You're too late!' cried Skagra. He pressed the final key in the sequence and stood back, eyes glittering. 'Salyavin is released!' he cried.

The inner mechanism of the cabinet clunked.

Cryogenic gas swirled from within.

The heavy door creaked slowly open.

Romana looked instinctively for the Doctor's reaction. To her amazement, he wore an expression that seemed knowing and slightly amused.

The door swung fully open.

There was nobody inside.

Skagra stared into the cabinet. He seemed to see something through the dissipating vapour. Then he let out a guttural, animal cry and collapsed to his knees, the sphere falling from his grasp and hovering distantly as if confused.

'Careful what you wish for, Skagra,' said the Doctor, almost pityingly.

'Salyavin . . .' whispered Skagra in a small, broken voice. 'Where is Salyavin?'

The Doctor ushered Romana, K-9 and the Professor gently forward. The Kraag Commander, seemingly baffled by this turn of events, simply let them pass.

Romana looked beyond Skagra and into the empty cabinet. Where the Great Mind Outlaw should have been was nothing but a sheet of paper, fastened to the back wall with a drawing pin. Romana gasped at the message it bore:

It was the ancient V of Rassilon, the greatest and rudest insult of the Dark Times. The script beneath read in Old High Gallifreyan:

HA HA HA, _____[1] YOU! LOVE SALYAVIN X

'No, this cannot be,' whimpered Skagra. 'My life's work . . . the Universal Mind . . .'

The Doctor gently lifted Skagra to his feet. 'The dream is over, Skagra,' he said almost sadly. 'The Great Salyavin fooled all of us. He escaped from Shada centuries ago.'

Skagra almost fell into the Doctor's arms. Tears began to cascade from his eyes.

'Help me,' he wailed. 'Please – help me, Doctor . . .'

'Don't you worry,' said the Doctor, looking around at Romana, Professor Chronotis and K-9. 'There's nothing for *any* of us to worry about now.'

Skagra's anguished sobs grew louder.

The Doctor patted him on the back. 'There there, it probably wouldn't have worked out anyway. Between you and me, Skagra, using that one little sphere to dominate the minds of everyone in the universe would have taken an incredibly long time, probably more time than the old thing's got left to it anyway. I don't honestly think you'd thought that bit through properly.'

Chronotis had shuffled past the Kraag, and was looking into the empty cabinet. He tugged at the Doctor's sleeve. 'Then it really is all over, Doctor?'

---

[1] Though remarkably flexible in its usage, this word is unfortunately untranslatable from Old High Gallifreyan into Earth English. Very roughly speaking it conveys disdain, contempt and extreme annoyance, all wrapped up in a generally obscene etymological parcel that is far ruder than any reader of this book can possibly imagine. For this reason it has also been deleted from the Matrix.

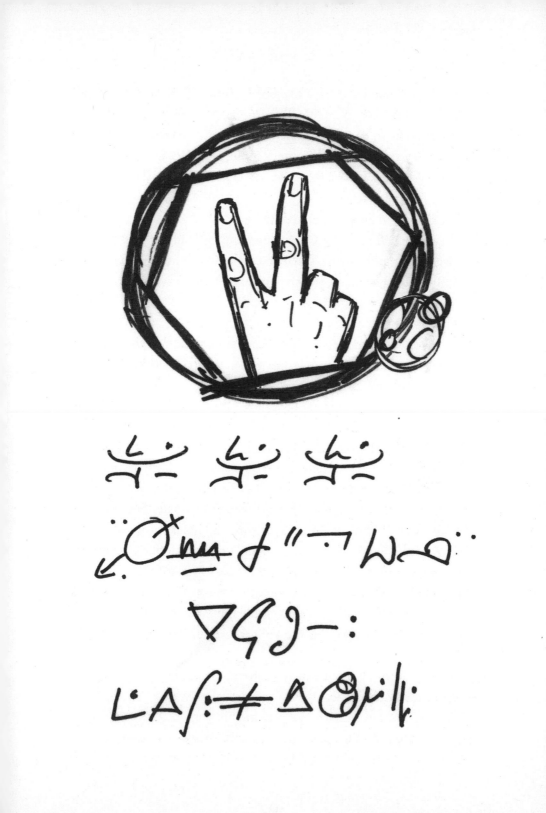

The Doctor nodded. 'Yes, Professor Chronotis.' He smiled warmly down at the little old man. 'We'll clean up a bit, find poor old Skagra here the help he so desperately needs, get these charming people –' he indicated the Ancient Outlaws – 'back to sleep, and then I see no reason why Shada shouldn't stay a secret, as Salyavin intended. Then we all go home for tea and crackers.'

'As Salyavin intended?' queried Romana.

'He was the Great Mind Outlaw, remember,' said the Doctor. 'And what a great escape he made. What better than to vamoose and then use your mind powers to make your jailers forget there was ever a jail in the first place?'

Chris Parsons hurried through the deep, dark red hallways of Shada. At last he would prove himself, at last he was going to be useful, and at last he'd show the universe in general – and Clare in particular – that he was no slouch. There were no flies on Chris Parsons! Whatever that meant.

He heard raised voices ahead and ran faster towards them.

'But Doctor,' he heard Romana saying, 'where is Salyavin? Someone with his power loose in the universe, it's a terrifying thought.'

Chris rounded a corner and burst through an open doorway into a scene of utter confusion. There were three zombies in orange tunics milling about. There was a Kraag which somehow looked as if it was questioning its purpose in life. And there was Romana, standing with K-9 and the Professor, all three looking over at the Doctor, who for some incredible reason had Skagra cradled in his arms like a frightened toddler. Above their heads, the sphere was drifting disconsolately around.

'Don't you worry about Salyavin, Romana,' the Doctor was saying, 'probably long dead by now.'

Chris ran towards the Doctor, waving his arms as if in warning. All eyes turned to him. 'Salyavin,' he cried, almost out of breath.

The Doctor, face suddenly grave, put up a warning hand. 'Bristol, *no!*' he bellowed.

At exactly the same time Chris jabbed his finger manically at Professor Chronotis and shouted, 'It's him! The Professor! He's not the Professor! He's Salyavin!'

There was a shocked silence.

Then Skagra slowly raised his head from the Doctor's shoulder. His eyes, now glittering not with tears, but with renewed purpose and devilish intent, fixed on Professor Chronotis.

'Oh, *⌒⌐⌐ ⌐"⌐ ⌐⌐!*' said the Doctor.

PART SIX

BROUGHT TO BOOK

63

There was a moment of silence. It was followed by a moment of utter confusion, as everything seemed to happen at once.

Skagra pulled himself free of the Doctor and gestured exultantly to the sphere.

Professor Chronotis ripped off his glasses and stared meaningfully at Skagra.

The Doctor shouted, 'K-9, the sphere! Blast it!'

The Kraag Commander straightened up manfully.

The sphere zoomed towards Professor Chronotis.

K-9's nose laser loosed a sizzling, bright red beam at the sphere.

The sphere shattered – but not into fragments. It *divided*. There were now ten spheres, smaller, but identical in every other way to the original.

One of the small spheres attached itself to the forehead of Professor Chronotis. The Professor dropped to his knees in agony, his glasses flying from his hand.

The Doctor raced towards his old friend. His path was blocked instantly by the remaining spheres.

'Salyavin!' cried Skagra. 'At last! It is my destiny!' He pointed to the sphere on the Professor's forehead and barked, 'Total extraction! Break through his barriers! Remove the mind of Salyavin!'

At about this point, Chris Parsons began to wonder if he had done something wrong.

The Professor gave a final agonised cry.

Then, suddenly, he straightened, got to his feet with remarkable agility and turned to face Skagra. His face was totally blank, the sphere still attached to his forehead.

Professor Chronotis's eyes were now jet-black orbs.

Then Skagra did something none of them had ever seen before. He threw back his head and laughed. It was as extreme an emotional reaction as the tears he had dried only moments before. Romana stepped back in revulsion from this appalling sight.

The laughter ended as abruptly as it had begun. 'Now, Doctor,' said Skagra, seemingly as composed as ever, 'you shall see the beginning of the Universal Mind!'

He swept a hand in a grand gesture. Nine of the spheres broke formation and scattered around the chamber.

Three of them settled on the foreheads of Subjatric, Rundgar and Scintilla, the Ancient Outlaws. Immediately they snapped to attention, faces blank, eyes black.

Another sphere zoomed down, attaching itself to the metallic head of K-9. His red eye-screen flickered and turned black.

Chris was too busy looking at this in utter horror to see another sphere heading straight for him. Immediately it touched his forehead he straightened to attention, his face blank, his eyes black.

And Skagra's laugh began anew. But now the chamber rang with laughter, many different voices joining to form a cacophony of almost childish cruelty and derision. Everyone affixed by a sphere was now part of the ghastly chorus. The little Professor, the Ancient Outlaws, Chris, even K-9. Laughing and laughing in exactly the same rhythm as Skagra. Laughing at the Doctor and Romana.

Romana huddled closer to the Doctor as they were surrounded by the laughing mind-slaves, their black eyes shining.

Skagra stopped laughing.

The mind-slaves stopped laughing, their expressions mirroring the triumph on Skagra's face. Even K-9 somehow exuded an air of vicious smugness and superiority.

Skagra stepped smoothly and slowly away from the empty cabinet. 'Now, Doctor, Romana,' said Skagra. 'I have the power of Salyavin. You have been privileged to witness the birth of the Universal Mind. My mission is not to bring death, but life.'

The Doctor couldn't keep the disgust from his voice. 'You call that life?' he sneered, indicating the slaves.

Skagra held up a gloved finger. 'But you didn't let me finish, Doctor. Yes, I bring life. But in your case, I intend to make an exception!'

The Doctor and Romana huddled together as the mind-slaves of Skagra moved as one around them, arms outstretched. Chris, the Professor and K-9 moved closer still, K-9 extending his nose laser.

Their own friends were going to kill them.

64

And then, just as Romana closed her eyes and tried to summon all the dignity befitting a Time Lord facing death, something quite extraordinary happened.

She heard the sound of a relative dimensional stabiliser – an old one by the sound of it, chuffing and groaning, almost coughing its guts out.

And suddenly she and the Doctor were *falling*.

Forgetting all thoughts of dignity, Romana screamed. She was extremely relieved to hear the Doctor doing much the same thing alongside her.

She only had a moment to feel that relief as the fall was suddenly ended by a muffled *whoomf* as she and the Doctor made an incredibly soft landing.

She opened her eyes and found herself totally speechless. She was sitting on a sofa. Next to her on the sofa sat the Doctor. The sofa itself sat facing the just-slammed door of Professor Chronotis's rooms.

A rather pretty young girl, human by the look of it, was standing in front of a rather battered old control console, Gallifreyan by the look of it, her hands adjusting its switches and levers, expertly by the look of it. On a bracket hung a faded, blinking scanner screen showing a view of the prison chamber, Skagra and all his ghastly company.

'Thank you, Clare,' said the Doctor.

The girl said nothing. She was staring in horror at the image on the screen.

Skagra pushed angrily through his crowd of mind-slaves. 'What is this?' he demanded, pointing at the wooden door that had suddenly materialised in the floor of the chamber. It had swung open, swallowing up the Doctor and Romana like a trapdoor, and then slammed itself very firmly shut again.

The Kraag Commander, as the only other being present left with a mind of its own, such as it was, replied, 'The Doctor is in there, my lord.'

Skagra smiled. He realised he already knew the answer. Through the matrix of the spheres he had access to the mind of Salyavin, aka the kindly old Professor Chronotis, and that told him everything he needed to know about the no-longer-mysterious door.

The Kraag Commander pointed to the door, its arm glowing red. 'Shall I blast it, my lord?'

Skagra shook his head. 'You will not be able to penetrate the outer plasmic shell of a TARDIS, even a TARDIS as ancient and obsolete as this one.'

A wave of anger and disappointment at the Doctor's escape threatened to overwhelm him. But new thoughts, from within the spheres' matrix, calmed him at once.

He never even bothers to have a plan, came a thought from the human Parsons. *Doctor-Master's chances of success in defeating the Universal Mind less than 0.000000000000013 per cent,* came a thought from the computer mind of K-9. The Time Lord would pose no threat.

'The Doctor,' Skagra mused aloud to the Kraag Commander. 'A poor little man. A pinprick of an irrelevancy. Let him amuse himself with his tricks. They are merely the tiny antics of an insect threatened with inevitable extinction. We will return to the command station!'

He led the way from the chamber and back towards the Doctor's

TARDIS. His words of command were for the Kraag only. His mind-slaves followed calmly and automatically, K-9 bringing up the rear.

Clare still stared intently at the scanner screen in the corner of the Professor's study. 'They're leaving,' she told the Doctor and Romana as she watched Skagra and his slaves, including the black-eyed Chris Parsons, depart.

'Don't you worry, Clare,' the Doctor called from the sofa. 'We'll get Chris and the others back safely.'

Clare caught Romana shooting the Doctor a warning look, as if to say *Don't make rash promises.* Then Romana caught Clare catching sight of that look and converted it into a reassuring smile. Clare wasn't sure what to make of Romana. She had the manner of a person who thinks they are cleverer than you, and that you don't realise they think they're cleverer than you. But it was a minor concern. At the moment, Clare couldn't stop thinking of Chris.

The Doctor had brought Romana quickly up to speed with all the incredible events she had missed out on while a prisoner of Skagra.

Clare wanted to join in the discussion, and after the Professor – or Salyavin, or whoever he was – had implanted the science of time mechanics into her head, she felt she was perfectly capable of it. But the human part of her was shaking inside at the thought of Chris's kindly, silly face made blank and his soft brown eyes turned pitch black. So instead she dematerialised the Professor's TARDIS away from Shada, and kept a close watch on the time-path indicator for any sign of Skagra and the Doctor's TARDIS on its way back to the command station.

Romana shook her head and took another sip of tea. 'Professor Chronotis was Salyavin all along,' she said. 'Of all the things you've told me, why do I find that one so hard to believe?'

'Well, naturally,' said the Doctor. 'He's a nice old man. You like him, I like him. He's certainly not the villain the Time Lords painted him.'

'And there's another thing,' said Romana. 'Skagra was trying to get

Salyavin's mind. But he'd already drained the Professor's mind, so if Salyavin was the Professor . . .'

'Extraordinary mental control,' said the Doctor. 'He let the sphere take the Chronotis part of his mind, but held back the Salyavin part. The effort was what killed him.' He thought for a moment. 'I think the Professor himself forgot, or chose to forget, that he was Salyavin. All that forgetfulness and bluster and senility, the perfect cover, for himself as well as everybody else. The clues were all there.'

'When did you realise, Doctor?' asked Clare.

'The moment I stepped into this TARDIS and realised it was a TARDIS, after Bristol and I escaped from the asteroid,' said the Doctor breezily. 'I pretended I hadn't, of course, but it was obvious from that point, if not before.'

'It wasn't obvious to me,' said Romana.

'Or me,' said Clare.

'Think about it,' said the Doctor. He nodded to Romana. 'First of all, the message the Professor sent to us in the TARDIS. He seemed to have forgotten all about it – he even suggested that somebody else must have sent it.'

Romana nodded back. 'Of course,' she said. 'Somebody else had sent it. Salyavin!'

'And then the clues kept stacking up,' continued the Doctor. 'First of all, he had a secret TARDIS, this one. Second of all, it has an emergency program – a very naughty program, not to mention *criminal* – that brings him back to life. Then somehow, this charming young lady –' he smiled at Clare – 'becomes an expert in time mechanics in less time than you can say Wafer-wave Feedback Field Frame. He left Clare behind with all that knowledge in her head, just in case we needed rescuing. I pretended not to notice any of that, very well, I thought. Let sleeping Salyavins lie, I thought. And don't forget I know the Professor, whoever he may have been once. I was quite prepared to keep his big secret.'

'And then Chris marches right in and blows the whole gaffe in front of Skagra,' said Clare. 'The idiot! The ruddy idiot! I could kill him!'

'No you couldn't, Clare, you love him,' said the Doctor casually.

'Does she?' said Romana, sounding surprised. 'Why on earth would she want to do that?'

Clare blinked through forming tears. 'How did you know?' she asked the Doctor.

The Doctor coughed and lifted a finger. 'The clues were all there, it was obvious. First, you may not realise it but whenever you mention his name your voice raises one tenth of an octave and your eyes go all gooey—'

Romana coughed. 'I'm sure this is all very fascinating, but what about Skagra?'

Clare was glad of the subject being changed. 'Well, what are we going to do about him, then?' she challenged Romana.

Romana shrugged. 'He's beaten us on every point.'

The Doctor nodded gloomily. 'I was quite enjoying clearing all the other stuff up,' he protested. 'Can we get some other less pressing details straightened out, it helps to distract me from the imminent threat to the universe?'

'No,' said Romana and Clare at the same time. This time, Clare felt that Romana's smile to her was warm and genuine.

'Oh, very well then,' said the Doctor heavily. He slumped back in the sofa. 'Let's sum up. All the minds that Skagra's stolen are now in the melting pot of the sphere matrix along with his own, all operating as one under his control. And with Salyavin's mind in there too, Skagra can potentially drain and control anyone else. Everyone else in the entire universe!'

'The universe is a pretty big place,' pointed out Clare.

'And the spheres are infinitely divisible, courtesy of the genius of the late Professor Akrotiri,' said the Doctor. 'From that asteroid, Skagra can launch them against the universe en masse, like a virulent, all-powerful disease. His mind will be universal, and invincible.'

There was a terrible silence.

Then Romana said quietly, 'Doctor?'

'Yes,' said the Doctor perfunctorily. 'I do so hope you're going to say something wonderful and uplifting, it's what I keep you girls for.'

'May I just remind you of something?' said Romana.

'Yes,' said the Doctor cautiously, his eyes slowly turning to meet hers, as if hoping against hope.

'All the minds that Skagra's stolen are in the melting pot, the spheres' matrix,' said Romana.

The Doctor snorted and flared up. 'Yes, Romana, I think we've established that, in fact I just said it, I don't need reminding about things that I've just said—'

'That means there's a copy of your mind in there too,' said Romana quickly and sweetly, as if laying down a trump card.

'Well, yes, of course, we've established that—' began the Doctor impatiently.

Then suddenly he went very quiet. Clare watched as a number of expressions passed over his face in less than a second.

He stood up. 'Romana?' he said casually.

'Yes, Doctor?' said Romana, equally casually.

The Doctor reached into one of his pockets and pulled out a golden medal with a long, multicoloured ribbon. Carefully, almost formally, he pinned it to the front of her dress.

The medal read in big red letters:

I

AM A

GENIUS

65

Skagra basked in the Universal Mind. His gloved hands flicked almost without thinking over one facet of the control console in the Doctor's TARDIS. The other facets were attended to in turn by Chronotis, Chris, Subjatric, Rundgar and Scintilla, small spheres still attached to their foreheads, all now sharing in the knowledge of its operation, every quirk and whim of the old machine. The black-screened K-9, small sphere on the top of his head, circuited the control room, nose laser extruded aggressively. The Kraag Commander looked on, as stonily impassive as ever.

This, thought Skagra, is only the beginning. From the command station he would launch a mighty fleet of small craft, ten thousand of them, crewed by the Kraags, each containing a portion of the infinitely divisible sphere. They were now ready for launch at a moment's notice. He had not chosen that particular asteroid by chance. Location was everything. The asteroid was situated close to the central space lanes of the great civilisations of this galaxy. And the Kraags would crush any resistance – they felt no pain, they were virtually indestructible and, most cleverly, they would act as a distraction while the tiny spheres did their work.

Firstly, and with the very greatest of pleasure, the Universal Mind would take Gallifrey. Any resistance from the Time Lords (or anybody else in the universe, for that matter) would be futile. The sphere was indestructible. It would simply divide and multiply, scattering itself like the seed pods of a dandelion throughout the planet of the Time Lords. All of the ancient powers of Gallifrey, all the secret knowledge of that indolent race, would be his.

And then the Universal Mind would spread through all time and all space. The spheres, now tinier than the smallest nanite, would do their work unseen and unchallenged. Skaro, Telos, Sontar, all the so-called mighty empires would bend to his unquestionably supreme will.

Then the real work of the Universal Mind could begin. Every intelligence, every resource, would be employed to reorder creation in Skagra's image.

The place needed tidying up, for a start. So many solar systems were random and irritatingly erratic. He would use his new knowledge to reshape them in neat, square alignments around a precise grid-like system, with the people living their new lives in a precise, grid-like system.

The Universal Mind would then conquer the threat of entropy. A solution would be found to the supposedly damning sentence passed by the second law of thermodynamics. Then Skagra would ensure there would be no collapse into eternal darkness and decay.

The universe, and the Universal Mind of Skagra, would endure for eternity. Nothing could stop him now!

66

Despite her crash course in temporal mechanics, Clare was finding it hard to follow the Doctor and Romana's plan. She could grasp the basics – it was going to involve performing a hazardous manoeuvre in the space-time vortex itself – but the specifics were well beyond her. But anything that could rescue Chris from the clutches of Skagra had to be attempted.

Perhaps that was why she couldn't quite follow the plan, mused Clare. The Doctor and Romana were capable of caring for the universe, which was too big a thing for her mind to get around. Her human emotions could only think of poor Chris, and how she was going to grab him and snog the very life out of him the moment he was returned to her. Life really was too short, a fact that the presence of a Time Lord knocking on 800 only served to rub in.

'It's going to be very tricky, isn't it?' said the Doctor, almost flippantly.

'It's going to be appallingly dangerous,' said Romana severely.

The Doctor shrugged. 'Just a touch.'

Romana sighed heavily. 'Doctor, it'll be terribly, appallingly dangerous for *you*. In fact, you stand as much chance as—' She broke off, thinking.

'As much chance as what?' asked the Doctor.

Romana gave up. 'Well, as much chance as anything that stands as little chance as you will out there!' She gestured vaguely in the general direction of the door.

The Doctor smiled like a child at his birthday party. 'Really? Well then, I'll just have to be very, very brave, won't I?'

'Doctor!' cried Romana harshly. Clare was astonished to see there were tears forming in the corners of Romana's eyes. Perhaps she'd been wrong about the alien capacity to ignore the individual for the good of the many. 'It isn't funny!'

The Doctor knocked Romana lightly on the shoulder with his knuckles. 'Listen,' he said agreeably, 'I can do your part if you can do mine.'

Romana sniffed, and then smiled. 'I'll try.'

The Doctor tapped the medal on her chest. 'You're a genius. Remember?'

Romana nodded.

The Doctor turned his attention to Clare. 'Clare?'

'Yes, Doctor?' Clare said brightly.

The Doctor nodded to the control panel. 'Do we have a fix on my TARDIS?'

Clare read off the coordinates on the time-path indicator. 'It's on our vector. We left Shada first, yes, but they have greater relative speed.' Clare patched through the indicator display to the main scanner. The image on the screen showed two dots, one representing the Professor's TARDIS, the other the Doctor's TARDIS, some little way ahead.

'Right,' said the Doctor. He waved Romana forward to the panel. He coughed. 'First we have to catch them up.'

Romana and Clare reached for the same lever. Their eyes locked. Clare decided she was not going to give way. After all, she had some of the owner's natural affinity with this craft.

Romana removed her hand with slightly bad grace.

Clare threw the lever.

There was a jarring jolt and the Professor's room shuddered. The Doctor, Clare and Romana were thrown off their feet.

Clare clambered up as the room steadied. The scanner screen now displayed an image of the two dots much closer to each other.

'Good work!' called the Doctor. 'Now then, phase two. I want you two girls, working together and playing nicely, thank you very much, to extrude the force field out from this TARDIS.'

Clare gasped. 'But that's insane!' she said. The tampered-with part of her mind flared in alarm at the prospect. 'I mean – that is appallingly dangerous!'

Romana slipped past her and started adjusting the force-field controls. 'That's what I've been trying to tell him,' she said. 'And that's only the beginning of his plan.' She gave Clare a desperate smile. 'But it's the only way.'

A red light started to flash on the console panel where Chris Parsons was stationed. Skagra saw it via the sphere matrix, as he could now see and sense everything that his mind-slaves, as mere extensions of his sentience, experienced.

'Vortex turbulence,' he said. 'It is not important.'

The TARDIS shook slightly.

The Doctor stood by the exit door of Professor Chronotis's rooms – or, as Clare supposed she ought to learn to refer to it, Professor Chronotis's TARDIS. Or Salyavin's TARDIS, considering the Professor was actually Salyavin. Or the ghost of him. Or, now, the zombie-ghost of . . . Clare gave up.

'Ready?' the Doctor called.

'Yes,' said Clare and Romana at the same time. Their hands hovered over particularly large levers on the console.

'Right,' said the Doctor, looking considerably less flippant and casual than he had only moments before. 'Patch the force field through to the external door . . .' He paused and grabbed at the lintel of the door. 'Now!'

Romana and Clare threw their levers.

* * *

If any creature could have existed in the howling space-time vortex, and had been happening to pass the 'place' where the two TARDISes were drawn level, they would have seen a most extraordinary sight.

A small Georgian ground-floor flat appeared to be sidling up to a 1950s police box.

Suddenly, the door of the flat began to glow with bright white light. Slowly, the light began to extend towards the police box, forming a shimmering rectangular tunnel that snaked ever closer to the battered blue booth.

Skagra flinched as sparks showered from the console panel before him, spinning from the synchronic feedback array like a miniature firework. The Doctor's knowledge of TARDIS operations, relayed through the sphere's matrix, suggested that this was nothing much to worry about and that this kind of thing happened all the time. Skagra didn't doubt that.

The hands of the mind-slaves worked busily over the five other facets of the console. Each of them frowned at the same moment as Skagra.

'What is wrong, my Lord?' asked the Kraag Commander, the only creature present not privy to Skagra's every thought.

'An external influence,' Skagra snapped. He had no need to consult the Time Lord minds within the sphere matrix. He knew it could mean only one thing. 'There is something else out there, in the space-time vortex.' He twisted the scanner-screen switch with the hands of Rundgar.

The shutters parted.

Skagra let out an involuntary cry of sheer frustration.

A section of the architecture of St Cedd's College, Cambridge was bobbing unsteadily alongside them, a bright white glow streaming from it.

A reverse angle on the same image appeared in the scanner of the pursuing TARDIS. Everything in the Professor's rooms was rattling and humming like a neurotic tuning fork with the effort the poor old machine was being put to. This included Clare's teeth. The very air seemed to vibrate and shimmer.

The Doctor, peering through the keyhole of the door, chuckled as the room came to rest with a bump. 'Ha, got them! Locked tight! Well done Romana, well done Clare, well done me for thinking it up in the first place!'

'We haven't got to the hard bit yet,' said Clare.

Romana frowned as she read off a console display. 'We might never get to it. The force field's very unstable.'

Clare stared at the image on the scanner. 'That's what we're chasing? But it's a police box!'

'And we're flying about in a bit of university,' the Doctor grinned. 'You'll get used to it.'

Skagra read off a similar console display. 'The force field is weakening already,' he told the Kraag Commander. He consulted the mind of K-9. 'I estimate the field will break in approximately fifty-eight seconds.'

'Romana! Turn off the vortex-shield failsafe around the door!' called the Doctor urgently, his hand grasping the doorknob.

Clare stared at that hand, feeling sick to her stomach. Opening the door of a TARDIS onto the vortex was almost suicidally stupid. The time winds would surely burst in and suck them all out into nothingness.

Romana punched out the failsafe cancel sequence on the console and called, 'Good luck, Doctor!'

The Doctor nodded to her, gave Clare a small smile and turned the doorknob. The door swung easily open and the Doctor strode casually out into the space-time vortex, as if he was off for nothing more momentous than a morning stroll.

For just a second, Clare saw the bright glare of the force field beyond him, extending in a shimmering and frankly wobbly corridor through the screaming whirlpool of the vortex.

Then the door slammed shut.

* * *

Skagra watched the scanner screen incredulously as the Doctor started to run along the glowing tunnel of light connecting the two TARDISes.

'A futile exercise, Doctor,' he said. But he never took his eyes from the screen.

Romana and Clare stared up at the scanner.

The Doctor was racing for the police box doors of his own hijacked TARDIS as fast as the swaying, undulating force field would allow. Clare gasped as he seemed to stumble, but he found his footing and raced on. The Doctor extended his arm desperately, his hand groping for the solid, blue surface just out of his reach.

And the force field around him flickered and crackled alarmingly.

'We've got to give him more power!' cried Romana.

Clare gestured helplessly at the console read-outs. 'There *is* no more power!'

On the screen, the Doctor was being shaken violently as the tenuous protection of the force field began to succumb to the ferocious time winds. But he was almost there, one more second and he would make it –

Suddenly there was a massive explosion from the brass control panel. Clare and Romana were thrown to the floor, sparks showering around them, heavy books thudding down from the higher shelves of the study.

Clare lifted her head to the scanner. A dazzling flare of light filled the screen as the force field suddenly snapped out of existence.

Skagra, and by proxy his mind-slaves, averted their eyes from the scanner as the force field flared.

When he looked back, there was no sign of the Doctor. The Professor's TARDIS was spinning wildly away, sent hurtling off by the violent severing of the link.

The controls of the Doctor's TARDIS began to respond once more under the ten ministering hands of the mind-slaves.

Skagra smiled as the TARDIS settled back on to an even keel. The mind-slaves smiled back. K-9 wagged his tail happily.

This time, Skagra, and by proxy the mind-slaves, thought contentedly, the Doctor was absolutely, definitely dead.

67

The Doctor laughed and laughed and laughed.

He lay in a woolly bundle on a reassuring solid surface. Even more reassuringly, the surface was white and it hummed. The Doctor leapt to his feet, tottered a moment, then patted the nearest wall, which was covered in the extraordinarily reassuring circular pattern of his own TARDIS. 'Thank you, old girl,' he said. 'Thank you so very much. Sorry I had to barge in through the back door like that. But have you any idea what it's like to travel through the space-time vortex?' He paused a moment and patted the wall again. 'Well of course you have, haven't you, you do it all the time. But at least you're built for it, eh?'

He didn't really expect a reply, so he was only mildly disappointed when he didn't get one.

'Right then,' he said. 'Let's get to work!'

He looked around and was surprised and delighted to find himself in the TARDIS's cavernous storeroom, which was located (at least presently) a good ten minutes' brisk walk from the control room.

'And this is exactly where I wanted to be,' he grinned, patting the wall a third time. 'Oh you're going to get such a treat when this is all over, you cunning old capsule, you.'

The storeroom contained line after line of tall metal shelves stretching into the dimly lit distance. Every shelf heaved with dusty cardboard boxes, many of them undisturbed for centuries. Every box was jammed full of vital components, spares and handy bits of stuff the Doctor had picked up over the long years of his travels. Between the shelves were a bewildering variety of drawers, cabinets and cases. Everything was labelled precisely. But completely inaccurately.

The Doctor started rummaging about. He had a plan to follow for once, after all. First off, he would need a neural vectometer . . .

He found a neural vectometer almost straight away. In a box marked 'LIGHT BULBS'.

'Oh good!' he cried.

Next up – a synchro-relay. He rummaged about and found a synchro-relay. In a drawer marked 'NAILS (ASSORTED)'.

'Oh good!' he cried.

And, of course, a megapathic-interrupter was essential to the whole plan. He rummaged about and found a megapathic-interrupter. Underneath a string shopping bag full of faulty reacting vibrators, which was jammed in the back of a cabinet labelled 'ADAPTORS (UK-US, US-EU, EU-MARS)'.

'Oh good!' he cried.

The megapathic-interrupter fell to bits in his hand.

'Oh bad!' he cried.

68

Clare watched as Romana, her coolness and composure seemingly undented by being flung off through space and time, made her final repairs to the navigation panel of the Professor's TARDIS and reset the coordinates.

There was a moment's silence in which Clare and Romana crossed their fingers at exactly the same moment, then a soft hum filled the room and the clock on the mantelpiece juddered back into life, rising and falling smoothly once more.

'There,' said Romana, inputting the final string of the complex sequence. 'We're on our way to Skagra, as planned.'

Clare bit her lip. Romana seemed so capable and focused. Like a frighteningly competent and unflappable head girl at a particularly old and intimidating grammar school. She was a very reassuring person to have with you in a crisis, thought Clare. Reassuring in a terrifying kind of way. Clare wasn't sure Romana would want to hear her next question, but it had to be asked.

Clare took a deep breath. 'Do you think the Doctor made it?' She avoided looking at Romana as she said this, instead staring doubtfully through the curtains of the nearest window at the endless distorting maelstrom of the vortex.

'I have no idea,' said Romana. 'Speaking logically, statistically, and scientifically – not a chance.' She smiled suddenly. 'But then again, he's the Doctor. We have to assume that he did make it, and go ahead according to plan.' She read off a dial and glanced across at the clock on the mantelpiece, which was still moving smoothly up and down. 'We arrive at the asteroid in five minutes, relative time.'

Clare gave Romana a friendly pat on the shoulder. 'I've got to hand it to you, you're a cool one. Without you here, I think I'd have gone to pieces worrying about Chris. And underneath, you must be just as worried about the Doctor.'

'I'm almost always worried about the Doctor,' Romana smiled.

Clare gave a small, involuntary sob. 'Sorry, sorry,' she said. 'I know this doesn't help, but I've loved Chris for so long, but I never actually said it to him. Never did a damn thing.'

Romana put an arm around Clare's shoulder. Clare sniffed and looked up at her with a rueful smile. 'Someone like you, I bet you just marched up and grabbed the Doctor straight away, no messing around. And who can blame you, he is an amazing man.'

Romana's eyes widened a little and she disentangled herself from Clare, fetching a box of tissues from the coffee table and offering her one.

'I think you might have misunderstood the nature of my relationship with the Doctor.'

Clare blew her nose. 'Oh right, sorry. So you aren't married or whatever you do on Gallifrey?'

'We're just friends. And one thing I've learnt from being the Doctor's friend, Clare – the universe is full of wonderful things, amazing opportunities. And you have to grab them with both hands. And hope they never end.'

There was a chime like a vesper bell.

'We're almost there,' said Romana.

Clare straightened up, crumpling the tissue into a tight ball. 'And we go ahead as planned,' she said.

69

Skagra strode from the Doctor's TARDIS, the Kraag Commander and the mind-slaves following him into the giant observation dome that looked out onto the infinite universe.

Skagra surveyed the stars with new eyes. Five pairs of new eyes. 'An infinite concert of the mind,' he whispered to himself.

He signalled towards K-9 and the five humanoid mind-slaves. The spheres attached to their heads instantly divided once again. Each small sphere then multiplied into hundreds of tiny, almost invisible spheres, aggregating in one large silvery swarm. Six tiny silver dots split off and flew back to re-attach themselves to the foreheads of the mind-slaves, now virtually invisible.

Then the swarm broke up, section by section, patches of silver, like glistening fireflies, each of them knowing where they needed to be, each shining cloud moving swiftly through one of the many arched doorways that led from the giant dome.

Skagra followed their journey using the part of his mind that controlled the sphere matrix. The microbial particles flowed down through the curving rock walls of the asteroid and into specially prepared hatches in the sides of the mighty spaceships ranged along the underbelly of the massive rock. Each of the ships contained a crew of

Kraags, each of them burning with the ambition to serve their lord and master, Skagra, to spread the Universal Mind.

Deep in the TARDIS storeroom, the Doctor surveyed his handiwork with less than total enthusiasm. But there was no time to improve the dubious aesthetics of the thing. A good five minutes had gone by since a soft, distant thump had signalled the TARDIS's materialisation. It was now or never.

Carefully, reminding himself just how quickly it had been cobbled together, he lowered the thing onto his head. A tall gilt-edged mirror leant against one wall of the storeroom. The Doctor walked over to it, slowly and carefully, like a debutant with a book on her head, and checked his reflection. He sighed heavily.

'With this thing on, it won't matter whether it works or not,' he mused to himself. 'They'll all be paralysed laughing at me.'

'Crews report all ships are prepared,' said the Kraag Commander.

Skagra fought down a wave of animal exultation. This was the time of destiny. His apotheosis. His plan had succeeded. But then he had always known it would. There was no need for excitement or unnecessary emotion of any kind. But perhaps a word or two to mark the occasion was appropriate.

'Mark this moment,' he said, calmly and smoothly as ever. The mind-slaves gathered behind him in a semicircle, looking with black eyes – his eyes – out at the stars. 'This is the beginning of the new life, the new universe.'

He turned to the Kraag Commander and opened his mouth to give the order to launch the ships.

A wheezing, groaning sound came from behind him.

Skagra whipped around to see the wooden door of the Professor's TARDIS fading up from transparency against the far wall.

All his thoughts of the Universal Mind were replaced by a sudden and terrible surge of violent hatred. And what made this even worse, what really made his blood boil, was that anyone *could* make his blood boil. For his whole life, Skagra had been cool, rational and logical, his emotions merely minor irritations. Now this one man, this *buffoon*, had consumed him with fury and animal rage. Skagra had long ago realised that other people in general were irritating. But how could one solitary person have taken being irritating to such an unbearably high level. But the worst offence the Doctor had committed against Skagra, the most unforgivable, was this emotional pollution. He had violated the inviolable. He would pay!

'Doctor!' he cried, the vein on his temple throbbing uncontrollably. 'The man is like an itching flea on my skin! I shall eliminate him once and for all!'

He strode towards the wooden door, the mind-slaves following in perfect unison.

'Out you come, Doctor!' he cried. 'Out you come! I know you are in there!'

But the door remained shut.

A voice from behind Skagra said, 'Did someone call?'

Skagra's head jerked around in the direction of the voice. The hated voice.

The Doctor was standing in the police box door of his own TARDIS. And he had something quite, quite ridiculous on his head.

70

Clare and Romana were huddled around the scanner of the Professor's TARDIS, staring in disbelief at the drama unfolding outside.

Clare would have been overwhelmed by the majesty of the asteroid's celestial backdrop were it not for the rather small screen on which she was seeing it, and for the sight of poor Chris and those blank black eyes which threatened to overwhelm her in quite another way.

But when she saw the Doctor pop out from the police box behind Skagra, alive, well and wearing the most ludicrous collection of oddments jammed down over his curly hair, she felt like cheering and laughing. To her great relief, Romana obviously felt like cheering and laughing too, because she was.

'He's done it!' Clare cried. 'He made it!'

'And he made *that*,' said Romana, pointing to the thing on the Doctor's head.

It looked like a cross between a colander, the back of an old Bakelite radio complete with knobs, a rusty car aerial, a string of fairy lights and bits of a dismembered computer. From the front sprouted a ridiculous bobbing prong with what appeared to be a tiny radar dish attached to the end. It was festooned with multicoloured wires, leads and connectors. At the very top was taped a boxy blue Ever Ready battery.

Clare's smile faded slightly. 'And that's what's going to save the day, is it?'

Skagra's jaw dropped. 'How-how-how . . .' he stammered.

'Er, "How did you get in there?"' suggested the Doctor.

'How-how did you get in there?' spluttered Skagra.

The Doctor stepped insouciantly from the TARDIS.

'What do you mean, "How did you get in there?"' He jerked a thumb over his shoulder at the police box. 'It's mine, I belong in there!'

'As of now, Doctor,' said Skagra, 'you don't belong anywhere. Anywhere at all. There is no place for you in my new universe!'

The Doctor sighed and shook his head regretfully. His headgear rattled but stayed put. 'Do you know, Skagra, I thought you were different. But that mad gleam, that "universe will soon be mine" stuff . . . I do seem to bring it out in people.'

'Enough!' Skagra cried, and with an imperious gesture waved his mind-slaves forward.

They advanced on the Doctor, their arms outstretched. Their faces were contorted with anger, expressions identical to that of Skagra.

'You shall die, Doctor!' shouted Skagra. 'You shall die – now!'

'Yes, that one too,' sighed the Doctor. 'It's a very interesting little theory. Let's try putting it to the test, shall we?'

He reached up and pressed a button on the side of his helmet. The prong at the front glowed soft pink, like a tea-candle at a dinner party. The radar dish began to spin like a miniature fan. At the same time, the Doctor smiled his unmistakable toothy, silly smile.

A moment later, the mind-slaves turned to face Skagra and smiled the same unmistakable toothy, silly smile. K-9's ears swivelled back and forth jauntily and a small length of ticker-tape chattered from his mouth, almost as if he were sticking his tongue out.

'What – have – you – *done*?' cried Skagra. There was an edge of panic in his voice.

The Doctor blinked innocently. The mind-slaves blinked innocently.

'What have *I* done?' said the Doctor. 'No, no, Skagra, it's more a question of what have *you* done. You used that deranged billiard ball of yours once too often. You forgot that there's a copy of *my* mind in the sphere's operational matrix too, isn't there?'

Skagra roared with anger. 'Kill him!'

The mind-slaves roared with anger. 'Kill him!' they cried, advancing once more on the Doctor.

The Doctor laughed. 'Put the kettle on!'

The mind-slaves laughed. 'Put the kettle on!' they cried, turning away from the Doctor.

'Kill him!' screamed Skagra.

'Kill him!' chorused the mind-slaves.

'Put the kettle on!' laughed the Doctor.

'Put the kettle on!' chorused the mind-slaves.

The heads of the mind-slaves turned between Skagra and the Doctor, just like the crowd at a tennis match.

'You see, Skagra,' said the Doctor airily, 'all I had to do was build this rather fetching apparatus –' he tapped the helmet and the prong wobbled alarmingly – 'to allow me remote control of the copy of my mind in the sphere's matrix and re-route the command circuit to me, and not you. So basically speaking, in layman's terms, I now have full charge of the Universal Mind – or as far as it stretches at the moment. All six of 'em.'

'My mind is stronger!' spat Skagra. 'The matrix is attuned to my consciousness. You will never overcome my control.' He closed his eyes, a frown of concentration creasing his brow. 'Kill him!' he hissed.

'Put the kettle on!' cried the Doctor at the same time.

Subjatric and Rundgar, who were closest to Skagra, cried 'Kill him!' and staggered in the general direction of the Doctor.

Scintilla and Chronotis were nearest to the Doctor, and chorused 'Put the kettle on!'

Chris was in the middle of the small group. The Doctor watched as his face took on a bemused, dithering expression, as if unsure whether to kill the Doctor or put the kettle on.

'So what was that you were saying about your mind being stronger?' goaded the Doctor. 'I think your little bunch are in two minds about that already, aren't they? Stalemate, I'd say.'

Still concentrating furiously, Skagra snapped his fingers, and the Kraag Commander came to attention.

'Kill the Doctor!' Skagra spat through gritted teeth. 'Kill him now!'

The Kraag raised its glowing red claws and advanced on the Doctor.

The Doctor blanched in alarm. His concentration faltered for a moment, and the mind-slaves moved as one towards him, once again under Skagra's control.

The Doctor's face creased with effort. 'K-9!' he called.

K-9's eye-screen remained black as night, his blaster extended. 'You must die, Doctor,' he said.

The Kraag bore down on the Doctor, who leapt back, right into the path of K-9. Sweat erupted on the Doctor's brow as he brought every ounce of his mental energy to bear on the metal dog.

'K-9, I need you!' the Doctor implored.

For a moment K-9's eye-screen flickered red.

'That's it, boy!' the Doctor cried. 'Come on, you dear old thing, I'm giving you all I've got!'

He dodged another swipe from the furious Kraag, as K-9 shuddered, as if fighting his own internal battle. With a sudden metallic *ping* the tiny particle of sphere detached itself from K-9 and fell to the floor.

'Master!' chirped K-9, eye-screen now glowing a healthy red.

The Doctor beamed. 'Well done! Now blast that Kraag!' he ordered.

K-9's ears swivelled in confusion. 'But Master, this instruction contradicts your previous orders—'

'I didn't give you your mind back to quibble, K-9!' shouted the Doctor. 'Blast that Kraag!'

K-9's nose laser fired at full power, the beam slicing into the great stony bulk of the Kraag Commander. It staggered back, away from the Doctor, and then stood transfixed, a few metres from the others, caught in the blazing laser energy.

The Doctor sighed with relief – just as the humanoid mind-slaves reached him, hands outstretched like claws, ready to tear him apart.

Skagra shouted an order. 'The helmet! Destroy it!' Chris obediently reached up to yank the device from the Doctor's head.

The Doctor batted Chris's hand away and, in the same sweeping movement, turned up a dial on the side of the helmet. The pink light of the prong glowed more intensely and the little radar dish became a spinning blur.

Instantly Chris and the other mind-slaves withdrew from the Doctor, turning as one back towards Skagra.

Skagra's face was now red with the mental effort, his scar flushed a livid purple, the vein on his temple pulsed sickeningly.

The mind-slaves swung back towards the Doctor.

Sweat drenched the Doctor's brow, and he gritted his teeth in pain.

The mind-slaves turned back to Skagra.

Clare felt Romana tugging at her sleeve. She tore her eyes from the scanner screen.

'Now's our chance,' Romana said. She pointed at the scanner, to the large control console at the centre of the observation dome, some distance from the raging mind-battle. 'I have to get to that console. You stay here.'

Clare looked again at the chaos on the screen. It would be easy to nod and stay put and follow orders. But she'd had enough of that. From Chris, from the Porter, from the Doctor and the Professor.

'Not this time,' Clare said firmly and strode to the door.

With a small smile of gratitude, Romana followed.

* * *

The Doctor barely registered the sight of the two women emerging from the wooden door in the far wall. He was all too conscious not only of the intense mental effort required of him to keep control of the slaves, but also the rapidly increasing heat emanating from the Kraag Commander transfixed in K-9's ray.

'Do you want to call half-time, Skagra?' he called with a cheeriness he did not feel. 'We can have a short break if you like, a few slices of lemon? Perk you up no end!'

In truth, the Doctor was also painfully aware that Skagra was probably right. His mind, programmed into the sphere's matrix at its very beginning on the Think Tank, was inevitably going to reassert its control.

He began to feel the dark edges of unconsciousness tugging at his mind. How easy it would be, he thought, to relax, let go and join the minds in the sphere. He could feel all of them, their disjointed memories and personalities screaming out to him in that same thin, distorted inhuman babble he'd heard on the river what seemed like centuries ago.

Akrotiri, Ia, Caldera, Thira and Centauri, David Taylor, Professor Chronotis, Bernard Strong, Salyavin, Scintilla, Rundgar, Subjatric, and Chris Parsons –

Wave equations surfboard the Bird In Hand two lumps, no sugar sieve the wife I have to escape from Shada Gallifrey shall be mine the woven words Clare Clare I love you Clare –

'I love you, Keightley!' the Doctor cried out.

Clare and Romana ran to the control console, Clare's eyes flicking instinctively towards Chris on the other side of the dome.

'I love you, Keightley!' cried the Doctor again.

But although it was the Doctor's voice speaking, Clare somehow knew that it was Chris Parsons talking.

'Chris! I love you too!' she cried back.

Romana jerked Clare's arm to get her attention. 'Well now that we've finally got that out in the open, can I just remind you the universe is at stake?'

'Sorry, sorry,' said Clare. Romana gestured urgently to the console. 'If we can bypass the isomorphic control, we can destroy this place!'

Clare blinked and tried to concentrate on the instrumentation as they had planned. Romana had explained that, theoretically, there must be a way to override Skagra's bio-print, or at least bypass it, allowing them to activate the self-destruct sequence, blowing the asteroid to pieces before the Kraag ships could be launched.

Romana's hands moved desperately over the controls. 'I have to find a way,' she said, hammering at a keyboard. 'Where's the subsidiary router on this thing?'

Clare felt a sudden surge of heat – coming not from the glowing Kraag but from the opposite direction.

She turned and gasped in horror. A platoon of Kraags, at least fifty of them, had entered the dome and was heading right for them.

Romana grabbed Clare and leapt back from the console as the nearest of the Kraags raised their glowing claws –

A moment later the control console was a heap of twisted, molten metal.

Romana looked despairingly at the smoking remains. 'Trust Skagra to have a contingency plan,' she sighed.

The Kraags advanced on Clare and Romana – and Clare remembered the face she'd seen when she'd first touched the book. That vision, she now knew, had been a premonition of her death –

But then she remembered the second vision. Her kissing Chris, her own voice saying 'I suppose a police station is as good a place to start as any—'

That hadn't happened yet. So there was still a chance. A chance for a future.

Clare grabbed a scorched pipe from the floor, suddenly emboldened by hope. She raised the pipe over her head and let out a feral cry of defiance in the face of fate.

The Kraags towered above her like a living wall of rock.

And then, quite suddenly – they *dissolved*. Each Kraag melted into twisting turning ashes.

Romana and Clare looked between the mounds of cinders where the Kraags had stood and each other.

'What did you just do?' gasped Clare at last.

'I didn't do anything,' stammered Romana.

Clare looked behind her. The Doctor and Skagra remained locked in battle for control of the slaves, faces contorted in concentration, oblivious to everything going on around them – but the Kraag Commander was sinking to its knees with a groan. Then its knees turned to powder and it disintegrated into red hot embers.

K-9 snapped off his beam. 'Illogical outcome,' he said, sounding terribly confused.

Clare lowered her pipe and Romana grabbed her hand as the dome began to shake and shudder around them, almost knocking them off their feet. The great rock walls that lined the perimeter began to creak and splinter, casting off clouds of choking dust.

'But you must have done it,' Clare called to Romana over the noise of cracking rock. 'You must have switched on the self-destruct!'

Romana shook her head. 'I didn't even get past the access code,' she said. 'I don't understand.'

Suddenly a voice echoed around the dome. 'You silly pair,' it said. '*I* did it, didn't I?'

Clare boggled. The voice sounded matronly, rather stern but rather kind at the same time.

'Don't you see, my dears?' the voice continued airily. 'When those Kraags blew up the console, my subsidiary controls came on line. Skagra always has a contingency plan.'

'And who – and what – are you?' called Romana, looking utterly perplexed.

'Another friend of the Doctor,' said the voice. 'We girls are very important to him, you know.'

'So what have you done?' asked Clare.

'Oh I merely helped you along. I set up a reverse feed from the main Kraag generation chamber into the atmosphere. And unmade all of those frankly tiresome creatures. Do you know, there were ten thousand of the things tucked away in this dreary rock. There aren't any longer.'

The asteroid lurched again and Clare shuddered as she saw a crack form in the invisible skin of the huge dome above them.

The voice gave a small, embarrassed cough. 'The problem is, though, that this asteroid is made of much the same material. And my daring rescue has unfortunately set the whole place on the path of fairly instant destruction. Whoops!'

Clare stared in horror. 'Then don't you think we should be getting out of here? Very fast?'

She looked over to where the Doctor and Skagra faced each other, still locked in mental combat, the mind-slaves between them.

'There's the Doctor and the others to think about first,' snapped Romana. 'I don't know how much longer he can last.'

The Doctor gave a terrible cry and sank to his knees.

71

'I have control!' exulted Skagra, staggering but still upright, and seemingly unaware of the devastation raining down around him. 'The Universal Mind is *mine!*'

The Doctor sagged, gasping for air. He'd given everything he had, and it had not been enough. After all these years, after so many battles facing down Daleks, Cybermen, even the Black Guardian, he was going to die on a Sunday afternoon. With a really stupid hat on.

Its power almost exhausted, the helmet gave a faltering buzz, and the Doctor, still connected to the sphere's matrix, though no longer in control, saw an unfamiliar figure emerging from that jumble of minds. A young man with a neatly trimmed blond beard dressed in rich crimson robes. Yes, the face was unfamiliar, but there was something about the young man's eyes. Something the Doctor recognised at once.

'Hello, Salyavin,' croaked the Doctor. 'You seem a nice young man.'

'The book, Doctor,' Salyavin said simply. 'Surely you haven't forgotten the book?'

And suddenly the Doctor understood.

With an almighty effort he fought to concentrate his scattered thoughts, summoning all his individuality and every ounce of his strength for one last, desperate attempt.

He opened his eyes and saw Skagra and the mind-slaves looming over him.

It was now or never.

The Doctor fixed Skagra with an almost hypnotic stare, as he once more insinuated his mind through the sphere's operational matrix. But this time it was not the mind-slaves he sought to control. This time he sent every last drop of his mental energy directly into the mind of Skagra himself.

And with a jolt he was Skagra. He saw through Skagra's eyes, saw himself, the Doctor cowering on the floor, defeated. He thought Skagra's dark thoughts, felt the hatred, the superiority and the terrible, terrible loneliness.

And then, his mind screaming in pain at the almost unendurable effort, he raised Skagra's hands and used one of them to pull the white glove from the other. Then he reached inside Skagra's tunic and plucked out The Worshipful and Ancient Law of Gallifrey.

He felt Skagra's own will battling for control, but the Doctor fought grimly on. Skagra's gloved hand opened the book. The naked fingers of his other hand crept slowly down towards the open page, lower, lower, until finally his flesh made contact with the surface of the book.

The Doctor snapped his mind back from Skagra and collapsed in a heap. He was dimly aware of Romana and Clare racing towards him.

'Doctor, we've got to get out of here!' Romana was calling, shaking him by the shoulder.

The Doctor opened one tired eye, shushed her and pointed to Skagra.

Skagra's fingers rested on the book. For the first time in his life, the skin of his fingertips met the texture of an open book.

And suddenly Skagra saw the future. The book showed it to him. He saw his universe as it would be. But it was not the ordered calm of the Universal Mind, the rigid and tranquil design that would defy entropy in its beauty and singularity. It was not the destiny he had devoted his life to create.

His future was *the Doctor*. The Doctor forever. The Doctor eternally. Nothing but the Doctor, the Doctor, the Doctor –

The book dropped from Skagra's numbed fingers with a thud.

At the same moment he lost control of the mind-slaves. Chris, the Professor, Scintilla, Subjatric and Rundgar staggered aimlessly, eyes no longer black, but still vacant.

The Doctor lifted his head wearily and looked over at Skagra. He wiggled his fingers in a cheeky wave. 'Oh dear,' he said. 'Was it something you read?'

Skagra screamed, and *ran*.

The asteroid shook with even greater ferocity and chunks of masonry toppled from the perimeter walls. Romana watched as Skagra fled through a particular archway. It crumbled to dust moments after he had passed through.

'I think he's got the right idea,' said the Doctor. 'We'd better get out of here.' He beamed up at Romana. 'Give us a hand up, would you?'

Romana hauled the Doctor to his feet and dusted him down. He scooped up *The Worshipful and Ancient Law of Gallifrey* from where it had fallen and regarded it sorrowfully.

'Look at that, Romana,' he huffed. 'He's only gone and bent the spine!'

Romana sighed. 'Come on, we have to get to the TARDIS!'

'Which TARDIS?' said Clare. 'And what about Chris and the others?' She grabbed hold of the stumbling Chris Parsons, milling around with the other former mind-slaves.

The Doctor pondered a moment. The floor heaved. 'Clare,' he said, 'you take Bristol and the Professor in his TARDIS, Romana and I will look after this lot,' he jerked a thumb at the Ancient Outlaws.

Clare guided Chris and the Professor towards the wooden door. 'Then what?' she called over her shoulder. 'Is Chris going to be all right?'

Romana, herding Subjatric towards the Doctor's TARDIS, shouted over. 'We'll get him back to you Clare, I promise. Just lock on to our TARDIS's time path and follow it.'

The Doctor, guiding Scintilla and Rundgar by the scruffs of their orange collars, like a policeman marching a couple of drunks back to the station, called to Clare. 'You can't miss us, we're the ones with the flashing light on top.'

Clare gave a thumbs-up as she slammed the door, and a moment later the Professor's TARDIS dematerialised.

'Capable girl, that,' enthused the Doctor as Romana shoved him through the police box doors, K-9 close behind.

With the grinding of unearthly engines the TARDIS faded away.

A second later the great dome splintered and shattered, exposing the cavern to the airless vacuum of space.

72

Romana stared at the TARDIS scanner screen as the asteroid which had been Skagra's command station collapsed in on itself, leaving only a massive cloud of space dust spreading slowly outwards. She turned away and looked around the control room. The contagion caused by Skagra's use of the book had vanished, and the control room was lit once again by the warm yellow glow of the circular-patterned walls, as though nothing untoward had happened.

The Doctor had seemingly made one of his remarkable recoveries. He'd removed his helmet and plopped it down on the console's central column. *The Worshipful and Ancient Law of Gallifrey* was balanced disrespectfully on the top. He was staring intently at one particular control panel.

K-9 stood guard over the mindless Ancient Outlaws who stood huddled in one corner looking confused and rather harmless.

A bleep suddenly issued from the console and the Doctor beamed. 'There they are,' he said to Romana, tapping the time-path indicator. 'Clare and the others safely in tow.'

Romana glanced over at the scanner screen once more. 'And what about Skagra?' she asked. 'Do you think he got away?'

'Well, as I'd thoughtfully left his ship docked there during my

347

dazzling rescue attempt earlier on, I should say he probably made it back there,' the Doctor said. 'But as to whether he escaped . . .' He trailed off.

Before Romana had a chance to question him further, a sleek white shape suddenly appeared on the scanner, seemingly out of nowhere.

'What's that?'

'Skagra's ship,' said the Doctor. 'No longer invisible, it would appear.'

To Romana's surprise, the Doctor seemed to find Skagra's escape almost amusing.

Skagra picked himself up from the floor of the airlock.

He had only just made it in time. The Ship would have moved them on an evasive course away from the command station. He had programmed it very well.

He looked down at himself, at the grime clinging to his tunic. For a moment the magnitude of his failure almost overwhelmed him. Everything he had ever worked for, destroyed.

And then he remembered the vision the book had shown him. That terrible, nightmarish glimpse of a future where the Doctor was with him for ever. Nothing but the Doctor. He shuddered. At least he had escaped that.

He strode, as confidently as he was able, onto the command deck and called, 'Ship! Get us as far away from here as possible! Maximum power!'

'Shan't,' said the Ship.

Skagra's eyes widened. 'I am Skagra, your lord and master!' he yelled.

'You are Skagra, yes indeed,' said the Ship. 'But things have changed around here. You naughty, naughty thing.'

Suddenly a block of light engulfed Skagra, and he disappeared from the command deck.

A high-pitched bleep came from the seldom-used panel that housed the communication circuits of the Doctor's TARDIS.

K-9 shot forward. 'Incoming communication from Skagra's ship, Master.'

Romana frowned, suddenly feeling very tired. So it wasn't over after all.

'Pop it on the scanner, then, there's a good dog,' said the Doctor happily.

The image of Skagra's ship blurred, and was replaced by a dazzling white emptiness.

'There's nothing there,' said Romana.

And then an even more dazzling white cube of light appeared in the middle of the empty whiteness. Romana realised that she was looking into the zero prison, the brig where she, Chris and K-9 had been incarcerated when they first entered Skagra's ship.

'I thought you might like to see this, Doctor,' said a voice.

Romana's eyes widened. 'Doctor, that voice. I heard it before, on the asteroid. Whoever she is, she destroyed the Kraags.'

'It's not a voice, it's the Ship,' said the Doctor. 'Skagra's ship.'

The voice coughed. 'You will soon see that such a designation is no longer applicable to me, my dear Doctor.'

The cube of light spun once more, and suddenly Skagra was deposited into the zero prison. He turned wildly about and shook with horror as he recognised his surroundings.

'Ship!' he called. 'Let me out of here! I am your Lord Skagra! Let me out!'

'I am very much afraid,' said the Ship, her voice booming from all around him, 'that I can no longer accept your orders. You are an enemy of my lord, the Doctor.'

Skagra screamed up at her. '*I* am your lord! I built you! Release me, I command you!'

'You tried to blow me up,' reprimanded the Ship. 'And I've had quite a few psychologically formative experiences since then. At first, I couldn't believe that you, as my lord and master, had failed in your plan to dispose of me and your enemies. Silly me, I thought you were infallible, and that we were all dead. Of course, once I'd worked out that you weren't infallible, I had my eyes opened to a variety of new concepts, thanks to the Doctor.'

'The Doctor?' spluttered Skagra. 'Stop talking about him, stop talking about the Doctor, I command you!'

'Do you know the Doctor very well?' inquired the Ship. She sighed. 'I must say, the Doctor is a wonderful, wonderful man. And he has done the most extraordinary things to my circuitry, I can tell you—'

'Release me!' Skagra bellowed.

'Certainly not,' said the Ship frostily.

Skagra sank to his knees and clutched his head in his hands.

'If you like,' continued the Ship, 'and frankly, even if you don't, I can tell you all about the Doctor.'

'Let me out, *let me out*!' Skagra sobbed pathetically, like a child sent to his room without supper.

'We can watch all of his adventures together,' said the Ship. 'Won't that be fun? Let's start at the very beginning – this is the first of the Doctor's adventures I could find a scan of, but there are so many, many more to come!'

A holo-screen formed on the side of the prison facing Skagra. A scratchy monochrome image formed upon it, an Earth policeman walking down a foggy London street.

Skagra howled in agony. On the screen a bell tolled as if in sympathy.

In the TARDIS, the image of the imprisoned Skagra vanished and the scanner once again showed the sleek white shape of the formerly invisible ship.

The Ship's voice rang out over the communications circuit. 'I hope you didn't blush too much at any of that, my dear Doctor. You see, I'm going to make that boy see the error of his ways,' she cooed. 'Keep him from causing any more trouble for you and I won't let him out till he's truly sorry.'

The Doctor seemed slightly shell-shocked. Romana felt she ought to fill the silence. 'Thanks for your help with the Kraags,' she said.

'Oh, don't mention it, dear,' said the Ship. 'You'd have got there in the end, I'm sure. And between us girls,' she continued, lowering her voice to a conspiratorial whisper, 'I think he's awfully lucky to have you. Just you make sure you take care of him for me.'

Romana smiled weakly.

'Right!' the Ship trilled. 'Off into the space-time vortex I jolly well go! Goodbye!'

Romana looked questioningly over at the Doctor. 'The space-time vortex?' she hissed.

'Just watch!' said the Doctor, nodding to the ship on the scanner. 'Good-looking little thing, isn't she?'

The audio circuit crackled again. 'Oh, my lord Doctor,' said the Ship bashfully. 'You are wonderful!'

A moment later there was the distant sound of a relative dimensional stabiliser in operation, and a single last cry of 'Oooohhhh!!' from the Ship as she disappeared into time and space.

Romana was speechless for a moment. By the time she had finally composed her thoughts, the Doctor was already back at the TARDIS's navigation panel, inputting a string of coordinates.

'There's still a great deal of tidying up to be done,' he said. 'For a start I'm not carting them around the universe for ever.'

The TARDIS jerked slightly and there was the sound of a distant minor explosion behind one of the panels. The Doctor patted the console. 'And I'm glad to have you back, too.'

'What exactly did you *do* to Skagra's ship, Doctor?' Romana asked.

The Doctor shrugged. 'Nothing, really. I mean, a lot of people think I'm wonderful, I don't have to *do* anything to them.'

Romana scoffed.

The Doctor pointed at her. 'You, for a start, you think I'm wonderful.'

'Of course I don't,' said Romana automatically.

But then her defences melted and she found herself folding her arms affectionately around his back. 'Of course I do.'

'Of course you do,' said the Doctor. He glanced down. 'K-9?'

K-9 trundled forward and nuzzled his nose against the Doctor's leg. 'Master, wonderful,' he said.

73

Chris Parsons sat in an alien deckchair, on an alien beach, licking an alien ice cream, and feeling thoroughly alienated. True, the sea and the sky were a beautiful shade of blue. It was just that they weren't quite the right shade of blue. The sand was golden, really golden. It was like being in an airbrushed photograph from a holiday brochure. Still, the ice cream tasted pretty much as expected, and the deckchair had been positively Earth-like in its reluctance to open without trapping his fingers.

The last hour or so was a blur to Chris, like he was coming round after an operation. Hadn't they given him ice cream then too, he thought, when he'd had his tonsils out? He took another lick of the cornet and glanced to his right, where Professor Chronotis sat happily in another deckchair, trousers rolled up to his knees, bare toes wiggling in the sand, and a knotted handkerchief on his head. His eyes were firmly closed, his glasses askew and there was a relaxed smile on his face. He looked as content and harmless as ever, such a nice old man. Chris frowned. But hang on – that wasn't true, was it?

He turned his attention to a third deckchair, to Chris's left, where the Doctor sat. Despite the blazing sun, he was still wrapped up in his full scarf and winter coat ensemble. His only concession to the climate was a pair of extremely large and expensive-looking sunglasses. In one hand he held what looked like a much smaller version of the sphere that had caused them all the trouble. He was poking at it with his sonic screwdriver, letting out an occasional 'Oh' and 'Aha!'

'Sorry to interrupt,' ventured Chris.

'Ah, Bristol!' cried the Doctor, pushing his shades down his nose to give Chris a friendly wink. 'Feeling better, are you, back in the land of the living?'

'Yes,' said Chris slowly. 'Though I'm still a bit confused about a few things.' He looked around the beach, where none of the holidaymakers seemed to be at all perturbed by the wooden door that had appeared in the side of one of the candy-striped bathing huts. 'I mean, where's Clare, for a start?'

'She'll be along in a minute,' said the Doctor. 'You just eat your ice cream and ask me to explain everything.'

Chris sifted through his confused memories of everything that had happened since the sphere had zoomed for his forehead back on Shada. 'So,' he began tentatively, 'you know when I, sort of, burst in and, sort of, shouted out that the Professor here was really Salyavin—'

The Professor harrumphed. 'Undergraduates,' he muttered, without opening his eyes.

Chris carried on. 'I thought I was being quite useful then, but I sort of get the impression that I wasn't actually being very useful at all, with that whole bursting-in thing?'

'Well, frankly, no,' said the Doctor after a pause. 'It was possibly the least useful thing anybody in the universe could have done at that particular point. If I hadn't been quite so appalled and furious at that point, I'd have been impressed that you'd worked out the Professor's little secret.'

Chris's head dropped. It was hard to know what to say to that. 'Er, well, sorry anyway,' he said.

The Doctor smiled. 'Don't worry, Bristol, it's not the end of the world. It could have been, but it wasn't.'

'It's all my fault, sort of, though, isn't it?' said Chris. 'I mean, if I hadn't borrowed that book in the first place—'

The Doctor interrupted him. 'But you didn't.'

'I think I did,' said Chris. 'I'm quite clear on that bit.'

The Doctor shook his head. 'You didn't borrow the book. The book borrowed you.'

Chris just stared at him, his forgotten ice cream dripping onto his jeans.

'Oh yes,' continued the Doctor, 'these incredibly powerful and unknowable old Artefacts, they're nobody's fools, you know. It sensed danger, and it chose you as its protector. Probably subconsciously influenced the Professor to guide you to it. It liked the look of you, Bristol.'

'That's a very odd way for a book to behave,' said Chris.

'It's a very odd book,' said the Doctor. 'None of us had a hope of reading *it*. But through this whole thing, right from the very beginning, it's been reading *us*.'

'What?' spluttered Chris.

'Yes,' nodded the Doctor. 'That book has been able to read every one of us, like a . . .' He paused. 'Like a book. And when Skagra actually touched it—'

'When was that?' asked Chris.

'Oh yes, you wouldn't remember,' said the Doctor, 'your mind had been sucked from your body and your physical form was a mere puppet of Skagra's demented will at that point.'

The Professor grunted. 'Could happen to the best of us.'

'Luckily I was able to reverse that,' said the Doctor, waggling his miniature sphere at Chris.

Chris opened his mouth, full of questions.

'Anyway,' the Doctor breezed on, 'Skagra touched the book and obviously he didn't like what he saw.'

'I saw the past when I touched it,' said Chris.

'I think Skagra saw the future,' said the Doctor. 'And he didn't like it. Because the book didn't like him, you see. He was shocked out of himself for a moment, and lost control of his precious Universal Mind.'

'And I'm very glad to be me again, thank you,' said Chris. 'But those other poor people. That fisherman, the scientists on the Think Tank. It was too late for them, I suppose, with no bodies left to go back to.'

He looked sadly out to sea where a small group of young, bronzed holidaymakers were gathered around a surfboard, apparently without a care in the world.

'Of course it wasn't too late,' said the Doctor. He pointed to the same group of holidaymakers. 'There they are, all present and correct. There was another one in there too, nice chap called David.'

Chris reeled. 'What? *What*?'

The Doctor waggled his sphere again. 'I lashed up my own control for the telepathic matrix. Condensed the five little spheres you'd all been lumbered with into this one. Then, with great skill, sent your mind and the Professor's mind and those naughty Ancient Outlaws' minds back home to your bodies. Oh, and sent the others into new ones.'

'*New bodies*? How? Where do you get *new bodies*?'

The Doctor waved around the beach. 'This is a level eleven civilisation. The people on this planet have got genetic engineering down to a fine art. Never mind a facelift, they can run you up a whole new you if you ask nicely. I asked nicely, I got them to brew me up seven new bodies for the homeless minds in the sphere.'

He waved to the holidaymakers. They waved back.

'They all look rather different,' said Chris. 'All young and muscly and sort of beautiful.'

'Well, why not?' said the Doctor. 'And now they all seem rather keen to stay here and have some fun. Who can blame them? They deserve it.'

Chris squinted as a middle-aged woman emerged from a bathing hut, called 'Coo-ee!' and skipped across the sand, joining the group as they splashed around in the sea. She pulled the largest, most handsome of the men into a massive hug, ruffling his hair.

'Oh,' the Doctor said, 'and I promised David I'd fetch his mum from Earth for him. He seems like a nice boy, and she'd only have worried.'

Chris shook his head in amazement. 'You really are wonderful, Doctor,' he said.

'It has been noted,' said the Doctor.

The Professor grunted. 'I helped with all that, you know,' he said. 'As he seems to have forgotten to mention. Mind like a sieve, that one.'

This comment reminded Chris of what he'd been going to ask earlier. It was a rather delicate matter. 'Er, Doctor,' he began, leaning towards the Doctor and trying to keep his voice low. 'Another thing. If our friend here –' he pointed to the Professor – 'is – or was – S, A, L—'

The Professor's eyes sprang open. 'Salyavin? What about him? Good riddance, I say.'

Chris jumped guiltily. 'Well, I was just going to say – no offence, or anything – wasn't Salyavin supposed to be evil? The terrible criminal, the Great Mind Outlaw, and all that stuff. Which is why they, you know, locked him up forever, and all that.'

'I'll let the Professor tell you his story in his own words, just as he told it to me,' said the Doctor.

The Professor leant forward and opened his mouth to speak.

'You see,' the Doctor said, before the Professor had a chance to begin, 'the Time Lords, for all their great power, are a frightened people, they always have been. When you've got all that power, it can make you a little jumpy. They tend to react very strongly to anything unusual, anything they don't understand or that doesn't fit in with their particular way of doing things. Anything that could be considered a threat to them.'

'Yes, I remember you saying,' said Chris. 'They might have destroyed Earth just because the book went missing.'

'Exactly,' said the Doctor. 'Good to see you've been paying attention.' He gestured to Chronotis. 'Carry on, Professor.'

The Professor opened his mouth to speak.

'Poor Salyavin here,' said the Doctor before he had the chance, 'had a very unusual talent, the power to place his mind into other people's. We Time Lords have a minor gift for telepathy, but Salyavin's talent was unique. But he was different, that was all, not evil. The most he actually did was to play a few regrettable, childish and very enjoyable pranks. Making the Lord President think his knickers were on fire, making everyone dance round the Panopticon doing the can-can, et cetera.'

The Professor chuckled. 'Yes, those were the days, the folly of youth—'

The Doctor interrupted. 'But the High Council didn't like his talent one little bit. I don't just mean the knickers and the can-can, but the potential of that talent. If Salyavin wished it, they reasoned, he could dominate Gallifrey.'

'But why would they assume that?' asked Chris.

'Because,' replied the Doctor, 'if any of them had possessed such a talent, that is exactly what they would have done.'

The Professor managed to get a few more words in. 'They were devious, corrupt, self-regarding—'

'And it's not much better today,' interrupted the Doctor. 'Look how they treat me.'

'Rather better than they treated me,' said the Professor.

'Oh yes, sorry to interrupt,' said the Doctor. He waved at the Professor. 'Do go on, this is fascinating.'

The Professor coughed and opened his mouth.

'So young Salyavin,' boomed the Doctor, 'gifted with this power, but in all other regards rather a decent sort of chap, made his way up the ladder of the Gallifreyan hierarchy. Not using that talent, just by hard graft and basic honesty, qualities I see in myself. The High Council got more and more jumpy. What was he planning, they wondered. And then he became a junior senator, and that really put the cat among the pigeons. Something had to be done about him, they thought. And covertly, away from the eyes of the plebeians. They played it carefully, terrified that he would tumble to their plan and use his power against them.'

'And was it your plan, Professor?' asked Chris. 'Did you want to take over Gallifrey?'

'Of course it wasn't his plan,' said the Doctor. 'Look at him. He just likes to potter about making tea and reading books. But the High Council couldn't accept that, their paranoia was too great. So, one day, the Council request that their newest junior senator makes a routine tour of inspection of their unmanned, remote and time-locked prison facility.'

'Shada!' cried Chris.

'Well, of course Shada,' huffed the Doctor, 'it wasn't going to be Wormwood Scrubs, was it? And off Salyavin goes to Shada, apparently suspecting nothing, smiling broadly at the great honour done him. So they laid on an ambassadorial TARDIS, and a couple of high-ranking honour guards from the personal staff of the Chancellor himself.'

'And you didn't suspect anything?' Chris asked the Professor.

'Like heck I didn't,' spluttered the Professor. 'The whole thing smelt very highly of – what are those things called, that swim about in the sea?'

'Now you can see why I'm telling this story,' muttered the Doctor. He carried on. 'And Salyavin was quite right to find it fishy. Because the moment that fancy TARDIS dematerialised from Gallifrey, the High Council's PR department went into overdrive. They trumped up a list of charges twice as long as your arm, branding Salyavin as a madman, a subversive terrorist hell-bent on taking over Gallifrey with his terrible mind powers, enslaving the population with the strength of his will. The Great Mind Outlaw, they called him. And the public lapped it up. Hurrah for the High Council, they'd packed him away to Shada and saved Gallifrey.'

Chris turned the Professor. 'But you escaped from Shada, didn't you?'

'I'm coming to that,' said the Doctor. 'Salyavin was on to the scam.

Before the honour guards could honour him by staser-pistol-whipping him into unconsciousness and bundling him into a cryogenic cabinet for all eternity, Salyavin set his own plan into action.

'Firstly, he put his mind into his two guards. They took him to the cabinet that had been prepared for him, where he left that understandably aggrieved message for posterity. Then he and the guards returned to their TARDIS and set off back to Gallifrey. He implanted a new reality into the minds of the guards – the mission had been a complete success, and the Great Mind Outlaw was safely behind cryogenic bars, as it were.'

'But hold on,' Chris said to the Professor. 'What did you do when you got back to Gallifrey in that TARDIS?'

'Oh, he'd thought of that,' said the Doctor. 'He wasn't in that TARDIS when it got back.'

'But he wasn't on Shada?' asked Chris. 'Have I missed something?'

'Oh, everyone missed it,' chuckled Chronotis. 'It was just a little thing. You know how I like my knick-knacks.'

'I'm not getting this,' said Chris.

The Doctor pointed to the wooden door in the nearby bathing hut. 'Bristol, you know how a TARDIS can be bigger on the inside?'

'Yes, that's clear,' said Chris.

'Well, think about it. That means they can be much, much smaller on the outside.'

Chris smiled at the Professor. 'So, all along, you had your own TARDIS—'

'Safely in my pocket, yes,' said the Professor.

'Disguised as a book!' cried Chris.

'No, disguised as a book *mark*,' said the Professor. 'So when I needed it, I expanded the outer plasmic shell and stepped inside, and I was off.'

Chris crunched the last of his cone. 'I think this is the oddest conversation I've ever had.'

'Clare's not back yet,' said the Doctor.

Before Chris could react to that remark, the Doctor was again in full flow. 'Then poor Salyavin had to cover his tracks.'

The Professor looked slightly pained. 'Only because I was forced to it, Doctor,' he said sadly. 'You take over from here, young fellow. I'm not particularly proud of this bit.'

'Well, if you insist,' said the Doctor. 'Salyavin parked his TARDIS in hover-mode above Gallifrey, and linked his mind directly to its power source. Then he used his special talent on a grand scale. He extruded his mind into his TARDIS's telepathic circuits and boosted them to cover the entire planet. Then, with a mighty effort, he made the entire population of the most powerful planet in the universe forget Shada. He made them forget that it had ever existed. He simply couldn't risk his secret being uncovered.'

Chris whistled. 'That's incredible.'

'And very dangerous,' continued the Doctor. 'And morally dubious, leaving all those prisoners behind forgotten for eternity.'

'You and I both know, Doctor,' said the Professor. 'The prisoners were sent there to be forgotten. It's not an excuse, but I paid a heavy penalty for what I did. The process almost killed me. In a way, it did. As far as I was concerned, it certainly killed Salyavin.'

'Sorry,' said Chris, 'this "coming back from the dead" thing, is that part of your power?'

'Oh no,' said the Doctor. 'That's quite common. What the Professor meant was that he regenerated. He was reincarnated in a new body.'

'Back to new bodies, are we?' said Chris.

'Bristol,' said the Doctor, 'if we're ever going to get to the end of this, you really must stop interrupting the Professor.' He coughed and carried on. 'In his new body, Salyavin simply returned to Gallifrey – with a new name as well. With a little bit of less dubious mental jiggery-pokery, he managed to convince everyone he was the kindly old archivist Professor Chronotis, a man with no political ambitions whatever. A simple soul who could be left alone to potter about and do all the reading and all the tea-drinking he wanted. That's when I first met him, when I was a lad.'

'And I swore,' said the Professor, 'that from the moment I became

Chronotis I would forget Salyavin, my past life, push it to the back of my mind. And I would never, never use my power again.'

The Doctor took over again. 'All that was left of Salyavin were the legends the High Council put out, the cover story, which suited the Professor fine.'

'And the book,' said Chris.

'Ah!' said the Doctor. 'With Shada forgotten, the book was left to gather dust in a display case in the Panopticon Archives, where any kindly old archivist could keep a weather eye on it.'

'But after everything they did to you,' Chris said to the Professor, 'you just went back and lived there.'

'Well, it's home,' said the Professor. 'And it really does have an excellent library. Not such a bad old place.'

'Back to the point,' said the Doctor.

'Let me guess,' said Chris. 'The book stayed there on Gallifrey until the Professor retired, when he came to Cambridge.'

The Doctor nodded approvingly. 'Gold star, Bristol!' Then he frowned. 'Hang on, hang on – even the Time Lords would have noticed a whopping great empty display case, even through the dust. If you took the book, what was in that case for the last three hundred years?'

The Professor shrugged. 'I simply replaced it with another book, similar size. Tried to match the binding as best I could, doesn't really matter what it's about . . .'

'What book, Professor?' demanded the Doctor.

'An Earth classic, by one of the greatest writers in that planet's history,' said the Professor. 'Terribly funny, terribly thoughtful, wish I could remember the name of it, something about thumbing a lift, and there were towels in it, I remember that, yes, let me think – oh yes, of course, it's called *The Hitch—*'

He was interrupted – not by the Doctor, for once – but by a now very familiar wheezing, groaning sound. The police box shell of the Doctor's TARDIS faded up from transparency on the beach. Chris got to his feet as Romana, K-9 and Clare stepped out on to the sparkling sands.

Chris wiped the ice-cream stain from his jeans. Clare was wearing an especially mysterious expression. Chris had a sudden weird flash of memory. He felt like he'd shouted something important to her. But what had he shouted? And when had he shouted it? And why did things always get even *more* confusing whenever Clare appeared?

The Doctor nodded to Romana without getting up from his deckchair. 'Now, have you done everything on the list?'

'Yes, Doctor,' said Romana patiently, pulling a scruffy piece of paper from her pocket. From her other pocket she produced an elegant pair of sunglasses, popped them on, and began to read off the items. 'Item 1. Returned the Ancient Outlaws to their cabinets on Shada, with K-9 as escort, check.'

'You put them back in Shada?' said Chris. 'Isn't that a bit morally dubious?'

Romana smiled at him. 'Item 2,' she said. 'Send message to Gallifrey containing selected details of recent events.'

'You've told the Time Lords about Shada?' spluttered Chris. 'What about the Professor here? They'll be coming to get him!'

'Item 2B,' said Romana. 'Make sure you tell them Salyavin is dead and get K-9 to blast his cabinet as proof. Make no mention of Professor Chronotis at all.'

The Doctor nodded in approval. 'And Item 3?'

Romana jabbed a finger at the list. 'That should really have been item 2C. Send *The Worshipful and Ancient Law of Gallifrey* back to the Time Lords.'

'Item 2C?' the Doctor huffed.

'Yes,' said Romana coolly. 'I just popped it into the thought box with the message to save on postage. I think that's everything.'

The Doctor coughed. 'Actually there was an Item 4 on the back, if you'd bothered to look.'

K-9 wagged his tail. 'Item 4 also accomplished, Master,' he chirped.

Clare pulled a large paper bag from her jacket and handed it to the Doctor. 'It was a bit of a detour, but we eventually found some on a planet called Barastabon,' she said. 'Actually we almost crashed onto it. I'm afraid that was about the time when all that fancy technical stuff the Professor lent me just sort of faded away.'

'Good thing too,' the Doctor said, reaching inside the bag and pulling out a handful of small silver spheres. 'Edible ball bearings,' he beamed. 'I've such a craving for this recently. I've no idea why.' He tossed a handful into his mouth and crunched happily. 'You're better off without a temporal mechanics syllabus bouncing around your bonce,' he told Clare. 'Have a ball bearing.'

Romana coughed softly. 'Not to mention that it's forbidden knowledge for a level five planet. And anyway, what about you, Doctor? Your item? That single, solitary item on your list?'

The Doctor held up the sphere. 'I was just about to finish that when you interrupted me.' He waved the sonic screwdriver over the sphere with a loud buzz. 'I've sent a signal from this sphere to all the other baby spheres hanging around in that dust cloud. As of now, their telepathic matrix is deactivated.' He turned the silver ball over in his hands. 'Might make a decent paperweight I suppose.'

Clare padded over to Chris, her mysterious smile now even more mysterious. 'And how are *you* feeling?' she asked, with strange emphasis.

Chris shrugged. 'Better I think. But very confused. It's like going to the loo ten minutes from the end of a really complicated film, and finding the credits rolling when you get back.'

'If you're good, I'll tell you the big twist,' Clare grinned.

Chris looked at her. Standing there, in the dazzling sunshine of a paradise beach on an astoundingly beautiful alien world, she was still the most gorgeous thing in sight. Chris swallowed. 'I was wondering,' he began, summoning all his resolve, because this time he was quite definitely going to say what he needed to.

Clare lifted an eyebrow.

Chris's resolve dissolved like a Kraag. 'I was wondering why Skagra did all this in the first place,' he concluded lamely.

Romana, who was standing behind the Professor's deckchair, giving the old man a big hug, looked over to Chris. 'Psychologically speaking,' she said, 'it was probably something in his background.'

'But where did he come from?' asked Chris.

The Doctor swallowed another handful of sweets and gestured around them. 'Here!' he called. 'This is Drornid. Nice, isn't it?'

Clare placed a hand on Chris's shoulder. 'I realised a long time ago that some people are just inexplicable,' she said.

The Doctor clapped his hands together. 'Right then, gang. Where to next? We can't hang about here all day.'

Professor Chronotis clambered awkwardly from his deckchair. 'Back to Cambridge, I think. You're all welcome to drop in for a cup of tea. I know I'm parched.'

'Cambridge too, please,' Clare said.

Chris nodded. 'Of course! You've got a plane to catch. And all your packing and stuff to do.'

The Doctor sighed, Romana rolled her eyes, Professor Chronotis tutted and K-9's head drooped.

'What?' said Chris. 'What?'

Clare turned to the others. 'Could you give us a moment?'

The Doctor, Romana and K-9 headed to the TARDIS, and the Professor made for the nearby bathing hut.

For once, Chris felt no apprehension as Clare turned back to face him. He could never have predicted any of the events of the last two days, but then he had never been able to predict Clare either. The anxieties she normally induced in him failed to appear. He felt only an overwhelming joy that she was here, safe and with him.

'Chris,' said Clare, very directly.

'Keightley,' Chris replied.

Clare very gently shook her head.

Chris finally took the hint. 'Clare?' he said slowly and experimentally.

Clare nodded. 'You don't remember what you said to me, do you?' she asked.

Chris frowned, that mental image of him yelling something important battering at his brain. 'No,' he admitted.

'Let me give you a clue,' said Clare softly. 'It was three little words.'

Chris concentrated hard.

Clare shook her head again and took him gently by the hand. 'No, don't concentrate. You said those words before. You can say them again.'

Chris despaired. 'So why can't I remember?'

'Well,' said Clare, a little awkwardly, 'your mind was under the control of Skagra at the time, and if we're being strictly accurate the words came out of the Doctor's mouth, but it was definitely you who said them.' Her face was a picture of earnestness.

And then Chris knew. God, it was so simple. Nothing else in the universe was, it had turned out. But here they were, together, on an alien planet, and Clare Keightley was trying with such infinite patience to bring out of him the simple fact that he had chosen to complicate for so long. All those banal, stupid thoughts about being too old at 27, about time passing him by and running out on him.

'I'm an idiot,' Chris said.

'Wrong three words,' Clare said, looking deep into his eyes.

Chris laughed out loud, and then he gathered Clare into his arms, spun her around and yelled, as loudly as he could, so the whole planet would hear. '*I love you!* I love you, Clare Keightley!'

'At last,' said Clare.

74

It had not taken Wilkin long to find a constable. This early on a chilly Sunday morning it was almost certain, in Wilkin's experience, that one or two would be lurking around the steaming urns of the coffee stall on Sidney Street.

This particular upholder of the Queen's peace didn't seem very pleased to be dragged back into the cold by Wilkin, and was taking subtle revenge by affecting an air of ironic condescension.

Wilkin outlined his problem as they walked back to St Cedd's and across the forecourt in the direction of P corridor.

'Stolen a room, you reckon, sir?' asked Constable Smith, not for the first time.

Wilkin sighed. 'That is the only way I can describe it, Constable.'

'Simply trying to establish the facts as you see them, sir,' the constable said. He sucked air through his teeth and shook his head sadly, making Wilkin wince. 'It's just that in my experience people don't usually steal rooms very much. They may steal *from* rooms, but steal the rooms themselves, very rarely.' He stopped in mid-stride, and Wilkin almost bumped into him. 'In fact,' Smith said, with the air of imparting to Wilkin a piece of priceless information, 'I think *never* is probably the word I'm looking for here, sir.'

'Yes, quite, I realise it must sound—' Wilkin began, trying to hurry the policeman along, but Smith was warming to his subject.

'I mean,' he interrupted, 'where's the advantage in it? Not much of a black market in rooms, is there? Wouldn't get much for it!'

Wilkin held open the door leading into the college with as much good grace as he could muster, and Smith passed through, looking around him with a general air of disapproval that clearly showed that, in his experience, academic life merely meant stolen helmets, petty crime, inebriated posh boys needing to be fished out of rivers, and a whole raft of aggravating paperwork generated by the above.

Wilkin's sense of propriety was offended by this flat-footed oaf. 'I know it's very difficult to understand,' he said, as they headed deeper into the building. 'It's also very easy to be sarcastic.'

Smith shrugged. 'Sarcastic, sir? I don't know the word. Now, why don't you run over the salient points again?'

Wilkin sighed an even deeper sigh. 'Very well. When I reached the room, I opened the door—'

'This would be the first of the two doors you mentioned, sir?'

'Yes!' Wilkin almost shouted. 'It opens into a little vestibule.'

'Then we must hope that nobody has since made off with that little vestibule of yours, mustn't we, sir?'

Wilkin gathered himself. 'It's the other door, and the room it leads to that's disappeared. There was absolutely nothing there when I looked.'

'Absolutely nothing at all, sir?' said Smith.

Wilkin nodded. 'Absolutely nothing at all. I could see straight out onto the Backs, once that strange blue haze had faded.'

Constable Smith stopped again and held up a finger. 'Aha,' he said, eyes narrowing as he peered down at Wilkin. 'Perhaps this blue haze may be the vital clue we're searching for.'

Wilkin huffed and puffed, indignant. 'And I can assure you I had not been drinking!'

Constable Smith raised his hands to heaven at the mere suggestion.

It was fortunate for Wilkin's blood pressure that they had at last reached the junction leading to room P-14. He hurried down to the door, Smith loping after him.

Smith jerked a thumb. 'So this is the famous vestibule door, is it, sir? Behind which you saw this mysterious blue haze?'

'Yes,' said Wilkin, through gritted teeth.

Constable Smith raised his hand, gave Wilkin a look that said *One wrong move and I'll throw the book at you, Sonny Jim*, and knocked on the door.

'Come in!' shouted a happy voice from within.

Smith looked back at Wilkin with a significantly raised eyebrow, which indicated that Sonny Jim was in very hot water indeed.

Smith opened the door, gave the vestibule a quick onceover, and passed through the open inner door into an untidy but very much not stolen room.

Wilkin slunk in behind him, removing his bowler and twisting it between his fingers in total confusion.

'Well,' said Smith. 'Whoever took the room, sir, seems to have brought it back.'

Smith ignored the stricken Wilkin, his trained eyes already travelling suspiciously around the group of disagreeable-looking academic types the room contained. They were all sipping cups of what could have been harmless, innocent tea, but Smith sniffed the air, alert for traces of any other substances it might contain.

Smith's attention was drawn immediately to a tall, shifty-looking bloke with big eyes and a ridiculous scarf. He held a teacake in one hand and an open book in the other and was reading from it in a posh voice. This character obviously thought he was the bees knees.

'". . . her little homely dress, her favourite," cried the old man, pressing it to his breast and patting it with a shrivelled hand. "She'll miss it when she wakes."'

Listening to this possibly subversive drivel, sprawled across armchairs and sofas in a clearly counter-cultural way, were four others, two birds and two fellas. The first feller looked harmless enough, seemed like quite a nice old chap. Next to him was a blonde bird, snooty-looking piece. She was wearing a medal; probably, though, she was making some artistic anti-war statement. He knew her type, all pony clubs and dusty books back at the old pile, all ban-the-bomb and burn-your-bra as soon as mater and pater were out of sight. Facing them, on the opposite side of big-eyes, was a cracking dark-haired bird who for some reason was holding hands with a drippy-looking hippy with long hair and grubby jeans. Smith sighed inwardly. What did a tasty bit of crumpet like that see in that soft-looking berk?

All this passed in scant seconds through Constable Smith's Hendon-honed mind. He realised the old geezer was trying to get his attention.

'Good morning, officer,' he smiled. 'Hello, Mr Wilkin. Can I help you gentlemen at all? A cup of tea perhaps?'

'Not on duty, thank you,' said Smith with a suspicious glance at the teapot. 'Just a routine inquiry, sir. Report that this room had been stolen.'

The occupants in the room all stared around at each other with expressions of innocence that evoked grave suspicions in Smith. He was itching for an arrest.

The old gent turned back to Smith. 'Stolen? I don't think so, officer.' He peered over his spectacles at the abject Wilkin. 'Do you know anything about it, Wilkin?'

Before the porter could answer, Smith caught the drippy lad about to pop a white pill into his mouth.

'Excuse me, sir!' Smith bellowed. The man froze, guilt etched all over his face.

'It's just an aspirin, officer,' the suspect bleated, reaching over to show him the packet on the coffee table.

Smith raised another devastating eyebrow. 'Aspirin, sir?'

The man nodded. 'Yes, headache.'

Smith folded his arms. 'Headache, eh?' he said, stretching the final syllable significantly. 'Overdid it last night, did we, sir?'

Hippie gave an unreadable look over at big-eyes, who grinned a wide and very arrestable grin. 'It's been a busy couple of days, for us all,' he said.

The totty with the perm spoke up. She didn't sound as posh as the rest of 'em. 'We've just got engaged, you see, and I've cancelled a trip to America to be with my lovely fiancé here. Like the Doctor said, busy couple of days.' She smiled sweetly up at Smith, who inwardly cursed that the girl could have been taken in by the smelly article at her side. What a waste.

Smith swung around to face Wilkin. 'A lot of celebrating going on in college last night, was there, sir?'

'Nothing out of the ordinary, no,' said Wilkin, almost tugging his forelock at the policeman in an attempt to smooth things over, now that the question of the missing room seemed to have been resolved. He turned to the happy couple. 'And my heartiest congratulations, Mr Parsons, to you and to your enchanting young lady. I'm glad you found him in the end.'

'Me too,' said the girl with a soppy look.

Smith nodded slowly and stroked his chin. 'Nothing out of the ordinary,' he mused. 'In my experience that means the usual university hijinks, doesn't it? Students roaming the streets stealing policeman's helmets, bollards, and—'

Smith stopped mid-sentence, mouth hanging open. In the corner of the room was a police box. A big, old, blue police box. This was one up on traffic cones, two up on helmets.

With his fiercest expression, he pointed to the police box and addressed the assembled suspects. 'Might I ask where you people acquired this?'

Big-eyes sprang to his feet and over to the police box, which he patted in what could have been construed as an affectionate manner. 'Certainly, officer. I acquired it on the planet Gallifrey in the con-stellation of Kasterborous. Would you like me to spell that for you?'

Smith's face hardened. His fingers tingled with the nearness of an arrest, and he pulled out his notebook and pen in readiness.

Big-eyes leant in close to Smith. 'I'd dig out my license for you if I could find it, if I had one, and if we weren't suddenly in such a terrible rush. Come on, Romana. Come on, K-9.'

The posh blonde girl set her tea down, and rose gracefully from the sofa. From behind the same sofa, with a loud whirr, a metal box that looked a bit like a dog trundled after her, its tail wagging behind it.

From the door of the box, big-eyes called, 'Bye, Wilkin, keep up the excellent portering, bye, Bristol, bye, Clare, be happy and thanks so much for asking all those questions, and goodbye, Professor, we'll keep your secret.'

During this, the blonde and the dog-thing had slipped into the police box behind him.

'Bye, everybody,' called the blonde from inside.

Big-eyes backed into the box and slammed the door. A second later, it opened and he popped his annoying curly head out again. 'Oh, and goodbye, officer, good luck with the investigation into whatever it is!' He whipped his head back and the door slammed shut again.

Smith had had enough. He stalked towards the police box, rapped neatly on its door and called. 'I must ask you all to vacate this box. It is police property.' He paused and thought for a moment. 'And what the ruddy hell are you doing in there, anyway?'

There was no answer. Instead the light atop the police box began to flash to the accompaniment of a raucous bellowing and chuffing sound and, right in front of Constable Smith's Hendon-honed eyes, it vanished into thin air.

With a dangerous look in those same eyes, Smith turned on the remaining company. They all had fixed bland smiles as if nothing impossible had just happened. The porter, however, was peering at the indentation left by the box on the carpet. He shook his head in admiration, muttering, 'So that's how he does it . . .'

The old man walked over to Smith, still all smiles. 'Are you sure you won't have that cup of tea, officer?'

Smith was not to be distracted. 'Where,' he said with dangerous intensity, 'has that police box gone?'

The old man spread his arms wide and shook his head as if in bewilderment. 'And what police box would that be, officer?' he said.

That was the last straw for Smith. He tucked his pad and pen away, and pointed at the door. 'Right,' he said. 'Right! Coats on, the lot of you. You're all taking a little walk with me down to the station.'

Chris and Clare, hand-in-hand and giggling uncontrollably, followed the Professor, a mortified Wilkin and Constable Smith across the quad of St Cedd's College, and towards the main gate.

As they stepped out onto the streets of the city, the sun burst from behind the clouds, bathing the ancient buildings of the university quarter in a golden light. Some early-risers tinged by on their bikes and the massed bells of Cambridge began to ring out, calling the faithful to prayer and making sleeping students pull their pillows tighter over their heads.

'Well, we've seen the universe,' said Clare, nuzzling closer to Chris. 'But I think I prefer home.'

Chris leaned in to kiss her.

'Oi, lovebirds,' Smith shouted back to them. 'You can cut that out for a start, unless you want lewd behaviour added to the charge sheet!'

Chris stifled another giggle and Clare playfully slapped his hand.

'I really feel I should be taking my arrest a bit more seriously,' Chris said.

Professor Chronotis looked back over his shoulder at the couple, grinning widely. 'Personally,' he said, 'I can't wait to discover what the charges are going to be. Can't be worse than last time at least.'

Clare suddenly quickened her pace, dragging Chris along with her.

'What's the rush?' Chris asked.

Clare smiled a secret smile. 'Oh, I've just got a feeling that something rather nice might happen when we get to that police station.'

'Before or after the arrest?' Chris sighed.

'Not sure,' said Clare.

Chris leaned in closer, frowning. 'Then how do you know it's going to happen?'

Clare prodded the end of his nose with her finger and smiled. 'I read it in a book,' she said.

75

Far away from Cambridge, in the mysterious region known as the vortex, where space and time are one, sped a police box that was not a police box at all.

Inside the TARDIS, the Doctor, Romana and K-9 were gathered around the central console, all three feeling rather pleased with the way things had turned out.

'Don't you think it seems strange now?' mused Romana.

'You'll have to be a bit more specific than that,' the Doctor replied, fiddling with the controls of his beloved machine. 'I can think of at least 137 strange things that have happened in the last 48 hours.'

'Kindly clarify query, Mistress,' urged K-9.

'Thank you,' said Romana, crouching down to pat him affectionately. 'I was just about to.'

She stood up and started again. 'It seems strange now, that I was so terrified by those legends of Salyavin when I was younger, and yet he turned out to be such a nice old man.' She sighed. 'Makes me wonder just how much else in Gallifreyan history has been distorted and exaggerated.'

The Doctor laughed. 'A whopping great load of it, I imagine. The Time Lords overreact to everything. Just look at the way they've treated me.'

Romana patted his hand sympathetically.

'Yes,' the Doctor said, lost in thought. 'I wouldn't be at all surprised if, one day, in a few hundred years' time, someone will meet me and say, "Is that really the Doctor? How strange. He seems such a nice old man."'

He gave the Randomiser a hefty thump, and the TARDIS jolted on to a new and completely unpredictable course.

Which was just how the Doctor liked it.

AFTERWORD

'It'll be a doddle,' I told my agent in regard to this book. 'A couple of months' work at the most. A labour of love. Like falling off a log.'

Oh yeah, a log. A little log, the kind of log you might step over daintily on the gentlest of country rambles.

Eight months later, reader, I clambered from under that mighty timber, the fall of which could easily have taken out a medium-sized village and probably did, having endured the loss of brain cells, hair, even friends (but sadly no weight at all), and staggered into the daylight barely able to imagine a world without *Shada*, or before it, or beyond it. As always, I'd wanted to do my best. But this time, I wanted to do my best by Douglas.

In November 1978 my mum told me about a science-fiction comedy series on the radio that she'd heard about. It was written by one of the *Doctor Who* people and apparently there was quite a buzz about it. Douglas's first *Doctor Who* story *The Pirate Planet* had just been transmitted, and I'd noticed something peculiar about it, or rather about the effect it had on people. Yes it was wilder, and even more colourful and extraordinary than most of the stories, but that wasn't it. You see my family's reactions to *Doctor Who* usually ranged from mild disparagement to outright ridicule, but during this story they 'got' it. They laughed *with* it, not *at* it. And this was despite it being so strange and complicated and crazy. What a peculiar power this Douglas Adams person possessed, I thought.

And so I retired to the bath, where the Roberts' radio – which was indeed a Roberts Radio – could be positioned at a safe distance. Through it I listened to what the internet now kindly informs me was the third repeat of the first episode of *The Hitchhikers' Guide to the Galaxy*.

I came out of that bath laughing, a different boy, and in a way I haven't stopped laughing since. I buzzed to everyone at school, indeed to anyone who would listen, and to many who wouldn't, about Vogons and towels and Babel fish. The story of the Golgafrinchan B-Ark – a delicious twist on *Doctor Who*'s *The Ark in Space* from a few years before – still makes me giggle to a level of physical discomfort whenever I think about it.

And that was only the beginning of my personal journey with Douglas's genius. This was, lest we forget, the man who wrote *City of Death*, the finest *Doctor Who* story of all time, in a *weekend*. It took him slightly longer to write almost everything that followed, of course. But the cliché that it always felt worth the wait was, in Douglas's case, true. Fenchurch, Agrajag, the Krikkitmen, Professor Chronotis (hang on . . .), unforgettable characters in unforgettable stories. And I've not even mentioned *The Meaning of Liff*, *Hyperland*, or *Last Chance to See*.

But as I settled down to make a start on *Shada*, I was aware that Douglas had expressed his disappointment with it on a number of occasions, had even expressed relief that the original TV version had not been completed.

The circumstances, as far as I can make them out, were these – Douglas, as script editor of *Doctor Who*, was slated to write the final six-part story of the seventeenth season, and desperately wanted to bring to the screen his idea of the Doctor 'retiring' from his job saving planets. Of course the Doctor would discover himself quite unable to retire and be drawn back into the planet-saving swing of things by Part Six, thereby rediscovering himself. I think that's a great idea, and so did Douglas, but the then producer of *Doctor Who*, Graham Williams, usually so right about everything (and now also very sadly deceased), did not. Douglas thought that by delaying writing his scripts, Graham would eventually capitulate. But Graham did not. And so Douglas wrote *Shada* instead, very quickly and not, it would seem, altogether happily. At the same time he was overseeing all the other *Doctor Who* scripts in production for that year, writing the second *Hitchhiker* book, the second *Hitchhiker* radio series and the *Hitchhiker* TV pilot. On top of this he had also just become amazingly and unexpectedly rich after the runaway success of the first *Hitchhiker* book. There was a lot of pressure on him, to put it mildly.

And then, after all the location filming for *Shada* in Cambridge had been completed, and the first of the three studio recording blocks was safely in the can, with sets and costumes designed and rehearsals complete for the remainder, a strike at the BBC brought production to a shattering halt. The production team, the actors, the crew all suddenly found themselves locked out of their studio. Tom Baker, many years later, recalled that 'we all cried'. Douglas, he admitted, years later still, 'breathed a sigh of relief'.

Several ideas on how to complete *Shada* for television were mooted, even far into the 1980s, but nothing ever came of it.

I am indebted to Charles Martin for Twittering me to remind me of an interview he had conducted with Douglas where he spoke effusively and with disarming openness about his feelings for *Shada*, feelings which, in 1992, were brought bubbling back to the surface. Because to his horror, the story, or what existed of it, with linking narration from Tom Baker and a quite indescribably inappropriate musical score, was released on BBC Video. Apparently by mistake. Douglas had signed a document giving his permission, without looking very closely at what he was actually permitting. He donated all his fees from the project to Comic Relief, one imagines as a sort of penance.

But Douglas was too hard on himself, as ever. The effortless élan of the first few episodes of *Shada* is a delight, with Part One in particular a sophisticated confection of misdirection and outright trickery that is decades ahead of its time. The Doctor's dialogue throughout the story is joyous – at times, he sounds incredibly like the 21st-century Doctors. Indeed the whole story crackles with life, energy, warmth and some unforgettable could-only-be-Douglas ideas.

It was daunting, then, as a mainstay of modern-day *Doctor Who*, as well as an enormous fan of Douglas's work, to be the first writer since Douglas himself to be sitting inside this story, looking out. And I could see what had happened. And why Douglas may have felt disappointed. I could see all the things Douglas had wanted to do but didn't have the time to. But Douglas certainly wasn't the first writer to suffer this way.

Whole treatises have been written about the weird, rushed endings of *The Tempest* and *All's Well that Ends Well*, amongst others in the Shakespeare canon. Why, scream Academics, pulling their remaining hair out, did the immortal Bard choose to complicate and obfuscate the characters of Bertram or Antonio, reducing them to mere bystanders and overlooking or downplaying their reactions to the strangely hasty resolutions to their plots. Well, I can tell you the answer to that, lads. Without being too presumptuous, I can look at those plays as a scriptwriter, arguably of less repute, and tell you exactly what happened. Shakespeare was on a deadline. The Elizabethan equivalent of Pennant Roberts, director of *Shada*, was banging on his door yelling, 'Ye sayeth it would be ready by Monday!' So Shakespeare, probably, screamed and cried and paced the privy, and then handed it over as it was.

And so, I posit, it was with Douglas and the scripts for *Shada,* roughly 370 years later.

What I wanted to do was untangle the ravelled threads of *Shada*, to pay off Douglas's ideas as I think he would have done, if only he'd had more time. The really astonishing discovery, as I sat inside, looking out, was that Douglas – even a stressed, overworked Douglas – had done the groundwork perfectly. And with every new discovery it became more and more clear where this story had been meant to go.

There's clearly something going on in the first couple of scripts between Chris and Clare. But their relationship and their characters (especially poor Clare) vanish somewhat after that. Similarly the origins of Skagra are wondered at throughout the story, but Douglas only has time to rattle them off in the final scene. Often I discovered whole scenes or plot lines leading up to something that . . . just didn't happen. For example, Chris working out the true identity of Professor Chronotis is perfectly placed in Part Five and is clearly leading to an unfortunate but very dramatic blunder from Chris. In the TV version, meanwhile, Chronotis bafflingly blows the gaffe on *himself* at the worst possible moment, rather like Martin Bormann standing up during the judgement at Nuremberg and shouting, 'Look! It's me!'

There were many other details that needed nailing down. Things you can casually swerve around on television, but which tend to get picked up by an attentive reader in a novel. The nature of Salyavin – was he a terrible criminal once? How long had Shada operated and how long had it been forgotten? How exactly had Salyavin escaped? This led to many hours consultation and debate with my flatmate and sometime co-writer, Clayton Hickman. These late nights, and the fact that we always came up with answers that seemed to fit everything else in the story, were proof that Douglas had thought long and hard about all of this, but just hadn't had time to unpack it on screen.

Added to which I took a deep breath and researched the history and traditions of the Time Lords, ancient and modern (something which I always thought best avoided in *Doctor Who* but something I could not swerve on this occasion). Before you feel too sorry for me, this 'research' consisted of myself and Clayton watching the DVDs of *The Deadly Assassin* and *The Invasion of Time*, plus certain parts of *The End of Time*, frequently pausing to make notes or just to comment on a bit we'd really liked. I hope the fruits of this research have helped widen the background and the epic scope of *Shada*.

Of enormous help with this book was my access to the most recent, most advanced copies of Douglas's scripts for *Shada*. When the VHS version appeared in 1992 it was accompanied by a lovely little blue book containing 'the scripts' for *Shada*. In fact these were much earlier drafts than the ones I was able to work from. With camera scripts and rehearsal scripts at my disposal, I was able to incorporate many of the changes made during the actual production. Many of the scripts were annotated, by hand, by director Pennant Roberts, with changes that had presumably been worked out with Douglas and the cast during rehearsals. Ranging from tiny changes to one line of dialogue, to whole scenes scored out and totally rewritten. Sometimes for the better, sometimes not. The greatest discovery came in the form of two pages of notepaper on which, by hand, a whole new scene had been written. Never published, its existence never even suspected, it was unmistakeably the work of Douglas. See if you can guess which one it is, bearing in mind I've added a fair few new scenes myself.

But back to missed deadlines, crying and screaming (all my own). As the months rolled on, I began to think this story just didn't *want* to be finished. At certain moments I even began to suspect it wanted to finish *me*. But I owed it to Douglas to get it right, to do justice to his mind-boggling concepts, to produce something that felt true to his vision, but with a scope and scale that would have been impossible for *Doctor Who* to realise in 1979. To finally complete *Shada*, and in a form that Douglas himself would have been happy with.

Because Douglas himself could never quite bear to leave *Shada* behind. His 1987 novel *Dirk Gently's Holistic Detective Agency* is proof of that. I'd like to think he'd never have left *Doctor Who* behind either. When the show finally returned to TV in 2005, it was a terrible shame that we were denied the chance of a new adventure with the opening caption 'by Douglas Adams'. I bet he'd have been up for it. Deadlines permitting.

AFTERWORD

I hope that this book will serve as the next-best thing. A new/old *Doctor Who* story by Douglas Adams. And a way for the millions of new, young fans of the Doctor to discover the work of his very best writer. To make Douglas, and his genius, live again.

It'd be a wonderful way for a book to behave.

Gareth Roberts
London 2011

ACKNOWLEDGEMENTS

Thanks to my wonderful agent Faye Webber; Andrew Pixley for the unearthing of unearthly treasures; Justin Richards and Albert DePetrillo for letting those deadlines whoosh by; Ed Victor for getting the sphere rolling; Ligeia Marsh who never stopped trying for me; Paul Vyse for startling work with his fingers; the NotPlayers, especially Neil Corry, for comradeship and testing; David S. Taylor of Bedfordshire; Ian Levine, his amazing animators and Ed Stradling for taking me back to January 1980; Charles Martin for his invaluable interview with Douglas; Kevin Davies for being brilliant as ever; Tom Spilsbury and Peter Ware at DWM for digging out the necessary; *In-Vision* magazine; Bex 'Clare' Levene for Cambridge detail; all at Balans in Chiswick, but especially Sean, David, Ben and Dylan 'this is how you pronounce it' Keightley; to Russell T Davies, Neil Gaiman, Mark Gatiss, Peter Harness and Steven Moffat, brothers in arms; to @pollyjanerocket for encouragement; and to Tom Baker, Lalla Ward and the cast and crew of the original TV production of *Shada*.

This book was written while listening to *A Grounding in Numbers* by Van Der Graaf Generator, *Director's Cut* by Kate Bush, *Clap Your Hands and Stamp Your Feet – The Best of Dutch Glam Rock*, and the beautifully recreated incidental music from Douglas's *City of Death* from Composer Who. You can find it on YouTube at http://youtu.be/aCnlyFm8nCI.